TAKING MORGAN

TAKING MORGAN

DAVID ROSE

QUARTET

First published in 2014 by Quartet Books Limited

A member of the Namara Group

27 Goodge Street, London W1T 2LD

A catalogue record for this book
is available from the British Library

ISBN 978 0 7043 7333 4

Typeset by Josh Bryson

Printed and bound in Great Britain by

T J International Ltd, Padstow, Cornwall

FOR JACOB AND DANIEL

THE LADS

Chapter One
Wednesday, March 28, 2007

For a woman who had to keep secrets, Morgan Cooper had a dangerous habit. When she felt stressed or anxious, she would voice her thoughts aloud.

What she actually said that fine spring morning in Tel Aviv was not in itself very reckless. She was stretching her tendons after her run by a bench that faced the beach, uncomfortably aware that her workout had done nothing to ease her frustration. It was not yet eight, and the sand was still scored by the tracks of the vehicles that groomed it each evening. But the sun was already rising above the line of hotels that flanked the seafront, and her skin was filmed with sweat. She wiped her face on the shoulder of her running vest and noticed a bulbous woman in pink velour. She looked about the same age as Morgan, thirty-seven, but was in markedly poorer shape. 'You go girl,' Morgan muttered. 'Or else it's all downhill from here.'

The unexpected response came from somewhere behind her right shoulder: a deep male voice with a strong Hebrew accent. 'You think my wife needs more exercise? I shall be sure to let her know.'

Morgan half-turned and looked up at the voice's owner: a tall man in his early fifties, with what was left of his greying hair cropped short. He was standing close, and she had seldom felt so embarrassed.

'Oh my God, I'm so sorry,' she began. 'I know this sounds ridiculous but I just didn't realise I was speaking aloud. I think it's just great that your...'

The man raised his hand and cut her off. He smiled. 'My dear, it is I who should be apologising. That lady is not really my wife. In fact, I have no idea who she is.'

'What did you say? But -'

1

'I was joking with you. A little stratagem. Forgive me if I'm mistaken, but I'm certain we've met before.'

Morgan squinted against the glare, noting his lean and rigid bearing: evenly tanned, he cut an impressive figure. Like her, he was wearing a vest and running shorts, though his skin was still dry. He looked utterly unfamiliar.

He held out his hand. 'Yitzhak Ben-Meir. I think it was a couple of years ago, at that New Year's party in Virginia. At the Watzmans' place. Am I right?'

Morgan had been trained to react to surprise encounters with outward equanimity. But even as she tried to exude a polite, uninterested distance, she felt off-balance.

'It's nice to meet you, Mr Ben-Meir, but I don't know anyone called Watzman, and it just so happens that I've spent the past three New Year's in San Antonio. Morgan Cooper. I'm here for a brief visit. A business trip.' She made a show of looking at her watch. 'I must be going, or I'll be late for my meeting.'

'Are you sure I can't get you a coffee?' he said, gesturing towards the beach. 'It's such a lovely morning, and the cafés over there are pretty decent. Or perhaps you'd prefer a juice?'

'I don't think so.' She shook her head, still smiling politely. 'Anyhow, I need to email my husband and make sure everything's okay with the kids. Perhaps we'll run into each other some other morning.'

She could hardly have given him the brush-off more decisively, but Ben-Meir was persistent. 'Even if we didn't meet before, we should have.' He was staring into her eyes. 'Are you quite sure you wouldn't like to sit and chat? I think you might find we have certain, how shall I put it, common interests.'

'Like I said, I have to get going.'

'Well if you change your mind, please, give me a call. You know what they say: it's not what you know, but who you know, and I know a lot of people in this country.' He pulled a business card from the pocket of his shorts and gave it to her. It stated his name, his title as director of marketing at a company in Herzliya, and an Israeli cellphone number. 'Make sure you

2

don't throw it away. You might decide you need it. Well, so long for now.'

At last Morgan took her leave, breaking into a gentle jog as she crossed the waterfront street, then turned left and ran on to her boutique lodgings, a Bauhaus former cinema on a quiet little square near the Dizengoff shopping mall. Whoever he really was, Yitzhak Ben-Meir had left her feeling deeply uncomfortable.

As she washed off the sweat in the shower, it seemed to Morgan that his silent approach and strange introduction were things he had practised. She hadn't been wearing her wedding ring, but he did not strike her as the type of man who would commonly hit on a perspiring woman at a beach. And then there was the business card. What normal person carried one of them in his jogging shorts? His interest had to be professional: he must have been sent to try to find out more about what he'd called their 'common interests'. That meant that her flimsy cover was blown.

Emerging from the bathroom, Morgan sat wrapped in a towel on the edge of her bed and connected her laptop to the internet. Within a few minutes, Google had confirmed it: Yitzhak Ben-Meir, a retired colonel – at least he was using his real name – had spent most of his career in intelligence, not with the Mossad, but Haman, the Israeli Defence Forces' intel section. The website of the firm on his business card, We Gotcha!, was a high-technology start-up, its board made up of a handful of retired intelligence officers and scientists. Its main product was a futuristic scanner, which was supposed to be able to spot potential terrorists by monitoring their biometric indicators when they printed their boarding cards at airports. Morgan knew all about 'retired' intelligence officers. His connections with his former employers were almost certainly still strong.

Downstairs, she sat on the hotel terrace, grazing lightly on a buffet breakfast of eggs, flatbread and salads. She knew the sensible thing to do would be to abort her mission, and return to her family in America. Ben-Meir's approach had given her a

3

compelling reason: her security had been compromised. Going home would mean she'd be there for the children during next week's school spring break. There could be picnics, hikes, a trip to a water park. It also meant she wouldn't have to upset Adam's preparations for his forthcoming Supreme Court date. She wouldn't have to make the phone call she'd been dreading: a warning to him that he'd have to find additional childcare, because she'd been detained in the Middle East.

She knew exactly how he would respond. Of course it was true that the case was important, both for Adam's career and because of the legal issues it raised. But so far as Adam was concerned, all the cases he had ever done always were significant, and his work more important than hers, as well as more important than the wearisome grind of raising kids, keeping a house, and ensuring someone had taken the necessary retail steps to ensure its occupants always had something to eat and well-fitting clothes. The biggest upside to going home was that she wouldn't have to experience Adam's inevitable resentment if she told him she had to stay.

At the same time, the thought of bailing was almost unbearable. Since the birth of her children, Morgan had spent years working behind a desk, first at Headquarters in Langley, Virginia, and then at an anonymous satellite building near the Tyson's Corner shopping malls. She had had to fight hard to be re-assigned to the field, and knew only too well that some of her colleagues were waiting for her to fail.

Before she made her final decision, she ran over the events of the previous day. She still couldn't figure what had gone wrong. She had left the hotel early, with just a purse and a small travel bag, telling the receptionist she had no need to check out, because she only planned to be away for two nights.

Mohammed, the Arab Jerusalemite driver she always used on her trips to the region, had been waiting as usual in his ageing white Mercedes, the air conditioning running. 'To Erez,' she had said, detecting in return a tiny intake of breath.

Erez was the gateway to the Gaza Strip, and she could well see why Mohammed might not think that this was an ideal time for an American woman to be visiting Gaza on her own. But Mohammed knew that Gaza was where Morgan often went, and he kept his doubts to himself. As always, she had been dressed modestly, in a plain long cotton skirt and a blouse with long sleeves. She wore little make-up, and on the seat beside her was a headscarf, ready for use.

The traffic through the Tel Aviv suburbs was heavy. Soon, however, the car was gliding down an empty highway through the lush, irrigated flatlands of Israel's south, the limestone ramparts of the Hebron hills far away to the left. In not much more than an hour, the Erez terminal loomed: an echoing hall of glass and steel, far bigger than necessary for its meagre flow of travellers. Mohammed parked the vehicle, and carried Morgan's bag to the external security gate. She showed her passport, and was swallowed by the turnstile.

On either side of the terminal lay the concrete slabs and razor wire of the Wall, Israel's security fence. Morgan knew that the infra-red and seismic sensors which ran along its length could detect any movement within several hundred metres, while the marksmen who occupied its many watchtowers were trained to kill anyone who appeared to pose a threat. The Wall penned Gaza's militants in, away from vulnerable targets in cities such as Ashdod or Tel Aviv. Should she run into any trouble, it would also be quite effective in keeping a potential rescuer out.

About twenty travellers were already waiting, and as Morgan stood there, last in line, they passed through the passport check without hindrance. But when it came to her turn, Morgan first had to wait almost twenty minutes while the girl, a listless Russian immigrant, conducted a long conversation on her cellphone. Its subject, so far as Morgan could make out with her rudimentary Hebrew, was which Ashkelon restaurant her boyfriend might take her to that evening.

At last the girl looked up: 'What is the purpose of your visit?
'Business.'

'What is your father's name?'

'Robert E. Lee Ashfield.'

'Mother?'

'Sherry Ashfield.'

'Her mother?'

'Janet Jones.'

'Are you Jewish?'

'No.'

'Have you ever been an Israeli citizen or resident?'

'No.'

The questions never varied. The clerk was looking for a Jewish name, for among the many curious features of the Israel-Palestine conflict was that though people still spoke of Gaza being under Occupation, Jews had been strictly forbidden from passing through Erez since Israel's disengagement of 2005 and the closure of the Strip's Jewish settlements.

The clerk's desk phone rang and she picked it up. She listened for a few moments, then put the receiver down and turned to Morgan.

'I'm sorry. You can't go today. The border is closed,' she said.

Morgan struggled to keep her cool. 'But you didn't say anything before! What's happening? Other people have already gone in. I saw them. Why can't I?'

The girl shrugged. 'Until now they didn't tell me. Maybe it will be open tomorrow. But you know in Gaza there is much trouble. Maybe tomorrow it will be closed again. Then comes Friday: if it opens then, it will be closed at one o'clock. The day after is Saturday, when it is always closed. Why don't you come back on Sunday?'

Morgan had asked Mohammed to wait for at least an hour, until she was sure she could enter Gaza, and it was with relief that she had noticed that he and his car were still there. That, however, was the only glimmer of light.

Twenty-four hours later, as Morgan drained the last of her coffee, she still hadn't made her decision. She could simply ignore her strange encounter with Ben-Meir, and pass her problem up her chain of command: if the US were to exert a little diplomatic pressure, it might well prove effective. That, however, would mean being delayed for days.

But the more she thought about it, the more she realised she did have an alternative opening – Yitzhak Ben-Meir. If she played him right, and told him just enough, maybe he would help her. His background with Haman must surely mean that he had the contacts to ensure her passage through Erez. The more she pondered, the less she saw any downside. So what if he'd figured out that she was a spy. It could hardly be news to the Israelis that the CIA was trying to develop its own Palestinian sources. Anyhow, the last time she looked, America and Israel were on the same side.

She stood up, walked into the lobby, and summoned the elevator. She had left Ben Meir's card on her bedroom desk. He answered the phone after two rings.

'Colonel Ben-Meir? It's Morgan Cooper, the American to whom you introduced yourself a little while ago. I wondered if I might accept your invitation after all. Shall we meet for lunch? I need to ask you something.'

Ben-Meir paused for less than a beat. His voice disclosed no hint of surprise. 'Of course, my dear Ms Cooper, it would be nothing but a pleasure. But I am busy until the evening. Why don't I meet you in your hotel lobby? We can decide where to go from there. Would seven-thirty suit?'

She hadn't told him, but naturally enough, he had known where she was staying.

This time, Morgan did not forget her rings: both her wedding band and the art deco diamond engagement ring that Adam had inherited from his great-grandmother, the glamorous Lottie Kuperwasser – a one-time star of German silent movies, who had escaped to Hollywood shortly before the Nazis took power.

She tried on several outfits. She had a grey linen business suit that she put with a skimpy tank top, but it looked both too formal and too provocative, as if she were planning to go wild at a corporate sales conference. Next she tried jeans, finding them way too casual. Finally she settled for a classic, black silk dress which ended just above the knee. Inspecting herself in the mirror, she considered it set off her honey blonde bob and bright blue eyes nicely. Despite her life's many pressures, years of competitive track and field and constant later vigilance had left her with a flat stomach and lithe, well-muscled limbs. For make-up, she used only foundation, an almost invisible lip gloss and a coat of mascara. She might feel desperate, but at least she didn't look it.

Ben-Meir had turned himself out in a pressed, green linen shirt and a pair of black designer jeans. He greeted her with gallant formality, then led her to a taxi he had left waiting outside. Their destination was a seafood restaurant a mile or two down the seafront, near the Hassan Bek mosque. Decorated with anchors and nets on the walls, it was already almost full. Ben-Meir had made reservations. There were tables outside, but so early in the season, the air was turning chilly. They took their seats by a panoramic window. The morning breakers had gone and the sun was a swollen orange, dipping to the milky horizon.

'It's beautiful, isn't it?' he said. 'Now, Morgan Cooper, before you ask me this question, please, tell me all about yourself.'

Ben-Meir, Morgan noted with approval, was wearing his own, gold wedding ring. What she had envisaged as a hurried drink was to become a leisurely dinner, accompanied by a fragrant Golan riesling. She had spent enough evenings dining alone not to savour it.

'I'm married, with two kids,' she began. 'There's Aimee, who's ten, and little Charlie: he's two years younger. My husband's a lawyer. He used to work for a non-profit law centre but now he's with Spinks McArthur: white shoe guys with offices in a dozen American cities and more overseas. In fact, I'm sure they've got a presence in Tel Aviv. But he does pro bono work. Sometimes it's kind of controversial. He seems to have a thing just now about defending the rights of Muslim terrorists.' Her candour was deliberate: much better that Ben-Meir hear about Adam's clients from her, and in any case, she presumed he already knew. 'We live in Bethesda, Maryland. Near enough to the Metro for the mortgage to be horrendous.'

Ben-Meir nodded. It seemed that Bethesda was not entirely alien to him. 'I understand the Bethesda school district has quite a reputation, though I'm more familiar with Virginia. I once spent a year there, living in Alexandria while I did my masters at NDU. But I've always thought Bethesda is one of the nicest DC suburbs.'

'Well, we certainly like it. But I'm really a lone star state girl. My mum's still down there, in toasty San Antonio.'

'Hence the New Years when you weren't at the Watzmans,' said Ben-Meir.

'Hence the New Years. We go most years to get away from the cold. In summer, we escape the heat in England. Adam – my husband – he's a US citizen, but his mother's English. His dad's from Boston, but Adam's education until he went to law school was over there. Both his parents are Oxford professors. Well, not just regular professors. So far as I know, they're nothing to do with the mafia, but over there they call them dons.'

Ben-Meir laughed at her feeble joke. 'So how did you two meet?'

'Harvard. Early in our first semester. We both needed some coffee and we shared a table at a place in Harvard Square. Adam was obviously brilliant, what with his first class bachelor's degree from Cambridge. Now he wanted to change the world by becoming a lawyer in the land of his birth, fighting for prisoners on death row – especially in Texas. Within a few minutes I'd told him that that was where I was from. My childhood had taken me a lot of different places: my dad was in the Marine Corps. But having seen a bit of the world, I wanted to change it too, which was why I was doing a masters in international public policy at the Kennedy School of Government, with a special focus on human rights.' She sighed. 'I suppose meeting Adam must have been fate.'

'And so what are you doing now? Putting your theoretical studies into practice?'

'I know you've done your homework Yitzhak. Yes. As I'm sure you're well aware, I'm with the State Department Bureau of Human Rights.'

'Tell me about that – and how do you manage to combine that with being a mother?'

'Well, the truth is, until quite recently I didn't. In the nineties I spent some time in former Yugoslavia. But once the kids came along, I kind of retired, at least from field work.'

'Field work?' said Ben-Meir. 'That is an interesting phrase. Did you know that intelligence officers use it?'

'Do they really? Well so do social scientists and college geology students.' Morgan looked back into his eyes, deadpan. 'And it's what the Bureau of Human Rights calls it, too.'

'So what did you do when you were stuck back in Washington?'

The true answer was that she had shown herself adept at the subtle art of clandestine operation logistics: indeed, her very success had become something of a problem when she did start trying to get back to the field, because some said she was indispensable.

'Admin, basically,' Morgan said. 'Anyhow, I hated it.'

'But now you're back in human rights field work?'

Morgan smiled. Despite this strange situation, she felt proud. 'Yes. And truth to tell, I love it. It suits me perfectly. The kids are a little older, and I know I want to travel, but also not too much. So my job right now is to keep an eye on Fatah and Hamas in the Gaza Strip. I don't need to tell you that neither of them is exactly a human rights poster child.'

Ben-Meir's face betrayed nothing. 'I don't have to tell you that Gaza is extremely dangerous. Are you sure you know what you're doing?'

'You don't have to tell me. Really, you don't. But I only need to be there a couple of days, and there are people there who'll take care of me. The thing is, yesterday I was stopped at Erez. I have no idea why, but as things stand I don't know when they'll let me in. I could cool my heels in Tel Aviv until someone way above my pay grade sorts the problem out, but it's really important I get myself home by the beginning of next week. I thought maybe you could help.'

'I don't get it. You're on your government's tab. You're staying at a nice hotel, and the weather is lovely. I'm sure you miss the kids, but they'll be fine for a day or two longer, and my suspicion is that like any working mother you could do with a rest. Why not go to Steimatsky's, buy a book that interests you and take it down to the beach? Or do some sightseeing. Have you visited Jerusalem, or the Negev? Perhaps we could go together. We could use my car. I'd be glad to show you round.'

Morgan took a deep breath. 'I'd love that. And in the old days, it's just what I would have done. But now it's not so simple. Look, this is going to sound pathetic, but next week is the children's school spring break. And apart from wanting to be at home for them, if I'm not, Adam is going to kill me.'

'Kill you? For being back a few days late?'

'I don't mean it literally. But he has a very big day coming up. For the first time in his life, he's due to be making an oral argument in the US Supreme Court. His cases are always important – at least, that's what he's always telling me – but this one: well, it's kind of a career milestone. He's going to need all the time he can get to prepare, and although we do have a part-time nanny, she's also a phd student: she picks them up from school and sometimes she makes them dinner, but there's no way she'll agree to take care of them full-time while school's out. So like I said, ordinarily, I could just wait until the border re-opens. But this time is different. You said you know a lot of people. So is there any way you could make a call and get the people at Erez to promise they'll open the gate for me tomorrow?'

Ben-Meir was silent for a while before he spoke. 'Morgan, I would not want you to remember me as someone who stoked any marital discord. But do you *really* understand the dangers? Gaza is a cauldron, no? So many people effectively trapped in

11

such a tiny space, with so few opportunities, so few ways to escape. And with tacit support from your government, we have penned them in. You could conclude that we have created a laboratory to cultivate extremism, a pressure cooker for hate.'

This time, she found it harder to meet his gaze. But she answered confidently. 'Yes. But there are ways to reduce the risks. I'm not new to this shit. And if I get what I want – well, maybe you'll be interested in meeting me again when I'm back.'

Surely she had given him his opening: his chance to question her about her mission.

'It would be my pleasure to hear all about your visit,' he said, 'perhaps again over dinner. Anyhow. It's true I may be able to help, and since if you stay here long enough, you're going to go there anyway, I might as well see if I can shorten the wait. Be at Erez by nine tomorrow morning.'

Ben-Meir raised his glass and clinked it against Morgan's. 'Let's drink a toast. To a successful visit to Gaza. And above all, to a safe and timely return.'

Over a decaf espresso, she asked Ben-Meir about himself. He told her his great-grandfather had emigrated to Palestine from Russia in the early 1920s, that his wife was a psychologist called Ruti, and that they had two sons who were serving in the military. But he wouldn't talk about his current work, nor his career in the army, and as she had expected, he refused her offer to pick up or split the tab. Afterwards, he hailed another cab and dropped her back at the hotel, where they parted with the same careful formality with which the evening had begun.

Back in her room, Morgan ran through her schedule. The weekly Saturday Erez closure meant that if she got through the gate next morning, Thursday, she wouldn't be able to leave Gaza until Sunday. But she could still make a plane from Ben Gurion airport that evening. That would mean three nights in Gaza, not two – a thought that triggered an involuntary, visceral thrill. She went online and changed her flights.

Finally it was time to call Adam, the call she'd been putting it off for the past two days. But thanks to Ben Meir, it was going to be easy. It looked as if her problems were resolved. The eastern seaboard was seven hours behind Israel: in DC, it was four pm. She dialled his familiar cellphone using the hotel landline. It went straight to voicemail: 'You've reached Adam Cooper. Please leave a message.'

Morgan was surprised to note she felt disappointed. For once, she'd really been looking forward to chatting with him: to hearing how his case was going, as well as all about the kids. 'Hi honey, it's me,' she said. 'Sorry to miss you. My trip got slightly screwed up, but I've managed to reconfigure. I should make the Sunday evening Continental flight through Newark and I'll be at BWI early Monday. I'll take a taxi home. Your Supremes case is safe. Tell Charlie and Aimee I can't wait to see them. Love to you all.'

Chapter Two
Thursday, March 29, 2007

Morgan did not have time to go running. In order to reach Erez by nine, she had to make sure she avoided the morning traffic, and that meant leaving soon after seven am. As she had done two days earlier, she kept her hotel room. 'This time, I feel pretty sure I won't be seeing you later. At least not today,' she told the desk clerk. Still a little bleary, she walked on to the street and slipped into the back seat of Mohammed's waiting car.

'You want Erez?' he said.

'Yes. Erez. It shouldn't take too long.'

'Insh'Allah.'

The roads were empty. A few miles from the border, with more than an hour to go before it would open, Mohammed pulled off the road at a gas station. He filled the tank and bought coffee. They sat in the vehicle drinking it, saying nothing, with the windows open to the warm morning air. She wondered whether to try calling Adam: she'd love to hear how the children were, and he often worked late. But he would be pissed if she woke him. Better not to take the risk.

Inside the terminal, the same listless agent was sitting in her cubicle. She looked as if she'd come direct from her boyfriend's bedroom: she hadn't time to brush her hair, much less take a shower. She yawned as Morgan approached, failing to cover her mouth with her hand. There was a speck of cigarette ash on the front of her khaki blouse.

'What is the purpose of your visit?'

'The same as it was when I tried to get through on Tuesday. Business. I am a United States diplomat.'

The girl shrugged. 'The name of your father?'

'Robert E. Lee Ashfield.'

'Mother?'

'Sherry Ashfield.'

'Her mother?'

'Janet Jones.'

'You are Jewish?'

'No.'

'Have you ever been an Israeli citizen or resident?'

'No.'

Saying nothing, she stamped Morgan's passport. With a dismissive tilt of her head, she indicated she could continue.

Just in front of Morgan, a group of aid workers was talking loudly in English about the effects of Israel's blockade of Gazan imports. Morgan hung back as one by one they pushed through the heavy, full-height steel turnstile at the back of the hall. Beyond, at the end of a short corridor, lay a walled, open courtyard. It looked as if there was no way out, although on the far side, there was a thick metal panel set into the wall. Morgan stood and waited, hoping these unsought companions wouldn't try to start a conversation with her.

'If we're lucky, someone will spot us on the CCTV screens, and this will slide open,' one of the aid people said, pointing to the panel. He seemed to be addressing one of his colleagues: a tall, earnest-looking girl with a long, mousey ponytail. Morgan presumed she must be making her first visit. 'This is it: the gateway to Gaza.'

Several minutes passed, and nothing happened. Morgan's cellphone rang, and she glanced at the number before answering: Mohammed. 'Is okay,' she said. 'Today no problem. You can go. I call you Sunday before I come back.'

At last the panel opened, then closed again after they had all passed through. They still had to trudge down a long, covered passageway on the far side, but here there were porters to carry her bag, urchins competing for the chance to make a few shekels. At its end, they waited to have their passports stamped at a Palestinian Authority security check, then emerged at a sandy parking lot on open ground, the watchtowers and fortified grey wall five hundred yards behind them. On either side of the lot

15

was devastation: smashed, blown out buildings, and seemingly random wreckage.

'What's this?' the neophyte aid worker asked. 'What the hell happened here?' She sounded Canadian.

'This is what's left of the Beit Hanoun industrial zone,' her colleague replied. 'The militants were using it as a rocket base, so the Israelis blew it up. Say farewell to the Gazan economic miracle.'

Morgan looked away and then, on the far side of the lot, she caught sight of a huge, unshaven Palestinian, his skin the same colour as his warm, brown eyes. He was smoking a cigarette, lounging against a Corolla. 'Akram!' she said. Her face lit up. Akram was Abdel Nasser's driver, a jovial father of six. He hurried towards her and bowed.

'*Habibi! Assalam aleikum. Keef halek?*'

'*Aleikum salam.* It's good to see you, Akram. *Alhamdulillah,* I am fine.'

They walked back to his car and got into it. Omar, one of Abdel Nasser's bodyguards, was already inside, occupying the front seat next to Akram. Young and surprisingly slight, he was clean shaven. His weapon, Morgan guessed, must be hidden in a pocket inside his western-style grey jacket: presumably some kind of handgun. As ever, he seemed taut, nervous. Morgan sat behind the two men, and taking a white cheesecloth headscarf from her purse, she shrouded herself, trying to look inconspicuous.

Omar turned to face her through the gap between the seats. 'Before is problem?' he said. 'You no come.'

'Yes, I had problem,' Morgan said. 'Israelis make problem for me at Erez.'

He tutted nosily and shook his head. '*Haram. Yehudi.*'

She hadn't been worried about the effect of her non-appearance on Abdel Nasser. She felt a little bad that Akram and Omar must have waited on Tuesday for hours until it became clear she would not be making an appearance. But Abdel Nasser understood Erez's vagaries better than anyone, and like any CIA officer handling an agent, she had taught him to memorise an agreed communications plan, a series of alternatives if either of them failed to make their planned meeting. The first alternative was that she would simply show up on the Palestinian side of the Erez crossing at the same time two days later, or if the border was still closed then, on the day it reopened. Now, thanks to her skill at manipulating Yitzhak Ben-Meir, the plan had been achieved. Any drive through Gaza these days was going to be a little sketchy: the next half hour or so would be dangerous. But she was in good hands. She could already feel her exultation rise.

Akram eased the car out of the parking lot and on to the Gaza Strip's main, north-south artery, Salah ad-Din Street. He kept his speed below thirty miles per hour, and it was soon obvious why: there were almost as many horse-drawn traps as cars, while pedal bikes and motorcycles kept pulling out without warning from the roadside. The road was covered in old pony manure, pressed flat by the passage of vehicles, and it looked as if no one had collected the trash for months. Between the shabby, off-white concrete buildings were piles of vegetables and peelings, some four feet high.

Barely a mile from Erez, they were stopped at a crude checkpoint: a dozen men in dusty fatigues standing by two piles of tyres which almost barred the road, leaving only a narrow gap between them. Akram wound down his window, and commenced a conversation in Arabic.

'Passport,' Akram said to Morgan. She gave it to him, and he handed it to the militiaman. His dark grey uniform was dusty and worn, but looked official: this must be the Palestinian Authority police service. After a few moments' study, her passport was handed back.

As they crawled along the road, they were stopped another four times: by the Hamas Executive Force, by the Preventive Security Organisation, and then by Force 17, the Palestinian Presidential Guard. These were easily the best turned-out. Dressed in black, wearing sunglasses and with much newer weapons, they were both sleeker and more aggressive, demanding that Akram get

17

out of the vehicle while they inspected the trunk. Morgan's Agency boss, Gary Thurmond, talked a lot about Force 17. He liked to refer to them as 'our guys,' because the unit he led had arranged secret training for them in the deserts of Egypt and Jordan, and was running a covert munitions supply line. According to Gary, Force 17 was the key to ensuring that Gaza stayed out of the clutches of the militant Hamas, and would soon be able to crush them. Morgan was unconvinced. They might look professional, but that didn't mean they had the will to fight.

The last stop, where the road passed through the fringes of the huge Jabaliya refugee camp, was the most unnerving. The roadblock had been mounted by five or six wild-looking men with ragged beards, frayed jeans and old, Soviet-issue Kalashnikovs, and as they approached, Morgan wrapped the scarf around her face so that only her eyes were showing, staring fixedly at her feet. She knew who these men were: members of the Dogmush clan, a local criminal mafia which controlled much of the camp and had lately begun to espouse its own brand of extremist fundamentalism. According to Abdel Nasser, its ideology was merely a front, and the kidnaps the clan was suspected of perpetrating had been carried out in order to make ransom money, not some political point. While they waited, a mother in a grimy purple coat with an infant balanced on her hip tapped on Morgan's window, bringing her free hand to her mouth in a gesture of imprecation. To her shame, Morgan felt too uncomfortable to unwind the window and give her a ten shekel note.

Finally the Dogmush commander waved them on. As the car began to move, Morgan exhaled loudly.

'Dogmush,' Omar said. 'Is bad persons, but they leave us alone. Today you have good luck.'

At last they were inside Gaza City proper. They drove past the handsome, nearly-new Palestinian parliament, and the streets became cleaner and wider, the buildings bigger and better constructed. The car made a turn round the wide green space of Unknown Soldier Square, with its fringe of lush palm trees, then headed downhill past the new culture centre towards the gleaming Mediterranean. Just behind the seafront, Akram headed down a shady side street, then came to a stop. He popped the trunk, took out Morgan's leather holdall, and opened her door.

He gestured expansively. 'Madam. We are here.'

'Thank you, Akram. *Sukran jazeelan.*' Making sure her head was still covered, she got out of the car and stepped into the marble lobby of an apartment building. Akram summoned the elevator, and they rode it to the fourth floor. Abdel Nasser must have seen them arrive from the window, for he was standing by the apartment's open door.

'*Marhaba*, Morgan Cooper. Welcome.'

There were several chairs outside on the landing, arranged around a small, portable TV set. This was a new development: in the past, Abdel Nasser had been happy to talk at the apartment alone with her, only summoning his bodyguards when they travelled outside. Khalil, Abdel Nasser's other guard, was already there, and stood when Morgan approached. As she went inside, he sat down again, and was joined by Omar and Akram. Abdel Nasser spoke to them in Arabic.

She entered the apartment ahead of him. At last he could close the door. He held out his arms. For a moment, even as she walked towards him, she felt a pang of guilt: an awareness of the pain her betrayal would cause if Adam or the children were ever to become aware of it. But she banished it, her incipient remorse driven out by the sheer pleasure of being with a desirable man who wanted her, and she stepped once more into Abdel Nasser's embrace. She closed her hands around his waist. 'Jesus, Abdel Nasser. It's getting scary out there,' she said into his chest. 'Couldn't you have chosen someplace else to live?'

'You know very well I could have done. But if I had, we would probably never have met.' He stepped back a pace and smiled. 'But I promise you, here we are safe. Very few people know I own this apartment, the whole building actually, and for now, the rest of it is still unoccupied. Later there are things we must do. But for now, you can relax.'

She breathed in the faint, citrusy scent of his aftershave. Abdel Nasser was wearing frayed but expensive jeans and an olive shirt that matched his skin tone. The phrase that had entered her mind that first time they met in New York came back to her, unbidden: this was a man who somehow always managed to look cool. But if she wasn't mistaken, he was tired.

'You sure you're okay?' she asked, looking up at him.

'I'm fine. It's just that the past few nights, there've been air strikes, and you know how it is – they do disturb one's sleep.'

She turned her face towards his and closed her eyes. 'Well hello properly, this time.' He bent his head, and for twenty lingering seconds, they kissed.

The building was not on the waterfront, but it was much taller than those on the other side of the street, which meant the airy, white-walled apartment had a view: children and donkeys on the beach; low rocky bluffs; the dark red Ottoman-style arches of the Al-Deirah hotel on its little promontory. Behind Abdel Nasser, the big window was half-open, filling the place with a fresh, onshore breeze. Beside him, on the starched white tablecloth, stood a fresh and fragrant feast: four kinds of salad, fried *halloumi* cheese, spicy *tabouleh*, hummus, calamari and flatbread.

'Come,' he said. 'I know it's still early, but let's eat. Omar texted me from the road so I knew when you were coming. I just warmed the bread and seared the calamari myself.' He poured them each a goblet of mint and arugula lemonade and handed one to Morgan. They clinked their glasses. 'Please, sit.' There was a scent of orchids. Erez, the Jabaliya refugee camp, Adam: they all seemed very distant.

They sat close to each other, their knees and thighs touching. He picked up a fat, gleaming olive in his thumb and index finger and popped it into her mouth, lingering a little to touch her lips and the inside of her cheek. When he withdrew she chewed it and swallowed.

20

'Mmm,' she said appreciatively, 'these are delicious.'

'Not as delicious as you. Not as delicious as what I am going to taste later.'

'I think you've been listening to too much Barry White, though you do say the sweetest things. But Abdel Nasser, I'm not going to be able make love to you with three of your men sitting right outside.'

'No. Of course not. And anyway, we have work to do. After we finish eating, I have arranged appointments. I will take you to meet commanders from both sides, Fatah and Hamas, people I trust, people who know my family. They will give you good information, and maybe you can tell your colleagues that what is happening here is madness. Then tomorrow we will meet the guy I told you about, the one who knows about the missiles from Iran. But there is somewhere else we can go later. I have another property no one knows about. In fact, I only bought it recently: an empty farmhouse, in the countryside. It was used by some Israeli settlers, but of course now they have gone. So far as such a thing is possible in this overcrowded place, it is remote. There we can really be together.'

She laid a palm against his neck. 'I'd love to spend a whole night with you. I've wanted to ever since… well, you know, since this started. But I can't. If I'm not at the Al-Deirah, my people will get to know. They'll assume something has happened to me, and believe me, that's not what we want. They'll launch a full-blown international woman-hunt.'

'I know. But all you have to do is check in. I know a way you can leave without being seen. There is a particular ground floor room which has a hidden terrace, and I've spoken to the manager, he is my friend. I'll meet you twenty minutes before the curfew. You can lie down in the back of my car. Where we are going is south of here, where there are no roadblocks. No one will ever know.'

'I'll think about it.'

Everything about what she was doing was already so reckless from so many angles that in some ways, this latest crazy plan of

21

his might make no real difference. But before she could begin to weigh it up, she started at an unexpected sound. She knew at once what it was: a high-velocity rifle, being fired extremely close. The building's heavy wooden door on to the street had been locked, but someone must have shot the lock out. Her realisation and fear were instant.

'Abdel Nasser! You said this place is safe! We've got to get out of here!'

Even as Morgan yells, she hears the sound of footsteps, thundering up the stairs. Their owners are moving quickly and then there are words being shouted in Arabic and agonised, guttural screams. A deafening crackling comes from the landing outside the door to the apartment, like someone eating a noisy bag of candy or chips in a movie theatre, but amplified. Morgan's training kicks in and she recognises what it is: the firing of Kalashnikovs. Abdel Nasser's face falls and he races for the door, knocking against the table and spilling his drink: his goblet falls to the floor and shatters. He leans against the handle and rams home a bolt. Someone is hammering on the other side, yelling. Morgan needs no translator. She grabs one end of the table and she and Abdel Nasser manoeuvre it across the marble floor to act as a barricade.

'We haven't got long,' she says. 'If they start shooting again, forget about the door: even these walls aren't thick enough to withstand many high-velocity bullets.' Abdel Nasser yells into his cellphone, trying to summon help. But no one seems to be answering. Morgan pulls out her own phone, trying to call the Agency night duty officer in Langley, then the station in Tel Aviv. But all she gets is a message in Arabic. The line won't connect.

Morgan looks out at the balcony. There's no drainpipe, no ledge, nothing that might offer a means of escape, and they are much too high up to jump. In any case, there's a black Mercedes parked outside. Wrapped up in her reunion with Abdel Nasser, she had not heard its approach. It probably contains more gunmen. The street is silent, devoid of passers by. In a place like Gaza, people know when not to look. Whatever it is that is happening, there will be no witnesses.

The men outside are battering at the door with something heavy and the wood starts to splinter. Abdel Nasser sounds hysterical, his voice two octaves higher as he continues yelling into his phone. Morgan knows it's useless. For a moment images of her children's faces fill her mind but she thrusts them away: if she is to survive the next few minutes she has to stay calm.

'Abdel Nasser. We should let them in. That way, they may not shoot us – at least not yet.' His eyes are panicked, but he nods his assent. She unbolts the door and opens it. Her stomach lurches at the sight beyond: the lower half of Akram's big, kind face has been blown away, and the remains of Omar and Khalil lie sprawled at the head of the stairwell. They aren't even holding their own, puny weapons, and it looks as if they were taken entirely by surprise. Even after the street door was opened, they seem to have done nothing to put up a fight. The explanation is still on the television screen: a soccer game. They must have been absorbed in it.

Four gunmen, in fatigues and black balaclavas, pour into the apartment. One menaces her with his AK47 while the others focus on Abdel Nasser. They scream at him in Arabic. She can only watch as one man kicks him in the back, and another behind his left knee, forcing him to the ground. Dazed, he's on all fours, close to the door, panting in his fear. One of the intruders clubs his ribs with his rifle butt. Then another slides the steel switch on the side of his rifle, changing its setting from rapid fire to single shot. He raises his weapon, and while Abdel Nasser half-struggles to rise to his feet, he shoots him through the back of each knee. Morgan sees the blood spurt, not much at first, at the points of entry.

She starts moving towards Abdel Nasser but one of the men grabs her arm, poking her chest with the barrel of his gun for emphasis. Abdel Nasser lies, his head to one side, his eyes meeting hers: a look of pain, terror and anguish she will never forget. His cries remind her of the music made by whales: high-pitched, other-worldly, involuntary. By now, his jeans are a mass of red, and a pool is spreading beneath them. His body jerks while the men follow the shots with further, brutal kicks to his kidneys. At last one of them clubs him again, this time around the head. His shrieks become groans. He seems to have lost consciousness.

'Abdel Nasser,' she screams herself, so stupidly. What can yelling now achieve? A hand is clamped across her mouth. It's followed by duct tape, wound tightly from her jaw to the back of her neck. She glances backwards as two of the men grab her arms and begin to frogmarch her out of the apartment.

They half-push, half-carry Morgan down the stairs to the lobby. Then they pull her outside. She catches the glint of the sun a final time, before they thrust her into the trunk of the waiting Mercedes.

Chapter Three
Monday, April 2, 2007

Adam Cooper knew it wasn't cool to feel impressed by his own office, but after a decade's toil in a dingy cubicle at the Washington Crisis Assistance Center, he simply couldn't help it. Even now, when he had been at Spinks McArthur for almost two years, he would catch himself gazing at his blondwood desk bearing two steel-framed photos of Morgan and the kids in childlike wonder. He had two big windows, all his own, and if he stood next to them and twisted his neck he could just about see the White House. Outside his door he had Estelle, his first-ever full time assistant. All this, plus more money than he'd ever imagined he'd make in his life, and still he was doing what his friend Ronnie called 'the Lord's work' – fighting the good fight against injustice in all its forms and its political handmaiden, the United States government. He liked that phrase of hers, though he wasn't in any conceivable way religious.

At the age of 39, Adam still possessed the broad, muscular frame that had made him both a mainstay of his Cambridge college rugby team and a successful Alpine mountaineer, with several daring first ascents to his credit. In older, happier times, when his hair was still almost black, Morgan had called him her 'silverback.' But now that his temples really were whitening, he still wasn't doing too badly. After all, George Clooney had also been turning grey.

It was Estelle who broke his reverie by ringing his office phone. 'Adam? I know you're real busy, but I've got Mila, your babysitter, on the line. She's already called three times, while you were in the meeting. Anyhow, she's says it's urgent.'

Adam fought against betraying his deep irritation. 'Hi Mila, hi. How are things? Aimee get off to her soccer practice? Is there a problem?'

'Adam, you told me Morgan would be home an hour ago. I can't go nowhere because Aimee will be home soon and anyway there is Charlie. I checked her flight and the Continental website says it landed on time, but she doesn't answer her cellphone. I know you are having a very important case this week, but I have my seminar and I only came this morning because you asked me a special favour. Please Adam, what are we going to do?'

Inwardly, Adam cursed. He knew how hard it was to find a reliable part-time nanny – they had been forced to let three go in just the past two years – but why Morgan had insisted on employing a bluestocking Czech who thought the psychological origins of Franz Kafka's story *In the Penal Colony* the most important thing in the world, he would never know. Outwardly, however, he could not have been more charming. After all, if Morgan was already one day late, she might as easily be two. Since she had gone back to working in the field, he was becoming used to it. He might well need Mila to do him more favours, later in the week.

'Mila, I'm so sorry. There must have been some kind of crisis that meant she couldn't make her flight. Maybe she got bumped. What time is your seminar?'

'It's at two.'

'Would it be okay with you if I get home by one?'

Mila paused ominously and Adam held his breath, hoping against hope that she was not concocting a reason for demanding his immediate departure from the office.

'Yes, Adam, that will be absolutely fine,' she said. 'I'll make the children some lunch. Don't worry. I'm sure Morgan will be home tomorrow.'

Adam plunged back into his legal research, working his way through the enormous stack of precedents with which he hoped to win over the Supreme Court. He knew that over at his office at the Georgetown University law centre, his co-counsel, the constitutional law professor Joseph Bright, would be doing the same thing. If he ran to the Metro, he could leave as late as twelve fifteen. Yet a break might do him good. Since Morgan

26

left, he hadn't been sleeping well, an unfamiliar experience. It wasn't simply the fact that in less than seventy-two hours, Adam would be on his feet in front of the nine men and women his colleagues flippantly called the Supremes. Adam had handled, and sometimes won, death penalty appeals on which men's lives depended. But *United States versus Mahmoud* was somehow different. It could change the entire legal framework of what the government called the war on terror.

Adam didn't know what Morgan was doing in the Middle East, and he didn't really want to know, either. But whatever it was, he reflected grimly, the likelihood was that he and his wife were on opposing sides. She would be trying to acquire information on one of the region's many brands of Islamist, perhaps by dubious means. He had spent the past several years fighting to protect the same people's rights.

It was true that Mahmoud, a US citizen born in the Lebanon, had given almost $100,000 to Zakat Relief, an Islamic charity. According to the Department of Justice, this was a front for Hamas. But Adam felt certain that Mahmoud, who currently resided at a federal prison in Ohio, was no terrorist. Now, for his final appeal, Adam had managed to get his case in front of the Supremes, and was trying to prove that his treatment amounted to abuse so outrageous that his conviction should be vacated.

It was not until his train left Tenleytown, two stops before Bethesda, that Adam finally started to give serious thought to his wife's non-appearance. Her missing her flight wasn't what made him feel uneasy. What did was her failure to send even a text or an email in explanation. He tried to work out when they had last spoken. It came as something of a shock when he realised that it had been almost a week, and that he had heard nothing since she had left a hurried voicemail on his cellphone the previous Wednesday. When she had first started travelling again, she had warned the kids that there would be times she would be unable to get in touch, that she would sometimes be in places where it was impossible to contact America. This, however, was by some way her longest radio silence. It didn't really seem likely that she might be in danger. How many times had he heard her say that she knew what she was doing? It was probably just some agent giving her the run around, or a chance to grab some exciting intelligence tidbit that she felt she couldn't miss. A shame she seemed to have forgotten he was about to make the biggest court date of his life.

Charlie's first words when he entered the house were predictable: 'Where's Mom?'

Adam's response was to drop his bag and wrap him in a hug, as if the expression of one parent's love could make up for the other's absence. It was futile. Charlie was trying to be brave, but his huge blue eyes, magnified by his spectacles, were wet with tears. Adam ruffled his tousled hair. He could feel a struggle going on inside his son's ribcage. He was fighting the urge to sob.

Aimee too was upset. She had always been hyperactive, her personality a baffling mixture of exceptional maturity and intelligence combined with an inability to deal with setbacks, and her relationship with her mother had long been vexed. But though she showed it in a different way, she was also missing her.

'But Dad, you promised, you promised! You said she'd be here in time to get me from soccer but instead Mila came, and she even gave us lunch. Where is she?'

'Sweetie, she's just a little late. I'm sure she's on her way...' Adam was doing his best to appear reassuring, but Aimee was as sharp as she was difficult, and she cut him off before he could finish his sentence.

'You don't actually know, do you, Dad? Jeez! Just what kind of husband are you?'

Adam's tone was harsh. 'I will not be spoken to in that manner, and it's time you remembered it!' Then he softened. 'Aimee, please, try to be patient. I'm sure she'll be home tomorrow.'

'How can you say that when you don't know where she is?'

'Look, she flew to Israel. You know that. She was due to fly back from Tel Aviv last night. Maybe she got bumped by the airline: it happens all the time.' He held out his arms. 'Come on. Give me a hug.'

Charlie was listening to Adam's exchange with his sister white-faced and open-mouthed. Adam sensed he had about three seconds to distract them before facing an emotional meltdown: 'Hey, what say we all go to the bowling alley?'

Mila was hovering, anxious not to miss her seminar. 'If you need me tomorrow, Adam, call me later. Now I must go – bye-bye Aimee, bye-bye Charlie!'

Getting into the car, the children still looked glum, but once at the alley, their competitive instincts took over. They played three games, and in the third, Aimee scored 138 points – 'my personal best,' she reminded Adam and Charlie several times, each requiring an enthusiastic round of high fives.

Adam had kept his cellphone with him, but the only call he got was a query about a document from the office. Twice, when he was able to slip away to buy sodas and to make an unnecessary visit to the restroom, he tried to call Morgan, but each time it went straight to her voicemail. On the second occasion, he left a message, trying to sound calmer than he felt: 'Hi darling it's me. Our time it's Monday afternoon. Please let us know what's happening. We miss you. Bye for now.'

Returning home from bowling, Adam directed the children to the deep, scruffy sofa in front of the TV set and went to his workroom. He checked his computer: as he expected, Morgan had sent no email. But as he came back down the stairs, he noticed that the light on the landline answering machine was blinking. The message had been left hours earlier, at nine o'clock that morning, when Mila would have been driving Aimee to her soccer practice.

'Hello? Hello?' The caller, a female Israeli, had initially failed to realise she was talking to a machine. 'This is Shoshana Gershon at the Cinema Hotel in Tel Aviv. I am looking for Ms Morgan Cooper. Please call me back.' The number followed. Adam felt a tremor in his hand as he punched it out. In Israel, it was nearly midnight.

'Hello? This is Adam Cooper in America. I received a message earlier from you. I think it is about my wife, Morgan Cooper. She is one of your guests.'

'Mr Cooper. Hold on please, let me see.' There was a pause, and Adam held his breath. 'Yes, the message, it is about your wife. She left here last Thursday, saying she would be gone three nights, and she asked us to keep her room open. But until now she didn't come back. Tonight is the first night of Passover and we are very busy, fully booked, so we had to close the room. We are putting her things in her luggage and the concierge has them safe. Did she come back to the United States already?'

'No, she didn't,' Adam said weakly. He swallowed. 'Do you know where she went?'

'I'm sorry sir, I have been on the night desk for these last days and I didn't meet her. I am reading a note on her file on the computer. Please can you call in the morning?'

It remained just possible that Morgan was already on her way back, but he could conceive of no circumstances in which she would have caught the plane without picking up her luggage. That meant she was almost certainly still in Gaza. A few clicks of the mouse and his computer soon told him that the Erez crossing was now closed for Passover, and would not reopen until Thursday. The best he could hope was that she would be home by Friday – by which time the Supreme Court oral argument in *United States versus Mahmoud* would be fading into legal history. What the hell was he going to do? To lose half a day was one thing, but more would be disastrous. As if on cue, the phone started ringing. Adam looked at the caller ID: his co-counsel, Professor Bright.

'Hey Joe. How's it going?' Adam tried to sound his usual, breezy self.

'I'm just fine. But how are you? I called the office and Estelle said you'd had to go home. Is everything ok?'

'Sure it is, Joe. Everything is copasetic.'

'Well I really think we must get together for a final session. Could you spare a few hours tomorrow afternoon? Shall we say one-thirty?'

'No problem Joe. I'll see you there.' Somehow he would have to manage it.

Adam's working schedule had never been more hectic. Once he was done with Ahmad Mahmoud, he was set to plunge straight into a case about detainees at Guantanamo. But the kids weren't due to restart school until the Tuesday of the following week, because spring break ran straight into Easter. He wondered whether to call Morgan's mother. But although he was sure she would book her ticket as soon as he put the phone down, the thought of her wafting aromatically through the house in her silks and kaftans made him wince. In any case, he told himself, he was panicking unnecessarily. This wasn't the first time Morgan had vanished without trace on one of her furtive little business trips, and it wouldn't be the last. She would almost certainly be home by the weekend, but once he let Sherry ensconce herself in their spare bedroom, she was likely to stay for weeks, cooking tasteless vegetarian meals and filling the kids' heads with half-baked New Age mysticism.

First he had to sort out the next few mornings. Adam picked up the phone and called Mila. To judge from the laughter and music at the other end, she was either at a bar or a cocktail party.

'Hey, Mila, it's Adam. Morgan's still not back, and it's not looking likely that she will be much before the end of the week. Is there any chance you could do some more filling in?'

'I know Adam. You have Supreme Court. I know how important that is.' She sounded giddy, maybe a little drunk. 'Excuse me. I invite my friends here after the seminar. Don't worry, Adam. I'm there tomorrow seven-thirty.'

Adam realised with a start that Aimee was standing in front of him.

'Daddy? Are you really sure mom's ok?'

'Yes honey, I'm certain.'

'Where mom is, there's a lot of bad people, right?'

Adam tried to stick to the politically progressive script that had sustained him for so many years.

31

'They're not bad, sweetie. They might disagree with America, but history is complicated, and they feel that in the past, we've treated them unjustly. Of course, that doesn't make all Americans bad, either – even if some of us have been misguided.'

'Dad. I'm ten. I've read the *Washington Post*. But sometimes the people who live where mom's been working do cruel, mean things, and I just want to be sure they haven't been doing them to her.'

Adam's throat was tightening. 'So do I Aimee. So do I. But honestly sweetie, I'm sure she's fine. Just busy.'

'Anyhow Dad, we should have been at Sarah and Ben's house ages ago.'

Adam looked longingly at the digital clock on his computer screen. It didn't seem likely he would even start to look at Mahmoud's case again until both the kids were asleep.

Ronit Wasserman lived less than five minutes' drive away, in a spacious split-level home that was almost a mansion. Her son, Ben, and daughter, Sarah, were the same age as Charlie and Aimee, and went to the same school. Ronnie, as her friends always called her, was a year older than Morgan, but though like Adam she was also a qualified lawyer, the only career she had pursued lately was that of homemaker. For the past five years, she had born the burden of raising her kids alone. Her husband, Theo, twenty years older than her, had been chief litigation partner at Adam's law firm. But Adam never knew him. A year before Aimee and Sarah started school, Theo Wasserman had died from a bleed inside his brain after being mugged while out jogging in one of the remoter sections of Rock Creek Park. His assailants were never captured. Thankfully, he had been well-insured.

Ronnie opened the door in jeans and a pink cashmere sweater, and the moment she did, all four children disappeared – Charlie and Ben to play computer games upstairs and the girls to kick a soccer ball in the Wassermans' enormous garden. Ronnie gave Adam a warm, unforced hug: 'So how's my favourite crusading advocate today?'

32

He returned her embrace in kind, noticing the fresh, apple scent of Ronnie's glossy, dark brown hair. 'I've been better,' he said. 'Morgan's job has bowled me a bit of a googly.' In previous conversations with him, she had found affectedly English metaphors amusing. 'Or as you say on this side of the Atlantic, a curveball.'

As he had hoped, she led him into the kitchen, where she handed him a bottle of Chablis. 'Open this,' she ordered. 'The sun is almost over the yardarm. You can tell me about it while I cook.'

Ronnie's spacious kitchen had been extended into the garden, a homely jumble of potted palms and chef's-standard pans hanging from hooks: a full-blown *batterie de cuisine*. While Adam perched on a stool with his wine, his elbow leaning on one of the Tuscan tiled work surfaces, she stood wrapped in an apron preparing spaghetti bolognaise - not just any bolognaise, but one made with meat and fresh tomatoes of such superior quality, and so intensely flavoured, that no adult or child could resist it.

In Washington's so-called 'mommy wars,' Ronnie and Morgan were on opposing teams, and Adam knew that Morgan disapproved of her. 'For chrissakes the girl went to Vassar and Stanford law,' Morgan had exclaimed one evening, as she and Adam were getting ready for bed, 'yet once she hooked up with Theo she seemed to lose all interest in paid work for the rest of her pampered life!'

Adam knew he shouldn't tell Ronnie anything about where Morgan was, nor encourage her to speculate as to why her return was delayed. At the same time, complaining to her about the inconvenient burden he now faced gave him a pleasurably disloyal frisson.

'I'm sure it's not her fault, and I know her work is important,' he said. 'It's important to me, too, and we always agreed that when the kids were a little older, she shouldn't have to feel tied to an office in Washington. But I wish it didn't have to be this week.' He sighed. 'Anyhow, I just hope she makes a success of it.'

Ronnie produced a terracotta bowl of perfect, plump green olives. 'Here, help yourself. So how do the kids feel about her being away?'

'Of course they miss her. But usually it's fine: all her other recent trips have been when they've been at school. But to tell you the truth, this time I am a little worried about how they're going to react – especially Aimee.'

'I guess you have to tell her how sorry she is, and promise she'd be home if she could possibly help it,' Ronnie said gently. 'And whatever we might think about the present US government, I guess it's encouraging that part of it still takes human rights seriously. Where is she this time? Back in the Middle East?'

Adam did his best not to sound evasive. 'Yeah, I guess. Well let's hope her hotel is near to a place she can jog, or by the time she gets back she'll be impossible.' He tried delicately to change the subject to his own contribution to the cause of human rights, aware that in this he faced an unqualified admirer. As he started to expand on the arguments he planned to deploy with the Supremes, the tension he had felt since taking Mila's call that morning began to dissipate.

Ronnie's own legal background made her the perfect audience, and when she made a pithy observation drawn from a case from the Lincoln era when the Supremes' distant predecessors had placed limits on a president's power, Adam scribbled a note on a memo pad that happened to be next to the olives. At the same time, she shared his own righteous anger about the suffering Mahmoud's incarceration had caused his family.

'I mean he's got kids under ten just like us, they were born in this country and never questioned their place here,' she said. 'And then it all disappears – father, livelihood, finally their home: all gone. Sure we have to fight terrorism, but not like this. You're a credit to the firm, Adam. I only wish you'd known Theo. He always said that this is the kind of work which makes us proud to be lawyers.'

Finally she made the offer of assistance he had not felt able to request. 'Look, I'm sure Morgan will be back soon. But you're

34

in a bind, and what you're doing is simply too important. Why don't I pick up Charlie and Aimee from Mila after lunch and look after them here for the next few days, We can go swimming, hiking, to the movies: whatever. It'll be a blast.'

Adam could have fallen to his knees and kissed her feet. 'Ronnie, I don't know what to say, but thank you. I owe you one.'

She flashed him a smile. 'Adam, for you and those kids of yours, it's nothing but a pleasure. Now go call them. It's time for dinner.'

After the bolognaise and homemade ice cream, it was time to go. On the doorstep, with the children already buckled up in the car, Ronnie put her hand to Adam's cheek and looked into his eyes. 'It's going to be ok,' she said. 'I promise you.' Withdrawing her hand, she chastely kissed the place where it had lain. Back home, he finally felt able to work. Aimee and Charlie put themselves to bed. When all was silent, Adam walked across the landing and found his son asleep with the light on, lying on his back, his thumb in his mouth, clutching the stuffed toy dog that had accompanied his every sleeping hour since the day of his birth. Adam kissed his forehead, then turned out the light.

For the next four-and-a-half hours, he inhabited the Supreme Court jurisprudence of the fifth, sixth and eighth amendments, and when he did decide to turn in, it wasn't because he felt tired, but because he knew that if he left it any longer, he'd be exhausted the following morning.

By the time the sandman came, it was almost three. He found himself almost immediately in a recurrent nightmare. He was back in the cave, a hole in northern England's Yorkshire Dales into which he'd been led by an instructor during a high school trip. The entrance was literally a dustbin lid over a length of piping. Then came a flat-out squeeze over stones, half-submerged in muddy water. That was just the start of a vast, incomprehensible labyrinth that extended for miles beneath the hillside. Adam was panicking, he wanted out, to be back home with Morgan, but she wasn't there and suddenly he knew he was trapped. He shouted: an unintelligible, guttural exclamation.

Then his eyes blinked open and he heard the sound of his cellphone, impossible to ignore. He registered the time on his bedside clock: five forty-five in the morning.

'What the fuck?' he said into the device.

'Adam? Adam? You there?' The voice on the other end of the line sounded distant. 'This is Mitchell. Eugene Mitchell. You remember me, right?'

Of course Adam remembered him: a buttoned-up Yalie a few years older than Morgan who, he was convinced, had tried to hit on her when she was doing some kind of training course at the Farm, the CIA school in Virginia. The three of them had gone out for beers a few weeks before his and Morgan's wedding, an evening that came as close as any to making him wonder whether he really was doing the right thing in marrying her at all.

'Adam, I'm in Tel Aviv. I'm really sorry to be calling you so early but Morgan was supposed to let me know she was safe before flying home on Sunday. I haven't heard from her. At first I though she was just held up, but I've made some inquiries with our own assets in Gaza, and it seems she never checked into her hotel there. You'll be getting an official call from Langley later this morning, but I figured you deserve a heads-up. I'm sorry, buddy, but it doesn't look too good.'

Chapter Four
Tuesday, April 3,
and Wednesday, April 4, 2007

The speaker was the one in the pressed twill trousers, blazer and an open-necked white shirt, fifty-something and a little overweight, the one who called himself Gary. Adam was sure he had met him before, before Morgan went to the Balkans. 'I realise that you, of all people, are going to find this difficult,' he was saying in his light Virginia drawl. 'But if this is going to end well, you're going to have to trust us.'

It was noon. They were sitting in the airy coffee shop at the Hamilton Hotel, an old place downtown, which though now run by one of the chains had maintained an endearing period individuality. Nursing his third double espresso of the day, Adam struggled to attain the clarity he needed to cope with what Gary and his sidekick, 'Mike,' a slim African-American in a Brooks Brothers suit, were trying to communicate.

Eugene Mitchell's unsought wake-up call from Tel Aviv had ended any chance of sleep. Somehow he had managed to get himself and the children out of bed and into their clothes, and had handed them over to Mila. But everything else was a blank, his final preparations for *United States versus Mahmoud* included.

In an attempt to clear his head, he had walked ten blocks to the Metro, found a seat on the train and stared at the *Washington Post*. But the words had danced in front of his eyes, seemingly bereft of meaning. Reaching the office, Adam had tried to appear normal, and to concentrate. He had managed to do neither. The call from Gary inviting him to the Hamilton had come as a relief, and when Adam left for their rendezvous shortly afterward, he could see the concern on Estelle's face.

It had not started well. As they sank into black leather armchairs around a small round table in a discreet corner of the room, Adam had insisted that Gary tell him what her mission was, and whether it was he who had made the decision to assign her to Gaza. Gary had remained polite. But although he acknowledged that he was the leader of her Agency section, he had calmly refused to answer any of Adam's other questions, and in so doing conveyed the impression of dealing with a troublesome insect. He kept saying the same thing: 'That information is classified, and I'm not at liberty to disclose it.'

'The thing is this,' Gary went on. 'We don't actually know yet that Morgan has been kidnapped. There are a hundred things that might serve to delay an officer in her position, and all we know for sure is that she's late in returning from Gaza to Israel. So the crucial thing now is that we don't overreact. I know this is also going to be difficult for you, but that means your continuing to go about your usual business.'

'That isn't all you know,' Adam said. 'I understand you're also aware that she never checked into her hotel in Gaza.'

'That's not something I can discuss. Anything regarding our assets in the Gaza Strip is classified.'

'Gary.' Adam's voice remained perfectly even. 'You're giving me bullshit. Please don't. Okay?'

The CIA man visibly flinched: it seemed he was not used to be being challenged. He ploughed on regardless. 'Anyhow, carrying on as normal includes your preparations for taking on the government in *United States versus Mahmoud*. You probably suspect that you and I take differing views about how to fight the war against terrorism. But like Voltaire said, however strongly I disagree with you, I will defend to the death your right to be wrong. And I promise you, I am passionate in my belief that everything we Americans do on behalf of our government must always be strictly legal.'

'I'm sure you are, Gary. I'm sure you are.'

For a glorious, solipsistic moment, the idea flashed across Adam's mind that the whole situation was some kind of set-up: that Morgan's CIA colleagues had mounted a stunt to distract him from his work. After all, he had been causing them plenty of embarrassment ever since 9/11, with cases involving alleged torture, secret prisons and 'extraordinary renditions.' It was Gary's colleague Mike who brought him back to reality.

'There is a further reason why we're worried. She was carrying a GPS chip in the lining of her purse. It's supposed to be hard to detect, and to enable us to locate her by satellite anywhere in the world. It's been off our radar since Thursday. That may mean someone knew they had to look for it – and once they discovered it, had it destroyed. All the same, we do have to keep our cool. The more worried we make ourselves appear, the more we give the potential kidnappers an advantage should it come to trying to talk to them.'

'Does that mean you're just going to do nothing?' said Adam. 'Is that what you're saying?'

'On the contrary,' Gary said. 'Sure: in public, we're going to keep our mouths shut. But let me assure you, behind the scenes, we and our colleagues in DC, in Tel Aviv, Cairo and throughout the Middle East are going to be working every line, every asset. If – and I do still emphasise that word, if – your wife has been abducted, that is not a trivial thing. We should know soon enough what's really happened to her. And once we do, if she really has been kidnapped, we'll be using every bit of diplomatic muscle America possesses to get her back. We do not take the abduction of one our officers lying down.'

'I am enormously relieved to hear that, Gary.' Adam could not keep the sceptical edge from his voice.

'The really critical thing at this moment is that there must be no, I repeat no, publicity. If Morgan has been kidnapped, our best hope of getting her back safely is to preserve the deepest secrecy, so that when they do release her, her kidnappers do not lose face. We intend to make them very, very fearful of the consequences of failing to set her free, but no one can let that be known in public. I know your job means you are familiar with members of the news media, but Adam, I cannot stress this strongly enough. However hard it gets, you've got to maintain her cover, and to tell anyone who asks she is simply delayed by her business.'

Adam folded his arms. 'I get that. But what do I tell the kids?'

Mike and Gary exchanged a look of bewilderment. This was a problem that apparently had not occurred to them.

'Tell them she's sick, delayed, whatever; that she can't call them because of the time difference with America. I'm sure you'll come up with something,' said Gary. 'But just make sure that whatever you do say, it isn't the goddamn truth. Once they start talking to their friends at school, you might as well put it on the front page of the *Post*.'

Mike put a hand on Adam's arm. 'And trust us Adam.' That phrase again. 'This will come out right. We're on the same side, working for the same ends. Please, my friend, trust us.'

Adam left the Hamilton in a daze. He hadn't eaten, but stumbled back to his office without purchasing any sustenance. 'Trust us.' That's what his own domestic representative of the CIA had been telling him for years, since the day their first Harvard spring when she had casually mentioned she was going to spend the summer as a CIA intern, and that if that worked out, planned to make the Agency her career. To say that Adam, already one of Harvard law's most vocal liberals, found this difficult, would be an understatement, and if they hadn't both been walking around Cambridge in a permanent erotic haze, they would probably have broken up over it. But the idea of losing her had been unbearable, and he had overcome his doubts.

Still hungry, Adam spent the afternoon at Joe Bright's cluttered law school office near Union Station, trying to spot the questions that might come from the Supremes next day and rehearsing answers to them. The whole time he was fighting to suppress the fears and anxieties that bubbled inside his stomach. Meanwhile, he tried to banish another thought that kept on trying to barge its way in: that if the government was correct in its assessment of his client Ahmad Mahmoud, that would mean that Adam was trying to win freedom for a man who probably held beliefs very similar to the kidnappers who had deprived his wife of hers.

40

***

Lawyers about to appear before the Supremes are required to wait for their moment in oak-panelled anterooms to the side of the great, marbled court. Adam, soon joined by Professor Bright, arrived early next morning, before the first, ten o'clock docket – an argument about the constitutionality of Alaskan fishing licences. He had hoped to steady his nerves. But it meant that when he walked out into the arena at eleven, ready to slay the Department of Justice lions, he had no idea who might be sitting in the public seats behind the bronze barrier that divided the room. The first person he saw, leaning gently forward in his seat, was CIA Mike from the Hamilton Hotel. Adam caught his eye and Mike raised his palm, mouthing the word 'later'. Adam's body jerked involuntarily. He could feel the perspiration breaking out at the back of his neck.

Then he saw Nuha, Ahmad Mahmoud's sister. She was wearing a new, smart suit, but looked exhausted. Adam's focus returned. Whatever he said, whatever he did for the next sixty minutes had to be for his client. The clerk read the name of the case and docket number and Adam walked to the lectern. He surveyed the crescent of judges. He was ready.

There was nothing very novel about the arguments Adam tried to present in his introductory speech. This, he told the court, was a case about the limits of executive power, and whether it was acceptable for an administration to change the constitutional rules that governed a person's liberty. But the central legal issue concerned the statute under which Mahmoud had been convicted.

'The government has only asserted that the charity to which he gave money, Zakat Relief, is a front for terrorism,' Adam said. 'It has offered no evidence to support this proposition, and it bases its claim on information which it says is classified. The result is that Mr Mahmoud has not been able to answer the case made against him, for the simple reason that he does not know what it is.'

41

As one of the newest recruits to the Supreme Court bar, Adam had already been taught a lesson by older hands: that although advocates were supposed to be allocated a five-minute speech before answering the justices' questions, in practice, they were often interrupted much sooner. 'I'll give you ninety seconds,' Joe had told him the previous night. In the end, he got seventy-four. As Adam had expected, the first intervention came from the court's leading conservative thinker, the ferociously intelligent and intimidating Justice Antonin Scalia.

Adam had just reached his first rhetorical flourish, a citation of Magna Carta, when Scalia cut across him. 'We are all well aware of the ancient great charter,' the justice said. 'But are you seriously proposing that every time the government wants to bring a case that links an individual to an organisation, it must start by proving that organisation's alleged character from first principles? What if I were charged under the RICO statutes of involvement with the mafia – would the government have to establish that the mob is not in fact concerned with the welfare of children and the elderly?'

After that, the next fifty-eight minutes felt like being an involuntary passenger on an intellectual helter-skelter. Some of the time, Adam seemed almost irrelevant, a pig in the middle of a ferocious legal contest that had already lasted for years, between Scalia and the liberal Justice Breyer on the opposite side of the dais: two great jurists fighting yet another battle in their years-long war of attrition.

And then, just when it seemed almost over, the words he had been hunting for to seize the justices' full attention came tumbling from his mouth. He started citing the very case that Ronnie had mentioned two nights earlier, when the Civil War Supreme Court had decided that the powers assumed by Abraham Lincoln to intern the Union's enemies had been unconstitutional. 'No doubt those wrongfully interned after Gettysburg were regarded as enemies of the United States, just as my client is now,' Adam said. 'But the requirement to test such propositions has not been diluted by the passage of the years, nor by the possibly even greater scale of our present jeopardy.' He sat down, and for more than a second there was silence.

At last the ordeal was over. Adam knew the press would be waiting for him outside on the white marble steps, and he resolved to say nothing, other than that he had made his client's case and would be awaiting the response from the Supremes. But first, as he gathered his papers and turned to leave, there was Mike, dressed as on the previous day in an anonymous, chain store suit.

'Hey Adam. I'm just checking in. How's it going? Are the kids all right?'

'Is there news? Have you had confirmation she's been kidnapped? Do you know anything more?'

Mike touched his arm. 'I'm sorry buddy. Nothing more to tell you yet. But anyway, you did great. Morgan would've been proud of you.'

To Adam's amazement, Mike gave him a toothy grin and winked, then placed an index finger in front of his lips. 'Shhh. Don't tell Gary, but not all of us in my business feel the same way about these issues. Like I told you yesterday, you, me, Morgan: we're on the same side.'

Before Adam could reply, he was gone.

Ronnie had known that like her husband in days of old, Adam would return from his high judicial combat feeling frayed. Tonight, she had said, she would bring over the ingredients and make dinner at the Coopers' house. That way, he could drink without having to worry about driving home. While she prepared a cassoulet, he had a gin and tonic, and over dinner, most of a bottle of Cabernet. Finally the children disappeared again. Ronnie and Adam sat in the conservatory dining room, staring at the debris of the meal.

'If the way to my heart was through my stomach, I would be madly in love with you,' said Adam. 'And I may have wrecked the case, but if Mahmoud still has any prospects at all, they're thanks to you.'

'That's bullshit and you know it,' she said. 'You haven't wrecked anything. You've had a normal day in the United States Supreme Court, is all. And as for the kids, I haven't done anything that any friend worthy of the name wouldn't have.'

'That's actually not what I meant – grateful as I am. No. I was talking about when you pointed out the relevance of that Civil War case the other night. I cited it in front of the justices, and to be honest, it was the highlight of my argument.'

Ronnie had been to the hairdresser. In place of her usual jeans, she was wearing a short and clingy cream knitted dress, and in the fading evening light, her eyes were dark, mysterious pools. He stared at her unashamedly as she crossed her firm, tanned legs, beaming with a pleasure that was entirely unfeigned. Still smiling, she pressed his right hand with her own.

'Now, Adam Cooper, you really have made my day – no, my week, my year! I'm thrilled that you used it – and even more that it worked.' Still covering his hand, Ronnie paused. 'And thank you for being generous enough to mention it – I used to know too many hotshots who liked to claim that the ideas they got from their colleagues were all their own. But Adam. Don't you think it's time we started to talk about what's going on here? I know this is a difficult time for you. I think it's pretty awesome that you managed to get the case ready and stand at that lectern at all. But it can't help to keep it all in. Let me be your rock. I know what it's like to lose someone. Talk to me Adam. Even if you just want to vent.'

For the second time that day, Adam felt a rush of perspiration. 'It's probably not what you think.' He was mumbling. 'It's kind of hard to talk about.'

'This isn't the first time Morgan's been late back from a business trip, is it? I seem to remember she was two days late last time she went, in February. And okay: you weren't about to make your first Supreme Court argument then, though you were pretty busy. But to do it now? Has it occurred to you that maybe she's trying to send you some kind of message – as in, husband, go fuck yourself?'

44

Ronnie gave his hand a squeeze. 'When I've seen you together lately, it's been obvious that things haven't been good. You used to seem so close. Outsiders never really know what goes on in a marriage, but to me it looks obvious that something's changed. You might have at least half of a British stiff upper lip, but talking does sometimes help. And if I've got this totally wrong, I apologise.'

Adam swallowed. 'You haven't got it wrong. I just don't seem to be able to figure out what Morgan wants from me at the moment. It's like everything I do or say is somehow selfish or inappropriate. So, I think I've tried to make it easy for her to travel again, but she says the way I talk about it, I've made her feel guilty. When I say we really need to work all this out, she'll admit we have our problems. But then she'll say that they're all my fault, because of my attitude, not just recently, but going back years.'

'Oh Adam. You don't seem like such a selfish bastard to me. You've spent most of career fighting for the rights of the underdog. I'd say that's quite admirable.'

'Well, I don't suppose Morgan would deny I've taken on some unpopular causes in my professional life. But when it comes to family life and childcare, she says I'm just as unreconstructed as her dad, who assumed her mother would follow him anywhere. But listen. This is beside the point. The problems in our relationship aren't the reason why she's not home. I'm certain she'd be here now if she could be.'

Ronnie touched the inside of his elbow and leant towards him. Her smell was intoxicating. 'You've been together a long time, haven't you? And your paths have grown very different. How has it been between you in the bedroom?'

Had it been anyone else, Adam would have been appalled. But there was something about the combination of Ronnie's alluring physical presence, her unqualified admiration, and the alcohol in his bloodstream that kept him talking.

'It used to be fantastic. I guess sex was the glue that kept us together, even when times were tough. But lately, not so much,' he said glumly. An unpleasant memory flashed across his mind.

45

'It didn't even happen at all on the night before she left for this trip. I kind of wanted it to say goodbye, but she turned me down.'

'I hate to be the bearer of bad news, but mightn't there be a rather obvious explanation? Are you sure she's not seeing someone else?'

'No. No.' He shook his head. 'That's just not Morgan, and anyway, she wouldn't have the time.'

'So why wouldn't she fuck you the night before she left?'

'She said she felt tired; she said was tense about the trip. I guess she knew I was worried and she was too, about having to go to Gaza.'

Ronnie's mouth was open. 'Where? Where did you say she was going? You know half my family lives in Israel, right? Oh my God. Gaza. Why has she gone there, of all the world's Godforsaken places?'

The spell was broken. 'Oh shit. I shouldn't have said that. Please, please, keep that to yourself. Promise me Ronnie - if it gets out, it can only increase the level of risk.'

'What are you saying? You know she is trouble? Have you been told, like, officially?'

He could hardly avoid telling her more, and if anyone deserved to know at least some of the truth, it was Ronnie.

'Kind of. But you really have to promise me you won't tell anyone what I'm about to say.'

'Is there anything my relatives can do to help?'

He touched her wrist. 'It's sweet of you to offer their help, but no, that includes your family.'

Ronnie nodded. 'You can trust me with your life. And hers.'

'She was in Tel Aviv, but she had to go to Gaza last Thursday. She never came back through the border, and no one's heard from her since. It looks like she's been kidnapped.'

Ronnie talked about alerting the authorities, and Adam assured her they were already on the case. She promised she would carry on taking care of the children as long as this thing took.

46

She agreed to share Adam's oath of secrecy, accepting his echo of Gary's argument that if it were true that Morgan had been kidnapped, any public leak would increase the chances they might never see her again.

On the doorstep, she hugged him tightly. 'You can call me any time, day or night. I'm going to be here for you, now and when after this problem is over, and however it ends.'

Adam stood in the porch, watching her get the kids in her car before setting off for home. His stomach tingled from the warmth of her breasts where she'd held herself against him.

Before turning in, he checked his email. There were messages of congratulation from Estelle and the bigwigs at the office, and from just about every constitutional rights lobby group in America. Apparently his argument in court hadn't been so dismal at all. He counted twenty-seven requests for interviews before he gave up, some from important TV shows: all the US networks, as well as Jon Stewart and good old BBC *Newsnight*. He hadn't turned his cellphone on again since the hearing: no doubt his voicemail was jammed. Ordinarily, the attention would have made him euphoric. Now his only sensation was relief that he hadn't had had to deal with this shit, and that all the people who really mattered knew how to reach him at home.

But there was one email he knew he couldn't ignore: a message from his mother in law. 'Hi sweetie been trying to reach my darling daughter and you. Kisses and congratulations. You're a superstar.

'Would love to see the little ones. I was thinking of coming up for a few days next Wednesday. Would that be okay with you? Peace and love to all, Sherelle xxx.'

As he wondered how to reply, Adam was lost for words.

Chapter Five
Thursday, April 5, 2007

She knew it must be still very early, because although her cell had no natural light, the sounds from the world outside the building were audible, and she had not heard the *Fajr*, the pre-dawn call to prayer. Eight days in and counting, and still the movie was running through her head, sometimes fast, sometimes in slow motion. Each time it started, she wanted to stop the projector, but try as she might, she couldn't.

It always began so peacefully, with memories of Akram: his genial presence; his addiction to Egyptian cigarettes; his preternatural skill at dodging Gazan roads' many obstacles. But then it swiftly degenerated: the indelible image of his body on the apartment landing, with the jagged, bloody hole that had permanently destroyed his smile. Khalil and Omar strewn lifeless across the stairs. And then the moments – the whole thing can only have lasted seconds – of her abduction, and the crippling of Abdel Nasser. The dark red of his blood, and its unexpected viscosity as it flowed across the tiled floor. The final blow from the rifle butt that had silenced his terrible cries. Her own nauseating, suffocating journey, trussed and gagged in the trunk of the black Mercedes, where they had kept her until long after dark, forcing her to soil herself. Each time the parade of images finished, there was a pause, in which she fought her own consciousness to stop it coming back. Sometimes she managed to think about Charlie and Aimee for many minutes, long enough to picture them vividly and to hope that this time, the movie wouldn't be coming back. But then it always started again. Against this inner projector, she seemed powerless.

Nights of trying to sleep on thin plastic matting on the floor had left her muscles sore. But today, she could feel something different, a familiar ache in her belly. 'Oh my God,' she said aloud. 'I'm getting my period.'

Morgan still had little idea who had taken her, nor where she was. Her room – her cell - was less than eight feet square: she guessed it had been some kind of storeroom or walk-in closet. Before she could use the toilet each morning, she had to await the arrival of the only female guard, who would apply a blindfold and escort her through the building. Morgan sensed that the corridors were narrow, the walls thin, and suspected she must be deep in one of Gaza's refugee camps, teeming mazes of concrete shacks thrown up after the Israeli-Arab war of 1948, each box separated from the next by narrow, dirt-floored alleys.

After the abduction she had been driven, cuffed and shackled in the Mercedes trunk for more than half an hour. That meant she might be somewhere in Jabaliya, the huge camp next to Gaza City. She might just as easily be miles to the south, in Rafah or Khan Younis. The best she could hope for today was that the female guard, a woman in her early thirties whom Morgan had heard called Zainab, would arrive in time to prevent her soiling her orange, Guantanamo-style jumpsuit. Somehow she had to make her understand she needed some sanitary protection.

Morgan heard the muezzin's call at last: it must be close to five in the morning. Only another two or three hours before Zainab's arrival. How come they never covered menstruation at SERE school? The answer was obvious: because the course was designed by men. Her mind drifted back to the Farm, and the faraway autumn of 1993. Her syndicate's instructor for SERE training – Survival, Evasion, Resistance, Escape – was a Vietnam special forces veteran who went by the deceptively cuddly name of Bud, and made no secret of his view that the Agency should not even consider deploying women in locations where they might need his skills. 'Bud, you were a bastard,' Morgan said to herself. 'And why the fuck did you never show us how to make a tampon from a piece of plastic matting?' Despite everything, she had made herself laugh.

Bud told his students at the start of their course that it would rank as one of the most stressful experiences of their lives, and having been mock-kidnapped, deprived of food and sleep,

49

subjected to relentless interrogation and tied for hours in stress positions that cut off their circulation and made their muscles feel as if they were being eaten by fire ants, Morgan and the rest of her class agreed. Yet however tough it was, it was also only make-believe.

'I can deal with this,' she told the walls of her cell. 'I'm a professional.' She knew that psychologists had conducted studies which showed that those who had been prepared for captivity, and taught to recognise its perils, tended to cope with it better, and could recover more quickly afterwards. Yet every day she experienced times when she felt the proximity of a black, gnawing terror, a bottomless lake of fear opening up beneath her.

The worst moments tended to come when the movie had stopped and she had been thinking about the children. One night she had awoken in the cell from a dream in which Adam was telling Charlie and Aimee that their mother was dead. Even after she wrongly thought herself fully conscious again, the dream had continued, the lurid scene playing out, its characters grieving though she tried to yell at them that she wasn't dead at all. She saw their tears and heard their sobs, but there was nothing she could do that would make them stop. When she finally awakened for real, at first she dared not embrace her own relief, in case it, not the nightmare, were imaginary. There was no CIA course on earth that could have prepared her to deal with such visions. She simply had to fight to banish them.

She must have dropped off, because Zainab had turned on the bulb in the ceiling and was shaking her awake. As ever, she was wearing a long dress and an Iranian-style manteau, a waistcoat that covered any lurking signs of femininity, while her head was wrapped in a scarf. 'Toilet now. You go. You wash. Clean clothes.' She was holding a neatly folded pile: a new orange T-shirt, orange jumpsuit, and a pair of orange, men's boxer shorts. With impressive attention to detail, her captors had also provided a pair of orange flip-flops. Morgan had been wearing the previous set of clothes for three days. Before that, she recalled with a shudder, she had spent almost three days and nights in her own blouse and slacks, their fabric spattered with gobs of Abdel Nasser's blood.

'Please,' said Morgan. 'I need sanitary towels. It's my time of the month.'

Zainab looked blank. 'Time? It is morning time. You wash.'

Morgan mimed a pain in her stomach, holding her belly, bending over and grimacing.

'You sick? No doctor. No having doctor today.'

'It's my period! Sanitary towels!' Morgan could not prevent herself from raising her voice. She mimed again, pointing to her crotch, trying to enact the idea of liquid flowing from between her legs. She fought the tears: 'There's no point in giving me a new fucking jumpsuit if you can't get me some sanitary protection!'

Recognition dawned in Zainab's eyes. 'Ahh! Kotex! Yalla. When you come back, we have.'

Morgan submitted herself to the blindfold, and held out her hands for the cuffs. As Zainab propelled her towards the grubby bathroom, she was docile again. Zainab handed her a towel and some soap, removed the cuffs, pushed her inside and locked the door.

'Ten minutes,' she said. 'You have ten minutes. You wash.'

There was a plastic chair. Morgan disrobed, draping her uniform over it. Quickly she used the lavatory, then stood beneath the shower. The water was barely warm, but for a precious little while, she could try to wash away her predicament.

For the rest of the day, as during the days before, there was nothing. Nothing to see, nothing to read, nothing to do except pick at the trays of food that Zainab brought twice each day, and when Zainab allowed it, to pay visits to the toilet. There was no one to talk to: when she wasn't directly attending to Morgan's needs, Zainab was elsewhere, beyond the cell's locked door. Morgan knew there were always others. Sometimes Zainab didn't tie her blindfold quite securely, and she would catch a glimpse of a man's broad back in the corridor. She would hear the thudding of their boots, and sometimes their voices; what sounded like arguments in loud, guttural Arabic. But none of them had once tried to speak to her, not even during the kidnap.

The cell was too small to pace around, and fearing that she might be under clandestine observation, Morgan felt too embarrassed to attempt any kind of work out. So she sat, cross-legged, on the bare floor, surrounded by bare, peeling, light-green walls, or she lay on the plastic mat, using her single thin blanket as a pillow. Sometimes she sang softly to herself, remembering songs from summer camps long past, or the traditional country and western tunes beloved by her father. She wished that her education had extended to learning poetry, but it hadn't. So she lapsed into reverie, brooding on her children, her marriage, the likely identity of her captors and her chances of release.

Years earlier, Morgan had read Brian Keenan's account of the five years he spent as a hostage in Beirut. He had called his book *An Evil Cradling*, a title that had left her slightly puzzled. Now she knew what he meant. Just as he had done, she felt as helpless and bewildered as a baby, with the sights and sounds of her restricted universe as strange as the sensations that entered the consciousness of a newborn. She remembered with a grimace that back in America, in a life impossibly remote, she used to complain so bitterly about her sense that she had no control over her destiny, and that circumstances – her children, and marriage to a driven, workaholic lawyer – had left her subordinate to other people's wishes and needs. How strange that now seemed. Here she had no control over anything. If Zainab decided to be cruel to her, there was nothing Morgan could do; if she were to be pleasant, then that would be her gift. Somehow Morgan had to get her talking. But the only thing to look forward to now was that point in the evening when Zainab would come to turn off the light, whose switch lay behind the locked door. If she was lucky, the cumulative effort of hours of inactivity might be sufficient to bring sleep.

At some point after the second call to prayer, she thought about Adam, reflecting on his own ordeal with a tenderness that felt unfamiliar. By now it would be clear to him that something had gone very wrong. Had the Agency been in touch? Almost certainly. No doubt Gary and one of his blue-eyed acolytes would soon arrange to meet him, exuding a breezy, bogus confidence that they knew how to rescue her. Like so much in their lives of professional duplicity, their attempt at reassurance would be based on lies. They would have no greater idea as to her kidnappers' real identity than she did. What had Adam told the kids? How had he coped with his long-sought date with the Supremes?

She felt herself beginning to disassociate herself from her surroundings, as if her mind had left her body and she were somehow floating free. So vivid was this waking dream that she seemed to be hallucinating. She was at home again, the floor shaking from the vibration of Adam's clumsy footfall as he clumped down the stairs. Then she was smelling his fresh perspiration as he came in from a run, and hearing his effortless, English baritone, the first of several reasons why Morgan had decided the very first time she laid eyes on him that she would definitely be seeing this slightly awkward young man again.

A week after that first coffee in Harvard Square, they had gone to bed together for the first time: a night of revelation. Any sign of awkwardness Adam Cooper might have had had vanished entirely the moment he became her lover.

'So this has never happened before?' he said as she recovered, moist and glowing, the first time he gave her multiple orgasms. 'Not even once with the boys you knew in Texas?'

'No,' she mewed. 'It hasn't.'

She doubted there was anyone in the world with whose body her own was so naturally compatible. How sad it was that in almost every other way, they had grown so far apart.

Morgan had noticed that Zainab's spoken English was variable. There were times when she barely seemed to grasp what her prisoner was trying to communicate, and others when she seemed quite competent. Cautious as Morgan knew she had to be, Zainab's chattier moments were nonetheless a relief.

'You have childrens?' Zainab said, standing in the cell with a tray of food.

'Yes. I have two. And they need me.'

'What are their names?'

'Aimee and Charlie,' Morgan said. 'Aimee and Charlie.' Her voice caught. 'She's ten. He's eight. They're good kids and I know they miss me. Do you have children, too?'

Zainab ignored the question. 'You like boy or girl childrens best?'

'I like them both. I love them. I must see them soon. Can I call them?' A momentary surge of hope filled her heart. 'When will your friends let me go?'

'Maybe you don't see them soon. I think it's not possible. I think to call is also not possible. You know, in Arabia is many childrens whose father is in Guantanamo. Long time he doesn't see them. He doesn't talk on the phone. Maybe for you is long time, also. And in Gaza, many childrens don't see their mother because she is dead, because the Israelis, they kill her.' She put down the tray. 'After now, you eat. But why you leave your childrens to come to Palestine? This is not your war.'

Morgan struggled to control herself. Why *had* she left Aimee and Charlie to come to this place, in pursuit of a mission she could barely understand? And why had she spent so many years when she should have been enjoying her comfortable life in Bethesda just longing for the chance to put herself back in harm's way? She mustn't let Zainab see she had got to her. 'Get a grip,' she told herself inwardly – a phrase from Adam's oh-so-English mother. She touched her face. Thank God. Her eyes were still dry.

'You know why I'm here,' Morgan said, trying to smile. 'I am here to investigate human rights abuses. The people of Gaza are my friends and I am trying to help them.'

'Friends? Your friend is Mr Abdel Nasser. He is collaborator. He help no one, only Israelis. Why you his friend?' This was beginning to sound like an interrogation.

'He knows many people. He works with me.'

Zainab raised her head and clicked her tongue: a gesture of contemptuous disbelief. She left and locked the door.

Alone once again, Morgan found herself remembering the time Adam met Gary Thurmond. Adam would probably not remember him. Poor dear Adam had never been good with faces: another reason, as if one were needed, why he would not have been much use as an intelligence officer. But he and Gary had been introduced after the SERE course, when most of the class had joined their tutors at a cheerless tavern near the Farm. They had even conducted a brief, spiky dialogue on the uses of the death penalty, which left neither of them much impressed with the other's opinions.

Gary had been standing at the bar, in those days much slimmer, sipping Coors Light from the bottle, getting a read on the students' performance from Bud and the other instructors. 'That was the day I decided that you and I were made for each other,' Gary told her months later. 'They said you knew how to keep your mouth shut – even if you were hell-bent on sleeping with that pinko young lawyer.'

Morgan had been assigned to work for Gary a few weeks after the SERE course. 'Normally, the hardest part is making your cover credible,' he told her. 'With you, it's going to write itself. From now on, human rights ain't gonna be just an academic exercise. It's your job.'

The State Department's Bureau of Democracy, Human Rights and Labour conducted investigations, issued reports and sent staff to testify at Congressional hearings. But unlike most of its far-flung personnel, Morgan's section had been entirely the CIA's creature. It had consisted of just four people: besides Morgan, just Gary, Eugene, now her colleague in Tel Aviv, and Alicia Phillips, a cheerful, fresh-faced woman from Milwaukee.

Gary was their leader and point man, a veteran of behind-the-lines operations in the 1991 Gulf War and the anti-Soviet jihad in Afghanistan. But while he mostly stayed in the United States, Morgan, Eugene and Alicia spent months at a time in the

Balkans, living an intense, comradely life in a shared apartment in Sarajevo. Enabled by their cover, they soon developed an enviable network of contacts among the Muslim victims of Serb aggression. Gary was convinced that what they were seeing in former Yugoslavia – a new generation of young Muslim fighters, many of them veterans of Afghanistan – was the start of something that would one day threaten America. For Morgan, gathering intelligence about atrocities was a noble end in itself, and she wanted to see it influence American policy. For Gary, as he put it one day during one of his flying visits, that was simply 'bullshit'.

'You need to remember something,' he told Morgan, his finger jabbing towards her chest. 'Your cover is not the same thing as your mission. You need to remember what we really want to know – who are these Muslims who keep showing up to fight with no discernible link to Bosnia-Hercegovina? Where do these motherfuckers come from? Telling us that is your mission. Where do they get their arms? Who is their emir? Is that understood?'

'Yessir. Understood.'

It wasn't long after that conversation that Morgan managed to get herself embedded with a unit of the fledgling Kosovo Liberation Army, ostensibly to document the first stirrings of what threatened to be the last and worst wave of ethnic cleansing. For three gruelling weeks, she shared their camps, their marches, their hideouts, constantly at risk of discovery by Jugoslav army or Serbian irregular patrols. The KLA guerillas came to see her as one of their own, and showed her an audacious new smuggling route, a supply line for weapons and ammunition purchased from corrupt Jugoslav National Army contacts at bases in Montenegro. It ran through networks of trails in the forested mountains by the side of the Tara river canyon.

By the time she got back to Sarajevo, Morgan felt triumphant. She'd done everything Gary wanted and more: among her KLA companions had been several veterans of the Afghan war, citizens of countries such as Sudan and Syria who seemed to have become Islamist soldiers of fortune, devoted to never-ending jihad. Her sense of glory lasted only hours. On the day of her return to the Sarajevo apartment, Alicia was hit by a sniper in the plaza outside on her way to buy food and plum brandy for a celebration dinner. Morgan and Eugene saw it all from the apartment: her puzzled half-turn as she heard the sound of a rifle shot, and then the flower of blood spreading on her cheesecloth blouse as she fell. They rushed down the stairs and tried to staunch the flow, kneeling at her side as she moaned. She managed to get a few words out: 'I'm sorry to spoil your party.' By nightfall, Alicia was being treated at an American military hospital in Frankfurt. But a bullet had lodged in her spine, and she'd been in a wheelchair ever since. The following summer Morgan visited her in St Paul. Still cheerful, Alicia had explained that her fiancé had decided he couldn't face a life with a paraplegic, but her parents had helped her convert an apartment. She'd gone back to school, and was working on a doctorate about the most effective way to protect human rights in the Balkans.

The menu was the same as the previous day, and the days before that: hummus, rice, beans and a few gritty vegetables, and a small triangle of baklava, washed down with half a litre of water. The seal on the bottle had been broken: Morgan could only hope it really was bottled. If she was lucky, Zainab would be back once more before nightfall with another sanitary towel, and to take her to the toilet. The evening prayer call had come and gone.

Hours passed, and then the door was unlocked again. But for once, Zainab was not alone: with her was a man, his face wrapped in a red *keffiyeh* scarf. They were carrying a cheap, foam mattress and an olive coloured sheet. They manoeuvred the mattress into the cell and laid it on the floor.

'You sleep better now,' said Zainab. 'This is bed.'

The man left them alone, and once again Zainab tied the blindfold and led her to the bathroom. She must have been feeling generous: she gave Morgan not one but two new Kotex, as well as a plastic bag in case she needed a change before morning. Soon enough Zainab was gone again, leaving her back in the cell, with the door locked and the only light a thin line from the corridor through the gap beneath the door. In fact, the mattress made it no easier to sleep. If anything, it seemed more difficult, as if the bed were a sign that her detention had become more settled, less temporary. The other westerners who had been kidnapped in Gaza had all been released after less than a week. This was the end of her sixth day, and somehow, it didn't seem very likely that she was about to be freed.

As she tossed and turned in her restlessness, she picked up a sound from the streets outside which she hadn't heard since the day of her abduction: high-velocity weapons. She guessed that the clashes between Hamas and Fatah had restarted. It was oddly comforting to be reminded of them, because Gaza's violent, unsettled politics meant her own situation was less likely to be permanent.

She had done better today. For some of the time, she had kept the movie at bay, but as she faced the night it returned. Again Morgan saw the blood, heard the blows and Abdel Nasser's screams, felt the pressure of the duct tape gag inside the trunk of the Mercedes. As sleep finally came, she consoled herself with the thought that having lived through that reality, she really ought to stop being frightened of nightmares.

Chapter Six
Sunday, April 8, 2007

Adam hadn't slept properly for days. He knew he had to reply to Sherelle's message, but he didn't even know where to start. He scrolled through the possibilities in his head: 'Hi Sherry, it would be lovely to have you come to stay but this isn't a great time because your daughter has been kidnapped. CIA says it's doing all it can but not yet sure how this is going to pan out. Love Adam. PS, don't tell a soul about this, okay?' That didn't seem quite to do it. 'Sherry! No, please, stay at home! My nerves can't quite take it right now.' Not so good either.

He stared at his computer screen, and as he had so often since his wife's disappearance, felt powerless. That he, Adam Cooper, rising star of the human rights bar, should have to be reliant on the CIA was intolerable. Mike, the young African-American, had at least struck him as sincere. Only yesterday, in the course of a long phone call, he had impressed on him the Agency ethos: that no officer must ever be left behind. 'Think of it as Saving Private Ryan, but with almost unimaginable technology. It may take time, but I promise you, we're going to find her.'

But there were things about Gary, who was evidently much higher in the CIA hierarchy, that made Adam deeply uncomfortable. His anal, restrictive approach to information; his insistence that the 'trust' he kept on talking about seemed to require total inaction on Adam's part. The mere fact that his wife had been kidnapped meant that, ultimately, Gary had fucked up. Why hadn't he done more to ensure her security? And yet the man was still pretending that she might not have been abducted after all. On top of it all, he was asking Adam to tell a series of elaborate lies about Morgan's unexpected absence to everyone he knew, including his own children: lies which would surely unravel the longer time went on. He remembered the case of William Buckley, the CIA chief in Lebanon, who was kidnapped and tortured to death after fifteen months in captivity in 1985. For all Gary's talk of working his lines and assets, Adam feared that he and Mike knew no more about what had happened to Morgan than he did.

The inaction was all the harder to take because Adam had always seen himself as a person of action, someone who tried to direct and influence events, rather than merely be swept up in them. He'd never been scared of taking risks: hence his record as a mountaineer. In the courtroom, he had always been equally bold. Sometimes the outcomes of trials and appeals left him saddened or disappointed. But at least he would have tried, fought the good fight. All Gary seemed to want him to do was to be passive, to wait.

At the same time, Adam felt pretty certain that Mike and Gary had not met many Islamists. He had. He had a network: a web of contacts stemming from his work which made it much more likely he could find sources in Gaza than any Agency officer. His deliberations over how to reply to his mother-in-law subsided, and in their place, he began to devise a plan. He picked up his cellphone and thumbed a message to Nuha, Ahmad Mahmoud's sister. 'We need to meet,' was all it said. 'I'll be at your apartment at nine o'clock this morning.'

Afterwards, Adam dozed, waking as soon as it was light. The kids had been expecting a lazy morning, but he had them out of bed, breakfasted and dressed early. He told them he had to meet someone involved with his Supreme Court case, and because their mother was still away and Mila didn't come on the weekends, they'd have to accompany him. By eight-fifteen, they all were piling into the Volvo.

'Dad!' said Aimee as they headed on to the Beltway. 'Why are we doing this? And why now? What if Mom calls? And how come she hasn't sent us emails?'

'I'm sure she will very soon. I guess she's been busy. And maybe she can't use the internet.' He knew how lame his words must have sounded.

Aimee snorted. 'But she usually stays in hotels! Dad, she's on a business trip, right? You ever stayed in a hotel where you can't get on to the internet?'

They spent the rest of the journey in silence. The kids were tired and sullen, and Adam felt too distracted to say anything that might reassure them. Then, responding to their fears and anxieties had always been more Morgan's role. She would know what to say. He frankly didn't.

Nuha, who worked as an emergency room nurse, lived in a functional but humble apartment in Alexandria, Virginia, on the edge of the housing projects. By now, she had once told Adam, at the age of twenty-seven, she should have been married, with children of her own, but while her brother remained a prisoner, that was impossible. 'How can we celebrate while he is being tortured?' she had asked. Her building stood in an open area of scruffy grass and earth. An abandoned plastic tricycle lay on its side next to the elevator, which appeared to be broken.

'Is this safe, Dad?' asked Aimee.

'Sure it is, honeybunch. Apart from anything else, at this time of day, anyone dangerous round here is still asleep.' He offered a fake laugh, but it only seemed to make Aimee more anxious.

The lobby and the bare concrete stairwell were plastered with graffiti. Four flights up, they knocked at Nuha's door. Entering, Adam blinked, trying to get used to the gloom: the curtains were closed. The room was almost bare of adornment, the only decoration a small oriental rug and a few pieces of Syrian brassware which rested on cheap, self-assembly furniture. Adam knew that Nuha gave a substantial portion of her wages to help support Ahmad's children. As usual, dressed in dark trousers and a hand-knitted sweater, she looked well groomed. But each time he saw her she seemed thinner than the last.

The children sat quietly on a sofa, close together and uncharacteristically meek.

'Why don't you watch the TV while Nuha and I talk?' Adam said. Nuha passed Aimee the remote, and she found a Scooby-Doo rerun. She kept the volume low.

'I'm sorry, I wasn't expecting you,' Nuha said. 'I only picked up your text half an hour ago. So what's up? Is it about the case? Has something happened?'

'No, no – it's all going fine. All we can do is wait for the judges to make up their minds. But actually, this visit is about me. I need to ask a favour. But first, please promise me that whether or not you find out anything, you'll be discreet. You mustn't tell anyone we've even spoken about this.'

She turned up her palms. 'Of course. You have my word.'

'Do you have friends, relatives, anyone, who is close to the struggle in Palestine? Anyone you could put me in touch with who might be in a position to lead me to people who know what's going on?'

Nuha's expression was unmistakeable: unadulterated fear. 'Adam, you know that since Ahmad's arrest, I have had nothing to do with politics. I do my job, I practise my religion, I try to help my family. I support Ahmad, but that's all.'

'I only need a name, a number – '

'Please don't ask me this.'

Adam felt he had no alternative. 'I wouldn't ask you unless I honestly believed I had to. It's just that I think my wife may be in trouble. It's possible you can help.'

'Your wife? What kind of trouble?'

Adam had already said too much. 'Well - it would just be useful for me to be able to talk to someone who could help me check something out.'

Nuha breathed deeply. 'Maybe I can get you a name, a number. But I don't want to talk about such things on the phone.'

Adam had already created a new, web-based email address for himself. He wrote it down on a scrap of paper and gave it to Nuha. 'If you get something, make a new email account on a computer you don't normally use, at an internet café or wherever. Then send me a message to this address here. Put

"Russian lady seeks business opportunity" in the subject line and I'll know it's from you.'

Adam had not noticed that all the time he was talking to Nuha, Aimee had been listening intently. They were barely back in the stairwell before he grasped his mistake.

'Dad,' she said, 'what's happening? You told that lady that mommy might be in trouble. What did you mean? What trouble? Is she going to be okay?'

'We were talking privately. I think you misheard.'

'Dad. Do you think me and Charlie are deaf?'

'Look, I can't tell you anything you don't already know.' Adam said. 'But I'm hoping that my friend might be able to help us bring her home.'

'I don't get it. A woman who lives in a housing project in Alexandria, Virginia? What do you mean?'

'I know some things are hard to understand right now. Let's get back to the car.'

Aimee had evidently been working herself up to this for days. Her anxiety and wretchedness served only to underline that Gary's demand he keep the truth from the children was ridiculous and unsustainable.

'Dad, we're not toddlers any more,' she said as they walked back across the grass. 'You've got to level with us. You send us to the best schools and you help us with our homework and talk to our teachers and you know we're actually both pretty smart. So stop treating us like we're dumb. What trouble is she in?'

Adam glanced at Charlie. He was walking, his eyes fixed straight ahead, as if trying not to listen. But the tears were watering his cheeks.

'Just get in the car,' Adam said. 'Then we'll talk.'

He had no alternative. They had to know the truth. Once they were all inside the vehicle, he twisted round to face them from the driver's seat. 'Aimee, Charlie, I'm sorry. I should have told you this earlier. But what I'm going to say has to stay our secret: you mustn't tell anyone else. Is that understood?'

Aimee could only nod, suddenly silent. Her eyes widened. She was trying not to cry, and bit her lip.

'As you know, your mother works for the US government. Right now, her boss has asked her to make trips to a place called Gaza. It's next to Israel, and the people there are called Palestinians. We – that's me and the people Mom works with – think it's possible she may have been kidnapped: captured by someone and locked up against her will, like in a prison. We're going to do everything we can to find her: not just the people she works with, but me. I think I may be able to help, because of the people I know from my job. That's why we came here to see my friend. Her family are Palestinians too, and I think she can put me in contact with someone who might know something.'

Charlie's eyes betrayed a mixture of pain and amazement, and for a moment, amazement held the upper hand. 'Do you mean cool secret agent people are looking for our mom – like from the CIA?'

'Yes, Charlie. That's exactly what I mean. And I'm telling you, these guys are good!'

'Wow, Dad.' A few moments passed while Adam's words sank in. But then Charlie started to sob. 'Daddy, daddy.' He was wailing. 'What if they can't find her? I want Mommy home!'

'So Mom has been kidnapped by terrorists' Aimee said. 'The kind of people who hate America and attacked us on 9/11. Is that what you're saying?' she asked quietly.

'Yes sweetie. We can't be sure yet, but that's what may have happened.'

Now Aimee started weeping, too. With his children buckled into the back seat of the vehicle, Adam couldn't even given them a proper hug, but watched in the rear view mirror as Aimee reached across and held Charlie's hand in hers. Adam had to swallow hard to compose himself.

Morgan came round from her nap with the *maghrib*, the sunset prayer call, a little after seven o'clock. It had been the hottest day yet: inside the cell, over ninety degrees Farenheit. She hadn't been given a shower for two days, but the heat was the least of her worries. As she lay on her back, she felt the room gently heaving, as if she were standing on the deck of a ship, while the ceiling started to spin. She sat up and breathed deeply, struggling to contain her rising nausea by focusing intently on a spot on the wall. Minutes passed and it didn't seem to be working. Apart from a half-empty bottle of water, there was nothing in the cell but her bedding; nothing she could use to vomit in, but several times she heaved. At last the dizziness began to lift. She had been prone to vertigo – the doctors called it labyrnthitis - ever since a teenage infection had left her with scar tissue in her left middle ear. Sometimes her bouts lasted only hours, but sometimes several weeks.

For a few more minutes she stayed motionless, the only noise her own subsiding hyperventilation, as she fought to take control of the panic within her. When it really seemed that all was still she stood and banged on the door. 'Zainab!' she yelled. 'Zainab! Please, come, I need help!'

Silence. There were no sounds of footsteps, no voices, anywhere in the house. For the first time since her capture, she was really alone. She yelled again, and as she did so, heard again the clatter of automatic fire outside, sounding very close to the house, then the cries and groans of someone, apparently a man, who'd been hit, followed by shouts.

'Zainab! Help!'

Again nothing. As she shouted, Morgan had lost concentration. Her mistake was to look at the floor, in the hope of detecting a slight flicker of the light that came through a narrow gap at the bottom of the door: the sign of someone passing. It brought a new wave of dizzy nausea surging through her head and stomach, and this time, Morgan could not contain herself. As she heaved, first hot bile, then her wretched, half-digested lunch poured from her stomach on to the floor. There was still no Zainab, but now Morgan was trapped amid her own filth and stench.

It brought to mind a recent memory. Charlie, tough little trooper Charlie, hardly ever got ill, but a couple of weeks before

Morgan left for Gaza he'd picked up a nasty virus. Adam had been working in his study next to Charlie's bedroom, but, as usual, when he cried for help, it was Morgan who rushed to his side: too late to stop him being sick all over her slippers and the floor. She'd cleaned him up, given him some water and children's Tylenol, and he'd gone back to sleep, but he'd woken almost every hour throughout the night.

All through that almost sleepless night, as she held him and soothed him and stroked his face, Morgan had felt herself suffused with a love so intense that it almost made her son's suffering worth it. That night, while Adam slept undisturbed, she had wondered seriously for the first time whether she should ask the Agency not to give her any more dangerous assignments in the field, at least not until the kids were grown. She hadn't, she recalled ruefully, given that idea a moment's further thought until now.

Curled in the corner of the cell, Morgan wondered who was comforting Charlie now. Suddenly the stink of her own, adult puke seemed especially repellent, and she heaved once more.

After Adam's shocking disclosure, the kids said very little, and once they were all back home, the routines of family life reasserted themselves. Aimee had a soccer practice. Charlie went to play video games with a classmate. Adam climbed the stairs to his computer. He didn't expect to find anything yet from Nuha, but to his surprise, a message was already waiting for him. 'You can try this number,' it said. 'Probably better if you travel before you use it.' Adam immediately recognised what followed: the number of a British mobile telephone, beginning with the code 07711. It only confirmed what he had already almost decided: they should all go to England.

The reasons were obvious. The CIA's insistence that he maintain secrecy was impossible. But now the children knew the truth, the idea that they could simply go back to school when the Easter holidays finished was inconceivable. Several of their classmates' parents worked in the media. As Gary had warned him, it would not be long before Morgan's plight was plastered across the front page of the *Washington Post*.

His finger a little shaky, Adam dialled a number in England.

'Hey Dad. It's me. How's it going?' He was trying to sound as normal as he could.

'Adam!' He heard his father yell down the stairs of the rambling north Oxford house. 'Darling, pick up the extension! It's our prodigal offspring.' There was a pause while his mother tuned in. 'So, tell us all about the case. How's it feel to be a Supreme Court advocate? How come you didn't call before now, did you think we weren't interested or something? How're the kids? And how's Morgan?'

'The Supremes' argument went fine, I think, though I guess it didn't feel that way at the time. I'm sorry I haven't called: things have been a little stressful. But the kids are great. As for Morgan: well, I think she's okay, but she's had to make, like, an extended business trip. But yeah, I'm sure she's fine.'

There was a pause while Adam's words sank in. 'A business trip, huh?' said his father.

'Yes. Well you know how it is: sometimes these things take longer than expected. Actually that's the main reason I called. We're all going a little crazy here without her and I wondered if we might come over for a bit.'

'Don't they have to go back to school?' The speaker was Adam's mother, Gwen. 'Are you sure this a good idea, darling? I mean, the university term doesn't start for another fortnight but once it does, your father and I are going to be awfully busy. You don't think they're going to miss their friends and get bored? Are you sure the school won't mind?'

'Mum. I'm sure by the time the Oxford term starts Morgan's trip will be over. I just thought it might be nice if we could escape for a week or so.'

Jonathan, Adam's father, brushed away her objections. 'It's fine. You can have your old room. The kids can have the spare. When do you want to come?'

'Let me see what I can get online.'

67

Half an hour later, Adam had booked them all on a British Airways flight from Dulles to Heathrow that left the following evening. He would call Gary, the school, Mila, and his office once they got to England: Monday was a public holiday, so he still had plenty of time. That left only Sherelle. He opened an email.

'Dear Sherry,' he wrote, 'I'm awfully sorry to be so late in getting back to you. Please accept my apologies. I did not mean to be rude.

'Aimee and Charlie have very busy calendars for the next few days, as do I, and Morgan is away on a business trip. We'd all love to see you, but it would be a lot more convenient a little later in the month. Let's talk in a week or two to see about fixing dates.

'I hope you're having a lovely spring on the Alamo. The blossom here is heavenly. With much love from us all, Adam.'

Hours had passed. It must be late, after ten o'clock, Morgan thought, but there was still no sign of Zainab, nor a sound of anyone else. Gaza went to bed early, and outside, the alleys of the refugee camp would be deserted, shadowy strips between the buildings, illuminated only by the stars. She had finished her water, and she needed both a pee and a new sanitary pad. Thankfully, the odour had diminished a little, or maybe she had merely got used to it. For the moment at least, she had stopped feeling dizzy. At last she heard the key being turned in the lock.

It wasn't Zainab but two tall, burly men, their features masked with *keffiyeh* scarves. They took in the state of the cell and its prisoner and visibly recoiled, shouting at each other in Arabic. One of them grabbed Morgan and hoisted her to her feet, then roughly pulled her arms behind her back and bound them with plastic cuffs. The other produced a thick, dark canvas hood and pulled it over her head, leaving her blind and disorientated. Inside, it too seemed to smell of human vomit.

'We go! You move!' one of the men shouted, his voice muffled, as if coming from a distance. He prodded her in the back, while the other man guided her out of the cell by the arm. Morgan sensed they were in the corridor. They descended a short flight of stairs and she heard another door being unlocked, and then they were outside: even through the hood, she could smell garbage and a hint of sewage, while on her hands she felt the faint waft of a Mediterranean breeze. For a moment she considered the possibility of escape, or at least screaming. But wherever she was – Gaza City, Jabaliya or Khan Younis – there was little chance of anyone coming to her rescue.

They made their way down an alley: there was no room for her captors to walk by Morgan's side, and instead, one of the men grabbed a handful of her overall and dragged her along behind him. Beyond, they seemed to have reached a road. She heard a car door being opened, and another man, presumably the driver, held a short conversation with the man holding Morgan. This time, thankfully, they did not put her in the trunk. She felt a hand pressing down on the top of her head, like a cop with a suspect, pushing her on to the passenger seat. Someone got in beside her and shoved her head down further, until it rested on her knees, presumably so it wouldn't be easily visible through the window.

After another burst of Arabic, the car began to move. As it lurched, bumped and decelerated, Morgan was once again nauseous, and she fought to keep calm, gulping air through the stinking, stifling hood. After what felt like an age but was probably not much more than half an hour, the vehicle stopped. Someone pulled her out, then frogmarched her across what felt like some kind of yard. Wherever she was, it felt more open: maybe she was somewhere in Gaza's rolling countryside. She was guided inside a building, and half-pushed, half-carried down a flight of stairs. Finally the hood was pulled off. Dazed by the light, she saw she was standing in a sparsely-furnished white-walled room. Facing her was a large bearded man in early middle age, dressed in a white turban and a knee-length robe – not the flowing *jallabiya* favoured by the Bedouin, but shorter, of the type common in southern Egypt and the Sudan. Morgan recognised it from a crash course in Islamist style she had been given by Abdel Nasser. It usually denoted not a member of Hamas – they tended to wear well-pressed trousers or suits with plain dress shirts, and sometimes even neckties – but a Salafist, a fundamentalist inspired by Osama bin Laden and al-Qaeda. Hamas beards were short and trimmed. This man's was long and ragged, shaggy like a black lion's mane.

'Mrs Cooper. It is so nice to meet you,' he said, in a lightly-accented voice that could easily have been European. 'In a moment you can clean yourself up. Soon we will ask you some questions. And then you will make a video, a nice little DVD.'

Chapter Seven
Friday, April 13, 2007

When Adam had called the number Nuha had given him, a warm, cultivated voice had answered it at once. Its owner seemed to be expecting him, and asked Adam to meet him on the first available occasion – at ten o'clock that Friday, in the lounge of the Lanesborough Hotel. The man assured Adam he would have no difficulty in recognising him, but to put his mind at ease he promised to be carrying a camel hair coat and a copy of that day's Times. Adam had taken an early train from Oxford, and having walked across Hyde Park from Paddington station, he saw straightaway that his interlocutor was standing by the bar - a dapper man in his early thirties in a brown pinstripe suit, with olive skin and a full, trimmed beard.

'You must be Adam,' he said, holding out his hand. 'Imad al-Saleh. And before we go any further, let me express my admiration for everything you've done. A lot of people say they support the concept of human rights. Not so many have fought for them the way you have. You must have made some powerful enemies.'

Adam shrugged, modestly. 'Well, one tries to do one's bit. So... you know Nuha and Ahmad?'

'Let's not talk about whom I know and whom I don't. The important thing is that you have asked for help. Let me see if I can provide it. But first, let's find a table and get some coffee.'

After they had ordered, Imad told Adam he was a doctor. 'My family is still in Gaza, but I'm working and studying here at St Mary's. I want to specialise in reconstructive surgery – trying to rehabilitate patients with blast and gunshot wounds. Back home, those skills are in demand.'

Adam began to describe Morgan's human rights bureau cover, her journey to Gaza, and her last voicemail message. Imad sat with his elbows on his knees, listening intently.

71

'Do you know the name of her point man? Surely, she must have had a fixer, some kind of go-between, to help her make contacts?'

'I don't know. She never told me much about her work. But I do recall one name – I think it was Abdel Nasser. Does that mean anything to you?'

The expression on Imad's face suggested that it did.

'Abdel Nasser is not an uncommon name. A lot of our people bear it in honour of President Abdel Nasser Hussein of Egypt. But I can think of one who is the sort of person a State Department official would find useful, and if it's him, I've known him since we were kids. Abdel Nasser al-Kafarneh – we were at the American high school together. He's from a very prominent family. He even went to school in America – Columbia, if I'm not mistaken. To be frank with you, he used to be a bit of a playboy. He'd hold parties in his parents' villa when they were away. There were Christian girls and alcohol: not what I was used to. But he is well connected.'

'So he's not very likely to have had anything to do with the type of people who'd want to abduct an American?'

'No way. Absolutely no way.' Imad looked quizzical, and tapped his fingers against his lips. 'I presume you've been to the US authorities. Surely they must have some ideas?'

'Of course. I've spoken to them almost every day since Morgan disappeared. My problem is that I don't think they really have a clue where to look. They promised me they'd know who was holding her within forty-eight hours. That was almost two weeks ago.'

Imad nodded. 'I'm not surprised. In Gaza, they talk to Fatah, no one else. And Fatah will not know anything. So. What do you want to do? Do you want to go to Gaza to see if you can find her yourself? If you do, I can make sure you meet the right people.'

Adam wasn't sure that was what he did want. Travelling to Gaza would mean leaving the children with his parents. It would be emotionally difficult for all of them. But at the same time, he felt convinced that if he didn't start to take matters into his own hands, he might never see Morgan again.

'Do you think I might make progress?'

Imad pursed his lips. 'Why not? So long as the Israelis let you in. And don't worry that you will also be kidnapped. We will do our best to keep you safe.'

'We?'

Imad touched Adam's shoulder. 'I think you know what I mean. You are here because you know I have influential friends. They can both assist your search and protect you.'

Adam knew he was taking an irrevocable step. 'Yes. I will go to Gaza.'

Imad looked at his watch. 'I need to get back to the hospital. I'll be in touch.'

After dinner, while Gwen tried to put the children to bed, Adam and his father sat on the deck in the garden, the remains of a bottle of a classed growth Bordeaux between them. The light was starting to fade, but the weather was unseasonably warm, and though most of the trees were still bare, the big magnolia at the head of the lawn was in resplendent bloom. As they sat, they could hear laughter and conversation: someone must be having a drinks party in the Lady Margaret Hall garden.

'Oxford,' Adam said. 'I'd forgotten how much I miss it.'

Jonathan Cooper stared at his son over half-moon spectacles. Thirty years as a fellow of Christchurch had eradicated almost every trace of an American accent, but when he felt agitated, as evidently he did now, it was still noticeable. He twisted the stem of his wine glass, and waved away what Adam thought was an imaginary insect.

Finally he spoke. 'So. Here we are, then. Are you going to tell me what's really happening, or do I have to guess?'

'Guess? What do you mean?'

'Adam. You're my son. You may live four thousand miles away, but I know you. You've just appeared before the Supreme Court in a case that even made the newspapers here, and yet you've barely mentioned it. You seem to have taken indefinite leave from work, and though you say Morgan's away on business you've not told us where. And so far as I know, you haven't even spoken to her since you arrived two days ago.'

'Yes,' Adam said, his voice cracking. 'That seems to sum up the situation admirably.'

'So tell me about it.'

Adam stared into the twilight for several minutes, struggling to find a reply. 'First let me ask you a question. What do you think it is that Morgan does for a living?'

Jonathan did not miss a beat. 'I suppose I've always assumed she's an intelligence officer. I mean, when you put it all together: months working on mysterious missions in the Balkans; a desk job in Washington that she never spoke about; now some scheme to monitor human rights in the Middle East – well, if you join the dots…'

Adam did not demur. There didn't seem to be any point, and if he had, his father would not have believed him anyway.

'It must have been difficult for you, keeping her secrets,' Jonathan said. 'How long have you known?'

'Quite a while. Since Harvard.'

Jonathan whistled through his teeth. 'It's not as if you're exactly a neocon now. But then – Jesus. You were a long, long way to the left. How did you deal with it? I mean, didn't it feel as if you were sleeping with the enemy? Come to that, now that you're doing all these war on terror cases, doesn't it feel as if you're doing it now?'

Adam shrugged his shoulders: a gesture of helplessness. 'I was in love with her. And some things might have changed between us, but underneath the day-to-day shit most working couples with children have to get through, I still am.'

'I'm sure you are. But all the same, how did you deal with the politics?'

'I'll never forget the day she came out to me. We were lying in bed, late: an early spring weekend. I started talking about how we could make a summer trip to Asia, and she told me she couldn't come because she'd signed up to be a CIA intern. And if that went well, she wanted a permanent job.'

'How did you react?'

'Not very well, frankly. I couldn't believe it at first: I actually thought she was joking. When I realised she wasn't, I started yelling about how the CIA had sponsored death squads in Central America, and then I slammed the door of the apartment and went for a walk. I thought she'd be gone by the time I got back, but she was still there, still in bed, wearing one of my T-shirts. I could see she'd been crying but when she spoke she was calm, kind of steely. What stopped us breaking up was that she made me a promise.'

'A promise?'

'Yes. First she made this little speech, saying we had more in common than it looked. According to her, my problem was that I failed to understand that she could be both a patriot and a liberal, and that underlying both our paths were the values of the US Constitution. The only real difference was that I would be trying to uphold them in court, while she would be protecting them by working at the Agency. What she said next I can still quote almost verbatim: "I know I can't be sure I'm right that the CIA can be a force for good. But I give you my word. If I find I'm wrong, I won't just leave, I'll blow the whistle. I'll give you the material for the biggest fucking case of your career."'

'And has she?' Jonathan smiled: he already knew the answer. 'But that was then, the nineties. It was easy for her to make that argument: I mean, who would quarrel with American foreign policy when it was trying to stop Balkan war crimes? But what about now? How have the two of you dealt with the fact that while you've been representing the victims of waterboarding and extraordinary rendition, she's been working for the organisation accused of perpetrating them?'

'We haven't been discussing our work, to be honest. There are subjects that are kind of taboo. But right now this is irrelevant. Our marital difficulties aren't exactly the point.'

'I'm sorry. I'm being insensitive. So: tell me what is the point. Fill me in.'

By the time Adam had finished relating what he knew, it was dark. Gwen came out to join them, carrying a cup of herbal tea. She sat down, trying to be cheery: 'There, darlings, the kids are in bed. Charlie's had his story and Aimee says she's still tired from the flight. We thought we might go up to Waddesdon Manor tomorrow – we can let Charlie try out the adventure playground. So what have you two been talking about?'

Jonathan put his hand on hers. 'I'm sure Waddesdon will be lovely. Meanwhile, it seems that as you've always suspected, our daughter-in-law is a spy, but unfortunately she's been kidnapped by Islamic extremists. We're not supposed to talk about it, because the CIA says they're petrified of what might happen if her case gets any publicity. Adam brought the children here because he couldn't conceal the truth from them, and once they knew, they wouldn't be able to hide it from their school friends.'

'Indeed not,' said Gwen. 'I don't suppose they would.'

'What do you mean?' asked Jonathan.

She turned on the bench to face him. 'Darling, they've already been here two whole days. Did you really think they weren't going to tell me? If the CIA was worried they might blurt it out to their school friends, I can assure you that there really wasn't much prospect they would hide it from their granny.'

'No,' said Jonathan. 'I guess not.'

'Well, who knows, maybe I'll be able to help you, Adam. I've taught a lot of interesting people over the years, and I like to stay in touch with them. At any rate, I can try.'

Morgan was losing track of time. 'Sal,' as she had named the anonymous Salafist she had met on the evening of her move to the countryside, had kept his word about allowing her to wash that first night. But ever since, she had been kept in total darkness. Someone – she was pretty sure it was Zainab – still took her to the toilet at irregular intervals. But whenever she went, she blindfolded and hooded her before they left the cell. Occasionally she would get a chink of light when someone opened the door to leave water and a tray of food. But as soon as her meal had been deposited, it would be dark again, forcing her to eat as best she could by touch. The cell itself was, if anything, larger. But no one spoke to her. She knew several days had passed. She had little idea how many. As to her whereabouts, she couldn't help but wonder whether she was being held in the very place that Abdel Nasser had promised to bring her for a tryst on the day of their abduction. No one knew he owned it, he had said. They kidnappers obviously did, but presumably they had had him under surveillance. If she was right, that meant there was little prospect of the kidnappers being disturbed.

She felt for a piece of flatbread and her water bottle, and reflected on the course of events that had brought her there. Since the summer of 2003, Morgan had been working with Gary Thurmond again. For a long time, it wasn't the fieldwork she had craved. But compared to the dark period after 9/11, when the Langley corridors had seemed to surge with the force of pure, patriotic rage, and a sense of mission and collective purpose greater than anything they had known for decades, it was paradise: at least she was making a difference. Her mind went back to a Friday in June 2003, at one of the Headquarters 'vespers' gatherings when she and her colleagues would gather to swap stories and drink beer. She hadn't seen Gary for several years. He looked heavier, but cheerful, and his deep mahogany tan was evidence of the fact he hadn't been spending too much time inside the Washington Beltway.

'Hey, Morgan. You're looking good,' he said. 'How's my favourite officer mom? I hear Aimee's got a little brother. Anyhow. Your career is doing amazingly! Keep this up, and one day you're going to be in charge of all of us.'

'I'm okay, thanks.' She tried but failed to stifle a sigh. 'The kids are great. And I know it won't be so long before they're more independent. But however important my work at Headquarters, it just doesn't quite do it for me.'

'You want to come back and work for me?'

'You know me Gary. I'm the gal who marched with the KLA. I'm the one who identified some of these jihadist motherfuckers' networks for the first time. Look, I can't take an assignment that would mean leaving home for months. But mightn't there be something more part-time – in terms of travelling?'

Gary looked at her carefully. 'You mean it?' He gestured round the room. 'You really feel you're ready to give all this up for the chance of getting shot at and contracting diarrhoea?'

Even as she spoke, Morgan knew she would say nothing about this conversation to Adam. 'Yes, Gary. I do.'

'Right now, there's nothing doing. But if I get the chance, I'll bear you in mind. Like you said, you're the gal who marched with the KLA.'

A few weeks later, Morgan had found herself transferred to an anonymous office building in Tysons Corner, Virginia. She was still working from behind a desk and facing a murderous commute from Bethesda, but Gary had promised that if he got the chance, he would find a suitable fieldwork assignment. In the meantime, she was now playing a critical logistical role in some of the counter-terrorist operations that were the war on terror's front line. Some, involving unfamiliar terms like 'enhanced interrogation techniques' and 'extraordinary rendition,' she found ethically questionable. She recalled her long-ago promise to Adam: that if she ever came across evidence that the Agency was not living up to the constitutional values she had joined it to defend, she would blow the whistle and give him the 'biggest fucking case of your life'. But this was wartime, the depths of a struggle against a pitiless enemy, and Morgan kept her mouth shut.

Her job meant she knew some of the details of her section's personnel and operations worldwide – information which, in the wrong hands, could be highly damaging. It also meant she had a certain familiarity with the unpleasant techniques her own captors were using now to soften her up: not only the darkness, but the deafening noise that filled it for many hours each day, a single album by the rapper Eminem, piped into her cell at high volume. As she munched her bread, it started again. She knew she could expect it for hour after deafening hour, the same recording played again and again on a continuous loop.

Relentless and inescapable, it made sleep all but impossible. Only once had she known time pass so slowly. Years earlier, when she and Adam had taken a skiing trip to Colorado, she had broken her leg and was forced to spend five days in the hospital, awaiting and recovering from surgery. The days were bad enough: hours of discomfort, alternately dozing and watching the trashy television that seemed to enthral her roommate. But the nights – a few minutes of sleep punctuated by long sessions of trying new positions which put less stress on her injury – were interminable. She would look at her watch, then fight the urge to do so again, until she gave in and saw with dismay that less than twenty minutes had passed. But now she had no watch, and the only way to compute the hours was by counting the times that *The Eminem Show* went back to the beginning.

Despite everything, she felt thankful for two things. The first was that after the move to her new prison, her vertigo had not returned. The second stemmed from her knowledge of a CIA facility in Afghanistan that had subjected detainees to similar audio treatment twenty-four hours a day for periods of up to three months. As far as she could tell, she never had to put up with it continuously for more than about fifteen hours, after which Sal and his comrades would switch it off for few hours. Perhaps they were short-staffed. In any event, it gave her vital respite.

The music had just been switched off now: at last an opportunity to rest. But outside her door, she made out the sounds of a conversation between several men. She was evidently its subject, for among the words she caught were '*Amriki*', 'human rights' and her own name. Palestinians often dropped English phrases into conversations held mainly in Arabic, and then came one that chilled Morgan's blood – 'CIA agent'. Had her cover been blown? Had they found the GPS chip in her purse? But even that would not prove anything: a State Department official could be easily be carrying the same device. Had Abdel Nasser broken while being interrogated? All she could do was wait.

79

A few minutes later the darkness was replaced by overwhelming light as the cell door was flung open. But the glare was short-lived, for the two men who entered placed another thick hood over Morgan's head before they dragged her out, marching her down a corridor into the same sparsely furnished room where she had confronted Sal on arrival. There the hood was removed, and to her unaccustomed eyes, the walls and furniture looked as if they were shining from some inner fluorescence. She blinked like a new-born kitten, screwing up her eyes. Morgan sat before him cuffed and shackled, keenly aware of not having been able to shower or wash her hair for many days. Next to him was a video camera mounted on a tripod.

'I told you when we last met we were going to make a DVD,' he said. 'We have a script for you. Please take some time to read it.'

It was typed neatly in double-spaced, 14-point lettering: in one sense easy to read. But speak it to a camera, and then have it broadcast round the world? After examining the first sentence, Morgan knew she never could. It said: 'My name is Morgan Cooper, and I am a CIA agent.' If she made that admission, she would be endangering the lives of every officer and every agent she had ever worked with. All the bad guys would have to do is work out who had been her associates. And if they were smart, that minimal confession would only be the beginning. They would try to extract whatever she knew about Agency methods and operations in ways she preferred not to imagine.

Somehow, she told herself, she had to feign the indignation of the truly innocent. Her reply to Sal came laden with contempt. 'You must know this is completely unacceptable. I am not going to confess to something I am not, in private or in public. You know very well that I am a diplomat. I work for the Bureau of Democracy, Human Rights and Labour, and I am trying to help and protect the Palestinian people. My business is not espionage. It is freedom and human rights.'

'Of course you have a cover. But I do not think this script is untrue at all,' Sal said. 'It is not, how do you say, the whole truth and nothing but the truth. But it is a start, and we are going to build on it.'

'We are going to do no such thing. And before you threaten me, let me give you a warning. Gaza is not Afghanistan. You do not control this place. Once news of my abduction gets out, every rival faction will be trying to find me. And you will not want to be around when they do.'

Sal motioned to one of the guards. The blindfold and hood were replaced, and she was taken back to her cell. She might have been imagining it, but Eminem seemed louder than ever.

Chapter Eight
Monday, April 16
and Tuesday, April 17, 2007

An Eminem lull: time to get her thoughts straight. For days and weeks Morgan had tried not to think about Abdel Nasser, because when she did, her mind filled again with the horrifying mental movie of the day of their capture. But now, facing interrogation, she forced herself to consider his likely fate. Had his wounds been treated, or had they already killed him? Perhaps, she reflected with a shudder, it would have been easier for him if they had. She didn't know why, but for some reason, she had a sense it was the middle of the night. Some vestige of her body clock must have survived, and she felt dizzy and disorientated, as if her vertigo were about to start again. Her eyes searched the room for a chink of light she could use to orientate herself, and so keep the dizziness at bay. The Eminem had gone on much longer than usual: she had counted nineteen repetitions of the album, an onslaught on her senses that she had found difficult to endure.

She was disassociating herself from reality again, hallucinating. A perfect Maryland spring day. They had all gone to Great Falls with Ronnie Wasserman and her kids, and after a stroll beside the surging Potomac they were having a lavish picnic beneath trees in fresh leaf. She could smell the wild flowers, and having forgotten her sunglasses, she was squinting against the sunlight. Ronnie, so lithe and energetic in pink shorts, sneakers and a revealing vest, was leading a game of Frisbee. All the children were enjoying it, whooping and running, and Morgan was taking special pleasure in the fact that Charlie seemed to be able to throw and catch more accurately than anyone. But she didn't like the way Ronnie seemed to be looking at her husband, while seldom speaking to her. She might be a widow, but her behaviour was frankly impertinent. Afterwards she would tease

82

Adam about it: 'I mean it! That woman's got a crush on you.' Then who was she to complain, after all that had happened with Abdel Nasser? Abruptly she was back in the darkness, a chill in her stomach.

The music stopped and the door burst open. Again she was hooded, then marched in chains down a corridor, back into what she was coming to think of as her interrogation room. They forced her into a chair and she sat facing Sal again, her hands cuffed behind her back. A length of chain ran from her handcuffs to a bolt fixed to the floor, and her legs remained shackled. She had been given nothing to eat or drink since their last meeting, and her mouth and throat were so dry she could barely speak. As the season had advanced, the Gaza weather had been getting perceptibly hotter every day. The room was airless, and she felt the sweat pooling at the back of her neck and armpits. She was starting to stink. As usual, Sal was flanked by guards. 'You get water when you talk,' he said. 'That's our new rule. So tell me. When did you join the CIA?'

'I've told you I am not a CIA agent,' Morgan said, her voice an arid whisper. 'I am a diplomat.'

'You are lying. What is more, I know you are lying. And soon, I will prove you are lying. But we will start with some easier questions. Where did you study?'

'I did a bachelors at the University of Texas. Then I went to the Kennedy School of Government at Harvard. My focus was the study of human rights.'

'And what did you do when you graduated? What does a "western woman" do with a degree in government?'

'I went to a place where Muslims were being abused and murdered. Former Yugoslavia. And I tried to get something done about it.'

'Very good Mrs Cooper. So where did you live in Yugoslavia?'

'I lived in Sarajevo. I shared an apartment with friends and colleagues. We tried to bring the world's attention to what was happening, and maybe we succeeded, because as you know, eventually my government stopped the murders.'

83

'With that you deserve some water,' Sal said. He spoke in Arabic, and the guard stood over Morgan with a brimming tumbler from which she drank greedily. 'If we continue to make this kind of progress, next time we meet I will allow you to sit with your hands cuffed in front of you, instead of behind your back, and then you will drink more easily,' Sal said. 'Now who was it you worked for in Sarajevo? Amnesty International? Human Rights Watch?'

'No, just as now, I worked for the State Department.'

'And where did you operate? Just in Sarajevo, or throughout the region?'

'As I said, we were based in Sarajevo, but we tried to gather data from right across the Balkans. We documented the massacre at Srebrenica, for example, and the slaughter at Gorazde.'

'Anywhere else Mrs Cooper? How about Kosovo?'

What did Sal know? Morgan's throat felt like the cracked bed of a dried-up reservoir, despite the precious gulps she had been allowed to drink. Her head was beginning to pound through dehydration, and she was battling a weeks-long deficit of sleep. Yet she had to think. If she said anything about what she had done in Kosovo, she could only expose herself. But how could Sal possibly know that she had spent time with the KLA? Not even Adam knew that, and it remained one of the most highly-classified parts of her career. Once again her mind drifted back to the Farm, and the course she had taken in resisting interrogation. 'Never say anything that can easily be shown to be false,' Bud had told her. 'Much easier to hide part of the truth than to explain an outright lie.'

'Yes, I did go to Kosovo,' Morgan said. 'The Serbs were just beginning to make life really difficult there, and we wanted to see what was happening.'

'Is that right? And you don't think it's a little strange that a woman who spent weeks travelling in secret with the KLA, at constant risk of betrayal or attack, pops up years later in another global trouble spot?'

84

Morgan gulped for breath. 'I work for the Bureau of Human Rights. Trouble and human rights abuses go together. There wouldn't be much work for me in Paris.'

'Not many people have heard the story of your march with the brave Kosovar guerrillas, have they?' Sal said. 'I wonder, is it still classified as a compartmentalised special access programme at CIA headquarters? "The Bureau of Human Rights." I love it. You didn't get trained to do that stuff at Harvard, did you? I don't think they teach the skills you need to embed with fighters there, do they?'

'I don't know what you mean,' Morgan said. 'Yes, I spent some time with the KLA, but only in order to document Serbian abuse.'

'Once again you are lying,' Sal said softly. 'You barely spent any time inside Kosovo at all. You were taken on a march through deepest Montenegro on secret paths through the forests, by men who trusted you. Anyhow, there is someone I want you to meet.' Sal made another gesture, a door opened, and a man entered the room, dressed in khaki military trousers, a black polo shirt and highly-polished boots. 'You know this man?'

Morgan kept her face blank, but as she looked into his eyes it all came flooding back.

'Have you forgotten me?' the man said. 'You don't know my name?'

'Yes, I know you. I never forget a face. You are Muhammad. Muhammad Zahar al-Falestini. You and your friend, he was also Palestinian – you were the leader when we went through the forest.'

'Good. Very good. Muhammad Zahar was my war name. My real name is Karim. Then I had big beard. It was cold, and I wear the same jacket like when I fight the Russian *kufr* in Afghanistan and Chechnya. I know you were CIA then. We all know. We have seen human rights people, and they are not like you. But we let you come with us because we think you help. We think America will stop ethnic cleansing in Kosovo. And now you are here, still a CIA spy. I look at your photo and

85

I know you.' He spat on the floor. 'Here in Palestine, no one thinks you help us. You help only our enemies. The Zionists. Tell the truth. Then maybe – maybe – we let you live.'

It seemed that Sal was better educated, but he was evidently deferring to Karim. 'Look, whatever you think is mistaken. I have always been committed to fighting for human rights, and in the Balkans I almost lost my life doing so,' she said. 'My best friend was shot there: she will never walk again. You have probably heard of my husband. He is a fighter too. His name is Adam Cooper, and he has spent the last few years fearlessly defending Muslims at places such as Guantánamo.'

'We know who your husband is,' Sal said.

'And you, you speak of husband, but you are whore, you make sex, you fuck with Abdel Nasser,' said Karim. 'You are prostitute.'

'I am no such thing,' Morgan said, her voice rising, hoarse from thirst. 'You can insult me all you wish, but you will not persuade me to incriminate myself with lies.'

'But you were making sex with Abdel Nasser, weren't you?' Karim's eyes bulged as he spoke, and his prurience disgusted her. 'He fuck you in his apartment, where you think you were safe. And then you wanted to fuck him right here, in his house. You know this? Now, we are in his house. His secret Gaza house. I think he wants to take you to make fuck with you. Is it different for you to fuck with Arab man? But his skin is light. Maybe is the same as with your husband. Why you do it? You like making sex with him, or for you is only work?'

Karim spat his words in her face, then crept behind her chair. He reach around it and cupped both her breasts, and moved a hand to her inner thigh and rubbed her crotch. 'Perhaps you like fuck me, Morgan Cooper? Is good?'

As Morgan's heart rate rose, she succumbed to rage, pushing her feet to the floor and thrusting the chair back against Karim's body. 'How dare you! You filthy bastard, you can take your racist stereotypes of western women and the porno fantasies you found on the Internet and stuff them up your ass!'

Karim stood up, a little winded, glanced at one of the guards and spoke to him in Arabic. He handed him a glass and a pitcher of water. 'I think you thirsty. Have a drink. Cool down. It do you good.' As he spoke, he filled the glass, then tipped its contents over Morgan's head.

Startled by the water, she felt the beginning of tears, pricking at the corners of her eyes. But she pulled herself together. 'You will learn nothing from me except the truth: I am faithful to my husband, and I am here to monitor human rights.'

'Now you can go,' Karim said. 'But soon, you come back.'

Alone again with Eminem, Morgan ponders the varieties of fear. First comes sheer physical terror, her imagination fuelled by her knowledge of what terrorists like these have done to other prisoners. She thinks of Daniel Pearl, his head sawn off after his pitiful last video message, and the many captives murdered in Iraq. If this happens to her, will she meet her end with dignity? Or will her personality start to dissolve while she still lives, her bodily fluids leaking out across the floor, as trussed and bound she begs in vain for her life? Bud used to call his SERE training 'an inoculation against stress,' yet his programme was conceived in the gentle conditions of the Cold War. She does not know whether his vaccine was strong enough to resist an ordeal such as this. She feels certain of one thing: that next time the guards come to fetch her, it will be to do something much worse than anything she has experienced so far.

Ineffective as it may well prove, at least she has had training to deal with the fear she feels for herself. But when she thinks of Charlie and Aimee, and the crushing loss that they will feel if her body, like so many victims in Iraq, is found dumped by a Gazan roadside, she feels a black, encompassing terror that smothers her like a shroud, a cloak so thick it banishes the booming music. Then, as she struggles to regain control of herself, despite the darkness, she sees Adam. He's in front of her, lit by warm sunlight: this can't be disassociation, but real. He's wearing a suit she's seen many times, a white shirt and the red tie he uses when he knows he's likely to be on television: someone once told him those colours will make him look reliable.

She cries out. 'Adam! What are you doing in this awful place?' Have they got you too? Have they brought you all the way from America? For God's sake, get out of here, before it's too late! What are the kids going to do if we're both in captivity?'

He doesn't speak, just stands. He looks reassuring, kind, and a little worried; but he's not angry. He must have forgiven her. But it's frustrating that he won't put his words into feelings, though like many wives, she's experienced this before.

Still he's silent, and then his image starts to melt away. Her pulse races, and Morgan remembers her training again. It makes her tremble. She's just had a full-blown psychotic vision, and while it lasted, she was quite unable to recognise it. She breathes deeply, trying to relax, and many minutes pass. Slowly her brain returns to detachment. She observes herself, documenting her own emotions. But as she does so, she creates the space for a new anxiety – a worry that if she simply dies or disappears, Adam will not be able to cope. Who will remember all their relatives' birthdays? How will he break the habits of the past decade and learn how to make the children's lunchboxes before his busy day at work, or pack their luggage before vacations? How will he know which of their garments have become too small, and which still have to be grown into?

At least they have given her a little food and plenty of water: three litre bottles, not the usual one, and parched, she drinks all of it. She's been so dehydrated, she feels no need to urinate. In any case, there is no Zainab: no offer of a trip to the toilet.

The men come for her again after the album has been played a further fourteen times.

And so she is back in the familiar room, with both Sal and Karim in front of her. This time, when the hood is removed, they ask her to stand. Between her and them is a wooden board, tilted downwards at an angle of some twenty degrees. There are straps made of nylon webbing attached to it at regular intervals, and a short distance from its lower end, two pieces of wood have been fixed at right angles, so giving the whole the appearance of a crucifix. Her pulse quickens. Now she knows what they are going to do.

'You can see what this. The CIA uses it, and maybe you have,' Sal says. 'I have read that in the middle ages, the Inquisition used to show the instruments of torture to the prisoner before they began to question him. Occasionally the mere sight was enough to persuade him to talk. So I show you this, and I ask you once again: will you confess? Will you read the statement I showed you before, and admit you are a CIA agent? I must warn you, this is not an exercise. It is not training, and we have no doctor here to call a halt. If this goes wrong, or you try to hold out in order to try to prove something, you may die.'

Morgan looks straight at him. 'Never,' she says, 'never. I have nothing to tell you except the truth.'

'Do you know why we do this?' asks Karim.

She looks at him closely and shivers. His face bears a look of pure hatred.

'It not just for confession. It is punishment. For what you do in Kosovo.'

'Punishment? I don't understand. All I did in Kosovo was try to help you.'

Karim snorts derisively. 'Help? You call this help? So I tell you my story. I think you know it, but I tell you, anyway.'

'Story? What story?'

'You already say: in Kosovo I was with my friend, he was also *Falestini*. Listen. He was not just my friend. He was like my brother. I give him anything. We are from here, in Gaza, we are friends when we are children. His name was Khalid. You remember?'

'Yes, I remember him,' she says softly.

'You march with us, and then you go: back to Sarajevo, back to America. But Karim and Khalid, and the Kosovar *mujaheddin*, we go back to Montenegro. We get more weapons, and we go back to the forest. It is cold, but the sun is shining, the sky is blue. It is beautiful, and I am happy. Soon we will fight the Serbs in

Kosovo. And then, we are walking, I look at the trees and I hear it. First I think it is insect. It is so quiet. But it gets louder, louder and louder, and I know that sound. I have heard it before. Do you know what it is?'

His intensity is terrifying. Morgan begins to guess what must be coming, but she pretends to be ignorant. 'No, how can I know? What was it?'

'In Afghanistan, we call this thing *Shaitan-arbat*. You know this word?'

Sal interjects. 'It means "chariot of Satan". It's what the Pushtun *mujaheddin* called the Soviet Mi-24 helicopter gunship. Truly, it is a weapon from Hell. At least in Afghanistan your CIA friends gave them Stinger missiles so they had a chance of defending themselves. But the Serbs had these gunships too, and in the Balkans, you gave the *mujaheddin* nothing. When the gunship appeared above the trees over Karim and Khalid, there was nothing they could do.'

'I'm sorry,' Morgan says. 'But what does this have to do with me?'

'Everything,' Karim says. 'Everything. You come with us, and then, after one week, ten days, we get the *Shaitan arbat*. How does it know where we are? Because you tell the Serbs – you or the CIA. Before you came, our way was secret. After, the Serbs find us, they know where we are. Because I know this *arbat*, when I hear it I tell the *mujaheddin* to take cover. But there is no cover. It has rockets, and a twenty millimetre cannon. We have animals, ponies: I see them hit. There is nothing left. They are like red steam. And then, how you say, I am sleep.'

Sal breaks in again: 'He was hit by a blast wave. He hit his head on something hard, and was rendered unconscious.'

'When I wake up, it is night. There is moon, but it is raining. All the animals, all the *mujaheddin*, all dead. I find Khalid. His head, his face: they are okay. But his body...' Karim grimaces. 'It is mess. His body, it is open. I look at him, and I remember so many days. I see his eyes for the last time, and I remember: when we are children, at school, the time of *intifada*. I remember

90

how we fight the *jihad*, in Afghanistan, in Chechnya, in Bosnia and Kosovo. I remember his sister, Zainab. You know her. She is here. Yes: Khalid's sister, she fight with us now. But I don't cry for him. He died a *mujahid* fighter. I pray, the *janazah*, the prayer for dead peoples. I close his eyes, and I run, because I know soon the Serbs are coming.'

Morgan knows she has no chance of persuading him that the revenge he seeks is misplaced; that the betrayal of the KLA supply line was not down to her. But she has to try.

'This was not my doing.' She cannot eliminate the quaver from her voice. 'I did not betray you. You have the wrong person. I work for the State Department.'

Karim stands, walks around the room, stands by his torture equipment, and then, after what feels like minutes, he folds his arms and he laughs.

'Not my doing. The State Department.' His voice rises in pitch: 'Now you stop the lies!' He looks at Sal and speaks in Arabic.

Sal translates solemnly, as if at a business conference. 'He says the reason why he laughed is that you are still claiming you are not from the CIA, and that the betrayal of his brother Khalid was not your fault, and for telling these lies you will be punished more severely. And he wants you to know something else. The hardest thing of all that he has had to bear is that Khalid did not trust you. On the last night in their safe house in Sarajevo, he tried to persuade Karim not to take you with them. But Karim was the commander, the *Emir*, and he overruled him. All these years he has blamed himself, as well as you, for Khalid's death.'

Sal looks directly at her, and adds with renewed urgency: 'And now allow me, please, to give you some advice: not from Karim, but from me. Start to tell the truth. It is the only chance you have to save your life.'

Karim speaks in Arabic once again and the guards take her arms and force her down on to the board. She feels the straps tightening across her legs and torso, and then her arms are pulled out on to the horizontal pieces of wood. They tie her again at the elbows and wrists. Karim takes a last strap and fixes it across her forehead. She is immobilised. He brings his face very close. 'This your last chance, Morgan Cooper,' he says. She says nothing.

Karim stands over her with a jug. The water is icy cold, and the first splashes, which land on her cheeks, are almost refreshing. But then the stream begins to hit her mouth and her nose, and she feels it entering her body. She tries to drink, because the jug doesn't look very big, and though her stomach is already full from the water they left in her cell, drinking will give her space to breathe and there must surely be a pause when he has to refill it. So she gulps and gulps, and swallows, but the stream keeps on coming, and at last she cannot help herself and takes water into her lungs. She feels her gag reflex as she starts to choke, and then an urge to vomit. Hot tears form in her eyes and run from both sides onto the floor.

There is a pause. Her breath is rasping, painful, and she remembers the time at a teenage party when she mistakenly inhaled a mouthful of Kahlúa and spluttered for breath for several minutes, terrified she was about to drown in coffee liqueur. But this time she doesn't have minutes to recover. After 30 seconds or less, Sal hands a second jug to Karim and the pouring begins again. This time, she finds herself able to drink much less. So the choking goes on longer, and is more intense, and for the first time she sees that Sal's warning was not empty – that she may be about to die. Some of the men on her SERE course were waterboarded as part of their training. A few had already endured it before joining the Agency as members of the military. But women were always exempt. Not, she finds herself able to reflect, that having had prior experience would have done much good.

Karim bends over her again. 'Have you had enough? You will talk?' Again she says nothing.

'That was just a warm-up,' says Sal. 'Now you will learn what it means to enter the submarine. You still have a chance. Please, take it.'

She says nothing, and she does not move a muscle. The submarine. That is what they called this treatment in Argentina under the junta. It was used by the Inquisition. And because she has studied the files of cases she once helped to facilitate at Headquarters, she knows what is coming next. In training, the CIA uses the method she has already experienced - the pouring of water directly from a jug. But the technique authorised in 2002 for real-life interrogations of al-Qaeda suspects involved the placing of thick cloths over the prisoner's face to form a suffocating, wet blanket, so that even in the gaps between pourings, the subject finds it almost impossible to breathe.

She knows her bravery will remain unsung. Gary, Adam, her parents, her children: they will never see or know how she determined that death was preferable to giving up her secrets. But having heard Karim's story, having felt so close to his primal need for revenge, she feels sure that whatever she says or does, they will kill her anyway. There remains for her only one mystery: the exact moment of her death.

There is another, tantalising pause. But as Karim lays the thick piece of material over her face, so completely covering it, Sal does not ask again if she wishes to confess. This time, the pouring begins very gently, so that although the cloth becomes soaked, at first she can move her tongue in order to create an air pocket, which she uses to take tiny, shallow breaths. But then the flow becomes relentless. As she fights in vain for air, the cloth seems to cleave to her skin, like some ghastly amphibian, a malevolent, slimy frog that fills her respiratory orifices. Gravity is her enemy, the twenty degree tilt of the board ensuring that none of the suffocating liquid runs harmlessly on to the floor; that it all flows inexorably to the entrance points of her body. There is water in her nostrils, in her sinuses, filling her mouth, in the back of her throat, all the way down her oesophagus, in her windpipe, and in her chest and lungs. She is upside down in a waterfall, then being flung into the depths of the black pool that lies at its bottom. She loses control of her bladder, and now hot urine flows backwards, mingling with the water, down the relentless slope, pooling in the small of her back, then flowing onwards, until it gets into her hair. Some tiny remnant of her inner voice tells her that the end is near, as she feels the darkness creeping inwards and her legs, arms and torso begin violent, involuntary spasms.

She cannot see or hear it, but Sal and Karim remove her mask and cease their pouring. The board is on a pivot, and they tilt her to an upright position and massage her abdomen until she coughs, vomits, and slowly returns to consciousness. But the respite lasts only minutes. Morgan has barely grasped that she is still alive when they return her to her previous downward sloping angle and Karim asks her if she wants to go through it again.

'Fuck you,' Morgan says.

She does not know where she finds this strength: she barely knows why. Two, three, four more times they repeat the process. Each time she blacks out, and each time she is astonished on coming round to discover that her life continues. She has read in waterboarding's strange and dismal pseudo-scientific literature that while in most cases, victims will say anything to make it stop, whether it is true or not, a small minority appear to decide that they would rather die than cooperate. Once they have been to the brink, permanent oblivion comes to seem preferable to continued suffering. Each time Sal and Karim swivel Morgan back to the vertical, her will gets stronger. Having almost drowned so many times, she finds it impossible to conceive that actual drowning can be worse.

Once again she sees Aimee and Charlie. In her mind she gazes at them. Her life with them, their lives since their births, the moments when first they crawled, walked and spoke in sentences: all seem to flash before her. Surely for their sake she should stop now, capitulate? She imagines their agony when they realize they must pay their last farewells; the grief they will still feel in the years to come, as adults. She feels her own deep loss, of never knowing how their stories will develop. But still she is certain that nothing she does will make any difference. The only factor that counts is that Karim is going to avenge

Khalid. Better that she dies with her honour and her secrets intact.

They torture her a final time. But afterwards, Karim asks the guards to untie her. She is drenched, and she stinks. Shivering uncontrollably, she is allowed to sit down on a chair, for the first time unshackled.

'There is someone else I want you to meet,' Sal says. 'Well, not meet, for you already know him well. Your friend and agent, Abdel Nasser.'

Morgan's eyes betray her horror as they drag him in. It does at least look as if they have dressed the wounds on his knees, and as far as she can tell, he does not carry the stench of gangrene. But it is evident that he has been tortured too. He is dressed in rags. He is cadaverously thin. His face is black with bruises. He looks dazed, and at first, he seems not to recognize her. Morgan cannot stifle her cry.

Sal speaks again. 'You appear not to care about your own survival. Now the question you have to answer is whether you are prepared to be equally foolish when it comes to the life of your friend.'

Another guard enters, carrying a huge curved knife, a scimitar not so different from the kind used to carry out public executions in Saudi Arabia. He hands it to Karim, who weighs it appreciatively.

'It is good,' he says. 'Very sharp.' He picks up a large metal bucket from the corner of the room, and Morgan realizes he will use it to collect Abdel Nasser's blood when he draws the blade across his throat, as in a *halal* abattoir. They are going to slaughter him as if he were a sheep or a goat. She has heard that this is what they did to Danny Pearl. Gary once boasted he had seen the video. There is a fire in Karim's eyes. It looks as if for him, executing Abdel Nasser will be a source of pleasure.

Morgan does not care if she saves herself, but from somewhere within, at the core of her being, she feels an instinctive, biological urge: she must save him. She cannot stand by and watch another human being, any human being, let alone this one, decapitated. She cannot stay silent while watching him drenched and choking in his own hot blood. If she can only preserve life, maybe there will still be hope. The dazed reverie induced by the torture suddenly ends and again she is living in the moment, aware and engaged. Her voice fills the room, authoritative and commanding. 'Stop! If I confess, will you spare him?'

Sal looks at Karim, who nods. 'You will read the text to the camera?' Sal asks.

Morgan looks at her sodden, puke-slimed feet. 'Yes,' she says. 'I will.'

Sal produces the camera, mounts it on its tripod, and points it at Morgan. Karim is suddenly manic, dancing round the room, and he cannot stop grinning. 'One take! One take,' he says with a cackle. 'You say it right or I still kill him!'

Morgan takes the printed text from him, and looking at the lens, trying to sound as unexpressive as she can, she begins to read: 'My name is Morgan Cooper and I am a CIA agent. I came to Palestine to betray its people. My mission is to defeat their resistance, and to give support to the Crusaders and Jews.'

She shivers, a violent, involuntary shudder. She knows it will show on the video.

'I will only be released after the government of the United States releases all Muslim fighters from Guantánamo Bay, Bagram and at the black sites run by my employer, the CIA. I call on the President to make this possible so that I may one day see my children again.'

Chapter Nine
Friday, April 20, 2007

As was his habit, Adam checked his email early. There was an overnight message from Gary. It had landed in his in-box at two-thirty in the morning, British time, and its tone was brusque. 'Adam, I need to speak to you. Call my cell after five am, eastern. I'll be up.'

Before he could make that call, he had things to do. Recognising that their return to America remained out of the question, his mother had managed to get Charlie and Aimee places at the local primary school, which Adam had once attended - Phil and Jim, as it was usually known, or, more properly, Saints Philip and James. They had started earlier that week. The roll, as always, was full, but the head of its English department, the marvellously-named Kelly Brain, was a member of Gwen's book group, and she had pulled strings to get them in. Once they were settled, Adam planned to embark for the Middle East. Gary could send all the imperious emails he liked, but there was still little sign that the Agency's search for his wife was becoming more effective.

He knew that leaving Charlie and Aimee was going to be difficult, especially if, as he hoped, he would be making his own trip to Gaza. How could he justify his absence, and, perhaps, putting himself in harm's way? Two nights earlier, it had been Aimee who had crystallised his decision as he sat on the edge of her bed before switching the light out.

'Dad? Are you planning to go look for Mommy soon?'

'Yes. Or at least I'm thinking of it.' At the time, it had seemed she was reading his mind: the subject had, at that very moment, been weighing heavily on him.

'You remember that lady we saw in Alexandria? You said she had friends who will help you. You must make them help you, Daddy. Mom's on her own. She needs you.'

97

Already, a new family routine was emerging. Each morning, Adam got the children up, made them breakfast and a packed lunch, and they walked together through North Oxford's affluent, Victorian streets in the fine spring weather to the school. After that, Adam sometimes had a work-out at a local gym, but until the kids were ready to come home again, there wasn't, truth to tell, very much to keep him occupied. He spent a lot of time brooding, After three-and-a-half weeks without his wife, Adam had grasped something important: that whatever the problems between them, he missed her deeply.

Part of it was sheer physical need. He might have rejected Ronnie's advances, but they had left him aroused, and when he did get to sleep he often woke early from intense, erotic dreams. In their wake, anxiety flooded in. It wasn't just the fear he might not get her back. He wasn't sure how things would be between them if he did.

The fights that had disfigured their lives in recent months hadn't varied much. Usually they began when Adam expressed his fears about Gaza, and rose in pitch when he said that they didn't have access to enough reliable childcare to enable him to do his own work in her absence. Her riposte was in essence always the same: that his claims down the years that he wanted to support her career were a sham; that he had always put himself and his own needs first, and now, whether he liked it or not, it was her turn.

Adam knew she had a point. In times past, before his move to Spinks McArthur, when he'd had to go away for weeks at a time in order to dig for fresh evidence to use in some death row prisoner's appeal, he had simply presumed that Morgan would be able to cope: after all, she had a desk job, and worked regular hours. Right at the start, when she first fell pregnant, he had offered to become a stay-at-home father in order to let her stay in the field. But both of them had known he hadn't really been serious. All those years, she'd felt thwarted, and was only now beginning to fulfil her potential. He, on the other hand, was doing about as well as a *pro bono* human rights attorney in a white shoe DC law firm possibly could, and that description happened to represent the fulfilment of his dreams.

But the tension between them wasn't just a product of the usual process of work/life negotiation that seemed to afflict every family with two working parents. As his father had guessed during their discussion in the garden, underlying it was another, bigger issue that neither felt able to discuss: Adam's belief that if Morgan were true to her principles, she should never have joined the CIA at all, and ought certainly to leave it now. Ever since the spring of 2004, when details of the dark side of America's war on terror had begun to leak, drip by caustic drip, into the public domain, Adam had nurtured a growing suspicion: that his wife might have played a personal role in supporting operations that he considered both illegal and unspeakable. She had never been exactly forthcoming about her work, and that was to be expected. But her absolute refusal to discuss any aspect of what she did, nor to give him the least idea of the nature of her current mission, had made him fear the worst. He no longer trusted her to do the right thing. If she had merely betrayed him with another man, that might have been more painful, but also easier to deal with. But if his fears turned out to be well-founded, and she really had betrayed the values he had always thought they shared, their marriage, he felt, was almost certainly doomed.

Their worst row of all had taken place across their kitchen table, three nights before her departure. After the usual escalation, Morgan said she was tired, and simply wanted to sleep. But Adam charged on, insisting that they finish what they'd started, and that he couldn't rest unless they finished having it out.

Morgan had lost all patience. 'Don't you think I feel bad enough about leaving you and the children already?' she demanded. 'Why are you trying to make it worse? Or are you simply trying to upset me so much that I won't be able to sleep, despite the fact I've got a huge amount of work to do before I leave, and then a long and tiring journey? All this talk about my safety is pure bullshit. The only reason you keep going on about my going back to fieldwork is that you seem to need to exert power and control in our relationship. It's not really about my work or even my safety; it's about me not being permanently on hand to service *your* life and *your* career.'

Finally she had uttered the one sentence that seemed calculated to make him stop, and so compelled his retreat into wounded silence: 'Adam, you've changed. I don't think I love you any more.'

Within ten minutes, as they got ready for bed, she was trying to reassure him that she hadn't been serious, and had only been searching for a way to dam his torrent of words. But they hadn't made love in the days that remained, and on her last morning, while the taxi waited to take her to the airport and they were saying their farewells with a last, quick squeeze, she had mentioned it again:

'Adam. What I said the other night. You know I didn't mean it. I was angry. I just wanted to wake you up from your complacency, from taking me for granted. I'll be back in ten days and then we'll make things different. We'll work this out. I love you very much.'

Back then, before she was kidnapped, Adam hadn't been sure whether that was true. All he knew now was that he desperately wanted it to be.

Ten o'clock. Adam had been home for half an hour. It was time to call Gary. Sitting in his parents' kitchen, he punched out Gary's number, and took a tiny pleasure in the fact that he took a while to answer, and when he did, sounded as if he had been asleep.

'It's Adam Cooper,' he said. 'You asked me to call.'

It didn't take long for Gary to compose himself. 'Uh, yes, I, Adam. So. Would you mind telling me what the fuck is going on?'

'Excuse me? Like I told you, I've brought the kids to England. We're all just settling in.'

'That's not what I meant. The reason for my email is that CIA public affairs got a call last night from a writer in San Antonio, asking whether it was true that an operative named Morgan Cooper had been kidnapped in the Gaza Strip. Do you have any idea why that might have happened?'

Adam felt a visceral lurch. 'A reporter? I don't understand. I haven't breathed a word of this to anyone. That's why we came to England, remember – to make it easier to prevent the news from getting out.'

'But you do know someone in San Antonio. Are you sure you haven't said anything that could have somehow allowed her to make two and two make – I was going to say five, but of course it's really four.'

'Sherry? My mother-in-law? She's the last person on earth I'd confide in – not unless I wanted it broadcast everywhere.'

'Yes. I get that part. So how do you think she could have found out?'

Adam had no idea. 'Is it possible that Morgan told her something? But Sherry doesn't even know she works for the Agency, let alone the details of her assignments. I did send her an email saying Morgan was away on a business trip, but that's all. And believe me, I don't know any writers in Texas. But you must be able to keep a lid on this. I mean, can't your public affairs guys tell this reporter it's bullshit?'

'We have. It's never been our policy to confirm or deny the names of field officers, and unless he's got some incredible inside source, he won't be able to run a story. But it would be kind of helpful if you could get Sherelle Ashfield to keep her mouth shut.'

'I'll do what I can,' Adam said. 'In the meantime, now that you've finished accusing me of spilling the beans to someone I haven't spoken to for months, maybe you can tell me whether you're getting any closer to finding my wife.'

There was a long silence. Adam heard Gary yawn.

'I could give you crap,' Gary said finally. 'I could spin you a line which would let you nurture false hopes. But as of now, I don't have anything. All I can say is what I've told you before. We are doing our best.'

If there was anyone in the world Adam might have expected not to get along with, it would have been Morgan's father, Robert E. Lee Ashfield. There was, to begin with, the fact of his long career in the US Marine Corps, which he had left with the rank of colonel, having served with distinction in every major combat operation from Vietnam to Desert Storm. There was his chairmanship of the National Rifle Association chapter for the state of New Mexico, where these days he ran a highly successful agricultural seed business. Finally, there were his staunch conservative beliefs.

Yet from the moment Morgan had introduced them fifteen years earlier, they had simply hit it off, bonding over beers and a mutual love of outdoor sports. They had gone on long hikes together in the mountains around Rob's home in Taos. Adam had taken his future father-in-law rock-climbing, and Rob had taught him to shoot handguns and rifles at the range he had at his ranch - an activity for which Adam had displayed a surprising aptitude. Adam had been yearning been to speak to Rob and confide in him, but before his conversation with Gary, he had held back. Now he suspected he might be the only person capable of persuading Sherry to keep quiet.

It had always seemed a marvel that Rob and Sherry had ever got together at all, much less managed to stick out life together for more than fifteen years. They would never have met if Rob had not lost a chunk of his right leg amid the carnage of Khe Sanh: spending some time at the University of Texas in Austin had been supposed to help him recuperate. When their eyes first met across the human debris of a Kappa Kappa Gamma party, Sherelle was already a senior, a yearning, dissatisfied soul who had been swept up in the sexual, political and psychedelic upheavals buffeting America while First Lieutenant Ashfield was serving his country in Asia. He liked churches, guns and Johnny Cash. Sherelle preferred the tarot, The Velvet Underground, and

102

pot. Yet somehow they had fallen into bed together, and when it turned out she had forgotten to take her pill and fell pregnant with Morgan, he had had no hesitation in getting down on one knee and offering her the life of a military wife and mother.

Of that, reflected Adam, the best that could be said was that from what he heard, the living hell which ensued was equally unpleasant for both of them. But once soothed by the balm of divorce, they had managed to build a kind of friendship, founded on their mutual devotion to their daughter.

As soon as he felt he decently could, Adam called Rob in Taos – by local time there, six o'clock in the morning. A sleepy woman's voice answered: Rob's girlfriend, Cathy.

'He's not here, sugar. He left last night to drive to see Sherry in San Antonio. She called and said she had something to tell him about Morgan. It sounded serious. You mind telling me what it is?'

'I can't. Not just now. What time do you think he might get there?'

'Shit, what time is it now?' There was a pause, presumably the result of Cathy checking her bedside clock. 'He left at six. Depends if he stopped for the night. He took the pick-up. If he didn't stop, and you know what he's like, he probably didn't, then he should have got there an hour ago.'

Damn. That meant Rob wasn't going to hear it all first from Adam. 'Thanks Cathy. Sorry to disturb you. Take care.'

He pictured Rob's arrival at Sherry's house in Alamo Heights: her gushing torrent of words while he sat among the Indian silk throws and drapes as she doubtless cast Adam as the villain. God knows what she'd heard, or how, but this was a situation he needed to get ahead of.

He was too late. His own cellphone rang. He looked at the display. A 575 number: the Taos, New Mexico area code. However, the voice on the line belonged not to Rob, but Sherelle. She must be borrowing her ex-husband's phone.

To begin with, she sounded relatively calm. 'Adam,' she began, 'I had to wait until Rob got here because I didn't have your cell number. And obviously, I couldn't call you at home. You want to know how I know that?'

'How's that, Sherry? Listen, I'm really sorry I haven't kept you in the loop, but just let me explain-'

She appeared not to have heard him. 'It's like this, Adam. I found it very obvious that you were avoiding me. More than avoiding me: there was something seriously wrong and you wouldn't tell me what it was. I have a right to know these things: in case you've forgotten, I am Morgan's mother. Well, I got your email and I thought about it. Finally I just got on a plane and I flew to DC. I got the early flight yesterday morning, and I was back last night. I took the plane and a Metro and a cab to your house and there was nobody there, and somehow it seemed that you weren't just gone for the afternoon, but for weeks. I sat on the porch and wondered what the hell I was going to do, and then I remembered your friend, that nice young widow, Ronnie. I remembered how to get to her house and the taxi driver had given me a business card, so I called him back and he took me there. Well. Can you imagine what she said?'

'No,' he said wearily. 'But you'd better tell me.'

'She invited me in and made coffee, and I could tell straightaway she was pissed. She said Morgan hadn't come back from a business trip, and was still missing. She said she'd given you all kinds of help with the kids, but you'd disappeared without a word and she'd only known that because you'd sent her an email when you got to England. Finally I got the truth, and I swear I almost fainted. She told me my daughter had been to Gaza.'

Sherry sounded as if she was trying to stifle her sobs. 'Gaza! What did the State Department think it was doing, sending a woman there? And what about you? How could you have let her?'

'I didn't "let her," as you put it,' Adam said gently. 'I didn't have a lot of choice. She's an adult, Sherry. I wasn't happy, but it was her decision.'

'Before I flew back I called Rob and Gerry, this guy I've been dating, who writes for *Texas Monthly*. I told him what had happened and he said, well, that sounds like she might be CIA. So he called the CIA public affairs people, like he was going to do a story, and asked them if it was true that Morgan had been abducted. They didn't tell him anything, Adam. But you're going to have to. I have rights.'

'Sherry, I'm sorry. I know I should have spoken to you but there were reasons, really good reasons, why I couldn't. I feel bad and I know you must be furious but please, hear me out –'

'Hear you out? When my daughter's been missing for close to a month and instead of telling me what's been happening, you send me a kiss-off email, then fly across the ocean with my grandkids? If it hadn't been for Ronnie, I'd probably have gone straight to the police, and told them my daughter had been buried beneath your garden patio. Are trying to tell me this is normal?'

'No Sherry, it's not normal. It's not normal at all. But if you don't mind, could you please put Rob on the line.' For a few moments, he heard the muffled sounds of what must have been an intense discussion between Rob and Sherry. Finally he heard Rob's voice.

'Hey Adam. How you doing?'

'Could be worse.'

'What do you need me to do, buddy?'

'Well, to begin with it would be helpful if you could calm Sherry down a little.'

'I copy that. But what's happening? Hey, you know I've got your back. But you've got to fill me in a little.' Adam could hear his voice begin to crack. 'How can I help my little girl? What can I be doing?'

'Rob, I'm so sorry I haven't told you all about this. God knows I've wanted to. Look, I don't want to say too much on the phone. But there's a reason why I've been so uncommunicative. Morgan's colleagues have been pretty clear on something: that the one thing likely to jeopardise her safety is publicity, and they keep on telling me their greatest fear is of something leaking out. They seem to think that if I tell anyone, even people I really trust, it's more likely to happen. Anyhow, that's why I haven't been in touch. It's also why I sent that email to Sherry, and why I've brought the kids to England.'

'Shit. Well, whatever happens, we'd better make sure we talk to each other now.'

'I know.'

'So what are your plans? You just going to sit there in England and wait for the Agency to do something?'

'No. I'm going to Israel. And if I can, Gaza. If the CIA can't find her, maybe I can.'

'I knew she could count on you. Jesus, this is taking some time to compute. What she must be going through doesn't bear thinking about, and I'm not finding it easy: if we ever get our hands on these motherfuckers, well...' Rob's voice tailed off, then rallied. 'Well just remember, I know a lot of well-connected people. I don't need to spell out what I'm trying to tell you, but if you think you need some assistance, call me. Any time, day or night.'

It was not until much later, just before midnight, that Imad's email appeared in Adams in-box. 'I apologise that it will be Saturday, but tomorrow we must meet again,' it said. 'Same time of day and location. I have news, and a contact for you. Try to book a flight some time early next week.'

Chapter Ten
Wednesday, April 25, 2007

Adam had done his research, mainly by interrogating his wife over the kitchen table, and so he knew that Eugene August Mitchell III was the closest thing the CIA had to aristocracy. His grandfather, Eugene Mitchell I, had served with its World War Two forerunner, the OSS, and went on to become one of the Agency's first recruits. His son, Eugene's father, met an early death from a haemorrhagic fever contracted during a mission to supply anti-Communist rebels in Africa. But while all three generations had gone to Yale, and the first two Agency Mitchells were still revered as swashbuckling, glamorous risk-takers, the pale and lanky Eugene III came across as bureaucratic and socially awkward. The first time Adam met him, before he and Morgan were married, the word 'geek' was not in common use, but if it had been, he would have applied it to Mitchell. It seemed he possessed an uncanny gift for saying the wrong thing. So far as Adam knew, he wasn't gay, but he had never had a wife or a serious girlfriend.

Having flown in to Tel Aviv on the red-eye, Adam had grabbed a taxi at the airport and checked into the same hotel as Morgan had the previous month. He managed to sleep for a couple of hours, and then, having showered and breakfasted, phoned Mitchell's office at the embassy. He had not warned him he was coming. The assistant, who introduced herself as Crystal, put him straight through.

'Adam! Are you in Israel, or are you calling from America? I guess not, it's still the middle of the night there.' Adam guessed that Mitchell was trying to give him the impression that his movements were not under surveillance.

'I'm in Tel Aviv. I just got in. I'm staying at the same place Morgan used – the Cinema Hotel. When can we meet?'

107

'Get yourself a shower, and a nap if you need it.'

'I already did that.'

'Then I'll see you at twelve. Just come to the embassy reception and ask for me. Make sure you bring your passport. In case you don't know, my official title is Regional Affairs Director. I'm not exactly undercover, but a nondescript moniker helps me avoid too much attention.'

When Adam arrived, he was struck by how much older Eugene looked. He also appeared to be slathered in factor 50 sun cream, which had left white streaks on his chin and cheeks. He ushered Adam into his clean, airy office.

'I won't ask you how you've been: I know you've been going through hell,' Eugene said. 'I mean, we all have too. But for you and the kids, it must have been far worse.'

Still a little dazed from the journey and the unexpected brilliance of the Mediterranean light, Adam only nodded.

'First I need your passport – we need to have it photocopied,' Eugene said. He took it, and asked Crystal via his office intercom to collect it. 'Strange the paths our lives take. You remember when we met before? The Shenandoah Tavern: you were the fledgling radical attorney and I was the greenhorn spook. I guess it was inevitable things between us felt a little tense. It can't have been long before your wedding, and all I could think was how the hell was a pinko like you managing to bang a righteous babe like Morgan Ashfield. Boy, she was hot. Still is, I guess, despite popping out those kids.'

Abruptly, Eugene seemed to realise that his discourse was making a less than favourable impression on his missing colleague's husband. 'I'm only kidding, right? Sorry. Maybe that wasn't quite appropriate.'

'No Eugene. Maybe it wasn't. So. Morgan's whereabouts. What have you been doing? I'm hearing nothing from Gary and Mike. No doubt you're aware I met them in Washington after you called me that morning.'

'Soon enough you'll get a chance to discuss it all with them face-to-face. They're on their way here as we speak. But don't worry yourself. This thing has gone up to the National Security Council and the President has made it clear he expects to see results. Mike and Gary are the men to deliver them.'

Adam stared at him. 'But there's no sign of them yet, is there? Do you guys actually know anything – such as, just who is it who might be holding her?'

'Well. We didn't. At least, not until recently. But yesterday something happened. Sometime after lunch, a package was delivered to the embassy front desk. It wasn't addressed to anyone in particular: all it said on the front was "Regarding Morgan Cooper," and thankfully someone down there in security had the presence of mind to send it to me. Of course, we've got CCTV coverage in the lobby and the street outside, and we've circulated the image of the courier to our Israeli friends. But so far, no hits. In any case, the courier was disguised. He looked like an ultra-orthodox Jew, complete with ringlets, beard, and a black, widebrimmed hat. I'd be prepared to bet that's not really what he looks like. The package bore no fingerprints, and though we're having it tested for DNA, I suspect we aren't going to find any. Inside was a DVD.'

'And this DVD… it shows Morgan?' Adam felt hesitant.

'Yes.'

'Is she ok?'

'I got to admit, she's not looking her best. But so far as we can tell, she hasn't been seriously harmed.'

'But how did it get out of Gaza? From what I've heard, the security for anyone leaving Erez is extreme. Surely the Israelis would never have let a homemade DVD through without checking what was on it?'

It seemed that the same question had been bothering Eugene. 'I don't know. It's possible it wasn't smuggled out in that form at all. It could have been sent electronically. Or it could have been smuggled through the tunnels into Egypt, and then somehow passed on here. The DVD itself doesn't seem to bear any clues.'

'Can I see it?'

'You can't see the actual DVD because it's already on its way to America in a diplomatic bag. Our labs over there may be able to tell us more. But I've copied it on to my computer.' Eugene turned his monitor so that Adam could see it, then clicked his mouse.

As Adam watched the image of his wife deliver her stilted message, he could sense Eugene looking intently at him. But all he said when the video finished was: 'Can I see it again?'

Eugene let him do so. Adam searched the screen, trying to take in every detail.

'She doesn't look very good at all,' Adam said when it finished the second time. 'A very long way from her best, I would say.' He was finding it hard to speak.

'I guess not.'

'She's lost weight. She's gaunt, and obviously exhausted. But her hair looks wet, and it looks as if water's been poured all over her clothing. She's sodden. What do you suppose that's that about?'

'I don't know. Maybe it's just sweat. My hunch is that wherever they made this recording, it doesn't have air-conditioning.'

'That's bullshit, and you know it. They've been torturing her. She's been waterboarded. And she's wearing an orange jump suit. Not exactly coincidence, huh?'

'Whoa!' Eugene said. 'You can't be sure of that, and neither can I. And you getting on your highly principled horse isn't going to do any of us much good, okay? Just so you know, of all the thousands of Agency personnel, almost none of us have ever had anything to do with waterboarding. Right? Anyhow, I'm not an interrogator, I'm the station chief, and I'm doing all I can to help your wife. So cut me some slack, okay?'

Adam's anger subsided. 'This banner behind her. What's it mean? I don't read Arabic.'

'We think it's the name of the group that's kidnapped her: the *Janbiya al-Islam*. They're new on the scene, but from what we can tell, they're Salafists, allied to al-Qaeda. A *janbiya* is a kind of curved knife, like a dagger: people wear them a lot in Yemen. I guess you could translate their name as "the daggers of

110

Islam". According to one of the Palestinian newspapers, a little while back they bombed a supermarket and an Internet café in Gaza.'

'If the group's already been mentioned by a Palestinian newspaper, then Hamas must know about it. So what about them? Have you been trying to talk to their security people? Aren't they more likely than anyone to be able to help?'

Eugene looked irritated. 'We don't speak to Hamas. Why would we, for Chrissakes? We work with the Palestinian Authority of President Abbas, and his party Fatah, and we're in touch with their leadership every day.'

'Well they don't seem to have come up with much so far, have they? Why not work with Hamas too?'

'Hamas is a terrorist organisation, sworn to destroy Israel. We don't think it's in US interests to have them thinking we owe them any favours.'

'I see. So what shall I tell Morgan's family? Shall I say I've seen this video? And what about the Israelis? Are they going to want to meet me?'

'No. Leave the Israelis to us. As for the video: yes, tell the family, so long as they're discreet. Look, for all I know, this video is about to lead the news on Aljazeera. But it hasn't surfaced yet, and our judgement is that it probably won't. I pray to God it doesn't. If the whole world finds out that Morgan works for the Agency, it might make it impossible to negotiate her release. It might force the kidnappers to murder her.'

Morgan counted three blessings. First, she was still alive, and so far as she knew, so was Abdel Nasser. Second, ever since her forced confession, she had had light, even when the mains power went down, because they had given her a floor-standing battery lamp. She could see the dank, grimy room that had become her home. Finally, there was no more Eminem. She also had Zainab – if, that is, she had ever been without her during the period of darkness. At first, when Morgan came back from that terrible interrogation with her jumpsuit soaked in water and urine and blood-flecked vomit, her throat and lungs raw, she had been almost solicitous, cooing and clucking with apparent concern as she took her for a shower and gave her clean clothes. But as each day melted into the next and time passed as slowly as ever, Zainab reverted to type.

'Today I think you see the mens,' she said, putting down another tray of dreary food. 'You tell the truth or you know what happen. Abdel Nasser, he finish.' She drew a finger across her throat.

Morgan's boredom was still almost unendurable, and as before, she sometimes spent hours disassociating, living vivid daydreams. She took Charlie and Aimee to school, helped them with homework and organised fun, family outings: all the things, she reflected ruefully, she had not done nearly enough of in her earlier, real life. But at last she also had a real-world pastime. One morning, Zainab had brought her an orange. With exquisite care, she fashioned a miniature chess set from the peel, with one's side's pieces delineated in orange, the other's by the white, inside pith. She had scratched out a board with her fingernails, carving the shapes of the squares through the grime on the floor, and hour after hour she challenged herself, working through exotic and standard openings remembered from her days on the chess team in high school.

Orange was just mounting a cunning left flank attack when two of Sal's guards came back, and though they chained her, this time there was no hood. As they walked her down the blue painted corridor, Morgan took a mental note. Seven paces beyond her cell, there was a closed wooden door on the right, and after another five, a door to the left. There was a left-hand, right angled bend, and then, six paces further, the door to the interrogation room. Morgan remembered she had gone down steps on the night of her arrival. The slight dampness and absence of windows suggested she must be in a basement. Could the stairs be behind one of those doors? Maybe she would get an opportunity to find out.

This time, Sal was courteous. 'Please sit, Mrs Cooper. I assume you're not going to try anything stupid, so unless you do, we can do without the shackles.' He made a gesture, and at once they were removed. 'We're not going to meet every day, but for a while, it's going to be quite often. I imagine you've had plenty of time to think about what happened last week, and I hope there will be no need to repeat any of that unpleasantness. You are comfortable?'

Morgan sat on her hard wooden chair and flexed her limbs. 'It will do. But please bring me some water.'

Sal spoke in Arabic, and one of the guards left the room, reappearing with a half litre bottle. 'You see?' Sal said. 'From now on, with your assistance, I will be, as they say, the good cop. You and I are going to establish a rapport, and as a result, our sessions will be far more productive. In the words of the US military's own interrogation field manual, "the use of force is a poor technique, as it yields unreliable results." So let us have a pleasant conversation, and this time, you will tell me only the truth.'

Morgan had spent hours thinking about a strategy for getting through this interrogation. Her rise through the CIA's ranks at Headquarters meant she knew secrets that really must not be given up, including details of officers who worked in places such as Afghanistan and Pakistan under non-official cover, and of operations which had resulted in the deaths of 'high value targets.' She also knew a lot about the Agency's communication and computer systems.

Paradoxically, her strategy for survival was to talk, for outright denial would get her and Abdel Nasser nowhere but the grave: as Zainab had just reminded her, if she didn't tell the truth, she 'know what happen.' That meant she couldn't go back on her critical admission that she worked for the Agency: they would never believe her, anyway. Instead, rather than to lie, her approach must be to tell a limited quantity of truth. She had sifted her knowledge into categories, determining what she knew that should be of interest to Sal and his colleagues, but could divulge without inflicting real damage. She planned to disclose this information as slowly as she possibly could, but eventually to go into prolix, embroidered detail, in the hope that if she kept on talking long enough, someone would find this house and rescue her.

'Of course, when we start, I will be asking you the questions,' Sal said. 'But today we are only setting out the ground rules. If there is anything you want to ask me, go ahead.'

'How much longer do you intend to keep me? You must surely know this can't go on much longer.'

'Mrs Cooper,' Sal said wearily. 'Let's not go there. How and when this ends is entirely up to you. Is there anything else?'

She thought of the murderous Karim, and the longing she had sensed in his eyes when he had been about to cut the throat of Abdel Nasser. 'Just one. You and Karim. The man who knows me from Kosovo. It doesn't seem you have very much in common.'

'Mrs Cooper, you are mistaken.' Sal looked solemn. 'Our parents inhabited different lands. I have had much greater material and educational opportunities. But both of us have dedicated our lives to this struggle, which we believe may well be *al-Malhamah*, the great, last battle between Muslims and Romans of which the Prophet Mohammed, peace be upon him, foretold.

'And next to Karim, I am only a footsoldier, his servant. I have sworn *bayat* to him, an oath of allegiance, and he may do with me as he pleases. Karim is my leader, my *emir*.'

When he left Eugene's office, Adam's mind was in tumult. While he was still in front of him, he had managed to restrain his feelings, but once he was back in the brilliant Tel Aviv sunshine, they threatened to overwhelm him. He was relieved that now at last there was proof she was alive – or had been when she made the video. But as he made his way back to his hotel, the horrifying mental picture of the Morgan he had just seen was all the while in front him. Intellectually, he had always known it was likely she was being maltreated. Emotionally, he had clung to the hope that she was still in reasonable shape, that the kidnappers had merely been trying to make some symbolic political point, and once they had done so, would let her go unharmed. Seeing the reality had been far worse than he had feared. Her voice, usually so clear and mellifluous, had emerged on the recording as a grating rasp, as if the mere act of speaking had been causing her physical pain, and she looked as if she had been sick. Her eyes were opaque, devoid of their usual vivacity. And then there had been that violent, horrible shudder halfway through her statement. What had those bastards done to her? The video had no date stamp: how long ago had this happened? Was she being tortured still? And what was this shadowy group, the *Janbiya al-Islam*? Adam had researched the many varieties of Gazan extremism on the Internet, but he had not come across any mention of them.

As soon as he got back to his room, he called Rob, and told him everything.

'I'm talking to my friends,' the colonel said, his voice an icy calm. 'We can't let them do this to her without suffering consequences.'

Adam did not inquire who those friends were. His cellphone and hotel landline were probably being eavesdropped.

'Be careful what you tell Sherry.'

'Don't worry. I will.'

Afterwards, Adam felt drained. He had not slept through the five hours spent sitting upright in British Airways economy the previous night, and when he lay on his bed to rest, he soon sank into oblivion. By the time he awoke, it was dark. It was almost time for his rendezvous. At their second meeting in London, Imad had given him precise instructions, and he followed them to the letter.

He put on a black T-shirt, black jeans and running shoes and walked down to the seafront. He went across the sand to one of the beach bars, where he sat in a deckchair under the black, Levantine night, a sputtering candle on the little plastic table beside him. He ordered a soda and sipped it, until his eyes were accustomed to the darkness. When he arrived, the only other customers had been a pair of American tourists, talking loudly about a trip they were planning to make to Bethlehem next day, but soon three others joined them: a pair of young lovers, who looked utterly absorbed in each other, and a middle-aged man in khakis and a dark, plain T-shirt. Finishing his drink, Adam got up and walked to the shoreline. After a few moments he could see that the couple had also left their seats. Could they be following him? Adam increased his pace and turned away from the water, heading back towards the road. When he reached it, the man in the T-shirt was already there, leaning against a parked Mercedes, smoking a cigarette.

Imad had warned him he was likely to be watched, but Adam had not expected it to be so blatant. He hailed a taxi, and asked to be driven the handful of blocks to his hotel. But when the car was almost there he leaned forward and told the driver he had changed his mind: instead he wanted to be driven in the opposite direction, to the flea market in Jaffa. There he got out and walked past some trendy restaurants further into the market, along the lines of empty pitches where the stalls would be next morning. The street was almost deserted, and he could detect no sign of pursuit. At last he spotted a three-storey Ottoman building, its walls covered with peeling yellow stucco. A man in a Yankees baseball cap lurked at the entrance to an alley beside it and beckoned to Adam.

'You are Cooper?' he asked.

Adam nodded, then followed him down the narrow passageway. It opened out into a square where another taxi was waiting. Adam got into the back seat. The man was the driver. As the vehicle began to move, Adam instinctively ducked his head until it rested on his knees. To a casual observer, he would not have been easy to recognise.

By snatching glances through the window, Adam could see they were heading out of the city towards Lod, the industrial town near the airport. At last they stopped outside a concrete apartment tower. The driver punched a code into a keypad to admit them to the lobby and summoned the elevator. He held the door while Adam entered, then reached round the side and pressed the button for the seventh floor. He shook Adam's hand. '*Yalla*, bye-bye Sir,' he said.

When the elevator doors opened, Adam found himself looking at a sallow-skinned, clean-shaven man in his early thirties, dressed in pressed blue jeans and a white, short-sleeved shirt. He looked like an off-duty IT sales rep.

'Welcome,' he said. The door across the landing was already open, and they entered a clean, studio apartment. While Adam sat down in a leather armchair, the man plugged an iPod into a dock and selected some Rachmaninoff.

'The music is in case there is anyone trying to listen,' he said. 'You can call me Bashir. I wish I could offer you coffee or tea, but this is not my apartment and there doesn't seem to be any. How was your journey?'

'It was fine, thanks.'

'Your first time in Palestine?'

'Yes.'

'You are missing your wife?'

'Yes, I am.'

'And your children? They are okay?'

'As well as can be expected. My parents are taking good care of them.'

'You are lucky. So. I think you went to the US embassy this morning. Did they tell you anything?'

For just a moment, Adam wondered what Eugene would say if he knew he was about to pass on the contents of their talk to a member of the Hamas underground in Israel. The thought did not detain him long.

'They showed me a video. It had been sent by the kidnappers. She looked as if she had been tortured, waterboarded, and on it she confessed to being a CIA agent.'

'Is that true?'

Adam said nothing.

'From your silence, I suppose that it is.' Bashir whistled. 'You must know that merely by agreeing to meet you, I am taking an enormous risk. If the Shin Bet knew anything about my associations, they would lock me up in a heartbeat. And you, Adam Cooper, are asking me to help free an American spy. Just be aware that if you were anyone else, I would refuse even to speak to you.'

'I can't thank you enough.'

'No, maybe you can't.' Bashir's eyes flashed with anger. 'Do you know what is happening in Gaza? Hamas has offered a ceasefire with Israel. We contested the elections last year, and we won. But when we tried to form a government, the foreign aid that should have funded its salaries was stopped. Israel complains that rockets get fired from Gaza, but most of them land in empty fields. But every so often, the Israelis decide to retaliate. They send in their tanks and their aircraft and they kill people. And we do not face only the external enemy. We are also forced to defend ourselves against armed Fatah gangsters, collaborators with Israel, friends of America. They set up roadblocks, arrest young boys on their way to school and university, and torture them. Even when they do not kill them, we find them afterwards, shot with bullets in their kneecaps. And the CIA is part of this chaos.'

'But I am not responsible, and neither is my wife.' Adam said. 'Anyhow, on the video, the group that has kidnapped my wife calls itself the *Janibiya al-Islam*. Have you heard of them?'

Bashir looked pensive. 'Yes. We know who these people are. They are followers of bin-Laden and al-Qaeda. I will make sure this information gets through. It is important.'

'Can you give me a contact inside Gaza? Someone I can link up with?'

'I don't think you should try to enter Gaza now. The situation is very dangerous, so dangerous we cannot promise to protect you. Your children have already lost their mother. What will they do if they lose you, too?'

'I can't just do nothing. I have to try.'

118

Bashir stood. 'I must be going. Wait here ten minutes, then leave. You will see a driver outside who will take you to your hotel.' He took a piece of paper from his pocket, scribbled on it and handed it to Adam. 'This is the number of someone in Gaza. His name is Khader. Do not call him unless you are in Gaza too. Make you sure you remember it, then put this paper in the toilet.'

As he left the apartment tower, Adam's spirits sank as fast as the elevator. He had travelled five thousand miles, and was physically much closer to his wife. But what was left of the road ahead still seemed long, and the only thing he knew for certain was that nothing he had ever done in his life had prepared him for such a journey.

Chapter Eleven
Thursday, April 26 – Sunday, April 29, 2007

After so many days in darkness and gloom, Morgan had almost forgotten what sunlight looked like. But now, early on a gleaming, breezy morning, the world was drenched in it. They sat facing each other in white plastic chairs, in the shade cast by a huge, spreading date palm – 'it won't just keep us cool,' Sal had said, 'it will prevent us from being seen from above.' The guards were hidden around the side of the building, a spacious villa, which had three storeys above the ground as well as the basement she knew so well. On the table between them, Zainab had left plates of hummus, flatbread, olives, *tabbouleh*, boiled eggs, pastries and dates, and two large glasses of Palestinian mint tea. She could not see over the compound walls, but she sensed the proximity of the sea, feeling its tang in her nostrils. They must, she reasoned, be somewhere north of Rafah, the least densely populated region of the entire Gaza Strip. Occasionally she made out the noise of vehicles or an aircraft, but they sounded distant: the house must be set back some way from the road. Her defences remained on alert. But if this was Sal playing the 'good cop,' it was something she could learn to live with.

'It's time I told you a little about myself,' Sal said, finishing the last of several pastries. 'You do not yet know my name: you can call me Abu Mustafa. Maybe you have guessed that I have spent time in the West. In fact, I studied in America. I am forty-one years old, and like you, I have children, two boys and a girl, and I do not see them enough. I am not from here, but from one of the neighbouring countries: *insh'Allah*, when we are done here, I will be able to go home for a while. It is hard, isn't it, to be away from one's family?'

Morgan nodded. This she had not expected: Sal – Abu Mustafa – trying to be charming and empathetic: a jihadist in touch with his feelings. This was a man who had helped perpetrate her torture, and the contrast was almost too much to comprehend. But then the memory of her CIA interrogation course, taught by a man named Phil who was both a spy and a PhD psychologist, began to bubble up. 'The guy you're interrogating may well hate Americans,' the lecturer had said. 'Convince him that you're a member of the same human species, and his mental door is already halfway open. How can I do that? I monologue. I talk about myself, to establish the perception that we have common ground, shared experiences. The important questions to which I want answers can come later. We call the goal here "adjusted cognitive reasoning" – to shift the subject's perspective towards that of the interrogator.'

There had already been signs they were planning a change of strategy: they had begun to let her take a shower every day, and to wear clean clothes – not the orange jumpsuits of the first days of her captivity, but loose-fitting T-shirts and sweatpants. Abu Mustafa's fond words about his family were merely another step. Yet as he described his children's various accomplishments, he did not seem to be faking. 'As I am sure you know, the fact I am called Abu Mustafa means my eldest child's name is Mustafa. He's almost sixteen, and though he loves his sports, *insh'Allah*, he will be a doctor or an engineer. Then comes Fatima: she's only thirteen, but already she knows English, French and Arabic. Finally there is little Osama. He is still just an imp. He is seven.'

Morgan wondered whether she could turn this abruptly different treatment to her advantage. Here was a chance to find out more about Abu Mustafa. For example, if his daughter was learning English and French, she probably went to a private school, and the family must have money. Where did Arab children still learn French these days? Lebanon? Jordan? Maybe Syria?

'Your youngest must have been born in 2000 - well before September 11,' she said. 'Were you already committed to waging the jihad then?'

'My son's name means "lion", but it has nothing to do with bin Laden. Many Muslim babies were given it, long before 9/11.'

She tried again. 'And where did you study in America? What was it that got you so mad?'

'Mrs Cooper, I do not mean to show you disrespect, but having seen the ways of the *kufr*, I became outraged. And when I started to see that the Muslim lands were also occupied by the *kufr*, some literally, others only spiritually, and that the law of Allah was being uprooted while the *kufr* stuffed their jails with the Muslim fighters who had striven to restore it – it was then that I understood the duty imposed on every Muslim, to practise *jihad*.'

It was a familiar narrative, one to which a long line of extremists had conformed, from Sayyid Qutb, al-Qaeda's ideological godfather, to Khalid Shaikh Mohammed, the 9/11 planner, currently a guest at Guantanamo. Having sampled the West's delights, they had become disgusted by them.

'So tell me about your wife,' she said. 'How does she manage when you're far from home, fighting your glorious struggle? I'll bet that this wasn't the life she signed up for.'

Abu Mustafa took a sip of tea. 'You are very perceptive. She is also an educated person, a doctor. She would much prefer our lives went back to the way they used to be, when I worked in an office and was home every night. However, in our culture, ultimately the woman will obey.'

'That doesn't mean she's happy.'

'She is a good Muslim. We share the same values.' Abu Mustafa spread his palms. 'And at least she is safe. But you also turned your back on physical security. What made you do that?'

Unexpectedly, Morgan felt a surge of emotion. What *had* made her act in the way that she had? Why had she been so bent on returning to the field that she had disregarded every warning, and ignored the effect her decisions had had on her marriage and her children? The answer had seemed obvious: that it was simply what she wanted, that it defined who she was and needed to do in order to feel fulfilled. Now that seemed hopelessly self-indulgent. She breathed deeply, fighting for composure, hoping that Abu Mustafa would not notice the effect his question had had on her battered psyche.

'I'm sorry. I didn't mean to upset you,' he said. 'Well, I know how it is because sometimes I feel the same way. In two days Fatima will be fourteen, and I will miss her birthday. I cannot even call her, in case your American friends or the Zionist entity locate my phone signal and send us a missile. How do I keep going? Because I believe that what I am doing is right, that it strikes a blow for justice. And I believe it is Allah's will.'

Morgan rallied. 'Well, Abu Mustafa, I happen to believe in my mission too, and in the great experiment in human liberty that the United States of America represents. And let me assure you, this doesn't make us similar, but more diametrically different than you'll ever understand.'

After that first session in the compound, they met on the next two mornings. Morgan had remembered another lesson from Phil's course on basic interrogation: 'When you're still trying to get a subject to the decision point, the point where they break, techniques like isolation and sleep deprivation have their advantages. But once you've got past that and they've started to talk, you want them well-fed and rested. Otherwise, they may simply be too exhausted to remember vital information.'

When she wasn't with Abu Mustafa, she was still being kept in the basement. But although down there she had no natural light, they had moved her to a bigger room with a single bed. They had let her bring her chess set. So far as she could tell, there were no hidden cameras, and for the first time since her capture she felt able to try a little exercise. Every morning, she did crunches, push-ups and Pilates on the kelim which covered part of the floor. Her muscles, she had noticed, had been atrophying: she needed this limited routine. The food had improved a little. Occasionally, Zainab even smiled.

Morgan remembered the Stockholm syndrome, the bond that can grow between terrorist captors and their prisoners. First came the loss of control, and total dependency on her captors;

then gratitude for the least unexpected kindness, and thence a sense of obligation that would make her give up her secrets. Her first, violent encounters with Abu Mustafa had made it seem impossible that she could ever feel such a relationship developing with him. Yet she was beginning to enjoy his company, and even looked forward to their meetings. So far she had given him nothing, but she had to wonder whether he too had been professionally trained. Had he once been an intelligence officer?

Once again, they were sitting beneath the date palm. As well as the usual Middle Eastern breakfast, today there were glasses and a pitcher containing a dark red juice. 'It is from the pomegranate,' Abu Mustafa said, pouring Morgan a glass. 'A Gazan speciality.'

Morgan was thirsty, and took a large gulp. 'It's delicious, really delicious.'

'Zainab made it specially. It reminds me of home. My wife makes it too. So what about you? Who does the cooking in your household?'

'Adam usually, when he's there. He's not bad at it.'

'So modern. So western. Does he travel often, too?'

'Not so much these days. Not like he used to. Occasionally he'll make a trip down to Guantanamo. It's not like it was in the old days, when the kids were small, and he'd disappear to the South to investigate some death case, sometimes for weeks at a time.'

'Didn't that bother you, him disappearing and leaving you with the kids? I mean, that's what you asked me about the way my wife regards my own absences from home.'

Morgan raised a hand to shield her eyes against a ray of the sun which had evaded the fronds of the date palm. 'Yes, it did. Of course it did. Look, I knew Adam didn't have a choice. He was driven to do this work, and men's lives depended on it. But all my life, through high school and college, I'd been taught to believe that men and women were equal, that the balance between them had changed. And suddenly my life didn't feel so different to my mom's, who never got the chance to establish a career because we were always moving, every time Dad was given a new posting. It might have been easier for me if our parents had lived near Washington. But Adam's were in England, and my own were long plane flights away. It just never seemed to get easier. I never had a moment to myself. My life was just work, kids, work, kids. I never felt I was devoting enough time to either of them, and I never had any for myself. I was falling into bed each night feeling utterly spent, and, far too often, alone.'

Abu Mustafa's dark eyes met hers with new intensity. 'In our culture, there would have been others to share the burden. The extended family, always ready to help. And did you have other anxieties when Adam was away?'

'What do you mean?'

'I mean, were you worried that while you were living a life of a drudge, devoting every moment to the kids and the CIA, your husband might have been diverting himself?'

His question was intrusive, but she had to keep talking. 'Yes. There were times when I was concerned about that.'

'Go on.'

'Look, I'm sure it's no different for anyone whose spouse spends time away. But those cases get very intense, especially when there's an execution date. People are thrown together. I remember there was one paralegal down in Georgia. Vicky. You know how it goes: younger than me, no children, able to commit every minute to the same cause which was obsessing Adam. It seemed like she was seeing more of him than I was for a while, and when I looked up her photo on the website of the local law firm Adam was working with, guess what, she was gorgeous. Meanwhile I was frazzled and exhausted. Finally Adam got this guy a stay and a new sentencing hearing, late in the afternoon on the very day he'd been due to die. That meant that instead of having to watch their client's execution, all the defence team were out on the town in Atlanta, celebrating.'

'And you thought they celebrated a little too hard?' said Abu Mustafa.

'Yes. Back home in Bethesda, Aimee had croup. Had Adam been there, I would have taken her to the emergency room, but I couldn't bring myself to wake up Charlie, who was still just a baby, and of course there was no one I could call to leave him with. I just wanted to hear Adam's voice, to get some reassurance. I called him at midnight, and at twelve-thirty, and every thirty minutes after that until at last Aimee stopped coughing and we both fell asleep around four. The next afternoon Adam bounded in, bursting with success, and a little bleary-eyed. He always insisted nothing ever happened, that they just stayed up late at a bar, drinking and chatting. I have to believe him.'

'You have to, but really you don't?'

'What difference does it make? Right now, I can barely remember what it was that once seemed so important.'

'And you, Mrs Cooper? Have you ever been tempted?'

Morgan detected a sudden beady prurience in Abu Mustafa's eyes. 'I already told you the answer to that question, the day before you and your friend almost drowned me. It hasn't changed, and I suggest you change the subject.'

Sunday morning: the start of Israel's working week. Adam knew that Mike and Gary had been in the country for several days, and he was surprised he hadn't heard from them. But he didn't much mind. Since his meeting with Bashir, he had been busy. He had discovered that getting into Gaza was not a simple matter. He couldn't just show up at Erez. He needed a sponsor, someone who had official access, and was willing to make the necessary arrangements and provide a measure of protection. A few months earlier, he and Morgan had been to a cocktail party in Bethesda. They had been introduced to Colin Reilly, a genial Canadian who was running a programme funded by the State Department, which was trying to teach the more amenable Palestinian factions the skills of modern political organisation.

Adam realised he might now be a useful contact, and two days earlier, he had taken a bus to Jerusalem, where he and Reilly had lunched at an Arab restaurant near the Damascus Gate. Reilly promised to acquire the paperwork and take Adam to Gaza with him as soon as he could. They would not be staying overnight. Adam didn't have much longer anyway. Every day he phoned Charlie and Aimee, and it was clear they wanted him back. The previous evening, his father had underlined their message. 'I know you have to do what you can. But don't stay away too long. You can always go back.'

Adam had been wondering whether he might finally get the chance to go to the beach when his cellphone rang. It was Gary.

'You doing anything, Adam?'

'Not just now, no.'

'Then perhaps you'd like to come by. We're in Eugene's office. You know where it is.'

Mike was waiting for him in the embassy lobby, dressed in khakis and a floral, Hawaiian shirt.

'Be careful,' he said. 'I don't know what you've done, but the boss sure seems pissed.'

Gary and Eugene were sitting at the glass conference table. 'Adam,' Gary said, without offering his hand. 'Sit down. And then, if you don't mind, since we're all working for the same end, I'd like you to give me an account of what you've been doing here.'

'What, everything?' Adam asked.

'Just the important stuff. I'm not interested in whether you've been sightseeing. But what have you done to try to find your wife?'

'I could ask you the same question.'

Gary looked at Mike and Eugene. 'Gentlemen, Mr Cooper is being a smartass!'

Mike and Eugene looked embarrassed. 'I'm not being a smartass,' Adam said. 'I'm merely stating that my last message from Morgan was left on my voicemail thirty-two days ago, and you seem to have made remarkably little progress.'

'Well, we might have gotten further if we weren't having to spend our time worrying about you.'

'What do you mean?'

'What I mean is, what the hell were you doing with a member of the Hamas underground in an apartment tower in Lod? With a man, I might add, who is now in Israeli custody?'

127

Adam could not disguise his emotions. He felt crushed. How had this happened? He had followed Imad's counter-surveillance instructions to the letter, and felt sure he had not been followed. But alas, he thought ruefully, unlike these men, he was no professional.

'In custody? Why? For agreeing to talk to me?'

'Oh Adam.' Gary's patronising, bogus sympathy was sickening. 'I know how hard these weeks have been. You've got guts, just like your wife, and that's admirable. I understand what you've been attempting. We don't talk to the Islamists, so you thought that maybe, thanks to your legal practice of representing them, you could. But listen to me, for Chrissakes. Listen to someone with almost three decades' experience. This region is a snake-pit. No one and nothing are as they seem. So your new friend Bashir al-Owdeh might have come across as ever so helpful, and no doubt he's promised he'll fix you up when you make your little trip to Gaza. Yes, my friend, we know about that too. But here's the truth. Al-Owdeh is a scumbag. He's been wanted by the Shin Bet for years. But you did them a favour. They were having you followed, and you led them to him. I guess that means at least some good has come of it.'

Adam stared at Gary, his expression fixed, saying nothing.

'Now, listen to the facts of life here. This group which claims to be holding Morgan, the *Janbiya al-Islam*. Well, I have good friends in this part of the world: seasoned Israeli intelligence officers who tell me things that they maybe shouldn't. Guys I've known for years. I've been spending time with them, and they're certain that the *Janbiya* are a fraud, a put-on.'

'They didn't look very fraudulent to me in that video. And the way they tortured my wife: that was definitely for real.'

'Sure it was. And I don't want to minimise it. But they're a front. The kidnappers want us to think they're some new bunch of radicals, way more extreme than Hamas. In fact, they *are* Hamas. Morgan's kidnap is being staged to suit Hamas's ultimate purpose – to take over Gaza and the West Bank. Whatever promises they might make, the last thing they'll do is help you. That means that by going to Gaza and trying to hook up with them, you aren't just risking your life. You're wasting your time.'

'What? How is kidnapping Morgan going to help Hamas? Sorry, but I don't get it.'

Gary sighed. 'It's complicated, like just about everything in the Middle East. So pay attention. What my sources say is going to happen is that Hamas will suddenly create a big media hoopla, saying they've found Morgan and liberated her. They'll parade her on television and send her home, while telling the world this proves they're no longer terrorists but a mature political organisation, fit to be recognised by the international community. But Adam. It's bullshit. Layer upon layer of lies and deception: that's the way this region works. It's all just an illusion, concocted to improve their image. You have got yourself in deep, way over your head. And now it's time to get out. Go home. Spend some time with your kids. And be a little fucking patient, okay?'

Gary sounded persuasive. But Adam did not believe him. His argument was far too convoluted, and if Morgan's kidnap was merely a piece of political theatre, why had its perpetrators tortured her, using a method which might easily have ended her life?

'I don't really care what your Israeli friends are saying,' Adam said. 'Maybe they're right. But maybe they're not, and if it's okay with you, and actually, even if it's not okay, I'd like the chance to judge things for myself. The Israelis can't go to Gaza. I can. And I will. And then, when I've made my own assessment, I'll go home. Or at least, back to England.'

'You don't work for me, so I can't tell you what to do,' said Gary, his voice almost a hiss. 'But I hope you're prepared for your kids to be orphans, Mr Cooper, because the way you want to play this, you're going to get yourself killed. Your life is your own. But what does piss me off is that if you go to Gaza and pander to Hamas, it will achieve nothing, except to expose more decent people to the risk of being kidnapped. So, go on your precious little trip with Mr Reilly. But bear the consequences in mind.'

Chapter Twelve
Wednesday, May 2, 2007

Adam had bought himself a pastry the previous night, and while he waited for Colin Reilly he ate it with a cup of instant coffee that he made in his room. While he ate, he looked again at a report of the capture of Bashir al-Owdeh in the previous day's *Haaretz*. He could not help feeling nervous that al-Owdeh's friends in Gaza might blame him for his capture, but he was determined to use the phone number he had given him. What else could he do?

He went downstairs at six-thirty, and almost immediately Reilly pulled up outside in his black SUV. 'Your papers are in order,' he said in a faux-German accent. 'You are free to enter Gaza – the place most people are desperate to leave. I'm sorry for the early start.'

The city streets were still deserted, and soon they reached the highway. As he drove, Colin set some ground rules.

'You have to understand that as a US government-funded programme, we are strictly forbidden from having anything to do with Hamas,' he said. 'I'll take you into Gaza City and you can come up to my office. But after that, you're on your own. I can't let you use my drivers, either. I'm not planning to go out. I've got some management issues to deal with. But you need to be back at the office by four. Otherwise, we'll be stuck in Gaza for the night. If you don't make it, I'll wait for you. But even if we manage to get into one of the hotels, you may not find it all that comfortable.'

'I thought Erez stayed open until six?'

'It does. But though I doubt it's more than five miles from the office, that's a distance that can take a while round here. You never quite know how it's going to go with the roadblocks.'

'Right.'

130

'Still, with any luck, we won't actually get caught in a fire-fight.'

Adam spent the rest of the drive lost in his own thoughts. What did he hope to achieve? Did he really think he was going to run into Gaza for less than twelve hours, meet some Hamas militiaman who would promise to drop everything and find Morgan for him? Soon enough, his reverie was brought to an end. They were at Erez.

'Here goes then,' said Colin, locking up the car. 'Remember, the Israelis will know exactly who you are, and why you're going in. But your papers say you're coming as my assistant. Just stick to that story if anybody asks. They wouldn't have given you permission if they really had any objection.'

They were early, and stood outside the terminal in the warming sun. As they waited, the air suddenly trembled. From somewhere that sounded worryingly close, came the gut-wrenching thump of an explosion.

'Take no notice,' Colin said. 'Some young would-be martyr just fired another rocket into Israel. Probably hit a lemon tree. Ah, look, the doors are about to open. We're first in line.'

Swiftly they passed through the formalities. Colin's driver, Omar, was waiting in the parking lot on the Gaza side. In the past few days, there had been something of a lull in the factional in-fighting, and though they had to negotiate the various roadblocks, none took much time. Yet though the main road was broad and comparatively clear, as he looked to the side Adam sensed the impenetrable and perilous warren of dwellings that lay beyond, the labyrinth jammed between the sea and the Wall. Often it was visible, a grey concrete rampart snaking its way along the brow of the low rise that marked the eastern boundary of the strip, no more than three or four miles away.

'Let's hope they're not holding her somewhere there,' said Colin as they passed the entrance to the Jabaliya camp. 'I don't think anyone would find her in that hellhole.'

Soon enough they reached Colin's office, a six-storey structure that could have been a bank. They parked on a side street, by the back entrance and took the elevator to the fourth floor. Adam hung back while Colin greeted a receptionist who wore a headscarf, as well some of the other staff. Big windows overlooked the grassy open space of Unknown Soldier Square. 'Make the most of it,' said Colin. 'This is as good as Gaza gets. The beating heart of the city.' He ushered Adam into an empty room with a desk and computer. 'Make your phone call. If they agree to meet you, they can pick you up downstairs. Tell them to come to the al-Kafarneh building on the east side of the square.'

Adam took out his cellphone and punched out the number al-Owdeh had told him to memorise. A guttural voice answered almost at once.

'Hello? Marhaba? Is this Khader? This is Adam Cooper. I've been given your number. I want to meet you to talk about my wife.' He was trying to prevent the nervousness he felt from being audible, but even as he spoke, he knew he had failed.

There was a pause, and it sounded as if the phone on the other end was being handed to somebody else.

'Yes. Mr Adam. Welcome. You are in Gaza?'

Adam explained his location.

'We will come in forty minutes. You will see the car. Be in the lobby.'

When they come, there are three of them, all dressed in jeans, T-shirts, and leather jackets: an unofficial uniform. They all have beards, and they pull up at the kerbside in another ageing Corolla. Outside, the sidewalk is busy, and no one seems to pay attention. The man next to the driver catches sight of Adam through the glass lobby doors. Adam spots the car, hyperventilates, then stands and leaves the building. It only takes a second to cross the sidewalk, and the passenger in the back seat leans across and opens the door. 'My name is Khader Abu Fares,' he says. 'Welcome. Get in.' He does not smile. Adam slides into the available space on the back seat, and as soon as he shuts the door, the car begins to move. A dozen blocks from the square, it enters a narrow side street. Adam smiles to himself as he makes a private internal joke: Khader the cadre.

'I'm sorry,' Khader says, 'but this is for security.' He takes a thick blindfold from a small leather zip-up bag in front of him and ties it round Adam's head. 'Now get out.'

Adam stands, still blindfolded. They are in the shade, and there is no traffic noise. He feels hands moving across every inch of his body, deftly removing his only possessions, his passport, wallet and phone. Adam hears Khader talking to someone in Arabic, and then the sound of another vehicle driving away.

'Now get in again. Get down, so you cannot be seen.'

Lying on the seat, Adam senses the car's bewildering motion: sometimes fast, sometimes slow; innumerable turns to left and right. Less than two hours ago, when he passed through Erez, he thought he had crossed the final frontier border between personal security and danger. Now he knows that that was only the beginning, and there may be many such barriers still to cross, each one leading to a deeper circle of peril. Finally the car stops.

'Please get out.'

Wherever they are, it is eerily quiet.

'You hear that sound?' Khader asks.

'What sound?'

'Listen. From up there.'

Adam makes out a buzzing, so faint he could be imagining it: high pitched yet muffled, like a faraway dentist's drill.

'An Israeli drone,' Khader says. 'A spy-plane. We cannot see it, but the sound means it is there, and its operator, who is looking at us on a screen in Beersheba, can send us an F-16 airstrike whenever he happens to feel like it. Remember this, Mr Adam. Even if the Israelis are your friends, this could be the day they kill you.'

As they stand, the calm is shattered for the second time that morning by an explosion. This one seems different. There isn't just the seismic bang: it comes accompanied by the sounds of things shattering, and within a few seconds, by screams, shouts and sirens.

'I don't know what's happening,' says Khader. 'We had better go inside.'

133

Adam feels himself being led into a building. Inside, the blindfold is removed, and he sees he is in the bare concrete stairwell of an apartment block. Despite the oncoming summer, it feels chilly. Khader motions to him and together with the driver and the man Adam thinks of as the guard, they climb the stairs. When they reach the third floor, Khader pushes at an unlocked door. Several men are already inside the apartment, preoccupied: rushing in and out of the main room. The furniture is sparse and utilitarian: a few rough shelves with some books and box files; a desk and a computer; some steel-framed chairs; and in one corner, a coffee table and a cheap brown couch and armchair. On the wall is a huge poster of Jerusalem, dominated by the golden Dome of the Rock, with a border of white Arabic letters printed on a background of brilliant green, the colours of Hamas.

'So. You are here,' says Khader. 'You will sit. You would like some tea?'

'Yes, thank you,' says Adam, trying to smile.

'I must ask you to give me a few minutes. There has been another attack, and I need to find out what is happening.' Khader heads into the adjoining room, and for more than hour, Adam waits. No one pays attention to him. At last Khader comes back.

'The situation is bad, and it is still developing. It started with a bomb near the Islamic University. Four of our people have been blown up in their car, and now there is firing. I think also some of the Fatah soldiers have been shot. Every day, it is getting worse.' He shrugs. 'Either it is Fatah, or the Israelis.'

Adam nods, as if a bombing and its attendant bloody chaos were just another everyday hazard. 'You know why I am here. Can you help?'

'Can we help find your wife?' Khader does not look encouraging. 'Please understand, I want to assist you, Mr Adam. You are my guest, and Ahmad Mahmoud, your client in America, is the cousin of one of my teachers. He is a very respected man. But you are here because Bashir gave you my phone number, and after you met him he was arrested by the Israelis. How did this happen?'

'I don't know. I swear to you, I have no idea how they found him, and the one thing I do know is that it was nothing to do with me.' Adam is aware he is gushing. 'I've gone over everything that happened that night and I just can't figure it out. I am sure no one was following me. I told no one where I was going. Look, if you're suggesting I'm working for the Israelis, surely you can see I would not have come here – especially after Bashir was captured. I'm here because I honestly believe that you want to find my wife, almost as much as I do. I am also convinced that she is being held by your enemies.'

'How would you know who is holding her?'

Of course: Bashir would not have had time to get a message about their meeting to his friends in Gaza. Khader doesn't yet know about the video.

'A DVD was sent to the US embassy. Morgan was on it, she looked terrible, she was wearing a Guantanamo-style orange jumpsuit and I'm certain she had been tortured. Behind her was a banner, which said she was a prisoner of the *Janbiya al-Islam*. Do you know this group? Is it connected to Hamas?'

'So many questions.' Khader shakes his head. 'No. It is nothing to do with the Islamic Movement. We know who they are. They are *takfiri*, extremists. They think it is fine to kill other Muslims in pursuit of their goals. But if they have your wife, it is not good news. You have seen a little of Gaza now. You have seen enough to know how hard it will be to find her.'

As they speak, another man in a leather jacket rushes into the room and whispers into Khader's ear, then hands him a small object. Khader's face darkens. He uncurls his fist, revealing a tiny circuit board.

'Do you know what this is, Mr Adam?'

Adam looks blank, and he shrugs. Before he can speak, Khader stands, raises his hand, and brings it down across Adam's face with sudden, shocking power.

135

'You do not know? You have been carrying this, and you don't know what it is?'

'I – I haven't seen it before.' Adam can feel his cheek swelling, but the shock prevents him from feeling any pain. 'I swear to you. What is it?'

'Well let me educate you, Mr Adam. This is an RFID, a radio frequency identification device: a tracker. After we searched you on the way here, my colleagues discovered it behind the leather in the wallet where you keep your passport. We have deactivated it. It is useless. But I do not believe you. Who gave it to you, Mr Adam?' He jabs Adam in the chest, with a force so strong he sprawls backwards across the spongy foam of the sofa, pushed off balance.

'I have no idea! This is nothing to do with me,' Adam yells. 'I'm here to find my wife, not take sides in your battles with Fatah or the Israelis. I'm a lawyer! I've spent the past few years of my career trying to defend your movement's supporters' constitutional rights, not get them wiped out in an airstrike.' Even as the words spill out of his mouth, he grasps their incongruous absurdity, and a first quiver of fear deep in his viscera. 'I wanted to meet you only to ask you for help. Why else would I take such a risk?'

'You want to find your wife.' Khader's voice is suddenly measured, calm, threatening. 'And is this how you plan to do it? By spying on us? *You* want to find Mrs Cooper. Well I think you must know that this is how the Israelis found Bashir – another man you asked to help you, who now faces years in prison.'

On the table there is an ashtray, and Khader puts the chip in it, then applies the flame from a cigarette lighter. In a moment, it is a blob of bubbling plastic. 'Now that we cannot be followed, we will go somewhere else. Who are you spying for, Mr Adam? Israel or America? The Shabak or the CIA?'

'If you don't believe me, speak to the family of Ahmad Mahmoud. Ask them how I have kept their hopes alive.' Adam has recovered his composure. 'I am truly sorry about Bashir. He saw me in good faith, and unwittingly, I betrayed him. But if I was carrying a tracking device, it was planted on me, and I do not know who was responsible. I have come to you because I do not believe the CIA has the slightest clue where Morgan is, and I feel certain that in time you will.'

Khader says nothing, but his eyes betray doubt. They get up and leave, Adam and the same three men as before. At the bottom of the stairs, the blindfold is again tied round his head. They march him to a car and push him in.

'You say your wife has been kidnapped by the *Janbiya al-Islam*,' Khader says as the vehicle begins to move again. '*Hallas*. If she is in Gaza, we will find the truth.'

Again the bewildering movement. This time, the drive seems to last longer, but the car is slower, sometimes barely moving. As they drive, Adam becomes aware that something is happening on the streets outside. At first the noise is distant and almost indiscernible, but slowly it grows louder: shouting, tumult, and then gunfire. He remembers a wild-eyed Australian he met at some Washington party, who had spent years covering the war in Iraq for one of the TV news networks. Unprompted, he had spoken about nothing except his life's many terrifying confrontations, his words an unstoppable torrent, as if he were unable to comprehend the miracle of his own survival. He recalls that the Australian called firefights 'stowshes' – a term, Adam discovered only later, from Australian and New Zealand military slang. With a squirt of adrenalin, Adam realises he's probably heading into a stowsh himself, accompanied not by trusted comrades but a possibly homicidal Hamas security cadre. He should be petrified. Yet mingled with the fear, he experiences a strange elation. Now no one can accuse him of not trying hard enough. Bizarrely, he recalls his adolescent reading of Jean-Paul Sartre. No longer a besuited litigator, he has seized his destiny.

The vehicle stops altogether, provoking a torrent of angry, frightened Arabic from the driver. Khader shouts back, and Adam feels the car begin to shake and rock. The invisible mob outside is screaming unintelligible chants and slogans, and on top of the men's deep roar there's a piercing descant: the shrieks of ululating women. A hand lifts the blindfold and Adam turns to look Khader, seeing that his eyes are wide with fear, and then at the scene outside the car windows. They're in a wide street, apparently close to the middle of the city, and in front of the car is a sea of men in *keffiyehs*. Most are clean-shaven, and that, Adam realises, means they're Fatah, not Hamas.

'We're going to have to run for it!' Khader's voice is an octave higher than it was when they were in the apartment. He tries to open the door, but finds it jammed by the pressure of the crowd. Through the windshield, maybe a hundred yards ahead, Adam sees three swaying coffins born aloft by mourners, draped in Fatah's colours. How did this happen? How can Khader's driver have been so stupid? They have blundered into a political funeral. According to Arabic custom, the bodies will be fresh, probably shot in an earlier phase of this burgeoning 'stowsh' earlier this same day. Now it seems that every eye is on their car, and fists are being raised: it's only too obvious that Khader and the others are Hamas.

'Lock your door,' Khader shouts. 'Maybe we can somehow drive out of this.' But the press of bodies only grows. Even were the driver able and willing to run people down, the car cannot move. Time seems to slow as Adam looks up and sees the incongruous trappings of normality: a balcony with plastic chairs; some laundry draped on a maiden; the usual square, concrete buildings. But so many people. So many of them young, and yet so angry.

Just ahead, a phalanx of the guards in black, the well-equipped guys who Colin said had been trained with American backing, emerges from a side street, and as he catches sight of them, Adam feels a surge of relief. At last: order.

'Khader, look.' Adam points.

But when Khader sees them, he pushes the door again with renewed, desperate force. 'They are Force 17,' he says. 'These are the worst. We must go now or we die!'

Adam doesn't see who fires the first two shots, but they seem to have come from behind, perhaps from a gunman hidden on one of the laundry-draped balconies. The Force 17 men scatter as the bullets thud into the concrete of the building above their heads, and he gazes in horror as one of them takes cover by the side of a van and raises his weapon. The crowd's screams are no longer coordinated and they rise in volume, while Adam pushes at the car door with his feet, his back braced against the front passenger seat, drawing on every reserve of his strength. With a surge of triumph he feels it open, and he keeps his legs rigid so it cannot close. He grabs Khader's wrist, and, dragging him with him, he dives from the car. But even as they make their exit, the Force 17 militiaman fires twice. The windshield shatters and the driver slumps forward, a cataract of blood pumping from his neck and forehead. As he leaves the vehicle Adam feels the spray, and for a fraction of a second he thinks he has been hit. He turns away as a third shot hits the Hamas guard who had been next to the driver. He may not be dead, but if they try to rescue him, they soon will be.

The shock of the shooting has made the crowd draw back in case more bullets, maybe not so well-aimed, are coming, and in the instant before the mob can regroup Adam and Khader start to run, away from the coffins, back down the street in the direction they drove in from. There is no more firing, and within two hundred yards the crowd has thinned. In a hundred more they have the street to themselves, but they keep on running, careless of the heat and the sun overhead. Away from the mob and the men with guns, the streets are empty, the windows shuttered. Adam has no idea where he is, a fugitive in an alien city. Then, through a gap between buildings, he catches the gleam of the sea, and mentally he orientates himself: he must be heading north – towards Erez! – parallel to the coast. He racks his memory for the Gaza maps he has spent hours poring over on the internet. Depending where he started from, he is either going to end up close to the haven that is Colin's office, or in the chaos of the Jabaliya refugee camp, the seething cauldron being fought over by a dozen militant factions. At last they reach a junction, and Khader stops.

'You go that way,' he says, pointing. 'Just go straight. It will take you back to Unknown Soldier Square. And you will need these.' He reaches into his jacket, and gives Adam his wallet and passport. 'I'm afraid we destroyed your cellphone. We had to be sure there was not another chip.' He holds out his hand. 'You saved me. Now, *habibi*, I believe you.'

'But what about you? Where will you go?'

'Don't worry. There is a Hamas house near here. I will be safe. Now go. *Insh'Allah* you will come back, and then we will find your wife. But it is for later. This is not the time for you to be in Gaza.' Khader waves, then walks quickly downhill, towards the beach.

Adam starts to jog again and makes his way along the wide, silent street. From somewhere behind, he can hear more gunfire, but soon, not so far ahead, he can see the square. Here there are still men sitting outside the cafes, and they look in astonishment at this sweating, bloodied westerner, running alone along the sidewalk. He pushes the plate glass doors and stumbles into the Kafarneh Building lobby. The air conditioning feels like a sudden immersion in a cool mountain waterfall. The security man says nothing as he summons the elevator, then rides it to Colin's floor.

Colin has been paying a visit to the rest room and happens to be on the marble landing when the elevator doors reopen. He scans Adam carefully, taking in the blood spilt across his safari shirt. 'Aha,' he says. 'I see you've been getting to know Gaza. You're going to need the washroom, and I can lend you a T-shirt. And then we'd better get you home.' Adam looks at his watch. It is three-forty five in the afternoon. He has made Colin's deadline Gaza with fifteen minutes to spare.

Adam had been warned that the security at Erez would be intense, and it lived up to expectations. He wanted nothing more than to be back in Tel Aviv, to take a shower and wash away his fear and frustration. First, however, he had to stand in the Erez security area, obeying the orders that were broadcast through a speaker system by staff looking down from a high-level viewing gallery, protected by blast-proof glass. 'Turn out your pockets. Place your wallet and passport in the plastic tray and put it on the conveyor belt. Remove your belt, watch and shoes. Now stand in the explosives detection booth ahead of you.' Even without a bag, it took forty minutes. Afterwards, back in the passport hall, he and Colin joined a long line of journalists, aid workers and a few privileged Palestinians. For almost an hour, it did not move, because there was no one in the inspection booth. It was almost six before they emerged, back in the land of Israel.

He felt disorientated and traumatised, trying to come terms with what had happened. On a few occasions while climbing in the Alps, he had, he knew, come close to death. Once an innocent snow-slope that he had just crossed was suddenly filled with a mass of falling boulders, some the size of cars, which had been melted from their icy moorings by a heatwave. Another time, he and a friend had been benighted while descending from a notorious ice-climb, the north face of the Aiguille de Triolet: had they not stayed active all night by digging an enormous cave with their iceaxes, they would have frozen to death. But somehow, surviving the worst that impersonal, implacable nature could throw at him seemed easier to deal with. The Force 17 men who had killed Khader's driver could just as easily have killed him, and they would have done so through an exercise of hostile, human agency. Worse, men who were equally dangerous, and just as culturally alien, were still holding Morgan. That he had gained a somewhat greater personal insight into what she what she was going through only intensified his anxiety.

Adam said little about his day on the drive back to Tel Aviv, hoping that when they arrived, Colin would join him for a beer. But he had to get back to his new wife in Jerusalem, and so after his shower Adam took to the streets alone, past the bars and restaurants thronged with tourists and on down to the seafront, where happy little clumps of young people were flirting as they always did in their flip-flops and shorts and miniskirts. He sat

141

and watched the sunset on a bench, and as darkness fell he walked to an outdoor café, picked at a pizza and drank most of a bottle of wine, but though the alcohol soothed him, his stomach could barely tolerate the food. He wondered whether Morgan could see the same evening stars. What seemed hard to believe was not Gaza, so near and yet so distant, but Tel Aviv. Three well-groomed American women in their early thirties sat down at the next table and tried to engage him in conversation, announcing they were from Milwaukee, and inquiring whether he could give them advice about the best way to arrange a visit to Masada. He answered politely but declined their request to join them, fearing that if he did, the only subject he would be able to talk about was how to survive your first firefight.

Before turning in, he checked his email. Among the spam was a message from Ronnie Wasserman, sent early that morning. 'Dear Adam,' it began, 'I spoke to your mother-in-law today and she explained you're in Israel. I imagine you know she came to see me a few days ago, and she gave me her number. Well, this is quite a coincidence, because I'm on the way there myself. Only for a week, unfortunately, but I really needed a break. I'll be staying with my sister in Ramat Hasharon, a few miles north of Tel Aviv. I'll be on my own: Theo's parents have agreed to take care of the kids. Anyhow, if you're free, it would be lovely to see you. I'm due to arrive tomorrow. Send me an email or call my US cellphone xxx R.'

He was already feeling a little hunted when he noticed an envelope had been pushed underneath his door. The card inside was signed by a man named Colonel Yitzhak Ben-Meir. 'Mr Cooper, I would like to meet you in order to discuss your visit to Gaza. You should know that I met your wife before she was kidnapped. I will call you in the morning.'

Chapter Thirteen
Thursday, May 3, 2007

After two solid days locked in her room in the basement, Morgan was relieved to be outside again in the open air. But from the moment she sat down with Abu Mustafa in their usual place beneath the date palm, she could see he was troubled. He seemed distracted, and had none of his usual appetite.

'What's wrong?' she asked. 'You're not yourself. Trouble at home?'

'As I told you before, I don't know what's happening at home, because I cannot speak to my family. And I don't know what you mean. I am fine.'

'You sure don't look fine. Well, I'm sure you must be missing them. I do know exactly how you feel.'

Abu Mustafa shrugged.

'So why don't you let me go? If you did, you could go home too.'

Before he could reply, the real source of Abu Mustafa's unease was apparent. Today, they would not be on their own. Morgan felt the ice enter her veins as a third person strode imperiously out of the house and across the yard to join them: Karim. A guard followed him with another plastic chair, and he sat down at the table, dressed in a Bedouin robe.

'Hello Morgan. Is nice to see you. You are thirsty today?' He giggled artificially, an unpleasant, high-pitched gurgle. '*Hallas*. Is time now for real questions.' He gestured towards Abu Mustafa. 'My friend he explain what I am saying.'

Abu Mustafa cleared his throat. He did not look happy, but his words betrayed no sign of disloyalty. 'As you would expect, I have been keeping Karim informed of our talks. But we feel we need to move now to matters of more substance, such as the true nature of your mission to Gaza. We have also been talking to Abdel Nasser. But we need to hear it from you.'

If anything, Morgan felt surprised that Abu Mustafa had already spent so long on what could only be described as distant background. It was finally time to put her strategy into effect: to try to protect the secrets she could never divulge by giving up what was safe. 'I was here to observe, and to make reports on what I saw. My mission was really no different from when I was in the Balkans. My government is heavily invested in the peace process, but in order for its diplomatic efforts to be effective, it needs up to date and accurate information from Gaza. We no longer have personnel stationed here permanently. The Agency knew I was anxious to return to fieldwork, and so it asked me to begin making frequent visits, while continuing to spend most of my time at home. So it suited us both and, well, here I am.'

'Here I am,' said Karim, aping her accent. 'No different from Balkans.' He snorted.

'Mrs Cooper, it is all very well saying you came here to observe,' Abu Mustafa said, trying to regain the initiative. 'But observe what? Aljazeera television is here all the time, and there are other correspondents. What did you need to find out that was so secret it needed the skills of an officer of the CIA's clandestine service, and the recruitment of Abdel Nasser?'

'Governments like to do their own reporting on the ground. But while it's true I work for the Agency, the kind of reporting they wanted from me here was much the same as it would have been if I had been working for the State Department.'

Karim got up, crossed the narrow distance to Morgan's chair, then bent down, placing his face just inches in front of hers. 'You are lying,' he said. 'And you lie, you know what happen.' He moved his fingers across his throat not once but several times, as if demonstrating a wood saw.

Morgan did not get the chance to reply, because Karim's features were suddenly frozen with terror. In the distance, she heard what sounded like the throaty engine of a grass mower trimming a college softball field. It rapidly grew louder. Karim yelled at Abu Mustafa in Arabic and they both stood up and started to run, Abu Mustafa pausing only to grab Morgan's wrist and drag her with them.

'An Apache,' he yelled, 'An Israeli Seraph! We must get undercover! Down the stairs, into the basement!' As they rushed for the house, Morgan caught sight of the helicopter's dark fuselage looming over the edge of the palm tree, as if seeking out its target. But it carried on moving, and they dashed down the narrow steps into the cellar and along the corridor, ending up in the only too familiar room where Morgan had been tortured.

There, moments later, she heard the muffled impact of a guided Hellfire missile. Wherever it was, it had not landed on their compound. Morgan remembered what Karim had been through in the Montenegrin forest. His reaction did not seem so disproportionate.

He looked at her sternly, still breathing heavily, apparently trying to recover his composure and authority, and brushed a fleck of imaginary dust from his robe. 'Now I go,' he said. 'But we talk again later.'

Yitzhak Ben-Meir followed up the note he had left at Adam's hotel with a phone call early the following morning. His voice, Adam noted, sounded unexpectedly hesitant: as soon as he had seen the note, he had assumed Ben-Meir must be some kind of Israeli spook. Adam invited him to the hotel for a late breakfast, and they met in the lobby at a quarter-to-ten. Loading their plates with hummus and salads from the buffet, they made their way to the back of the terrace. 'This is excellent,' Ben-Meir said. 'We can chat without being overheard.'

Adam was in no mood for small talk. 'I think you owe me several explanations,' he said as they sat down, 'so let's deal with them. Why the interest in me, all of a sudden? Morgan's been missing for more than a month, and yet this is the first sign of interest I've had from any Israeli. Oh, don't tell me. I can guess. You want to know what I discovered in Gaza. Well, that part's easy. I almost got killed.'

'Mr Cooper – may I call you Adam? – the truth is, we didn't get in touch with you before because our American colleagues asked us not to. Or so I understand. As for nearly getting killed:

I am sorry to hear this, but I'm sure you knew that Gaza is a dangerous place. I heard there was a bombing yesterday. The militants were also firing rockets at us – one hit a house in Sderot. Anyhow, I'm glad you managed to get out in one piece. What happened?'

'I got caught up in the aftermath of the bombing,' Adam said. 'A funeral for the victims where there were soon more dead bodies. One was the driver of the car I was sitting in when he was shot. But never mind about that now. You said in your note you met Morgan before she was kidnapped. How was that? And how was she?'

Ben-Meir sighed and played with his coffee spoon. 'Look, I really would like to tell you. But you have to promise that you will treat everything I say in confidence, and that means not telling your CIA contacts at the US embassy. So far as they are concerned, this meeting isn't happening.'

Adam looked at him quizzically. 'Why? What's the big secret you're trying to hide?'

'There's no big secret. I just don't think it's in either of our interests for them to know. Officially I'm retired, and that gives me more latitude. I feel it incumbent on me to help you find your wife. But actually, my own colleagues do not know I have sought you out. So do I have your word?'

Adam nodded. 'But my assurance that I keep this confidential comes with a condition,' he said, 'that you don't give me bullshit. If you can't give me answers for reasons of operational secrecy: fine. I get that. But don't fucking lie to me, okay?'

'I won't lie to you. You have my word.'

'We'll see how much that's worth.'

'Look, as I told you: this isn't business. It's personal. I liked your wife. You can have no idea how sorry I am that she's missing, and I feel partly responsible. I have had comrades taken prisoner, and I know a little of what it's like.'

Adam could feel his eyes were wide. This he had not expected. 'So,' he said. 'How'd you meet her?'

'For the first time, on the beach, the day before she went to Gaza. She had been out for a jog, as I had been told she does most mornings. One of my colleagues had asked me to do him a favour.'

'A favour? What kind of favour? You mean, he asked you to check her out? To see what the Gringos were doing in Gaza?'

'Of course, that was part of it. The Americans share a lot less with us than you might think, and I was asked to approach her because we needed to know what she was doing. Experience has taught us that we cannot allow foreign intelligence agency operatives to run around in the Occupied Territories without a degree of, how shall I put it, supervision.'

Adam snorted. 'She's a professional. I bet she didn't tell you much. She certainly never tells me.'

'No. She didn't. But you see, finding out about her mission wasn't really my main purpose, though I'm sure she thought that it was. Actually it was rather different.'

'Different? I don't understand.'

'She had encountered a certain problem the previous day. For some reason, when she got to Erez, although it had been open earlier that morning, she found the border was closed.'

'And? I still don't get it.'

'My colleague had told me there was a substantial risk that having been refused, she'd just give up and fly home – she couldn't afford to wait here in Israel. Something to do with being back in time for you to fight a court case. My job was to figure out a way to make sure that didn't happen, that she did make another attempt to enter Gaza. I don't know why it was so important. But that's why I feel guilty, and the reason why I'm telling you far, far more than I should.'

'Why didn't you just call her at her hotel and tell her and say, "it's okay, you can go to Gaza?"'

'My colleague wanted me to find some way of making her think that she was using her skills as an officer, and so creating her own opportunity. I know that sounds strange, but I suppose the idea was to stop her realising how much we knew about her. So when I first talked to her at the beach, I gave her a business card. I knew she'd find it easy to confirm I'd been in intelligence.

And I gambled she'd call me later, to ask what I could do for her.'

'And she did.'

'Yes, she did. So later we met for dinner. She told me a lot about her life, about you and your kids. We had a pleasant evening. And then she asked me if I could use my contacts to have Erez opened the next morning – so she could fulfil her assignment, and not get home too late. Well, of course I could do just that. It was the whole point.'

Adam was horrified. It seemed that this man had played his wife: manipulating her sense of urgency in order to consign her to the place where she had been kidnapped. But he tried to look deadpan: it was vital he find out as much as he could.

'But why? Why all the subterfuge, Yitzhak?' Adam said. 'You've told me what happened, but none of it makes any sense.'

'It doesn't really make sense to me, either. But I thought you should know. Look, this is a guess, just speculation. But the colleague who asked me to do this, he knows a lot of Americans. He worked with them years ago, in the same region that your wife was last in the field, the Balkans. My hunch is that one of his American friends was especially keen that she should make this visit, and asked him to do what he could. The little charade with me was a way of bypassing official channels. But like I say, it's speculation.'

'Who is this colleague? What's his name?'

'I'm sorry. I can't tell you that.'

'You have any idea who his American friends might be?'

'If I did, I couldn't answer.'

'I see. So how did Morgan seem?'

'She was excited about her trip. It was clear she took her mission very seriously, and was delighted to be back in the field. At the same time, she was desperate to get home, not just to see you and the kids, but because she knew you had this court case. She didn't want to let you down.'

Adam stood up. His eyes looked moist. 'Just give me a moment while I think about this.' He paced around the terrace, then sat down again.

148

'Part of me says I should just walk out and leave you to finish your breakfast on your own,' he said. 'And you must surely realise I don't trust you an inch. But you have to tell me this. Why did your people put a tracker chip in my passport? Why did you have me followed when I met Bashir al-Owdeh in Lod? Surely you must have realised that when I got to Gaza, that could have got me killed?'

Ben-Meir looked baffled. 'Followed? Tracker chip? I don't know what you're talking about. I had no idea you'd ever been to Lod, and as for al-Owdeh, my understanding is that his arrest was a simple operation by the local police, acting on an anonymous tip-off. I assumed it must have come from someone on his own side – someone who'd fallen out with him.'

Adam's face was white. 'And the chip?' he asked.

'You say there was a chip placed in your passport. I'll take your word for it. But ask yourself this: how would we have got hold of it? I'm sure you haven't been stupid enough to leave it in your hotel room. And why would we have gone to such lengths, anyhow? Of course, we knew you were going to Gaza with Mr Reilly. After all, he applied for the paperwork to get you in. But why imperil your safety?'

Adam appeared to be swallowing hard. 'I have another question,' he said.

Ben-Meir gestured for him to continue.

'Have you ever heard of the *Janbiya al-Islam*?'

'Yes. I believe they might accurately be described as a Gazan branch of al-Qaeda. They don't just want a Jew-free Islamist state, but a restored caliphate, run like early medieval Arabia.'

Adam nodded. 'That's what I've been told, too.'

'Well, what about them? Are you saying that they could be the ones who kidnapped Morgan?'

'You mean you don't know? Haven't you seen the DVD?'

'What DVD? My role in all this is very limited – as I'm sure you understand.'

'I was shown it at the US embassy. They told me it was hand-delivered there. Morgan was speaking, wearing an orange overall,

149

like the prisoners at Guantanamo Bay, and in the background was a *Janbiya al-Islam* flag. She looked really terrible.' Adam's voice filled with emotion. 'I'm pretty sure she'd only just been tortured. She confessed to the camera that she was a CIA officer. She'd never have done that willingly. I don't know what's really going on here, but tell me this. So far as you know, is this group real? I mean, is it possible they're some kind of front – that really they're a part of Hamas, which set up the kidnap because what they actually wanted to do was to claim the credit for eventually releasing her?'

'I don't understand. Why would they do a thing like that?'

'Well, if Hamas facilitated her release, it would earn them credit with the international community. It would encourage the diplomats and policy makers to start doing business with them. But I admit: it does sounds pretty convoluted.'

'Mr Cooper.' Ben-Meir sounded solemn. 'I can't commit myself to an answer here. I am not, as you say, in the loop. But what you suggest is most improbable. In intelligence, it's often wise to employ a version of Occam's razor. If you have to choose between competing explanations, the simplest one is usually – though alas, not invariably – correct. Believe me, Hamas has much easier ways of gaining acceptance abroad than setting up a bogus kidnap. The risks would be enormous for them, because the truth, as it so often does, would probably get out. I would have to conclude that whoever told you this is lying.'

Ronnie looked a little drawn, and had lost some weight. Her sister Rachelle lived up the coast, in a villa in the wealthy town of Ramat Hasharon, and she had asked Adam to take a taxi and meet her there in a restaurant close to the beach. She had already warned him when he phoned her after his meeting with Ben-Meir that she had spent the morning accompanying Rachelle on a visit to her oncologist. Two years earlier, Rachelle had had cancer, and though this had been only a routine check-up, such things were always stressful.

Ronnie had made an effort, nonetheless. She was wearing a green, cotton minidress and a dark bolero jacket, with high-heeled sandals that emphasised her long, firm legs. She slipped the jacket off once they sat down, revealing tanned, bare shoulders.

'So, mortality,' said Adam, after they had ordered. 'It's a bummer, I guess. How is she?'

'For the time being, thanks to God, she'll live. She's had another scan, and there's no absolutely sign of it coming back. Her general health and fitness have always been excellent, and that's definitely helped her beat it. But it doesn't look like she'll ever be able to have kids, and you just don't expect that to be happening to your little sister, especially when she's only thirty-five.'

Rachelle, Adam knew, was married to a somewhat older man who had made a considerable fortune by organising investment in some of Israel's high-technology start-ups. They had met when she was working on Wall Street.

'So how about you? The kids driving you mad?'

'Oh, it's the kids who keep me going. I didn't see it that way at the time, but when Theo died, having Ben and Sarah was the only thing that stopped me falling apart. But I did need a break. Speaking of which, I'm going to order a cocktail, and my diagnosis is that you need one too.'

Adam had not eaten since breakfast, and the two large mojitos they both downed before ordering their food went straight to his head. 'I've never actually told you that Morgan has been kidnapped,' he said. 'But since that's what you seem to have told my mother-in-law, you've obviously guessed.'

Ronnie put her hand on his: her signature gesture, Adam thought fuzzily. Somehow, out here, after so many weeks when he seemed to have been focused on only one thing, it didn't feel inappropriate. He shifted his position and his knee touched hers beneath the table. She held it there long enough for him to feel the warmth of her skin.

'I admit it: I was hurt when you just disappeared off to England without even calling me,' she said. 'I know that seems a bit petty: I had no right to expect you to. So I'm sorry about what I did, blurting everything out to your mother-in-law, but I had thought you might confide in me.'

'Ronnie, it's okay. It doesn't matter,' Adam said softly. He touched her arm with his remaining available hand. 'It's not like any of us affected by this business have had any kind of blueprint to guide us on what we should do, and as you know, it's not something they teach you at law school. Actually some good has come of it. Trying to maintain secrecy was killing me, and thanks to your talk with Sherry, I've been able to level with the one person I really feel knows what I'm going through - Morgan's dad. Just being able to share it with him has been an enormous help. He and I come from very different worlds, but he's a pretty decent guy. We've always hit it off.'

As night fell, they began to eat. Ronnie told Adam stories from her childhood with Rachelle, and of her sister's romance with Avram. Having been an investment banker with a promising career, now she did nothing more strenuous than sit on the boards of Jewish charities, and supported contemporary artists. He told her he'd been to Gaza, but little about what had happened there, and nothing at all about his mushrooming doubts about Morgan's colleagues from the CIA. It was an enormous relief to spend an evening mostly focusing on something else. Slowly the restaurant emptied. Adam looked at his watch.

'Jesus. It's nearly midnight. I'd better find a cab.'

'Wrong exclamation to use round here, my friend. Will you walk me home first? It's only a couple of blocks, and I'll show you how to get back to the main road heading back to Tel Aviv – you'll find a taxi there in no time, even at this hour.'

Adam paid the bill, and they stood. The street, a wide, two-lane boulevard with grass verges along the sidewalks, was deserted. Moonlight filtered down through the spreading, mature trees. As they walked, Ronnie took Adam's arm and placed it round her well-toned waist. Beneath the cloth of his shorts, he felt himself hardening.

Finally they stopped outside Rachelle and Avram's villa. The lights were off. She turned to face him.

'Hold me.'

His hands grasped the small of her back.

'Whatever you want, it's okay,' she said. 'If it feels wrong, I'll understand. And if not now: well, maybe there'll be a time when things are different.'

'I can't. I just can't, even though a huge part of me wants to, and it might do us both a lot of good. But I've had a wonderful evening. In fact the best for a very long time – since long before Morgan was kidnapped.'

She rested her head against his chest. She said nothing for what felt like several minutes. 'So will I see you again before you leave?'

'Why don't you come to Tel Aviv tomorrow. It's my last night.'

'If I can. So long as it's okay with Rachelle. Call me in the morning.'

He felt the dampness: her eyes were wet with tears.

'I'm sorry. I don't mean to be pathetic,' she said. 'It's not really me who's having to go through all this shit – what you and Morgan and Rachelle have to deal with. I'm just on the sidelines. But she did so want to be a mom. Thank God she has Avram.'

'You're not pathetic. Just human.'

She gave him a final hug, then kissed his lips firmly, breaking away from him without opening her mouth.

'Thanks Adam. Seeing you on your own for once was wonderful.'

'Maybe see you tomorrow then.'

'Like the Arabs say, *insh'Allah*.'

All the way back to Tel Aviv, Adam breathed the scent she had left on his polo shirt.

Chapter Fourteen
Friday, May 4, 2007

Adam awakes, only to realise with plummeting disappointment that the eroticism from which he surfaces is merely another dream - not of Ronnie, but of Morgan. They had been in their familiar bedroom in Bethesda, and she was on her knees, her legs straddling his face, maintaining her balance with a palm against the headboard. He was lost in her warmth, her nectar on his face as she moved her open vulva across his lips and tongue, and he was reaching up to pinch her nipples in the way he knew she loved. He could feel the tremor beginning in her thighs and buttocks that meant she was about to come. It wasn't just the immanence of her smell and taste that made the dream so vivid, but the sound, the involuntary, throaty whimper Morgan made only when utterly abandoned. How long has it been since he's heard it for real? Will he ever hear it again?

Returning fully to consciousness, he orientates himself. Of course, he's in Tel Aviv. Last night he was with Ronnie. She made it obvious she wanted to sleep with him, and he has never needed sheer physical release so badly. But if they'd finally done it, the emotion now washing over him would not be longing but guilt. It was lucky they met in Ramat Hasharon. They could hardly have gone back to her sister's place, and there was nowhere else to go. He remembers he asked her to come to Tel Aviv this evening, the last of his trip. Maybe he should call her and make an excuse. But first he has to prepare himself. A final meeting at the embassy. This time he will confront them, for now he knows that the chip in his passport can only have been put there by the CIA.

Karim did not come back the previous day, and now once again it was the two of them, Morgan and Abu Mustafa, back in the dingy basement instead of the airy yard. 'Karim says outside is becoming too dangerous,' Abu Mustafa said apologetically. 'I'm afraid he is right. The situation here in Gaza is deteriorating.'

'What's happening?' Morgan said.

'The usual, but worse. Factional fighting and Israeli air-strikes. It always goes up and down. You've been coming here long enough to know that. Now seems to be an up.'

'So let me go. The longer you keep me here, the greater the risk – not to me, but you.'

'First we have work to do. It's time to get back to where we were before the Israelis interrupted us. Let's start with Abdel Nasser.'

Morgan had known this must be coming. Days earlier, she had decided that this was a subject on which she could safely digress. After all, Abdel Nasser was already a prisoner. There didn't seem much she could say that would make his situation worse.

'If you want me to talk about Abdel Nasser, I need to know he is okay,' she said.

'He is alive. That is enough.'

'He was injured. Let me see him, so that I know his wounds are being treated.'

'That is impossible. In any case, he is no longer here. And if you do not want him to suffer, I suggest you continue to cooperate.'

'So what do you want to know?'

'It's a strange thing, recruitment. Picking someone you can trust, who can fulfil your objectives, and who has the right skills and abilities. You and I, and the organisations we represent, we are really not so different. If I am looking for talent in a university or a refugee camp, I need to spot certain qualities. I need fighters who do not fear death, who will guard our secrets, who are intelligent and resourceful. And I have to determine their motivation, the purity of their commitment: someone who cares about money or glory could pose a lethal risk. Only when I am sure do I make my pitch. As a case officer, I imagine

155

you go through a similar process. Tell me about how it went with Abdel Nasser. How did you meet him?'

Morgan knew she had no choice. 'There's a colleague based in the region. I've known him a long time. We trained together. He recommended him.'

'What did he say about him?'

'That he and his family really know Gaza. That they know the politicians, and the people who run the factions and militias. And because of their strong American connections, they understand ideas that matter to us, like the rule of law and human rights.'

'Good, Mrs Cooper. Now we are getting somewhere. So how did you make contact?'

'I emailed him. Because of my cover, I had a State Department email address. He replied in less than an hour, saying he'd be delighted to meet me in Gaza, but just then, he happened to be in California. He planned to be in New York the following week. This would have been early spring last year. A few days later, I took the train up from DC, and we met at an Italian restaurant.'

'Your first impressions of him?'

Morgan tried not to blush. 'I liked him. He was beautifully dressed, and he had perfect manners. He was obviously intelligent, and he had a sense of humour. His first words after we introduced ourselves were: "New York, it's great to be back. As you may have noticed, they named Gaza only once."'

'What did you eat? Did you both drink alcohol?'

'I had fish. Halibut, I think. I really can't remember what he had. And yes, we did drink alcohol. An excellent pinot grigio, if that means anything to you.'

'What did you tell him was the purpose of your meeting?'

'What you'd expect. I gave him my cover: that the State Department wanted me to begin independent monitoring of human rights violations being perpetrated by the main Gaza factions. I think he thought I was nuts. But he agreed to help if he could, and we arranged to meet in Gaza. A few weeks later, we did.'

'But arranging to meet is a long way from recruiting him as an agent. Gaza may be poor, but a member of the al-Kafarneh family would not be attracted by money. How did your acquaintance develop?'

'I made a few more visits, and truth to tell, we liked each other. I guess I was a point of contact to a world that he knew. Of course I never actually revealed myself to him as an Agency officer. But there was a definite moment when, if you will, our relationship shifted gear.'

'Go on. I am all ears.'

'It was an evening about ten months ago. We were sitting at a table on the al-Deirah terrace. We were gazing at the Mediterranean, drinking homemade lemonade with mint and arugula. The sun was just going down.'

'You make it sound idyllic. How lovely.'

'You can be snarky if you want, but the fact is that when you're sitting out there, this idea that people used to have that Gaza could become a Palestinian Singapore doesn't seem so improbable – so long as you ignore the sewage outlet pipe a little ways up the beach. Anyhow, I'd become aware that Abdel Nasser had a reputation as a bit of a playboy. But I'd also decided this was misjudged. Maybe he was different when he was younger. But when I got to know him, I could see was a man of principle, and a Palestinian patriot. And that turned out to be the way to, uh, take our association to the next level.'

'So you appealed to his sense of decency and persuaded him to become a spy. How very touching.'

'Do you want me to tell you about this or not?'

'I'm sorry. Please, go on.'

'So there we were on the terrace, and Abdel Nasser started telling me that my own country, America, was the key to solving the Palestinians' conflict with Israel – because many Palestinians, starting with him, shared our constitutional values. I can remember his words pretty much verbatim: "The thing I love most about the United States is your idea of a citizen state, in which race and religion don't determine your loyalties, your responsibilities. Everything else that's great about America stems from that – equality, freedom, opportunity. And that's what I want to create in Palestine."'

Abu Mustafa looked incredulous. 'Abdel Nasser, with all his wealth and influence, became a spy for *this*? For some half-baked vision that here on the soil of Palestine, you and he could reconstruct the American dream?'

'Yes, he pretty much did. He told me that what hurt him most was that by always putting Israel first, America was disregarding Palestine's potential. But he said he was convinced that if America's leaders only knew more of the facts, their policy would change. It was actually quite noble, even if it was based on a completely idealistic view of America.'

Abu Mustafa gestured for her to carry on.

'He said that when had been a student at Columbia, he'd campaigned to end the war in Bosnia, and eventually, America did. He told me it was always easy to predict failure: the daring thing was to hope and strive for success. Then he said: "I only wish I had some way to get this message across in Washington." And that's when I made my pitch.'

'And this was?'

'I told him he did have a way to get his message heard in Washington. I said he could do it through me. All he had to do in return was use his network of contacts to find things out for me. I appealed to his nature and his hopes for his country, and he readily agreed.' Morgan sighed. 'And now look at both of us. Maybe it wasn't such a smart move, after all.'

'Yes, look at you both. And that's how things are going to stay until you begin to tell me what was the real purpose of your mission: why you needed an agent as well-connected as Abdel Nasser.'

This too, Morgan knew, she had to disclose. 'I told you I was observing. That's actually the truth. It's just that it wasn't about human rights.'

'But instead?'

'It's hardly a secret that the United States did not welcome Hamas's victory in last year's Palestinian elections. So we set up a programme to see if we couldn't, how shall I put this, change the facts on the ground, to strengthen the forces loyal to Fatah. We wanted Fatah to be able to smash Hamas on the streets if it had to. We didn't ask them to start these violent clashes. But once they started getting aid, I suppose they were inevitable.'

'So what are you telling me? That you have been coordinating some kind of coup? But why would the CIA choose you? You have no military background. You're a woman. You're not even here most of the time.'

'I wasn't running the programme. I was sent here to evaluate the results. You know how it is: sometimes the guys on the ground get carried away. They know headquarters doesn't want to hear about failure, and so sometimes they exaggerate: they'll say things are swell when, in reality, they're turning to rat shit. My job was to figure out whether what Headquarters was hearing was true – that Fatah was becoming so strong that if it came to a final showdown, Hamas was finished.'

'And Abdel Nasser?'

'He listened and he kept his eyes open, and hung out at night drinking tea with the commanders from both sides. Every so often, I'd breeze into town, he'd tell me what was happening, and take me to meet some of his sources. We'd sit with them in their dingy apartment blocks, drink more tea and smoke some shisha, and then I'd form my assessment.'

'So did they confirm that the CIA's plan was working, and that Fatah was bound to triumph?'

'No,' Morgan said. 'Neither Abdel Nasser nor the people he introduced me to used to say that at all. All the honest ones said the same thing: that Fatah was set for disaster. That's pretty much what I said in my own reports.'

'And then?'

'And then my colleagues took no notice of them. But I'll tell you what I think. I think Hamas will be in total control of Gaza within weeks. And then, my friend, you and Karim had better watch out. If you haven't yet freed me and Abdel Nasser,

Hamas's guys will hunt you down like dogs, because the one thing they will not tolerate is a challenge to their power.'

All three CIA men are waiting for him, sitting around the conference table in the familiar station office: Gary, Mike and Eugene. But there's a fourth, whom Adam hasn't seen before: a fleshy Israeli in late middle age. Even before they've been introduced, Adam guesses that this must be the 'colleague' who asked Ben-Meir to meet Morgan, to make certain she would enter Gaza. They all stand as he enters, politely formal, and he shakes their proffered hands. How normal everything seems. Through the blast-proof windows, he can see the bikini girls and bodybuilders on the beach.

'Adam, I'd like you to meet an old friend and fellow combatant in the war on terror,' Gary says. 'Amos, Adam, Adam, Amos.'

Adam nods, trying to take him in. Grey hair, big black spectacles, a double chin; an air of inscrutability.

'It is my pleasure,' Amos says. 'I have heard great things about your wife. I am here to help us end her ordeal. But you must be very proud of her.'

'Yes, I am.' Adam gestures at Amos and Gary. 'So you two go back a long way?'

'You could say that,' says Amos. 'We long ago realised the mutual benefits of cooperation.'

'I understand you're leaving us,' Gary says. 'I'm sorry your trip hasn't been more fruitful. But you did your best, and that's what we're going to keep on doing. Now that you've been to Gaza, you can see it's not going to be easy. But you're leaving this job in the right hands, Adam. We're not going to rest until she's home.'

'I'm pleased to hear that.' Adam smiles, trying to keep his voice even and pleasant. 'And are you making progress yet? Any more messages from the kidnappers?'

Gary held up his hand. 'Hey: easy now. I know you're disappointed, but this is why I've asked Amos here to brief you. He's the expert round here. And what he says is classified. But we figured we need to trust you. So, Amos. The floor is yours.'

160

Amos looks at Adam, then at the CIA men round the table. He clears his throat. 'You've seen for yourself how tense Gaza is getting. And by the way, I'm am very pleased to see you are safe. From what I hear, you didn't choose the best of times for your visit.'

'Not exactly. I got caught on the fringes of a firefight. But as you've observed, I escaped.'

'You manage to hook up with Hamas?'

'You know I did.'

'I suppose your new friends tried to tell you that the *Janbiya al-Islam* is nothing to do with them.'

'Yes. They did.'

'And I dare say they seemed credible and sincere. But allow me to explain a little of how they operate. I have been observing these extremist factions for many years. This is a textbook example of what is known as *taqqiya*.'

'*Taqqiya?*'

'It's an old Islamic concept.' Amos looks smug. 'It comes down to the idea that it's not a sin to lie when talking to *kufr*, to infidels, if it helps the greater good. You could call it a licence to bullshit in the service of the cause. Gary has already explained to you that the *Janbiya* is a front, an illusion. I cannot tell you how I know this, but we – myself and my colleagues – we are certain he is right.'

'If you say so, Amos.' After what he has heard from Ben-Meir, how can he take him seriously? 'If you want to try to get me to swallow that, sure, by all means go ahead.'

'What do you mean, "if I say so?"' says Amos. 'You're suggesting that I'm wrong? That you know these people better than we do?'

'Adam,' Gary says reproachfully. 'Amos is our friend.'

'Yes. I think you're wrong,' says Adam. 'What's more, I don't really think you believe it either. Why look for a complex explanation when a simple one seems obvious - that Morgan has been kidnapped by a jihadist group called the *Janbiya al-Islam?*'

161

He watches Amos stiffen. His baggy jowls are reddening, but he keeps his voice low. 'I hadn't quite grasped that analysing the structures of jihadist terrorism was one of your specialities. Or perhaps you are one of those useful idiots who thinks these people are freedom fighters, with legitimate rights to express their murderous views. Of course I know about your legal work. But just listen to us for once. We can't stop you from associating with those who not so long ago were sending kids to blow themselves up inside Israeli buses and pizza restaurants. But I do see it as part of my job to warn you that you're wasting your time. Yes, Hamas knows where your wife is. But the very last person they're going to tell is you. And in the meantime, it's my duty as an Israeli officer to try to dissuade you from doing anything else that might get you killed.'

Gary interjects: 'Or to put it another way, leave finding Morgan to us. We actually know what we're doing. After what happened, it ought to be clear that you don't. But Amos does have one more thing to tell you. But he's not going to, unless you gave us an undertaking it goes no further than this room.'

'Fine,' says Adam. 'What is it?'

Amos clears his throat again. 'I can give you no details of what I'm about to tell you. But locating your wife may well be about to become a great deal easier than it is now, for one very simply reason: that Hamas's days as a force to be reckoned with are almost over. I can't tell you why, or exactly when. But it's going to be soon.'

'What do you mean?' Adam is incredulous. 'Are you trying to tell me that Hamas is about to be crushed by physical force?

'As I told you: no details. But go home, and be patient. Soon there will be good news.' Amos throws him a twisted smile, then stands. 'Gary, I must leave, or I'll be late for my meeting.'

'Me too.' Gary stands too, followed by Mike. 'Sorry Adam, we have work to do. I'll leave you with Eugene. He can make any necessary arrangements. So long.'

Adam remains seated, and watches as they leave. He doesn't offer his hand. He has been planning to confront them about the tracker chip, but frankly, what's the point?

'I'm sure we'll see you again soon,' Mike says. 'Hope everything's okay with the kids. Safe travels.' Alone of the departing trio, his voice betrays a little warmth.

The door closes. Eugene and Adam are alone. 'Can I offer you something?' Eugene says. 'Some tea? Coffee? A soda?'

Adam waves his hand and demurs. 'I'm fine.'

'Gary can be a hardass. I'm sorry. But…' Eugene shrugs.

'But?'

'We do have to follow his lead. His experience and his contacts, especially with the Israelis, are amazing. As you can see. That guy Amos – you know I can't tell you his last name. But in the circles in which we move, he's a legend.'

'Right.' Before Adam can say anything else, there's a knock on the door.

'Enter,' Eugene says. Crystal, his assistant, comes in. She's wearing latex gloves, and holding a padded envelope.

'This just came, addressed to you. It's been through the scanner. It looks like another DVD.'

Eugene gets up and walks behind his desk, opens a drawer and takes out a sealed packet of gloves. He puts them on, takes the package and examines it. Crystal leaves. 'Hmm. It looks different from the other one. Apart from the obvious fact it's got stamps on it and has been through the mail,' he says, squinting at the postmark. 'Looks like it was sent from Ashkelon.'

Adam stares as Eugene opens the packet and reaches inside. There's no covering letter, just the DVD in its clear plastic box. On the cover is a sign scrawled in thick, black felt-tip pen: 'Morgan Cooper 2.'

Eugene must have realised Adam has seen it. 'Shit,' he says.

'Can I watch it?' Adam asks.

'I'm sorry. I'm going to have to say no. I mean, this could be anything.'

'You mean, you're worried I don't have the stomach to watch a DVD showing my wife getting murdered.' Adam's voice is thick. 'You're right. I probably don't. But I think we both know

163

it's not that. It's too soon. Come on Eugene. I have a right to see this. Put it on.'

Eugene hesitates. 'The answer should still be no. I really shouldn't do this. But I guess you and I have known each other a long time, and since you're here… Well, I get the sense you're having trouble believing we're on the same side right now. So if I did say we could watch it together, would you take that as a sign of good faith?'

'A sign, yes.'

Eugene keeps a television and a DVD player on a stand at the back of his office. He uses the remotes to turn them on, and slots the DVD into the loading tray. He sits down again and he and Adam turn their chairs to face the screen.

First there's some static, but then it fills with the image of an airy, white apartment. To the left are big windows, with the glimpse of a balcony behind them, and facing them a table with an exquisite embroidered cloth. To the right again is a wide upholstered sofa. The camera position is static, and at first the owners of the two audible voices are invisible. But Adam knows one of them straightaway: Morgan. The other belongs to a man with a light Palestinian accent, whose English is perfect. They're talking about visiting with someone later that day, and discussing whether the place they've chosen will be safe.

'I think I know what this is,' Eugene says. 'Fatah's security services have bugged dozens of apartments and houses down there, places they think might be of interest. In fact, they've, uh, had some technical help from us. I think this comes from the apartment where your wife used to meet her main agent, a guy I hooked her up with. He's from a well-known, wealthy family – Abdel Nasser al-Kafarneh. He went to school in America. Ah, yes, look, there he is. Good looking fellow, I got to say.'

A tall, slim man in a finely-tailored suit has walked into view, apparently from a doorway off to one side: he's carrying two glasses of tea. Adam can't help noticing he is indeed unusually handsome, with animated dark green eyes, olive skin and a goatee. The words of his conversation with Morgan are strictly professional. But in her tone, and in her frequent laughter, Adam detects a warm engagement. At last she too is in shot. Her hair is longer than she wears it now – or wore it before she vanished – and he makes a rough calculation: these sounds and images must have been recorded last year, near the beginning of her mission.

The screen goes blank again. It seems the DVD is some kind of compilation, for when the images return, Morgan and Abdel Nasser are wearing different clothing, and the light is different. There is no disguising the lack of formality with which they address each other.

'Why can't your people see the consequences of the mistakes they are making?' Abdel Nasser says. 'We only held elections because you insisted we do so, even though it was obvious that Hamas was going to win. And now you think you can simply reverse the result. What do you think this does for those of us who try to argue that the route to prosperity and statehood lies through constitutional politics, not violence?'

Morgan sounds embarrassed. 'I know. I know. Look, I don't make the policy. I promised you I would get your message across in Washington, and believe me, I have.'

'I believe you, Morgan. But I'm sorry, I don't want to go on with this. It's just not working out.'

Morgan gets up and speaks from somewhere out of shot. Adam recognises what she's doing: she's making a last-ditch bid to persuade Abdel Nasser not to resign as her agent, and as she often does when she's fired up about something, she's on her feet, pacing around the room.

'If you want to know what I really think, I happen to agree with just about everything you've said,' says her disembodied voice. 'Yes. America is treating Palestinians with contempt. What we're doing is totally counterproductive. And while we're about it, I think my bosses are assholes.'

Eugene breaks in, as crass as ever: 'Shit. Gary's not going to like this much.' He presses the remote. 'I don't think we can watch any more. This is straying into classified territory.'

165

'Bullshit, Eugene,' Adam says. 'This isn't about national security. If it's anything, it's office politics. Jesus. This is a video of my wife. You owe it to me to let it continue.'

Eugene hesitates, then lets the recording play again.

This time, Adam knows when it must have been shot, because she's wearing a light knitted dress he bought for her last December. It must depict a meeting one or two visits before the one when she was kidnapped – a trip she made during Gaza's mild winter. They're on the sofa. Morgan's sitting cross-legged, her back to the camera, and Abdel Nasser seems so close they're almost touching. On the table, there's the debris of lunch.

'I'd better be going,' Morgan says. 'I can't afford to miss my spot at Erez.'

'I know you have to,' says Abdel Nasser. 'And the car will be waiting. But I wish you could stay.'

Abdel Nasser turns to face her and Adam sees her hand clasp the back of his neck.

'Be safe, Abdel Nasser,' says Morgan. 'Don't take any risks. Especially not for me. It's just not worth it.' She laughs, a little self-consciously. 'If I were forced to choose between my country and my friend, I hope I would be brave enough to choose my friend.'

'Casablanca,' Abdel Nasser says.

'Bogart channeling E.M. Forster.' She brings her other hand up to his face and kisses him on the mouth. For what feels to Adam like minutes, they hold each other, still kissing. Finally she pushes herself away, then stands. 'Until the next time. And by the way, every time we say goodbye, I do cry a little. But usually not until I'm safely back in my perfect little life in Maryland. I'll miss you.'

Eugene moves to turn the DVD off again, but Adam leans across and holds his wrist: 'Don't you bloody dare.'

Eugene sits back and for a final time the screen goes blank. When the recording comes back again, the picture is a little gloomy. It must be evening. They seem to be back on the sofa, and Adam takes in the back of Morgan's head and the outline of her body. She is moving: up and down, backwards and forwards, and the shocking thing is: she's naked. She twists a little and he catches sight of her breast, partly cupped by a man's hand, a hand at the end of a sallow, hairy arm, with manicured fingers that start to work her nipple. At the bottom of the screen he sees her bare buttocks, falling and rising, the rhythm and pace intensifying. She's supporting herself with a palm on Abdel Nasser's chest as she takes him inside her, and then she reaches behind his shoulder to pull him in more deeply, the way Adam knows she likes. At first, the recording is almost silent, punctuated only by heavy breathing, but then there's a sound that cuts through his skull like a laser. It's the sound which filled his dream this morning, the sound of Morgan intensely aroused, the sound she makes only when close to an orgasm. At the same time, he can see the start of an involuntary quiver in the lower part of her body. She's not merely fucking this secret lover, she's about to come.

'Turn it off!' Adam yells. 'For fuck's sake, turn it off!'

'A penny for them. You seem to be preoccupied.' Ronnie looks at him quizzically across the tablecloth of an Italian restaurant a short walk from his hotel, the candlelight reflected in her eyes.

'It's nothing. Well, not nothing, but you know how it is. I can't really talk about most of this shit. It's been a difficult day. Some setbacks.' Adam waves his hands. 'Enough about me. How are you?'

'I'm good. I've been taking it easy. Brunch with Rachelle, some shopping, a little trip to the beach. It's so nice to be able to spend time with her again. In fact, if it had been anyone else, waiting until five in the afternoon before calling to ask me out to dinner, I'd have said no, and spent the evening with her and Avram. But since it's you, and since it's also your last night… well, just this once, I was prepared to make an exception.'

'I'm jolly glad you did.' He takes a large gulp of wine. 'And by the way, you look ravishing.'

'You really feeling okay, Adam? It's not that I'm lacking in confidence about the way I happen to look, but you don't usually bother to comment on it. Actually, I got this just this morning.'

167

She pouts and twists her torso from side to side, emphasising her breasts while displaying her new, hand-embroidered top.

'It's great,' he says. 'And you're really in great shape. It suits you. Where'd you get it?' Even as he asks, he wonders why. Why is he asking her to talk about shopping? He stares at her even skin. She's wearing a different perfume.

'So I thought that was quite a bargain -' Ronnie breaks off. 'Adam, what's up? You're not even listening to me. What have you done with your head? You know, the one that contains that extraordinary brain which even impresses the US Supreme Court?'

He's got to try to relax.

'Is it Morgan?' asks Ronnie. 'Is there news?'

'No. Nothing. And the situation in Gaza only gets worse. But no. Nothing concrete.' He sighs. 'I guess I'm just feeling down because it feels I've put my normal life on hold and dropped everything for this Quixotic mission – and managed to achieve precisely nothing.' He decides to risk going just a little further. 'And all the while, I can't help thinking back to the problems we had. You know, the things you and I discussed back in America.'

He's given her a cue, and she takes it. She reaches across the table and holds a palm against his cheek. This time he does what he hasn't done before. He responds. He turns his head to her hand and kisses it.

'We deserve to live a little, too,' she says.

'Maybe we do.'

They finish their meal and pay the bill. Adam doesn't have to ask if she's coming back to his room: they both know she is. They slink past the receptionist into the elevator and as it makes its way to the seventh floor they face each other and kiss each other properly for the first time.

Once inside his room with the door shut behind them, everything's a flurry, lit by moonlight, filtered by the window blind. Her brand new top, lacy bra, skirt, panties and high-heeled sandals are already on the floor around the bed as Adam, now bare-chested, unbuttons his jeans and she pulls them down, followed by his underpants. She takes him in her mouth, touches herself to moisten an index finger, then uses it to tease his anus, jolting him with the fierceness of his pleasure. When he can't take any more, he moves away and starts to descend, while she spreads herself deliciously at the edge of the bed. He longs to taste her, but she stops him, placing a hand on his head: 'No, don't do that. Not this time. I want you to fuck me.' She's already taken a condom from her handbag and unsealed it, and now she reaches for it from the bedside table and unrolls it on to him. He'd like to fuck her like a stallion for the rest of the night, but it's been so long and he can't hold back. Rather more quickly than he'd wanted, he fills the condom and slowly softens.

Afterwards, she crouches over him, stroking his face. She lets him take her weight as she stretches out on top of him. 'I know that you know I've been wanting to do that for ages,' she says. 'You're a good looking, sexy bastard, Adam Cooper, as well as principled and brainy.'

'You didn't come. I'm sorry. I was too quick. But it's been a while.'

'It doesn't matter. I will next time. It was wonderful.'

He stands. 'I'd better get rid of this thing.' He goes to the bathroom, and disposes of the condom. When he gets back, Ronnie is sitting up, the sheet covering her breasts.

'I've got to get back to Ramat Hasharon. Rachelle will be worried. But we'll see each other soon.' She looks as if she's trying to read his expression. 'Is everything okay, baby?'

He sits on the bed beside her, and she touches his nose with a fingertip.

'Listen. I'm not going to turn into a bunny-boiler if Morgan comes back and you decide to make a go of it. But like I said before, what happened tonight – we deserved it.'

Part of him wants to turn her over and begin again, but he doesn't try to stop her getting dressed. He pulls on his clothes and walks her outside, where they soon find a taxi. Before she gets in, they kiss properly once more. But back in his room, a tautologous three-word sentence keeps on running through his mind. Ronnie isn't Morgan.

Chapter Fifteen
Thursday, June 14,
and Friday, June 15, 2007

Adam had been out all day, and had only just returned from a meeting in London with a British human rights group which seemed to think it might find a use for his expertise. He hadn't said anything to Spinks McArthur: so far as they were concerned, when the question of Morgan's absence was finally resolved, he would be coming back to work. But like so much else in his life just now, the idea of returning to America felt almost unbearable. On the rare occasions when he did consider the future, he made two assumptions: first, that there was a better than even chance he wasn't going to see his wife alive again; and second, that even if he did, they would not be together. No doubt Morgan would want to continue to travel in order to pursue her career. No doubt, he told himself, with each new mission she would take another lover. In all the circumstances, making plans to move to England with the children did not seem unreasonable.

His wretchedness was only compounded by what had happened with Ronnie on his last night in Israel. As she had promised, she was no bunny boiler: far from it. In the emails and calls they had exchanged over the succeeding weeks, she had been caring and solicitous, making it clear that she neither demanded nor expected anything. Their night together had been a 'lovely interlude,' she said, and if it led to nothing more, she would have no regrets.

However, Adam did have regrets. He might feel betrayed, but he was also steeped in guilt. A little of it was for Ronnie: he had used her to wreak a feeble, unseen revenge. But despite the agony of having witnessed the trysts between Morgan and Abdel Nasser, his guilt was mainly for her.

As he turned the key in the lock of his parents' front door, he could hear the television. He was taking off his jacket when

170

his father called him from the sitting room: 'Adam! Here, come quickly! You need to see this.'

He hurried into the sitting room, where his parents were watching the Channel 4 news. A view of Gaza City's Unknown Soldier Square filled the screen, taken from a balcony close to Colin Reilly's office. The open space was a rippling sea of people, many of them wielding green Hamas banners, their faces masks of euphoria. Adam had spent the past few weeks deliberately trying to block out news from the Middle East, but this was different. After three days of brutal conflict, the reporter was saying, Hamas had seized power. Fatah's troops had barely put up a fight, although some had been killed by savage methods, such as throwing them from the tops of buildings.

In the next scene, an earnest man in his thirties with a neat goatee and a suit was briefing reporters in fluent English. He said that documents and other evidence which Hamas had acquired earlier that day when its forces took control of the Gazan secret police headquarters proved that Fatah's militias, notably their Force 17 guards, had been armed and trained at America's behest. 'Some of you have asked why we have carried out a coup d'etat,' the spokesman said. 'We reject this label. It is now clear that Fatah, helped by its Israeli and American allies, had been planning a coup against us. We have simply thwarted that plan, and we have done so with the minimum of bloodshed. We have the support of the people, which is why there has been so little resistance. In the coming days we will work to establish a government which will restore order and the rule of law.' Almost next to the spokesman stood Khader, who looked rather sleeker than on the day Adam had saved him from the Fatah gunmen. He was wearing a pressed blue uniform. It looked new.

The report shifted to a line of villas close to the seafront, which had apparently been owned by members of the ousted Fatah elite. They were being wrecked by a mob. The camera focused on a man smashing a window by hurling a lump of concrete, then cut to a short interview with him, the mob in the background. 'This regime, this people, was corrupt,' he was

171

saying. 'Now we will have justice. They will pay for their crimes, and also their friends in America and Israel.'

Finally, the anchor in London conducted a live discussion about the meaning of the Hamas putsch with the channel's flack-jacketed reporter on a balcony above the square: visibly nervous, she expressed her hope that whatever the wider consequences, it might at least reduce the level of violence on Gaza's streets. Then he turned to the Washington correspondent: 'So, Matt, what has the Administration been saying? Is it making any comment on these claims that Hamas has thwarted an attempted US-backed coup by Fatah?'

'Well, Jon, that's certainly one of the questions everybody's asking. The truth is, no one really knows. But it has to be said that if Hamas's allegations are true, and the US was running some kind of covert programme, the new regime in Gaza isn't going to be in any hurry to do America any favours. No doubt the picture will become clearer over the coming weeks.'

With that, the broadcast turned to English politics. Gwen Cooper raised the remote and turned the television off, just as Charlie and Aimee burst into the room from the garden. She held out her arms and hugged them.

'Hello darlings. I hope you're hungry. Look, Daddy's home.' She gave Adam a sharp look. 'We can talk about what was on telly later, can't we, dear. Let's all go and sit in the kitchen. I've made a nice fish pie.'

Next morning, when Adam returned from taking the children to school, Gwen cornered him at the foot of the stairs. 'No arguments,' she said. 'I'm working from home this morning, and then I'm taking you out to lunch.'

He knew better than to demur. 'Okay. Where are we going?'

'It's not a bad day. I think the Cherwell Boathouse. At least that means we can walk. Be back down here, ready to leave, at twelve-thirty.'

Rain had been forecast, but when lunchtime came, there was no sign of it. It was a typical English summer's day, with ragged cloud and intermittent sunshine: not exactly flaming June, but comfortably warm nonetheless. Along Norham Gardens and past the Dragon School playing fields, the scents of early summer competed for attention, borne on a balmy breeze: the new-mown grass of the cricket fields, and in the gardens of the older houses, honeysuckle and wisteria. They walked down the alley towards the river without speaking, then stood for a while on the platform by the water's edge, watching the usual mix of capable and incompetent boat people as they tried to pole their flat-bottomed punts. A large party of raucous Americans in US college sweatshirts had rented two boats and were making them zigzag uncontrollably, their polers apparently certain to end their voyage by falling in. Beyond the melee, on the far side of the river, a languid youth in a white jacket and pedal-pusher shorts glided past from somewhere downstream. His companion, propped against the boat's blue cushions in a pale, floaty dress, sipped from a champagne flute, trailing her fingers in the water.

'I think we can risk a table outside,' Gwen said. They entered the restaurant and she greeted the maître d' with a kiss on each cheek. In moments, they were ensconced on the waterside decking, beneath a white umbrella.

'Plus ca change,' Adam said, picking up the menu. 'I see they're still doing that organic salmon in sorrel sauce.'

'I do wish that were true,' said Gwen. 'If only.'

'What do you mean? Look, it's right here.'

'Darling, as I've told you before, don't be deliberately dense. I meant, as you know perfectly well, that I wish it were true that things hadn't changed, starting, alas, with you. But first let's order. I'm going to have the hake.'

'I'd better have the salmon. To satisfy your yearning for continuity.'

She beckoned a waiter. 'I think we're going to need some wine. We'll take a bottle of the Meursault. That one.' She pointed. 'The 2002. A very good year indeed.'

Gwen buttered a warm bread roll. 'Darling, forgive the cliche, but when you've had a sip or two of your Burgundy, we need to talk. I don't think you're telling me everything that happened on your trip. Apart from when you're with kids, I've never seen you so miserable. So, not to put you on the spot or anything, I want to know what you've been leaving out.'

Adam coloured. The waiter brought the wine, poured a little for Gwen to try, then gave them both a glass, leaving the bottle in an ice bucket on a stand. Throughout the ritual, Adam stayed silent. Finally he opened his mouth.

'I don't know what makes you think I'm hiding something. Obviously I'm unhappy. My wife's been kidnapped, for Christ's sake. I went to try to rescue her, got shot at, and achieved precisely nothing. What do you expect?'

'But you seem to be making plans to stay in Britain indefinitely. Well, selfishly, I'd love that. I never imagined until they came to stay how absolutely lovely it is to have the children living with us. But Adam, your life, and Morgan's life, are in America. Do you really think she'd give it all up to become an Oxford housewife or something?'

'Probably not.'

'And are you really ready to waste all that training in the American legal system, and all those nights you spent in lonely motels while you hunted for missing witnesses in the South? We can't be certain she will get out of the hell she's in alive. But we've got to believe it's going to happen, we've got to keep trying to do what we can, and thinking too about how things will be when she's back. She's going to need a lot of support. The way you're acting, it's as if you've decided that even if she's freed, you're going to walk away from her. What have you have discovered that can possibly justify that?'

Adam drank his wine quickly. Ever vigilant, the waiter refilled his glass.

Finally Gwen seemed to sense he had had enough to feel relaxed. 'Alright. I'll go first,' she said. 'Of course your father told me about your talk with him that night just after you arrived. I think you actually used the phrase "marital difficulties," and it's been apparent to me for ages that things between you and

Morgan have not been good. It was all so much easier in our day.'

'I dare say it was,' Adam said.

'I suppose you've had to deal with the same boring issues that seem to divide every young professional couple nowadays – all that endless, tedious nonsense about careers and children; the rows over who's going to have to make sacrifices, who's not pulling their weight.'

'It's not nonsense. It's the way life is unless you're rich enough to pay people to do all that stuff for you. It's the price for the progress we've made towards gender equality.'

'Yes, darling. I know it is. But in your case, it's not the only thing dividing you, is it?'

'What do you mean?'

'It's not just that her work sometimes makes your own life more difficult. It's not hard to see that you fundamentally disapprove of what she does.'

'Not entirely,' said Adam. 'Every nation needs to defend itself against threats to its national security. But since the news broke that the CIA was running secret prisons and torturing people, the divide between me and Morgan has seemed rather big.'

'Well, my darling, you need to listen to me now, and listen bloody carefully. Because I think you might've been doing her a bit of an injustice.'

'Mum, I appreciate your standing up for her. But how the hell would you know?'

'Because I've heard something. Not all the details, but a bit. From one of my old political science students, a Rhodes scholar. We've always kept in touch. She went into the same line of work as Morgan, and she knows she's been kidnapped. Not that she's directly involved or anything, but it seems that as you might expect, around Langley it's fairly common knowledge. Well, she was in town yesterday, and we had a bit of a catch-up. I'm afraid I rather pumped her for information. I hope I didn't embarrass the poor girl. Anyhow, she did know something that might just be significant.'

The waiter appeared with their food. Having put down their plates of fish, he started to serve the vegetables, but Adam touched his wrist impatiently. 'It's okay, just leave it here. We'll sort it out ourselves.'

'Adam!' Gwen said. 'Let the poor man do his job.'

Adam motioned with his hands for the waiter to continue.

Gwen leant forward, adopting a confidential tone. 'How much do you know about the people Morgan works with? Or, for that matter, what they do?'

'To be honest, very little. She doesn't tell, and I learnt a long time ago that if she wasn't volunteering, it was better not to ask.'

'Well, so far as I can make it out, she's attached to some kind of free-floating specialist team that's supposed to be "taking the war on terror to the enemy" – or at least, that's how my former student put it. Anyhow, it seems that your wife had a bit of a falling out with her bosses.'

Adam had turned very pale. He felt his heart-rate increase. 'A falling out?'

'Yes. A spat. Rather a bad one. I don't have to tell you of all people that over the past few years, ever since that Abu Ghraib scandal, such things as "enhanced interrogation techniques" and what the Agency likes to call "extraordinary rendition" have become controversial. After all, that's how we started this conversation. On Capitol Hill, the intelligence committees and their investigators have been crawling all over this stuff. According to my student, there are more than a few CIA personnel who are simply terrified that if a Democrat wins the next presidential election, they're all going to be prosecuted.

'So in the midst of all that, this boss of Morgan's hatched a little scheme. I don't know all the details, but I believe it involved abducting a radical Muslim cleric. Apparently he keeps a mistress in Amsterdam or somewhere. Well, the plan was that the CIA was going to have him secretly filmed *in flagrante* with the girl, then ship him off to a place where the authorities maintain a rather laxer attitude to the treatment of prisoners than the Senate and House Intelligence Committees like to see displayed by Americans. Morgan was supposed to help arrange this operation, and if he didn't talk, leak the pornographic videos to the press.'

'I thought you said I'd been doing her an injustice,' said Adam. 'That doesn't sound like doing the right thing at all.'

'Don't be so impatient. I haven't finished. According to my student, Morgan made no secret of her belief that this whole thing was a really terrible idea, which was almost certain to blow up in the Agency's face. But her boss wouldn't listen, and so she blew the whistle. Discreetly, you understand. She didn't do anything dramatic, such as squealing to the media – nor, indeed, to you. But she wrote a report to the CIA Inspector General. He went right to the top of the Agency and put a stop to it. Naturally, he promised her that her identity would remain strictly secret. But my hunch is that if I've been able to find out about it so easily, her boss probably has too. Who knows: maybe that's why he sent her to Gaza – some twisted idea of revenge. After all, it's not a pleasant place, especially for a woman.'

Adam was struggling to get his words out. 'Are you're saying that this boss, whoever he is, might deliberately have put her somewhere where her safety was at risk?'

'I don't know. I have no evidence. I don't want to jump to conclusions. But I wanted you to know that she didn't betray the values you always thought you shared. She stood up for them.'

Adam could feel the tears welling, and dabbed his eyes with his napkin. 'My God. I've made quite some misjudgement, haven't I?' He shook his head. 'How could I have got her so wrong?'

'It doesn't matter. But it means you mustn't give up – not in your efforts to find her, and not, if you do find her, on your marriage. I've no idea if things between you will work out. But you can't just let it go.'

The lump in his throat was physical: a hard bolus of misery. 'Mum. You were right. There is something else.'

'What?'

It took him some time to be able to speak. 'She was having an affair out there. The CIA knows about it. And when I found out, I sort of had one – well, more a one-night fling – too.'

'Ah. Excuse me if I say I told you so. So are these new relationships of yours, how shall I put it, serious?'

'Hers? How can I possibly know? I had no idea that anything was going on until the day before I left the Middle East five weeks ago. Sure, she'd grown distant, cold sometimes, but I never dreamt she was seeing someone else. If I never suspected my wife was having an affair, how can I say what it meant to her? I don't know when it started, and I don't, to put it crudely, know how many times they slept together, though my hunch is it only ever happened in Gaza, so their opportunities were somewhat limited.'

'So what about you? Do you have strong feelings for this other person with whom you say you had a one-night fling?'

'I like her immensely. And to be honest, she's gorgeous. She's a widow, almost a neighbour, and she happened to be in Israel when I was. She'd already made it clear she was attracted to me. So when I found out about Morgan, I kind of went for it. But almost immediately afterwards, I felt terrible that I had, and as you've obviously guessed, I still do.'

Gwen picked up the bottle from the ice bucket and topped up Adam's glass. 'Have another drink. You need it. And from this moment on, you're to stop punishing yourself. These things will happen in the best-regulated families. Maybe it really is all over between you and Morgan, but equally, maybe it's not. The point is, you're not going to know, one way or the other, unless and until she's back. And unfortunately, her old colleagues seem to have made a bit of a mess of things in the Gaza Strip lately, if the news reports are true.'

They had some coffee, and Gwen paid the bill. Neither then, nor as they walked home and the sky went dark and produced the first of the long-delayed rain, could Adam bring himself to tell her anything more. After all: when it came to the DVD,

178

to use the spy's stock cliche, she had no need to know. But his mother's words had struck home, and as he walked, he gazed in silence at the pavement. Gwen's disclosure that the operation which Morgan had thwarted had included a plan to film its target having sex left him stunned and bewildered. That the very same thing could have happened to Morgan felt like more than coincidence.

As for himself, he was awash with remorse. How he regretted the lack of trust between them which had stopped her from telling him about going to the Inspector General. And for the past few weeks, he had simply been fooling himself. The notion that he could somehow move on and make a new start in England leaving everything unresolved was delusional.

Not long after they walked in, Adam's cellphone rang. The caller was CIA Mike.

'Hey. Long time,' he said. 'How are you doing?'

'In the circumstances, just fine.'

'We need to talk. I'm coming to London – I'm due in late Monday. Can we meet? Would Wednesday work?'

It seemed that Mike would not be his only transatlantic visitor. Late in the evening, after Adam had taken the children swimming and put them to bed, he opened an email from Rob. 'I've got a business trip to Europe,' it said. 'It's time we talked face to face. I'm going to make a little detour – see you next week, in Oxford.'

Chapter Sixteen
Wednesday, June 20,
and Thursday, June 21, 2007

Over the preceding weeks, Morgan had come to appreciate something for which she was thankful: that Abu Mustafa was not an effective interrogator. Since the day of the helicopter they had seen each other many times, almost always in the basement, and only once in the wonderful fresh air. He had been able to figure out that while the children were small, she had been a capable CIA desk officer. However, despite his questions, she had been able to hide the fact that she had been part of a specialised, counterterrorist unit. More important, she had revealed none of her deeper, more sensitive secrets. Arranging logistics for clandestine operations had given her a patchwork of knowledge about undercover officers and their agents in several countries. Should this knowledge fall into the wrong hands, at best those sources would be compromised, forcing the Agency to terminate whatever operations they might be involved in. At worst, lives would be jeopardised. In most cases, she did not know clandestine sources' real names. But as an intelligence officer, she was only too well aware of the jigsaw effect: the risk that if she were to give up something apparently innocuous, the enemy might put it together with some other piece of information gleaned elsewhere, and so use it to wreak grave damage.

However, rather to her surprise, she was confident that her discussions with Abu Mustafa really had been harmless. Once she had managed to waste most of a day discussing encrypted satellite burst radio communications, with Abu Mustafa seemingly unaware that the Agency had been using such methods since the nineteen-eighties. Another time, she diverted him into an involved discussion of the bureaucratic procedures governing payments to clandestine agents. It could, she mused, simply be that with the facts of her mission in Gaza already disclosed, he didn't really know what to ask. But she also wondered whether his behaviour might be deliberate: whether for some unknown reason he did not wish to probe more deeply.

Although they had spent hours together, there had sometimes been gaps lasting days between their meetings, and so far as she could ascertain, Karim was often not at the farmhouse, either. She suspected they were making plans to move her: the longer they stayed where they were, surely the greater their risk. Maybe their plan was that the real interrogation would start somewhere else at a later date.

Whatever the truth, the tedium and background anxiety remained intense. Her interest in solo chess was waning, and when another orange gave her the chance to make a set of chequers, she found that this too soon palled. There were power outages every day. They had left her with the same floor-standing battery lamp as before, but even when the batteries were fresh, its light was dim.

The only other way she had of passing time was exercise. Every morning, she did the Canadian Air Force routine she had used as a student on days when it was too cold to jog, as well as Pilates. The possibility of escape was always at the forefront of her mind, and should a chance present itself, she would need to be fit. But so as far as she could see, there had not been a single opportunity. Altogether, she had noticed at least eight guards, none of whom seemed to speak English. They followed a varied rota, and when she was allowed out of her cell, two or three of them were never far away. All but one of them treated her as a non-person, never looking her in the eye.

The exception was a sallow, overweight man with strange, green eyes named Aqil, whom she had sometimes caught staring at her with undisguised sexual longing. It made her shudder. The one ordeal for which she still felt unprepared was to be raped. If Aqil were ever to be given his chance, she felt sure he would leap at it.

In some ways she felt proud of herself: she was still holding up. At the same time, she felt numbed and disoriented, and filled with a dread that this ordeal might continue for months, or even years. At night, in the hot, dark hours she spent wide awake, she sometimes felt the absence of Charlie and Aimee as a sharp, visceral pain. But for much of the time, the normalisation of her captivity had grown so all-encompassing that she actually looked forward to such moments of sadness, because they reminded her that inside, she was still fully alive.

Sometimes she thought of Abdel Nasser. She reflected on the fierce, transgressive thrill that went through her when they first became involved, and his unexpected skill as a lover. She remained profoundly fearful of Abdel Nasser's fate, and blamed herself again and again for his predicament: that an agent for whom she was responsible had suffered in the way that he had she regarded as a crushing failure, a breach of her basic case officer's duty. But though she was aware that long before the affair had started, her marriage had been in trouble, she now felt baffled as to why she had decided to risk her career and her marriage on a fling which, so it seemed to her now, meant little to her. If she did see Adam again, she would have to tell him: the only way to rebuild their relationship would be on the basis of honesty. But what if he were to learn of her affair while she remained a captive – or died as one? If he had, it must surely have caused him pain. How would that affect their reunion, or the way he would remember her? If only she could explain it all to him, and ask for his forgiveness.

She had loved Abdel Nasser's attentiveness. He had made her feel wanted, not merely needed. The thought that he might be falling in love with her left her electrified. But she did not love him. Through the long watches of her incarceration, she had come to grasp what it meant to 'repent at leisure' – having slept with the man, she reminded herself, a total of just three times.

Aside from Abu Mustafa, the only person she saw was Zainab, who ever so slowly, was beginning to open up about herself. She too must have been bored, for instead of thrusting Morgan's food into the cell and leaving as fast as she could, had started to linger. Zainab, it transpired, was from Khan Younis, and her brother, Khalid, a hero of the first *intifada*, had fought the Soviets towards the end of the *jihad* in Afghanistan, but then, as Karim had already told her, died fighting overseas, on that trail through the Montenegrin woods. Zainab made clear that his death had left her shattered. But unlike Karim, she did not blame Morgan. 'Is war,' she said simply. 'Bad things happen.'

As the weeks went by, Zainab had started to ask her questions, too – not about her work and her mission, but her childhood, and life in America. Where had Morgan been to school? Who was her father, and what did he do? Did everyone there like George W. Bush? Some of her inquiries suggested that her indoctrination about the West had been very peculiar. One evening, a little embarrassed, she had asked Morgan something which had apparently been on her mind for some time: 'Tell me, why is normal in your country that men make sex with animals?' When Morgan had responded with horrified denial, she giggled nervously. Maybe, Morgan mused, she had picked this up from a Muslim televangelist. The Arab TV stations were full of such creatures, some of them saying extraordinarily bizarre and offensive things.

Their longest conversation had taken place on a hot afternoon, when both Karim and Abu Mustafa were absent. Placing her finger to her lips in the universal gesture of confidentiality, Zainab smiled and winked, then led Morgan up the stairs and into the sunlight. 'The mens not here,' she said. 'Come, we sit.' As ever, two of the guards were lurking, clutching their Kalashnikovs as they lounged by the door to the villa. But Zainab seemed to have obtained their cooperation, too, for at one point one of them disappeared, coming back with his gun slung over his shoulder and carrying a tray of cookies and fragrant Palestinian tea. For more than an hour, they sipped it beneath the palm tree's fronds and chatted. Zainab managed to communicate that her family had once been prosperous, and that in years gone by, before the waves of suicide bombing, the second *intifada* and the building of the security fence, her father had commuted daily from the Gaza Strip to a well-paid engineering job with an Israeli company in Ashkelon. But he had died young from a heart condition, leaving the family impoverished.

That same afternoon, Zainab revealed that as a teenager, she had harboured powerful feelings for Karim, and before Khalid's death, had assumed she would one day marry him. But since his return from the Balkans, he had changed, becoming fractious and withdrawn. 'In old days, we laugh,' Zainab said. 'After Khalid die, with Karim, he talk now always *jihad*, always *jihad*.' These days, she said, he usually called her '*akht sagheera*,' little sister, so making clear he had no romantic interest in her. That, she added, explained how it was that she, a woman, had been allowed to join a group of Salafist kidnappers led by a man who was not a close blood relative – something which should have been unthinkable. 'If Karim not think I am his sister, you have your food from a man,' Zainab told her. She blushed and giggled, remembering an earlier embarrassment: 'And maybe he not know Kotex!'

Morgan heard a knock and soon the door was being opened: another new morning. Zainab entered with a tray.

'Hello Morgan. You sleep okay?' Zainab smiled.

'Not too bad,' said Morgan. 'Not too bad.' Lately the food had deteriorated again: today there was only flat bread, a bottle of water, and some olives. 'Zainab. I want to ask you something. I hear a lot of shooting. Has something happened? Not here, but on the outside?'

Zainab looked nervous, and her eyes scanned the room, as if someone might be hiding there. She lowered her voice to a whisper and looked at the floor. 'Yes. In Gaza, Fatah finished.' She drew her finger across her throat. 'Many people die. Much fighting. My cousin, Hamad, he only 18, he is dead. He is not fighter, he die because he is in wrong time, wrong place. Hamas now king in Gaza. You not tell Abu Mustafa I say this, okay?'

'I promise. But what do Karim and Abu Mustafa think about this? They are happy, no, because they are strong Muslims and Hamas are strong Muslims too?'

Zainab shook her head. 'No, no, no. Not happy at all. Karim very unhappy. He is say now is very dangerous here, in this place.' She dropped her voice still further. 'I think they move you. We go from here. Is new place, very secret.'

Morgan had always believed that the last thing her kidnappers wanted was a Hamas coup, and though she knew it might also bring danger, she had to struggle to stop her face breaking out in a grin: at last, this must be her opportunity. Hamas could not countenance a radical Islamist rival: once their power was consolidated, they would surely hunt them down. She touched Zainab's arm. 'What time are we leaving? How can we move if Hamas has set up roadblocks?'

Zainab shook her head again. 'I not know anything more. Please, now eat. I go.'

Adam had arranged to meet Mike in the grand, high-ceilinged dining room at the Randolph Hotel on Beaumont Street. With relief, he noted it was empty. He was a little early, and as it turned out, Mike was late: his train from London, he explained apologetically, had been delayed by a signalling fault for more than thirty minutes.

'No surprises there, I'm afraid,' Adam said. 'I should have warned you. The service is appalling.'

'Shall we get some coffee?'

'Actually I'm hungry. I skipped lunch. Why don't we have an afternoon tea? Earl Grey, scones and clotted cream? And iced cakes and cucumber sandwich triangles, if you really want to push the boat out.'

'Since Uncle Sam is paying, that would only be appropriate. After all, it is one of your country's two greatest culinary gifts to the world, along with the full English breakfast. Outstanding. Just outstanding.'

'If you say so. Though I'd like to remind you that actually, I'm a US citizen.'

'Of course you are. My apologies.'

Adam summoned the waiter, and within a few minutes, their tea arrived. It was time for an end to the small talk.

'So where have you come from?' Adam asked. 'Washington, or the Middle East?'

'Both places. I stayed in Tel Aviv until just after the Hamas coup, then flew to DC. That's where I came in from. Look, I want to say that what happened that day before you left Tel Aviv, I'm really, really sorry, and Eugene should never have -'

Adam raised his hand. 'Enough. It's done. I'd really rather not discuss it. And right now, if you don't mind, it's not the fucking issue. But I'd like you to tell me a little about what is. Now that Hamas is in control of Gaza, exactly what do you plan to do rescue Morgan?'

Mike appeared to be in the throes of some inner struggle. But if he had been debating whether to disclose anything of substance, he appeared to have thought better of it.

'Adam, I happen to think you're a good guy, and I also respect your work,' he said. 'But I can't tell you anything that's classified. You know that.'

'You don't have to tell me everything. It's just that after everything that's happened over the past few days, I can't help feeling your chances of making progress now are round about zero.'

'You're wrong, Adam. Gary would say this more forcefully, but with respect, you don't know what you're talking about.'

'Oh really? You got a contact with one of the Hamas senior commanders, have you? With one of those guys who've been all over the news media claiming CIA had been planning a Fatah coup?'

'There are always back-channels. That's how this business works. There are channels not only to us, but to the Israelis.'

'Like that slob you introduced me to, Amos? The guy who told me Hamas was about to get whacked? That wasn't such a brilliant call, was it now, Mike?'

'There's really no need to get personal here.' Mike paused, and then his words came in a rush. 'As I said, I like you. So I'm going to say more than I should, and you're going to have to respect my confidence, because if Gary finds out I've told you this, he could make my life very difficult. We've made a genuine

186

breakthrough. I'm not going to give you all the details, but you can expect to see Morgan alive again very soon.'

'How soon?'

'I can't be specific. But soon.'

'Can you give me evidence for that?'

'No. It's classified. Adam, you don't have to believe me. It's your choice. But if you don't, you need to consider the downside.'

'What downside, Mike?'

'You seem to think you can do the Agency's job better than we can. I know what that means: that you're thinking of going back to Gaza. Well, see, here is the risk. Right now, we're in the middle of a very delicate negotiation. There's always a danger that something might leak, and that could cost Morgan her life. And our judgement is that if you go in, you increase that danger merely by your presence. I'm sorry to be blunt, but for Morgan's sake, I have to ask you: cease and desist.'

'Gary put you up to this, didn't he,' Adam said softly.

'He's my boss.' Mike shrugged.

'Yes. But that's not what I meant. I meant, he put you up to all of it, this whole fucking charade. You show up at my Supreme Court case, make out like you're the guy who shares my values, and who really has my back, pretend you're taking me into your confidence. And then you come here and threaten me.'

Adam could see he had got to him, but Mike remained outwardly calm. 'Think about what I said,' he said evenly. 'And let me make a suggestion. If Morgan isn't free by the end of next week, or if we can't show you concrete proof of our progress, by all means, make another visit to Gaza. Eight days is all I'm asking for – but for that period, stay away, or be prepared to face the consequences.'

Adam stood. He had left his scone was untouched. 'Sure, Mike, I'll think about it. I'll think about it very carefully. Jesus, you people. You really know how to pile on the pressure, don't you? In the meantime we're done. Why don't you finish your afternoon tea on your own.'

187

Rob had told Adam he planned to come straight to Oxford on his way from Heathrow to an agribusiness convention in London. He must have taken a shower and spruced himself up at the airport, for the lean figure in pressed khakis, dress shirt, navy blazer and cowboy boots who rang the bell at Adam's parent's front door at ten the following morning did not look like a man who had just endured a trans-Atlantic flight. Gwen and Jonathan stood side by side to greet him, with Adam just behind. Gwen gave him a hug, and Jonathan shook his hand firmly.

'It's been too long,' Jonathan said. 'Come in and have some coffee. Leave your bag in the hall.'

They sat around the Coopers' red oak kitchen table, and Rob promised that when the convention finished, he would come to stay for the weekend, to spend some time with the kids – 'I'm ashamed to say it, but it's nigh on two years since I've seen Aimee and Charlie,' he said. But all the while, Adam sensed that Rob wanted to talk to him alone, and he could see his mother had picked up the signal, too. After a decent interval, when their mugs were drained, she stood.

'Well, I'd better get off. My students await,' she said, gesturing with her eyes at Jonathan.

'Yup, me too,' he said. 'It's been a pleasure, and we look forward to seeing you properly.'

They left the room. Rob sat in silence for a moment, only starting to speak when he heard the front door close. 'Well here we are, son. How are you doing? I mean, how are you *really* doing?'

Adam shrugged. 'What can I say? It's all pretty shitty, which you already know. And now it seems that the CIA have fucked things up even more than I thought they had, because whatever it was they were planning for Gaza appears to have backfired. I'm struggling to think of a silver lining.'

Rob smiled, and put his big calloused hand on Adam's shoulder. 'I hear you. I've had some pretty dark nights of the soul myself these past few weeks.' He shook his head. 'I was never the greatest father. I did my best, but I guess I found a daughter hard to understand, though I was always so, so proud of her – prouder than ever now that I know all that human rights bullshit was just her Agency cover. But you know how it is: you may not always get your kids right, you may not always be able to meet their emotional needs, but the one thing I always thought I could do was protect Morgan from harm. I know this sounds stupid, but I kind of feel like I've failed.'

'You're right. It does sound stupid. But all the same, I understand.'

'Well you know me. I'm a practical guy. I don't just sit on my butt. And I haven't been. But even if the dawn is coming, this sure does feel like the darkest hour. The past few weeks have opened my eyes. Things I maybe always knew, but preferred not to face up to.'

'What things?'

'Well, in America we've grown used to politicians running for office who say things like "Washington is broken." But the folks who say those things, they're talking about lobbyists, and the sleazy process of law-making. What I've learnt now is that there's a different, much more dangerous way in which the system is broken. A way that means that a brave young woman who was serving her fucking country can be abducted by a bunch of extremists, and it seems that no one directly responsible for her gives a shit.'

'You're obviously not saying this without good cause. Tell me more.'

'I've been to DC twice in the past few weeks. I didn't want to tell you on the phone, because I'm fairly sure those motherfuckers are listening – to you, if not to me. I've met staffers from the National Security Council, and the CIA. But excuse my French, everything these motherfuckers said was total, fucking bullcrap. They seemed to have only one concern: that I'd keep my mouth shut. They said they wanted to avoid a situation where the kidnappers might lose face if they released

189

her. What they're really worried about is that if it becomes known that an American's been kidnapped in Gaza, it'll focus attention on their own fucked-up operation. So far as I'm concerned, they can all go fuck themselves in the ass.'

'We're on the same page,' said Adam. 'And they seem to be trying to keep me out of it, too. I had one of the Agency guys visiting me here just yesterday. He told me that if I went back to Gaza, I'd be as good as signing Morgan's death warrant; that there's some kind of fragile, back-channel negotiation going on, and if I go in, I'll fuck it up.'

'What do you think? You going to take his advice?'

'It's really difficult. I don't believe a word he says. But on the other hand, just suppose he isn't lying, at least about this – and I do end up wrecking things? Part of me tells me that to wait a few more days after so many weeks can hardly make much difference. On the other hand, what if something terrible happens as a result of that delay? I don't know, Rob. I just don't know.'

'Jesus,' Rob said. 'This isn't easy. Maybe what you should do is fly to Israel as soon as possible, so at least you're in position, and then you can decide about Gaza when you get the lie of the land.'

'That's what I figured.'

'Well when you do decide to go, I want you to be aware of something. I was on active duty a long time, and you know what they say: there's no such thing as an ex-Marine. I got contacts, Adam: people who stayed in the service and became general officers; who know their way around. Some of them even knew Morgan when she was growing up, and they're fucking proud of her too. So when you go back to Gaza, bear in mind me and my buddies, think of us all as family, we've got your back. If you think you need help, you're to holler. As I've told you before, you can call me any time, day or night. From time to time my friends and I have pulled off some shit that might surprise you.'

'Excuse me if I'm sounding stupid, but what kind of shit do you mean?'

'You ever hear of the incident at al-Qaim?'

'No. What was that?'

'This stays between you me. Okay?'

Adam nodded.

'It was nearly two years ago. I had met some Iraqis through the seed business. They were looking for quality strains of wheat. Well, we stayed in contact after the invasion. They hated America for occupying their country and killing their relatives, but they hated al-Qaeda even more. For a while, they bided their time. Then, when they could see that most of their fellow Sunni leaders were starting to feel the same way, they began picking fights with those motherfuckers. The first place where it came to a head was al-Qaim, a town in the desert, close to the Syrian border. Unfortunately, my guys had bitten off more than they could chew, and they found themselves outgunned, pinned down in the desert. There were two hundred of them, but more than twice as many al-Qaeda. Night fell, and it looked as if when dawn came next day, they were going to be wiped out.'

'What did this have to do with you?'

'In America, it was still daytime. I was on my porch, contemplating my navel, and I got a call on my cell – all the way from al-Qaim. One of my buddies asked me if I could help.'

'And?'

'I made a few calls. I don't need to tell you where. Anyhow, when the dawn came up in the al-Anbar desert an hour or two later, it wasn't my Sunni friends who got whacked, but their enemies – by three US Marine AH-1 Cobra helicopters.'

'You called in a helicopter gunship airstrike on the Syria-Iraq border while sitting on your porch in Taos?'

'Yessir. I surely did.'

'You're not suggesting I ask you to organise an airstrike in Gaza? I mean, don't you think the Israelis might just have something to say about it?'

'I'm not really suggesting anything, Adam. Except, like I said, to bear in mind that we can do surprising shit. That we're committed to this, and we will do whatever it takes to stop someone we love and admire go through hell.' He stopped for a moment, overcome. 'We're not going to let her die out there, okay? So just make sure to keep me on your speed dial. Oh, and there's something else.'

'There is?'

'My recollection is that for a liberal, you used to be a pretty fucking decent shot. You should get a little practice in. You never know. You might need it.' Rob reached inside his jacket pocket and pulled out a piece of paper with a name and number on it. 'This chick is a friend of mine. She runs a little, uh, facility not too far from here. Her clients are a little, uh, unconventional. She's expecting your call. Promise me you'll pay her a visit tomorrow morning, before you get on that plane.'

Adam reached across the table and clasped his father-in-law's hand. 'I will, Sir. You can count on it.'

It was a golden afternoon. At five past three, Adam joined the other parents outside Phil and Jim, the school on the edge of Port Meadow where Charlie and Aimee had now been pupils for almost two months. There were a few other fathers waiting for their offspring, but they were in the minority. To his relief, the women generally made little effort to engage him in conversation, and none to probe his circumstances. Aimee emerged in the company of Alice, her new best friend, a tall, precocious-looking girl with raven hair in a pony tail.

'Dad? Can Alice come back to ours? Just for a couple of hours? Her dad will come to pick her up.'

'Not tonight, sweetie. There's something we need to talk about.'

'Can't we do it after Alice has gone? Please?'

Adam was delighted that the kids were making new friendships. He knew how much they missed their mother, but in some ways they had never seemed so settled, and to them, Bethesda must seem an age away. He and they had passed more time in each others' company these past few weeks than at any time in their lives. Not having to obsess about legal filing deadlines had its advantages. His resistance to Aimee's request crumbled. 'Alright then. She can come.' He turned to Alice. 'Have you told your mother?'

'My mum's not here. She's away in Germany on business. I'm allowed to walk home on my home, but if you lend me your mobile, I'll call my dad to tell him. He won't mind.'

Charlie ran up, and gave his father an unforced hug. 'Daddy! Can I go to Tom's house? He says we can go catch frogs on Port Meadow.'

'Okay, Charlie.' A sigh. 'Let me talk to Tom's mum. I'll arrange to pick you up later.'

Hours later, Aimee and Charlie had bathed and were ready for bed. Adam sat with them in the sitting room.

'Guys. I know you hate it when I'm away. But I think I've got to make another trip. I'm leaving very soon – probably tomorrow evening.'

'You're going back to Israel?' Charlie's eyes were wide. 'Are you going to look for Mommy again?'

'Yes sweetie. That's the plan.'

'Do you know where she is? Will you bring her back? Will she be here for my birthday?'

'Well, I don't know exactly where she is. And I'm not certain yet about your birthday, although I'm going to do my best. But I wanted to be sure you two are happy with this – that you'll be okay with granny and grandpa.'

'Is it going to be dangerous? What if the bad guys shoot at you?' Aimee asked.

'I hope they won't. But I can't be sure.'

'What if you don't come back?' Adam could see she was close to tears. 'Who'll take care of us then? What if you find her but they say you can't have her back?'

Adam didn't know how to answer. But while he paused, his daughter spoke again.

'Can't someone else go and get her? Are you the only one who can find her?' Without waiting for an answer, she continued, picking at the skin at the side of her thumbnail. 'You do have to go. You have to find her Dad. Just promise you'll be careful.'

193

Adam gave her a one-armed hug. Sometimes her maturity astounded him. He wrapped the other arm round Charlie. 'I promise. I'll do everything I can to be safe. I wouldn't be doing this if I thought I had an alternative. I just wanted to be sure you're okay with it. And I'll keep my stay away as short as possible.'

'You have to go. You just have to.' She buried her face in his shoulder, and he felt the warmth of her tears. He stroked her hair, and after a little while, they stopped. She looked up again, her eyes still moist, bravely trying to manage a smile.

Adam turned to Charlie. 'What about you?'

'I just know it, I know it, this time you're going to get Mom!' His excitement was palpable. 'You are going to find her, and she will be back for my birthday, because anyway, it isn't for weeks! Aimee, Mommy's coming back!'

Adam knew better than to puncture Charlie's hopes. 'I'm going to give it my best shot, little guy. The very best I've got.'

Chapter Seventeen
Friday, June 22, 2007
and Saturday, June 23, 2007

Morgan had a sense that Zainab had been avoiding her – or at least, avoiding any chance of talking to her in private. She brought her food, removed her tray, and spoke to her politely. But she gave out no more information, and did not stay to chat. Her attitude only sharpened Morgan's growing anxiety. Hamas might have defeated Fatah, but consolidating its power and imposing order was bound to take time. As to the journey of which Zainab had warned her, she felt a deep foreboding. How did they propose to transport her? How would they hide her?

It was early afternoon when Karim and Abu Mustafa burst in, Karim jabbering excitedly in Arabic. He was holding a pair of scissors and a role of black, reinforced duct tape. Zainab followed, bearing a thick, white, cotton cloth. Morgan knew what it was: a Muslim funeral shroud. Now she knew the answer to the question which had been troubling her. They were going to move her as if she were a shrouded corpse, tightly wrapped in the Islamic style, but without any kind of coffin.

'I am sorry, Morgan, but we have to make a change,' Abu Mustafa said. 'We believe that this house is too conspicuous, and if our enemies try to find you, here will no longer be safe. But we have found a new place. It is not as grand as this villa, though I am sure that once we get there, it will not be too uncomfortable. However, we cannot take the risk of being stopped on the road. You will be on the back seat, wrapped in this shroud. If we are stopped at a roadblock, they will think you have passed away, and we are taking you for burial. But this requires us to ensure you remain completely still. You cannot move even a muscle. You must be totally immobilised.'

Karim was carrying a small, zipped brown leather pouch. He opened it and took out a hypodermic, filled with a clear chemical.

'This will not hurt,' Abu Mustafa said. 'It is just an intramuscular injection, a sedative. It will make you sleepy. Please, roll up your sleeve and hold still while Karim gives you the drug. When you wake up, you will be in the new place.'

'No!' Her voice was a shriek, impelled by sheer fear. 'I will cooperate, I promise! I will not try to escape, and I will be still for you. But, please, I beg you, do not give me this! I am allergic to this type of anaesthetic. If you give me this injection, I will vomit. Please, believe me, I am not making this up. But you don't need to do this. You have guns. When we are travelling, I will know that if I try to make trouble, you will shoot me.'

'Actually, we won't be armed on this journey,' Abu Mustafa said. 'We don't want to cause suspicion. But that means we cannot take the risk that you even twitch a muscle.'

'I can keep still. Absolutely still. I have been trained, for God's sake! I swear that -'

Saying nothing, Karim grabbed her arm, and forced her into a chair. She felt him squeeze her shoulder very hard, and then he took the roll of duct tape, wrapping it round her head several times, binding her lips tightly shut, and wrapping more layers over the bridge of her nose. He left only a tiny window, just wide enough for her nostrils. From her chin to her eyes, her face was covered. Then, while she fought a rising sense of suffocation and panic, Karim took the needle and jabbed it through the cloth of her long-sleeved top into her arm. Morgan remained dimly aware of being lifted, of being wrapped in the shroud, and being carried up the stairs, her head pointing downwards. In her mouth, she was starting to feel a flood of that strange, warm saliva that often accompanies nausea, when at last she lapsed into oblivion.

Morgan's return to consciousness was as sudden as if she'd been fired from a cannon from the depths of a black mineshaft. She was lying on her side on a narrow, dusty, couch, which was covered in a rough fabric. Her head was pounding, her throat lining burned and her stomach was sore from heaving. Not for the first time since she became a captive, she stank of her own vomit. Someone – presumably Zainab – must have tried to sponge it away, for her chest and stomach felt damp. Her whole body ached, and she guessed she had been kept immobile for a long time in an unnatural position. But the duct tape, though it still formed a hard, sticky clump behind her neck and head, had been cut away from her mouth, and she was breathing freely. If someone hadn't removed the seal, she would have inhaled the vomit and probably died. The shroud in which she had travelled – the cloth whose purpose might all too easily have become real - had been draped across her legs and lower torso as a blanket.

She half-opened an eye, finding herself in a small, dingy room lit by a single lightbulb. The walls were yellow, and in places the plaster was crumbling. It seemed to be night. There was a window to one side, covered by a plain, dark blind, but there wasn't even a glimmer of light seeping in around the edge. The room held three other occupants: Zainab, Karim and the creepy guard, Aqil. They had not noticed she was awake. Zainab and Karim were sitting at a table with a turquoise plastic, paisley-patterned cover, speaking intensely in Arabic. Aqil, as usual, was standing. Either they had found a way to move their weapons through the roadblocks, or they had managed to access an alternative supply: he was holding a Kalashnikov.

Morgan knew enough Arabic to understand that Karim and Zainab's conversation was becoming heated. Zainab was not raising her voice, but she kept on using the word '*haram*', a term that meant something unclean, religiously forbidden or simply wrong, often in sentences which also contained Morgan's name or simply '*Amriki*', the American. Morgan guessed that Zainab was talking about the treatment she had seen her endure at the hands of Karim, and that she was telling him that taping up her mouth had been both risky and cruel. It must have been Zainab who had cut away the gag when they were already on the move.

Karim did not appear to be taking Zainab's criticism well. Although his voice too was barely louder than a whisper, he was beginning to hyperventilate, and the colour in his face was rising.

Morgan closed her eye again. She did not want them to realise she was conscious. This little drama was too important to miss.

As the minutes went by, Karim's voice became harder. Morgan could not make out many of his words, but then he said something she recognised, and knew to be deeply insulting. He was calling Zainab '*magnun*', crazy, and using the term repeatedly. Morgan opened her eye again, just enough to watch Karim stand and make as if to leave. '*Hallas!*' he said, 'enough!'

But Zainab was not done. Before Karim could pass through the open doorway, she let loose an angry stream, her loudest utterance yet. So far as she could tell, Zainab was accusing Karim of associating with a '*yahudi*', a Jew or Israeli. Morgan caught another word: '*khawan*,' 'traitor.' In her fury, Zainab was accusing him of betraying his own cause.

Whatever their precise meaning, her words stopped Karim dead. His eyes black, he turned on his heel towards Zainab and bent down to where she was sitting. '*Bint ish zaniya*' he said: 'daughter of a whore'. He raised his right hand and struck her hard enough across the face to make her reel, then repeated the process against the other cheek with his backhand. Morgan heard Zainab's teeth crunch. As Zainab tried to stifle a squeal of pain, he turned away once more, and striding past Aqil without a glance, he left the room.

Morgan fully opened both her eyes and met Zainab's with a look of horrified pity. As she stared at her, Zainab reached for a Kleenex from a box on the table and dabbed away tears. Karim had must have cut her lip or tongue, for the corner of her mouth was beginning to well with blood. She touched it with her fingers and winced: it was evidently tender. Quietly sobbing, she shook her head. She was saying something that sounded like a moan, but was actually one of the words which had provoked Karim's rage. She uttered it repeatedly: '*Haram*.'

Soon Aqil left the room, locking the two women in behind him. A few minutes later, he returned with a bucket, indicating with a leery chuckle they would both have to use it to relieve themselves. Morgan struggled to a sitting position, and crawling across the floor, she crouched in front of Zainab. Gingerly, she touched her jaw. The bleeding had soon stopped, but her mouth was evidently still tender. Morgan took a piece of the toilet paper Aqil had left by the bucket and moistened it with some water from a drinking bottle, dabbing at the cut on Zainab's lip.

'Is okay. You not have do this,' Zainab said.

'Round here, sisters have got to be doing it for themselves,' said Morgan.

'It's just so weird, isn't it?' Ronnie said. She and Adam were treading water, a few feet out of their depths. On the gentle shelf of Jaffa's Banana Beach, that meant they were easily far enough out to sea not to be overheard. The lacquered harshness had gone out of the day, and the shadows were starting to lengthen. On the wide sandy beach, Rachelle was sitting on a lounger beneath an umbrella, reading a book. Avram, a strong, hairy, bear-like figure with a throaty laugh, had corralled Ronnie's children, Ben and Sarah, into a game of *matkot*, the Israeli version of paddleball. Their distant cries of excitement punctuated the seaside tranquillity.

'What's weird?' asked Adam.

'That we're here, where everything is so normal, despite everything that's happened. It's yet another gorgeous day. We've had a lovely lunch at the café, and apart from having to be on our best behaviour, you and I can live our lives as we please.' Beneath the blue water, where it couldn't be seen, she placed a toe against his crotch and wiggled it.

'Ronnie, I - '

'Shh. You don't need to worry. I'm not about to jump your bones in front of my sister and my children, much as I'd really love to. Anyhow, we'd probably both drown if I did. I just meant to say that I look at this coast, into the haze by that distant curve where it stretches away to the south, and it feels so strange that less than forty miles away, it's Gaza, where everything is so, so different. Where your wife is, and where you're going to be risking your life tomorrow.'

'Probably not tomorrow. It'll take me a day or two to make the necessary arrangements. But hey, that's Israeli geography. It's a small country.'

The schools in Bethesda had gone out at the end of the previous week, and after less than a month back home, Ronnie had decided to bring the children over to spend the summer in Israel, emailing Adam to inform him of her intentions. When he replied with the news he was about to arrive on the overnight flight that morning, she had invited him to recover from his journey at the beach. He hadn't required much persuasion. One way or another, their children's closeness meant Ronnie and he were going to remain entangled. Of course, they would never sleep together again. But they needed to be able to relate to each other as adults, and as friends.

Sleek and tanned in a dazzling white swimsuit, she stroked his groin with her toe again, forcing him to conceal his arousal by trying to start a water fight. Ronnie didn't seem very interested in that, but with a look of regret, she slowly withdrew her foot.

'We'd better be going in,' Adam said. 'Avram will want us to join the *matkot*.'

'Yes. In a moment.' She sighed. 'Look at us all. Lunch was a gas, wasn't it? Whatever this thing is between us, it could work, don't you think? But it's okay. I know you have to go back to Gaza, and that you can't give up on Morgan. But just promise me you'll be careful, okay? Don't do anything stupid, and don't ever tell those crazy Islamist motherfuckers that you have Jewish ancestors, because trust me, it wouldn't make them happy.'

'I promise. Solemnly. I get the point.'

'And if you do succeed in bringing Morgan back, you're going to have a lot to deal with. You don't need extra grief from me. So if you should both end up in Tel Aviv, I'll keep out of your way.'

Her voice was steady, but he noticed a teary pinprick at the corner of one of her eyes and his heart surged. 'You said we both deserved what happened between us. The truth is, I don't deserve you.'

'In fact, you don't have me. Well, you did have me, but so far only the once.' She twisted, agile as a seal, and reaching beneath the water she grabbed his penis through the cloth of his swim shorts. Instantly, he started to stiffen. 'But baby, though you may not realise it, you do deserve me. That is something very few people do.'

She disengaged herself from his genitals, and slowly they swam to the shore, saying nothing. It seemed to Adam that his life had become surreal. This time the previous day he had been with Rob's friend Amanda, a willowy blonde of a certain age in a green padded gilet and wellingtons, reacquainting himself with handguns and rifles at the underground firing range concealed beneath her Buckinghamshire farm. He surprised himself by how easily he had taken to handling firearms again. With a handgun, he found he could hit the middle of a body-sized target range almost every time. He looked up in time to dodge an oncoming pedalo. The water suddenly felt heavier, for Adam knew that every stroke was bearing him closer to Gaza.

Slowly the hours passed. Morgan, attempting to recover from her own ordeal, slept fitfully on the couch. The room was stifling, and although there was a fan, the power, as so often, was off.

At last Morgan began to stir. Her head throbbed: the after-effects of the drug. Soon she was fully awake. Her eyes went straight to Zainab's. She was still sitting in the same position, staring into space.

'You're still here? Are you okay?' said Morgan.

'I okay.'

'Your mouth? How is it?'

'Is okay. Until now, I not eat. But I think it is possible.'

'It would be nice if we could wash.'

'Here no shower.' She pointed at the bucket. 'You want toilet?'

Morgan grimaced, then stretched, yawning. 'I guess so. Sorry, Zainab.'

Zainab turned to face the wall, while Morgan began to handle this primitive arrangement. When she was done, they moved to the table and sat facing each other.

'Did Karim ever do anything to you like this before?' Morgan asked.

'No, no. Never.' She shook her head vigorously. 'He never touch me. He never yell at me. Before, he always give respect, because of my brother Khalid. But Morgan, before, always I follow him. I not say bad things, I not question him, because he is my emir. Maybe now he hit me because I am bad.'

'No! This is not your fault!' Morgan was passionate. 'No man ever has the right to do what he did to you. You hear me Zainab? You understand?'

She nodded.

'Are you a prisoner too like me, now?' Morgan asked softly. 'Are we both Karim's prisoners?'

'I not know. Is possible. But I think soon he let me go. I stay here in case you sick again.'

'Do you know where we are?'

'Yes. It is Yebna. Is very close to border, to Egypt. Very conservative place. It is camp, for refugees, near Rafah. Karim's people, his family, they live here, so he think he safe.'

'His tribe is from Yebna?'

'Yes. He trust the Yebna people.'

'Are there tunnels in Yebna, Zainab?'

'Yes. Many tunnels. The Yebna people is making much money. They bring the things from Egypt.'

There was a knock. 'Enter,' Zainab said in Arabic, and Aqil came in, bearing a tray with more water, flatbread and a dish of hummus. He set the tray down on the table, and left without a word, but this time, he left the door unlocked. They both began to eat.

'Zainab, I want to ask you something,' Morgan said. 'Do you know where Abdel Nasser is? Did he stay at the farmhouse when we went from that place? Was he also sleeping there? Did he come here with us?'

'I not see Abdel Nasser. Until now, I not see him. But maybe he is here. Maybe they take him to Yebna.'

Morgan chewed for a minute, then spoke again, her tone insistent. 'Why did you agree to join Karim? I mean, why did you agree to help him when he decided to kidnap me? Did you believe that this would help the Palestinian people become free?'

Zainab said nothing for a while. At last she took a deep breath: 'Before, I think yes. I believe him. He tell me, if we take you, it is good because we show we are stronger than Hamas, and they are *haram*. But now all is change. I think Karim wants you because it make him feel strong. Before, I love him, I trust him. Not now. He not think about Palestinian people. He only think about Karim.'

'You know, you could do something, if he lets you leave this house. You understand what I'm saying? You could tell someone where we are – someone from Hamas.'

Zainab nodded. 'I understand. Until now, I am thinking.'

By the time Adam left the beach, it was getting close to sunset. He strolled through the Bauhaus boulevards towards his hotel, enjoying the warmth and carefree summer atmosphere. Everyone he saw was wearing shorts and flip-flops. He planned a quiet evening on his own, to gather his strength for the encounters soon to come. He was staying at the Cinema Hotel again, and as he pushed through its bronze and glass Art Deco doors, the receptionist beckoned him over.

'Those gentlemen over there have been waiting for you,' he said in a thick, Brooklyn accent, gesturing towards a group of three men sitting at a table by the elevators. 'They wouldn't say who they are, but they said their business is important. I didn't really feel I had any reason to ask them to leave. I hope that's okay.'

Adam looked at the men and shrugged. He had never seen any of them before. 'I guess so. I'd better find out what they want.'

He strolled across the lobby and the oldest of the trio, a slim, balding man in his forties, stood. He was obviously Israeli, wearing sandals and a loose Hawaiian shirt.

'Mr Cooper?'

'Who wants to know?'

'Chaim Dore. I am the security correspondent for *Maariv*. And these are two of my journalistic colleagues.'

The second man was some years older. He wore a beard and a well-worn, khaki waistcoat of the kind favoured by photographers, festooned with pockets. He too stood and held out his hand. 'Stephen Pearlstein. I'm the Israel bureau chief for the *New York Times*. We're here to talk about your wife, Morgan. We understand she's been kidnapped in Gaza, while on assignment for the State Department.'

The last of the three looked altogether different: forty at most, a little overweight, and certainly overdressed: even in the air conditioned lobby, his Marks and Spencer suit and gaudy silk necktie were making him perspire. 'Derek Turner,' he said in a Thames estuary accent. 'Like you, I've only just arrived – sent out here at short notice, hence my incommodious attire. I'm a reporter from the *News of the World*.'

Adam blinked. 'I see. Who told you I was here?'

'I'm afraid I'm not at liberty to disclose my source,' Turner said. 'I hesitate to speak for my colleagues, but I imagine they would feel the same. But whoever told us you'd be here isn't really the point. As you can see, whoever it was, his or her information was accurate.'

'And just what is that you want?'

'A little of your time. An interview, somewhere reasonably private,' Pearlstein said. 'I apologise for the intrusion. I know we come at a difficult time. Is there somewhere we can go?'

'Can you give me a single reason why I shouldn't tell you all to get lost?'

Pearlstein looked at him with apparent sympathy. 'Of course you're perfectly welcome to tell us to get lost if you wish. But sir, it could be that we know things you don't, and if we could maybe sit and talk, you might hear something from us that could be useful. Plus, the mere fact that you've showed up and confirmed who you are is newsworthy. Like it or not, the fact of Morgan Cooper's kidnap is a story, and if you're here too, well, that only makes it more newsworthy. You might be more comfortable if we agree to talk on background. But think about it. What have you got lose?'

Adam felt helpless, and Pearlstein's logic sounded irresistible. 'Okay. We'll go to the breakfast room. It should be quiet in there. I'll see if I can get us some coffee.'

As a lawyer, Adam had grown used to dealing with reporters, and he liked to think he knew the rules of the game. The important thing was to control the conversation: to say the things you wanted to say, and absolutely nothing else. 'Okay,' he said as they sat down at a table. 'Unless we later agree something to the contrary, this is all on deep background. No attribution for anything I say to "friends of Adam Cooper" or any other such BS. Is that understood?"

Dore and Pearlstein replied in the affirmative.

'For now,' said Turner. 'For the time being.'

'I'm kind of surprised to find you here,' said Adam, looking at Turner with unconcealed disdain. 'I wouldn't have thought an American official being kidnapped in the Middle East is exactly staple fodder for a UK Murdoch tabloid.'

'Then that's where you're wrong,' Turner said with a fleeting snigger. 'We take, erm, international relations at both the political and the, erm, personal level very seriously, as it happens. And after all, in your case, there's also the kiddies to consider.'

'The kiddies? What do you mean, the kiddies? You leave my children out of this, or this interview is over right now. You got that?'

'Steady on! Adam, mate, I'm not trying to cause offence. All I'm saying is the fact that your kids are staying with your mum and dad in Oxford – and no, that didn't come from a confidential source, but a phone call to your father - gives the story an extra, erm, topicality for us, you know what I'm saying? A bit of a domestic angle, shall we say? We're not about to publish their photos or anything.'

'Anyhow, let's get back to the main issue here, shall we?' Pearlstein said with unconcealed irritation. 'Let me assure you, the *New York Times* isn't concerned with the details of your childcare arrangements, and neither does it wish to intrude on their privacy.'

'I'd like to begin by making something perfectly clear,' Adam said. 'There's a reason why Morgan's kidnap hasn't been reported thus far. It's that if you publish a single word about it, you will be placing her in jeopardy. I can't stress enough how critical this is. But I'll make you a promise: if you all agree to write nothing for now, I'll give you all interviews when she's free – to you and no one else.'

'That is not possible,' Dore said.

'What do you mean, it's not possible? You think you can just sit here and play God?'

'It's not possible because Israeli Army Radio is already carrying the story, and has been for the past three hours. Just the basic facts: that she was on a human rights monitoring assignment, that she has not been seen since late March, and that both the American and Israeli authorities have been doing all they can to secure her release. It's too late.'

Adam fought for composure. After the weeks of imprecations from everyone at the Agency that he maintain total secrecy, this! 'How has this got out?' he asked. 'Has there been some kind of briefing?'

'I'm sorry, but I can't disclose what I or other journalists may have been told on the same background conditions under which you're speaking to us yourself,' Pearlstein said. 'Naturally, the last thing any of us want to do is to endanger your wife's life. But as Chaim says: the secret is out.'

Adam knew the only thing he could do was somehow to limit the damage. At least he could try to avoid telling the world that he was in Israel to look for her.

'Alright. I'll tell you a little about Morgan,' he said. 'But only on one condition: that you don't write that I'm here, because if that gets known, it really isn't going to help.'

With seeming reluctance, the three reporters agreed, and for the next half hour, Adam answered their questions. He tried to sound weak and uncontroversial, and to stifle any hint that he planned to go to Gaza. 'I'm here because I wanted to be physically closer to her, and I'm optimistic that the chances of her being released soon are improving,' he said. He was also careful not to give the merest hint he had ever felt dissatisfied with the US government's efforts to free Morgan, and insisted he was clueless as to the kidnappers' identity.

'So I guess we're almost done,' Adam said finally. 'But I want to ask you something before you go. Have any of you been in Gaza since the Hamas coup? Not you, obviously, Mr Turner.'

Pearlstein shook his head. 'Not yet. Hoping to go next week.'

'For Israelis, it is impossible to go to Gaza since the withdrawal in 2005,' added Dore. 'Before, I went. But not now. I talk to people there on their cellphones.'

'So what do you all think?' asked Adam. 'You said maybe I'd learn something if I spoke with you. So tell me. What's really happening there? How will it affect her chances of freedom?'

'I am sure Hamas is soon ending the anarchy,' Dore said in his not quite fluent English. 'All the armed factions know who is the boss, and if they don't, they're going to find out. I would say this means her chances have improved.'

'One last thing,' Adam said. 'You've already made clear you can't betray your sources. But just tell me this. The person who told you I was in Israel, staying at this hotel. Were they Israeli, or American?'

Dore and Pearlstein exchanged a glance. They both shook their heads. 'Sorry,' Pearlstein said. 'We just can't go there.'

'I see. Well, gentlemen, I can't pretend it's been a pleasure, but thank you for your interest. And I'm sure I don't need to add this, but please, be careful what you write. Don't make it any harder for the kidnappers to free her. And this you can have on the record: we love Morgan, me, my children and all the rest of her family. We miss her very much, and we want her back safe.'

All four men stood, but as Dore and Pearlstein advanced through the lobby and pushed the doors open on to the street, Turner, who had said almost nothing after they first sat down, hung back. As the others beckoned to the taxi rank outside, he turned abruptly, once again facing Adam.

'Erm, there is something else. It won't take a moment. Could we just go back to the -'

'No, Mr Turner, we couldn't. It's been nice meeting you.'

'I didn't want to say this in front of the others. It's about a DVD. A rather, erm, *personal* DVD, if you get my drift. A DVD of Mrs Cooper.'

Adam was aware he had failed to keep the shock out of his eyes. 'What makes you think I'd want to discuss anything personal with you? Why don't you just fuck off?'

'Because, Adam, mate, I've got some pictures of you, taken today by an excellent Israeli photographer with a very long lens. They've captured you on the beach and in the azure Mediterranean, in the company of a lovely looking girl with long dark hair in a white designer swimsuit. She seems to have a rather stunning figure, and she looks, erm, like she might be extremely close to you. Pardon me, but I did think that looked like a funny way to be showing how much you were missing your wife. So let's go back to the lounge and sit down to discuss it, shall we?'

Chapter Eighteen
Sunday, June 24, 2007

To judge by the *News of the World* website, Derek Turner's article had not made the front page, but it was both prominent and humiliating. 'Belle Aviv!' the headline read, 'Gaza Kidnap Husband's Romp With Law Firm Stunner.' Illustrating the piece was a large picture of Adam and Ronnie in the sea. He was grinning manically, trying to splash her, and she had twisted herself into a strange but revealing position in her effort to get away. But while her body was trying to escape, her eyes remained locked on his, and her expression could only be described as one of adoration. In a second photo, he and Ronnie were depicted standing as he kissed her goodbye – thankfully, on her cheek. She had put on a gauzy, see-through shirt over her swimming costume, which served only to accentuate her impressive physical condition. She was also pulling him firmly towards her with a hand behind his neck.

Adam had stayed up until after two to wait for the article to go online. As he read it, he could see that Turner had at least stuck to the text of the vile agreement they had made a few hours earlier. Believing he had no alternative other than to speak to the man again, Adam had pleaded with him that to publish anything about the state of his marriage could only deepen Morgan's peril – after all, whoever her kidnappers really were, one thing seemed certain: she was a prisoner of fundamentalist Muslims, a category of men not known for their generous view of adultery.

'The thing is, Adam, mate, I can't un-know what I know,' Turner had told him wheedlingly. 'Believe me, we're on the same side. But I've been sent a long way, I've spent a lot of the paper's money, and I've got to have something publishable to show for it. I'll do what I can to lessen the impact, and so far as her safety is concerned, it's not as if I'm going to write that she's a CIA agent, now is it? She's a human rights officer with the State Department, and I wouldn't want to create even the tiniest suspicion that that might not actually be true.'

That too was a threat: Adam was sure that Turner's source must have been an intelligence officer, and it was only too likely that he had told him that Morgan was one too. It was also apparent that while Turner had been briefed selectively – he seemed to know nothing about the DVD of Morgan's confession to being a CIA officer, the *Janbiya al-Islam* or Adam's previous trip to Gaza – his information, where it mattered, was painfully accurate. It even included the detail that Adam had seen what Turner delicately termed 'a Morgan Cooper sex tape' for himself inside the US embassy. Thankfully, he seemed to know very little about Ronnie. 'So, erm, have you been shagging her?' Turner had asked. 'Excuse my directness, but in all the circumstances, and given the aforementioned photographs, I would be derelict in my duty if I failed to ask.'

Finally, they had agreed their sordid compromise. Turner promised he would not describe the DVD directly, nor imply that what he had been told about it was true. Instead, he would refer only to 'cruel rumours in Middle East diplomatic circles,' that she had been filmed having sex with a mysterious lover by her abductors before they kidnapped her. Turner promised he would write that these rumours were 'unconfirmed,' that investigators believed they were 'hampering inquiries into her disappearance,' and that 'sources close to her family' denied them.

In return, Adam was forced to give Turner Ronnie's name, adding that she was a friend of the family from America, and that she and her children were spending the summer in Israel for reasons unconnected with Morgan's disappearance. 'Don't worry,' Turner had said, 'I'm not going to imply that you two are having an affair.' Adam had to admit that in words, at least, he hadn't. The article described her as a 'widowed former hot-shot lawyer from Adam Cooper's top Washington firm,' adding that she was a 'long-standing girl pal' who had 'helped Morgan's husband by cooking his children meals and baby-sitting while he defended a terrorist in the US Supreme Court.' The pictures and headline were a different matter, leaving little to the imagination.

Adam knew he should have called Ronnie to warn her after Turner had finally departed, but he hadn't, hoping against hope that maybe the article would not turn out as badly as he feared. Of course, once it went online, it was far too late. Instead, he searched the Web for examples of Turner's previous *oeuvre*.

It didn't take long. Turner, it appeared, had spent several years based in Washington, alternating perfunctory coverage of American politics with trips the length of the Eastern seaboard to confront misbehaving celebrities. But while his bigger scoops tended to involve reality television stars, he appeared to have had at least one source at the Agency, who had briefed him about aspects of counterterrorism. Turner had obediently published what this source had told him.

The most egregious example dated from March 2004, when three British citizens detained at Guantanamo Bay returned to England. The previous weekend, as Adam vividly remembered, they had given an extensive interview to one of the London papers. They had made shocking allegations about the methods used to interrogate them, and conditions at the prison. Their story was picked up widely by media outlets around the world.

Turner, however, went against the general tide. His page one 'splash' cited anonymous 'US security sources' who complained that by releasing the men and sending them back to England, America had exposed its ally to a 'grave terrorist threat.' One of the three, he added, had taken part in the fierce hand-to-hand combat attending Osama bin Laden's flight from the Tora Bora caves in Afghanistan, and the *News of the World* published a photo which purported to depict this individual, lying wounded on the ground after the battle, still clutching a Kalashnikov. Days later, it became clear that the man in the photograph was someone else entirely, who was, in fact, dead.

But it was also apparent Turner hadn't simply made the story up. There were just enough telling, checkable details – such as what Turner described as exclusive new information about the men's arrest in Pakistan – for it to be evident that he had a genuine CIA contact.

By the time he stumbled to bed, exhausted, at almost four, his suspicions were close to certain. Derek Turner must have been briefed either by Gary Thurmond, or possibly, by Amos or one of his colleagues. Either way, they were doing all they could both to thwart his mission and to make his life unbearable.

Tired as he was, it took a long time before he sank into sleep. Much later than he had intended, he was woken by the hotel phone at his bedside. A quick peek behind his bedroom curtain confirmed that the sun was already high.

'Hello,' said Adam blearily.

'It's Belle,' said Ronnie. 'Belle fucking Aviv. Would you mind telling me what the hell is going on?'

'Ronnie, I-'

'Have you seen it? Do you know what I'm talking about? Have you seen the fucking London *News of the World*?'

'Yes. I've seen it. And I'm really, really sorry. But there was nothing, absolutely nothing I could do about it. The guy cornered me here last night. Obviously he already had the photographs.'

'And you didn't think it might have been an idea to warn me?'

'I know I should have. I'm really sorry about that too. But I just didn't know what to tell you until I saw the article, and by the time I did see it was the middle of the night. I was going to call you first thing this morning.'

'Yeah, well now it's ten-fucking-thirty, and I've already had my old college roommate on the line from London. She could barely stop herself laughing. I've managed to keep my kids away from it so far, but that's not going to work for long now, is it? And what about yours? Don't you think they read the *News of the World* at that school you've been sending them to in Oxford?'

'Well, er, actually not all that many people do read the *News of the World* in North Oxford. It's not that sort of place.'

'Well, Adam, I've got news for you: it's only going to take one. And how do you think this is going to play with your parents – and, oh my God, what about Morgan's?'

'Look, Ronnie, I can see very well why you're upset. And you're right, I should have called you as soon as I knew anything. But you're acting as if it's all my fault. I didn't leak the fact I was in Israel to the media. I didn't know there was some fucking paparazzo photographer ogling us both at the beach.'

'So, my name, Adam. How did they get my name? You think this slimeball reporter's "diplomatic sources" somehow knew that, too?'

Adam knew that any attempt to lie would be futile. He took a deep breath. 'I told him. I told him because I made a deal with him. In return for giving him your name, he promised not to write that you and I were having an affair, and he also agreed to say that this DVD of Morgan was just a cruel rumour. As you can see, at least he stuck by his word.'

For long seconds, Ronnie was silent. When she spoke again, the anger had gone. Her voice was much quieter, less animated, and she sounded wounded. 'So there is a DVD. Of Morgan having sex with someone, presumably not you.'

'Yes. There is.'

'And when did you first hear of it?'

'It was during my last trip to Israel. In fact, I've seen it. I was with an official inside the US embassy when it first arrived. It was labelled with Morgan's name and I guess he thought I had a right to see it immediately.'

The pause, this time, was longer. 'Suddenly it's all falling into place,' Ronnie said. 'That last night, when we had dinner and went back to your hotel. You'd promised you were going to call me but you didn't until after five. I can't remember your pathetic excuse, but it was because you'd seen this fucking tape that day, wasn't it?'

'Yes.'

Now she was quietly sobbing. 'My God, I'm such a damn stupid fool. I really thought I meant something to you. And when you did call, although it was late, I was just so happy, you know, that we were going to get another chance to be together, and maybe, finally, something would happen between us that night. But now I get it. All I ever was to you was a very handy babysitter and then, when your fucking male ego was punctured, a revenge fuck. A fucking revenge fuck for your fucking wife getting nasty with some fucking local on one of her business trips. It's okay Adam. I'm an adult. I will deal with this. But I will do so on my own. Just do me one favour. Please, don't ever call me again.'

After Ronnie got off the line, Adam's immediate impulse to deal with the reservoir of shame and fury curdling inside his stomach was to march straight to the embassy, demand the duty clerk summon Gary, and then confront him. But first, he wanted to see Yitzhak Ben-Meir, who seemed to be the only intelligence or security man he could even begin to trust. When he called, Ben-Meir said he was free that evening, and they fixed a rendezvous at a restaurant amid the glitzy splendour of Rothschild Boulevard. Having spent part of the afternoon listlessly dozing, Adam used the walk to get some much needed fresh air.

Ben-Meir was already waiting at an outside table with a glass of white wine, watching the Israeli version of the *passeggiata* – a nightly parade of effortless, summery style: of glossy, well-groomed women aged from sixteen to ninety. Most wore short but elegant dresses, carefully accessorised jewellery and elaborate high-heeled sandals. As they wove their course between the boulevard's cafes and the shady, spreading trees, some of them towed obedient-looking men or little dogs. There was a slight but welcome breeze. Ben-Meir stood and clasped Adam's hand with what felt like unfeigned affection. 'You okay?' he asked. 'You don't look like you've slept much.'

'I've slept, though not enough, and too late. Before we say anything, if you don't mind, I need a drink.' He beckoned to a waitress. 'I'd like a gin and tonic, please. A large one.'

'If you want to eat pork, this is the best place in Israel,' Ben-Meir said. 'They even do a Shabbat brunch special: a smoky bacon open sandwich made with traditional Ashkenazi *challa* bread. The true meaning of the secular Zionist tradition.'

Adam's drink arrived, and he gulped it thirstily. Both men ordered filet steak, and agreed on a bottle of cabernet.

'So what's happening, my friend?' said Ben-Meir when the food and wine arrived. 'What's wrong – I mean, apart from the obvious?'

'The obvious? You mean the ever-present background obvious, that my wife has been kidnapped, or the what's obvious today to several million Britons, thanks to an article in the country's biggest-selling tabloid newspaper?'

From his expression, it was evident that Ben-Meir did not know what he was talking about. 'A tabloid? What has that to do with you?'

Adam covered his face with his hands. Flushing deeply, he began to explain, telling Ben-Meir about his meeting with Turner and the other journalists, the *News of the World* article, and his belief that the very same senior CIA officer who was supposed to be leading the hunt for Morgan was probably behind the leak.

Ben-Meir listened without interrupting him, looking pensive. 'I can see why this is unpleasant,' he said. 'For your children, and the rest of your family, it may be a little difficult. And it may not be helpful that the fact of Morgan's kidnap has made the news, though to be honest, I don't think it will make much difference. But set against everything else, is it really so terrible? For a day or two, some uneducated people in England will be talking badly about you. Why is that a big deal?'

'You're forgetting the part about Morgan. This so-called sex tape.'

'You said the article refers to a rumour. Why take it seriously?

'I'm worried about the impact it could have in Gaza. On the kidnappers, and for that matter, Hamas.'

Ben-Meir laughed incredulously. 'The state of your marriage is no more their business than mine. In any case, I do not think that the *News of the World* is widely read by Gazan Islamists. You're worrying about the wrong thing here, believe me.'

'I'm relieved to hear you say that. So what should I be worrying about?'

'I would have thought it is obvious. You have made some powerful enemies. They are trying to upset you, and if you are to outwit them, you need to move fast.'

'Meaning?'

'You have no time to waste. They know you're in Israel, and if you're hoping to go back to Gaza, you need to leave as soon as possible, or they will ensure the border will be closed to you.'

'The CIA asked me to give them to the end of the week. I said I'd think about it. They said they're in the middle of some delicate negotiation with the kidnappers, and if I went to Gaza, I'm likely to screw it up.'

'And you believe this?'

'Not really.'

'Look, if they try hard enough, eventually the CIA will be able to deal with Hamas, though they'll have to start from a very low base. But last time we met, we agreed that it didn't seem likely that Hamas had anything to do with the kidnap, and I do not think it likely that anyone at the Agency is talking to the *Janbiya al-Islam*.'

'So where does that leave me?'

'You must go there yourself. As soon as possible. And there is another reason. I can understand why you have spent your day thinking about the article in the *News of the World*. But you are forgetting something. I didn't even know about the *News of the World*. But I did know that the story of Morgan's kidnap has also been reported by Israeli Army Radio, by *Maariv*, and most important of all, the *New York Times*. It's on the wires, which means it's everywhere. Other reporters will be after you. The President of the United States has already authorised his spokesman to say he is taking this business very seriously. Thankfully he is spending the weekend at Camp David or somewhere, but tomorrow he will be back in Washington. You have no time to waste. You're ready?'

216

'I guess so.'

'You need to be at Erez by seven forty-five tomorrow morning. Earlier if you can make it. Then – and only then – I think I can get you through. Don't tell anyone about this before you leave, especially not on the phone, and don't call your guy in Gaza until you're on the far side of the security fence. I have taken certain steps to ensure that you don't need any special paperwork, and someone is expecting you. But don't be late, not even by ten minutes. If you are, I am doubtful you'll succeed.'

'Thank you. I'll be there. But why are you doing this, Yitzhak?'

Ben-Meir cut a morsel from his steak, popped it into his mouth and chewed it ruminatively. He took a sip of wine, and avoided Adam's eye. Finally he was ready to speak.

'Because I don't like this business,' he said. 'They can't do anything to me: I'm retired. But I feel used, by a man I'd thought was a friend, and I do not think he was acting with honourable motives. I have no proof of this, Adam. But I've been asking questions, and I've reached a conclusion I find distasteful. I think there is a very specific reason why certain people – Israelis and Americans – may have been acting in the way that they have. I think it is possible that when Morgan went to Gaza two months ago, they knew she was going to be kidnapped.'

'They knew? They fucking knew?' Adam could not stop his voice rising in pitch. 'You mean this has all been a set up?'

'I told you, I don't have proof. But it is possible, yes.'

'But why? Why would anyone do that – deliberately put a loyal officer into harm's way? And with people like that?'

Ben-Meir wore an expression of helplessness. 'I don't know. I cannot imagine an adequate reason. And as I told you, I could be wrong.'

'This old colleague you thought you trusted, the guy who asked you to approach Morgan to make sure she went to Gaza, is he the same Israeli you think knew she would be kidnapped? And does he happen to be called Amos? If so, I've met him.'

217

Ben-Meir gestured apologetically. 'I'm sorry. I've said enough. I can't tell you anything more. Just make sure you're not late at Erez.'

It's evening: in the airless Gazan summer, it feels like the hottest part of the day. Morgan sits on the bed of the same room in which she returned to consciousness after her journey from the farmhouse, the room which has become her current cell. She's sweating, dizzy and dehydrated; her empty water bottle has not been replaced for hours, and her head is beginning once again to throb. She has had no opportunity to wash, and she wears the same grey sweatpants and grey cotton top in which she was forced to travel: she still smells faintly of vomit. For a moment, she fantasises about ice-cold sodas and beer, and then about a long-ago August hike in the Catskills, when feeling as dry as stick insects, she and Adam had peeled off their clothes and bathed naked in a waterfall, followed by a glorious *al fresco* fuck. At least her thirst means she barely needs to urinate: for this, there is still only the bucket. There is nothing to read, nothing to see, and no one else in the room. Noises penetrate from the outside world, but they seem to make no sense. The window is permanently covered by some kind of shutter that she cannot open from the inside, though she senses she is two or three floors above the ground, perhaps in some kind of apartment block. Earlier today she heard strange sounds, as if something heavy was being manhandled behind her locked door up a flight of concrete stairs: there were grunts of effort, and she thought she recognised one of those grunting as Aqil. Just as in the old days, the only person she has seen lately is Zainab, who once again seems to be able to come and go freely. What has become of Karim, Abu Mustafa and Abdel Nasser? She has no idea.

The old normality of her incarceration has been shattered, and the part of her brain that became accustomed to captivity gropes for a new routine. But the part that is still the mind of a trained intelligence officer knows that she is approaching an endgame. Several times during the day, she has heard Israeli

F16s flying low, their roars met with shouts of panic from the streets. An hour ago there was a helicopter, hovering for several minutes seemingly just tens of feet above her head. And there is almost no food: only flatbread and a little hummus. No tea, and nothing hot. The power is off for many hours each day.

She hears at last the only sounds that promise any relief: the key being turned, the heavy bolts on the outside of the door being drawn back.

'Morgan? I am here.' Zainab.

She comes in, Aqil with his Kalashnikov close behind. Zainab is carrying a tray. It seems heavier than usual. With a surge of relief, Morgan sees that Aqil is carrying a new, clean bucket, some toilet paper, and two big bottles of water.

'I have cucumbers,' says Zainab. 'More hummus, olives, dates and bread. This can, is tuna. Here, more water. Now I take bucket. Aqil has new one.' She sets the tray down beside Morgan on the mattress, and takes the impromptu chamber pot. As she bends, her face is momentarily hidden from Aqil. She looks straight at Morgan, grins, nods, and, with extravagant theatricality, she winks.

'Is done,' Zainab whispers. 'What we talk about. Is done.'

Chapter Nineteen
Monday, June 25, 2007

Adam needed no persuading to follow Ben-Meir's instructions. After they had finished their meal, he strolled back to the hotel through Tel Aviv's carefree streets, feeling tempted to call the children: he was likely to be gone for several days, and if anything were to go wrong, at least they would have heard him reassure them of his love. But he knew his communications were almost certainly being monitored, and so sent only a short email to his parents. In this he told a lie: that he planned to visit the US embassy at some point over the next couple of days, and afterwards would decide what to do.

To his surprise, he slept relatively well, then rose at five, slipping out of the hotel with only a light backpack, telling the sleepy receptionist he was going to take a walk. So far as he could ascertain, there was no one following him, but nonetheless he took basic precautions, strolling by a convoluted route to a taxi rank near the seafront. He bought some coffee and a pastry from an all-night kiosk, then woke a dozing driver. As they left the city, the streets were still deserted, and Adam was standing in the Erez parking lot by seven-fifteen. A uniformed IDF officer who had watched him arrive waved at him through the plateglass door of the terminal and unlocked it.

'Mr Cooper?'

'Yes.' There was no one else in the huge, echoing hall. The man took his passport, squinted at it, then unlocked the door to one of the booths with a bunch of keys which hung from a chain. He found a pad and stamped it, handed it back to Adam, and pointed to the door which led to Gaza.

'The CCTV will be off for less than five minutes. Don't look back.' Moments later Adam was in the yard, waiting by the sliding electronic door in the security fence. It opened and

220

he stepped through. This early, there was no one on the far side: no sign of the usual gaggle of drivers and hungry-looking porters. He strode down the walkway alone, and across the sandy wasteland beyond. Finally he reached the wooden shack that served as the Palestinian border checkpoint. A small group of armed Hamas militiamen dressed in blue fatigues stood by while one of their colleagues unlocked it. As Adam approached, one of them walked towards him, weapon at the ready.

'*Amriki?*' he said. '*Sahafi?* Journalist?'

'Yes, I have an American passport,' Adam said. The man beckoned him towards the shack, where a new printed sign warned that any alcohol discovered in luggage would be poured away on the spot. High above, invisible, Adam recognised the buzzing of an Israeli drone.

'You are early,' the Hamas militiaman said. 'Border is closed. How you come at this time?'

'I have, er, an appointment,' said Adam, ignoring the man's question. 'Please, I must call my friend, Khader Abu Fares.'

The Hamas man sounded impressed. 'You know Doctor Khader? You have his number?'

With a momentary stab of panic, Adam realised the only number he knew was the one that Bashir had given to him weeks earlier at their unfortunate encounter in Lod. Fortunately, he still remembered it. He reached for his phone, but the border guard offered his.

'Please. You can try.'

Adam punched in the numbers, and Khader answered almost immediately. As soon as Adam identified himself, he was effusive.

'Adam! *Habibi*! Welcome back to Gaza! You wait there ten minutes. I am sending a driver for you. I think this is a great piece of luck that you have come today. It is an excellent time for your visit.'

In less than twenty minutes, a black SUV with tinted windows was racing up the road towards them. It stopped beside the shack. Another man in blue fatigues emerged, opened one of the passenger doors, and motioned for Adam to get in.

Every trace of the anarchic chaos which had been so visible during his last visit had disappeared. There were no roadblocks, and despite the three-wheelers and the pony carts, the morning traffic moved smoothly. Along the road there were stalls, selling dusty fruit and vegetables, and bread shops with orderly queues. They passed a line of teenage girls on their way to school, neat in their dark blue uniforms and gleaming, white headscarves. Soon the vehicle was easing through the gates of a high-walled compound. It stopped at the entrance to a three-storey building, with a broad covered porch and a portico framed by bougainvillea. A sign stated that Adam was entering the headquarters of the Palestinian Authority Preventive Security Organisation. The description, he mused, was out of date: according to the news media, all the Preventive Security Organisation's members in Gaza were dead, in jail, or at home, having been fired and disarmed by the Gaza Strip's new rulers. Khader, who was also wearing the ubiquitous blue fatigues, was standing by the doors to welcome him. As Adam got out, he embraced him warmly.

'Come. We will go to my office. I have news.'

They climbed a pale marble staircase, then turned left along a corridor. There was a sense of bustle: officials came and went along the corridor and in and out of its offices, some in uniform, others in pressed trousers and smart, short-sleeved shirts. Most were clutching files. Towards the corridor's end, Khader opened the door to an anteroom and bid Adam go in front of him. He paused to exchange a few words with his assistant, a young woman in a long-sleeved dark grey dress and headscarf, then led Adam into a spacious office with air conditioning, a hardwood desk, a new computer and a large-scale map of Gaza pinned to the wall. Two black leather sofas and an armchair were arranged around a coffee table.

'You will take coffee or tea?'

Adam asked for tea with mint.

Khader gave orders to the assistant through the open door.

'Nice office,' Adam said.

'I think it has been built with the generosity of European Union taxpayers,' Khader said. 'So, thanks to them for that, and thanks to God you are here, anyhow.'

While they waited for the tea, Khader inquired after the children, and how Adam had been coping. When their drinks arrived, he stood, and closed the door.

'*Yalla*. So.' He looked up at Adam and fixed him with his dark brown eyes, smiling triumphantly. 'Our intelligence staff have been busy. Since we have restored order, we have checked many leads, many sources of information. The power of the criminals collaborators with the Zionist entity who controlled the place where we sit has been smashed. The people feel safe again, and they trust us. Because of that, they are happy to give us information. This is the reason that we now know much more about the *Janbiya al-Islam*. We know the name of their leader. It is Karim Musleh. He is a very dangerous man, and he has fought in Afghanistan, the Balkans and Chechnya. As I told you before, he is a *takfiri*: he believes that people who do not agree with him are not Muslims, and can be killed with impunity. We also know his deputy: he is a Jordanian Palestinian. His name is Abu Mustafa. And here is the best news. We know where they are holding your wife. I hope you are ready, because we are planning to free her very soon. Tonight.'

Morgan has spent half the night brooding on her conversation with Zeinab. Now, as she wonders whether she really has managed to set in train the events that may lead to a rescue, she hears a sound through the wall, a cross between a gasp and a whimper, as if an errant pet has been struck a cruel and unexpected blow. The thin masonry barely muffles what follows: thumps on the floor, the footfalls of someone trying but failing to get away from an assailant, the rattle of a door handle which has been locked, and a succession of yelps, first of anger, and then, unmistakeably of pain. There is sobbing, and Zainab's voice shouting in Arabic: as before, Morgan catches the word *haram*. A chair or some other piece of furniture is

223

knocked over, a booming vibration that makes the floor of her own room shake, and something else heavy falls to the floor: a softer impact this time, that of a human body. A guttural male voice yells, and increasingly, its owner sounds out of breath; it's the voice of someone who doesn't keep in shape, and relies on sheer bulk. It must be Aqil. She makes out a few more words: '*sharmoutah*,' the Arabic term for 'bitch,' spat out with terrifying venom, and *bint himaar*, 'daughter of a donkey.' He follows them with something worse: now he's calling Zainab *khoos umk*, 'your mother's cunt,' a phrase as taboo in Arabic as it is in American, and barking an order: *kol eyri*, 'eat my dick.'

This last evokes an anguished protest. Morgan hears the sound of another blow, and then a piercing scream. Thus far, none of these sounds transmitted across the lathe and plaster barrier which separates her from Zainab and Aqil has had any kind of pattern. They've been the sounds of a ragged, uneven attack. Now, however, they become more rhythmic. The man stops speaking, and his grunts are deeper, more visceral. As well as effort, there is pleasure in them, a gleeful slavering as the noises emerge: he is enjoying himself. Morgan imagines him sweating, his dirty breath and yellow teeth in Zainab's face, and she trembles as she hears Zainab's shrieks mount in their pitch and intensity.

Finally they find a rhythm. She is screaming now with all the air in her lungs, a metronomic, disembodied ululation, four high Cs to the bar, a hundred beats to the minute, *allegro fortissimo*, a song of pain and desperation. The blood rushes to Morgan's head. She cannot simply sit here while Zainab is raped. Whatever it takes, she must do what she can to stop this happening.

She starts by banging and kicking on the locked door, careless of her safety or the consequences. Let the neighbours hear her yelling in English: it can't make anything worse. 'Let me out, you motherfuckers! I am telling you, let me out! You call yourselves Muslims and you let this bastard commit rape, so stop, stop, stop, right now! This is *haram*. Let me out!' Nothing happens, and Zainab's cries continue, more distressing than ever. Aqil sounds as if he is close to his climax, and Morgan turns her attention to the wall. Picking up a chair, she begins to batter it, in the hope she will break it down. She sees the first layers flake, and she batters it again with redoubled strength: in less than a minute, she thinks, she will be through. With more blows, she feels it beginning to give. She swings the chair again and again, gasping with the effort; for a moment she pauses for breath. Zainab's screaming has stopped. Then the door is flung open, a shadow fills her horizon, and someone pounds her head with a rifle butt. The darkness is instantaneous.

When she comes to, she is lying on the floor, her hands bound tightly in front of her. With a stab of shame she realises she has soiled herself: her legs are wet, and there is the sharp smell of urine. Karim is standing over her. In one hand he holds a pistol, in the other three white tablets – a triple dose of sleeping pills.

'You sit,' he says.

She obeys, struggling to wrest herself upright.

'Now listen. I don't worry if you die. But you make this noise, is dangerous for me. You take this, or I kill you now. You will sleep.'

She takes the tablet from him. At least it's not another injection. She wonders whether she can only pretend to swallow it, but after handing her a bottle of water, Karim first watches as she takes a gulp, then forces her jaws open and inspects the inside of her mouth. He leaves and locks the door. As the minutes pass, she feels unconsciousness return.

When she finally awakes, she feels groggy and disoriented. There is no electricity, and outside the light has almost gone. But through the gloom, she sees that a belt-fed heavy machine gun on a black steel tripod has been dragged into the room and placed by the window. Her head throbs, both at the front and on one side: a combination of dehydration and the effects of the blow. The pain in her temple is sharp, and when she moves her jaw she cries out involuntarily: she prays her skull has not been fractured. She looks to the corner and she sees is not alone. Watching her wake is Abu Mustafa, the whites of his

225

eyes gleaming orbs. He moves across the room towards her, his motion almost silent.

'Are you okay?' he asks, softly.

'What the fuck do you care?' She feels her arms cramp. 'Can you at least untie my hands? These plastic cuffs are really tight, and I feel as if the circulation to my hands is being cut off. And give me some water?'

'I am sorry. I am truly sorry for what has happened.' He is whispering. 'You must know what I think. You surely recognise that I am not a barbarian. Aqil is an animal, and his behaviour disgusts me.' He grimaces, then helps her sit, unscrews the top from a bottle of water, and holds it to her lips. She drinks thirstily. He offers an arm, and she staggers to sit on the couch.

'I am sorry, but I cannot untie you. Karim will be back. Aqil is just outside. But Morgan, please, we must talk. We do not have much time.'

All afternoon and well into the evening, Adam has waited at Khader's headquarters, mostly on his own, in some kind of common room. A television fixed high on a wall plays Aljazeera in Arabic, and from time to time Khader's assistant brings him tea. He has nothing to read, so he has nothing to do but fret. At six o'clock, two men in uniform who speak almost no English took him down a corridor to the building's Spartan canteen, where they ate hummus, a finely-chopped salad, cold flatbread and chicken. Afterwards, Adam returned to the common room, where he snatched a nap on the couch. At around nine o'clock, Khader reappears. He is carrying a map and other papers. He sits down, and spreads the map out on a low table.

'I'm sorry I had to leave you alone for so long,' he says. 'But I know you will understand. We are planning our operation. *Insh'Allah*, in just a few hours, we will be celebrating success here together with your wife.'

'*Insh'Allah*. So tell me. What are we planning to do?'

'We? I do not think you can come with us. It could be dangerous. You should wait here.'

226

'No.' Adam is firm, insistent. 'I'm not going to do that, Khader. I've come this far, and I'm not going to back out now. And anyway, if I'm with you guys, when Morgan sees me, she'll know this is a rescue operation, not another attempted kidnap. My presence could really help. Who knows? Maybe she'll get some chance to escape.' Adam smiles. 'And besides, since you and I last met, I've had some shooting practice. Give me a gun, Khader. I know how to use it.'

Khader cannot stop the grin that spreads across his face, and he clasps Adam's hand in the Palestinian fashion, with wrists crossing: a gesture of solidarity. 'Okay, *habibi*. You will come. Welcome!'

'So what's the plan?'

'Soon we will travel south, first to Khan Younis, where I will hold a briefing, and then to Rafah, where your wife is being held.' Khader points to the map. 'She is in the Yebna refugee camp, in an apartment block. It is on the southern edge, right by the Wall and the border with Egypt.' He unfolds a larger-scale chart. 'The Wall is here, and the building is here – less than two hundred metres from the frontier. When we get into position, you will be able to see the houses in Egyptian Rafah, on the far side of the Wall. And on the Gaza side, between the Wall and the apartment building, it is open ground.'

Kahder's finger stabs the chart: 'Here, right in the middle of the open area, you can see there is a little shack. It has been constructed above the opening of one of the tunnels that run beneath the Wall. Beneath it is a vertical shaft, with a winch for the smugglers to bring up their goods. Before we move in, we will secure it. We cannot take the risk of giving the kidnappers any chance of moving Morgan to Egypt, because there we cannot operate: the Egyptian army is no friend of Hamas. I think it is better that you wait there with a few of my men. You will be able to see what is happening, and when it is safe, you can come.'

'Okay. If you insist.'

'We believe they will have at least ten men in the apartment building, maybe more. I do not know where they have

227

come from, but in the past few days, there have been more: reinforcements. They must have arrived through the tunnels. They have a heavy machine gun, as well as an RPG launcher, grenades and Kalashnikovs. But the kidnappers will not be expecting us. We will attack at five tomorrow morning. Probably they will have a guard keeping watch, but at that time only he will be awake. *Insh'Allah*, when the others wake up and realise they have no chance, they will surrender.'

'You really think that's possible? Won't they reach for their guns and fight? Don't they want to become *shahids*?'

Khader shrugs. 'If they wish to die, we are ready to assist them.'

'So how's it going to work? I mean, you're not going to be able to just walk in.'

'We will have three teams. The first will make a cordon around the building. That will stop them escaping. The second team will use a ladder to get across this gap' – again Khader points to his map – 'from the roof of the next building. They will cross the gap, and come down to the kidnappers' apartment from the roof. There is a stairwell, and Morgan is on the highest floor. The third group will climb the stairs from the ground. The apartment next to the kidnappers' is empty, but there is a locked door connecting them. They will smash their way through it at the same moment that the others come down from the roof.'

Adam whistled softly. 'But what about Morgan? There's going to be a lot of smoke, and it will be dark. How are you going to make sure that she isn't killed?'

'We will do our best, and put our trust in God. We have no choice.' Khader removes a handgun from his waistband and hands it to Adam.

'You say you know how to shoot,' Khader says. 'But you are not experienced in combat, so I will give you just one magazine. It is for emergencies.'

It's so dark now that Morgan can make out only shapes. Abu Mustafa takes a small, squat candle from his pocket, places it on the table, and lights it. Its light is feeble, but at least Morgan can see his face. She's still on the couch: he's sitting on a chair, facing her, the flame casting flickering shadows. 'Before you say another word, I want to know what has happened to Zainab,' she says in a whisper.

'She is alive. I hope she will be okay.'

'What do you mean, you hope she'll be okay?' Morgan's voice is rising again, as her anger surges. 'Are you out of your mind? She was raped! Has she seen a doctor? What else did that bastard do to her?'

Abu Mustafa looks helpless, his eyes registering defeat. 'Karim has let her go. She has gone to Khan Younis. *Insh'Allah* her people will take care of her.'

'You mean she's gone to her mom and dad? What the hell is she going to say to them? But I don't understand. Why has Karim let her go? Surely, the first thing she'll do is give away our location.'

Abu Mustafa touches Morgan's shoulder, and she twists away from him, shuddering involuntarily.

'Please. Don't be disgusted with me,' he says. 'I am not like Aqil and Karim. And however angry you may feel, you must not raise your voice. There are things I must tell you, but if we are disturbed it will not be possible. So listen. Zainab has already given away our location. Letting her go will make no difference. It is because she betrayed him that Karim told Aqil to punish her.'

'How did she do it?' Morgan asks. 'When?'

'When she left to buy food, she went to the house of a cousin who is a member of Hamas, and she told him everything. But Karim has his own network: people from his clan, people he trusts. One of Karim's tribe is an officer in the Hamas *mukhabarat*. He sent Karim a message. I don't know how. He told him Zainab had betrayed him, and that soon, almost certainly tonight, this building will be attacked.'

For a moment, Morgan is speechless, struck dumb by guilt and remorse. It is she who encouraged Zainab to give away

229

Karim's secret, and she who is responsible for her pain and humiliation. She feels the prickle of tears. 'So why didn't he just kill her?'

'He beat her, like before, to try to make her confess, but she said nothing. That's when he gave her to Aqil. Afterwards he let her live because he believed that to stay alive would be worse.'

'Jesus. You people are evil.' Morgan still speaks softly, but with fury. 'You, Abu Mustafa, you say you are different, but you have contaminated yourself by associating with Karim: you are tainted, stained, *haram*. And you know what? I hope that when Hamas does storm this building, that you get what's coming to you. I hope they shoot you and take you prisoner, or maybe torture you before they let you die. You and all of the rest of them. As for this conversation: we're done.' She twists and faces the wall.

But Abu Mustafa isn't done. In a voice of weariness, in measured, trembling words, he carries on speaking, addressing himself to her back through the sultry darkness.

'I know I will probably die tonight,' Abu Mustafa says, 'and I do not relish the prospect. But please. You must listen. I don't have much time. Maybe you have guessed this already. I am a Jordanian intelligence officer. I have a wife and family in Amman, and everything I told you about missing them so badly is true. And before anything more, I want to say I am so, so sorry for what has happened. I apologise, to you and your family, from the bottom of my heart. But also please believe me when I say that I never thought this operation would go so wrong.'

'Operation?' Her mouth is arid, her eyes wide. 'Operation? You're a Jordanian agent and you're telling me that this has all been some kind of operation?' She turns to face him again, hyperventilating. She can't keep the bitterness from her voice: 'What do you mean, Abu Mustafa? What fucking operation?'

'My assignment for more than a decade has been to infiltrate the extremists – not Hamas, but the crazy people, the *taqfiri*, like Karim. We began to suspect there were links between what some call al-Qaeda and radical Palestinian groups many years

230

ago. I went in search of them. I travelled to Chechnya, and that's where I first met Karim.'

'And? How did I come into this? Where do I fit in?'

'My agency was working with an Israeli colleague. His first name is Amos: that's all I know. I don't know whose idea all this was originally, but I heard it from him. Anyhow, it started with the clashes between Fatah and Hamas. He and his American friends wanted to help Fatah defeat their rivals, just as we did. We all gave them help, guns and training. But that wasn't enough. We needed a way to push President Abbas and the rest of the Fatah leadership politically, to exert enough pressure to make them act. So they asked me to go to Gaza, to reconnect with Karim, and to persuade him to kidnap an American. The original plan was that after a little time, maybe a couple of weeks, she – that is, you – would be released. Once you were free, and safely out of Gaza, America would have told Abbas that your abduction proved the chaos had become too much, that the time had come to use his forces to restore order. You could say your release was meant to be the signal for a Fatah coup. All the Hamas leaders would have been arrested, and their organisation destroyed. It was Amos who recommended you as the victim, by the way, though he told me you worked for the State Department, not the Agency.'

'You're losing me, Abu Mustafa,' Morgan says. 'You might have helped arrange my abduction, but how the hell did you intend to make sure that I was released?'

'Because Karim was in on it, too. He didn't know – he must never know – that I work for the Jordanians. But he knew all about my links with Amos, and he even met him. Three times Amos arranged for us both to pass through Erez. He gave us lunch in Ashkelon, and he and Karim made a deal. In return for carrying out the operation in the way I have described, Karim's little group, the *Janbiya al-Islam*, would be given money, far more money than he had ever dreamt of. About two hundred thousand dollars. Half upfront, and half to be paid after you were freed.'

231

'He kidnapped me for money? That was all he was interested in? I don't believe it.'

'It wasn't his only motivation. The plan always was that we would force you to make a video. You wouldn't have been tortured, but you would have begged for your life, begged the Americans to take the necessary steps to ensure your release. The film would have been shown on television across the world. It would have added to the pressure on Fatah and Abbas, but also given Karim what he craves most. He wants to be a famous a global jihadist, a *mujahid* in the same league as bin Laden. This would have helped him get there.'

Morgan's comprehension dawns. 'So he agreed to all this without knowing who I was. But then he recognised me, and he realised I wasn't merely a CIA officer, but the very woman he blamed for the death of Khalid. And from that moment, all bets were off.'

'Yes. But he didn't tell me, and he didn't tell Amos. But the truth is, I think he'd known for months. Amos had given him video equipment to bug the apartment where you used to meet Abdel Nasser. Karim used to collect the memory chips after you'd been there, and somehow he got the films to Amos: I'm not sure how, but maybe electronically. I guess he must have watched the videos and recognised you from them. Anyhow, a little while before your last visit, Amos promised he would tell us when you were coming next. He said Fatah was now strong enough to carry out its coup. You would arrive, and then we would pounce.'

'So what about Abdel Nasser's bodyguards? And his driver, Akram? Those poor bastards had families too. They were just ordinary guys from Gaza, and you had them shot. You had Abdel Nasser maimed. Was that also part of the scenario?'

'No. That was Karim and Aqil. They changed the plan without telling me. They were supposed to overpower them, but to leave them alone. I'm pretty sure they kidnapped Abdel Nasser for a reason. Karim suspected that you might not break, but if he threatened to kill Abdel Nasser in front of you, then you would start to confess. Well, he was right.'

Morgan shakes her head. 'I just don't know what to say. This "operation," as you call it, is the most fucked-up thing I've ever heard of. It's insane, criminal, deranged, and whoever dreamt it up deserves to be indicted. Jesus.'

Abu Mustafa looks wretched. 'I realise now how stupid it was. And I have paid a very high price. But you know, I never even thought about it going wrong until the moment Karim said he recognised you from Yugoslavia, and that he knew you were CIA. He didn't do that until the day before you were due to arrive, but he told me then that you were his chance to avenge the death of Khalid. I guess he was so excited, he couldn't keep it to himself.'

'He told you that? So why didn't you get a message to Amos? Explain what had happened, and tell him the plan was off?'

Abu Mustafa's voice is mournful. 'This has troubled me more than anything. As soon as Karim told me, I knew the operation had to be aborted: that the promises he had made to guarantee your safety would be broken. At that point, before the kidnap, we were still using cellphones, and so I did call Amos. He promised he would, as he put it, "act appropriately." You had been expected the following day, March 27, but you didn't show up. I assumed Amos had closed the border, and that everything was cancelled. I began to think about going back to Amman. But then, two days later, you did come. Karim had said we should keep on watching, and so as soon as you arrived, we were ready. It took me by surprise. There was nothing I could do without blowing my cover. But you see what I'm saying? Amos aborted the operation, but only for forty-eight hours. He put it on hold, but then someone decided it was on again.'

'Well if you couldn't stop the kidnap, why didn't you tell Amos where I was once it had happened, so that he could organise a rescue?'

'A little while later, I got a chance to call him again. I had hidden a phone for emergencies. But Amos's number had been disconnected. I tried three more times, but I could never get through.'

233

Morgan swallows hard. Her head is throbbing again, more painfully than before, and she feels utterly exhausted. 'Sweet Jesus. So whoever was controlling this fucked-up mess thought about it for a while, and then determined he not only wanted me kidnapped, but to stay kidnapped. Well, he got his wish. And here we are.'

'Yes. Here we are. Can I get you anything?'

'More water.'

Abu Mustafa puts the bottle to her lips.

'Thank you. And soon I'm going to need a trip to the ladies' room.'

'You probably understand something else now.'

'What's that, Abu Mustafa?'

'I was always trying to protect you. Even when you were being waterboarded, I was doing my best to keep you alive. Karim did want you to confess, but part of him really wanted you to die. But every time you lost consciousness, I made him stop. And afterwards, when he left questioning you to me, I wasn't really trying to interrogate you. I wanted to make it all last as long as possible, in the hope that someone would find us.'

'Well, gee, thanks, Abu Mustafa. You did a super job there.'

'That's not all. You must have noticed: Karim has been away a lot. He always knew it would not be safe to keep you in Gaza for very long, even before the Hamas coup. Once he had made the video, he had his calling card: his proof he had a CIA prisoner. So he went through the tunnels, to Sinai. He hooked up with jihadi groups in Egypt, people he knows who come from Yemen. I don't know where he plans to take you now, but I know he has a vehicle waiting for him. It all took a lot of organising. He had to make several trips. Wherever it is that you're going, that's where he plans to conduct your real interrogation. He knows I've got nowhere with you. He thinks I'm soft. Maybe he doesn't trust me.'

'So now he's going to spirit me away and torture me some more, then probably kill me. No doubt, he'll do it all on video.'

'That does seem possible.'

'Why the hell didn't you tell me all this weeks ago? We could have figured out some way to escape. We could have been working together. That would have given us a better fucking chance than we seem to have now.'

'Yes. It would have done.' His voice sounds sadder than ever. 'I was trying to preserve my cover, pathetic as that sounds. And also I was scared of Karim. He understands much more English than you think. He might have heard us talking, or bugged our conversations. If I had revealed myself to you then, he might easily have killed us both.'

'So now what? I'm tied up, awaiting an attack that will probably kill us anyway. And if I do survive, I'll be taken somewhere even worse. And where is Abdel Nasser? What the fuck has happened to him?'

'I am sorry once again. I do not know where Abdel Nasser is. And I do not know how to protect you. If I get the chance, I will try to kill Karim. But also let me give you some advice. When the shooting starts, keep your head down.'

Chapter Twenty
Tuesday, June 26, 2007

Adam has synchronised his watch with Khader's, and now he checks it again for the hundredth time since leaving Khan Younis. It's still only four-thirty. It already feels like the longest night of his life, but there are still thirty minutes before the attack is due to begin. The cordon is in place, with the apartment building at its centre. A squat, four-storey concrete structure, its pale outline shimmers in the light of a three-quarters moon. He hunches in the shadow of the flimsy shack which protects the winch above the tunnel shaft, feeling grateful for the buzz of the insects, for they hide the noise of his rapid, shallow breathing. Rafiq, the cordon team leader, a junior officer with a well-trimmed beard in his early twenties, crouches to Adam's left. There's a gentle breeze and it's pleasantly warm: about the same temperature as a summer day in England. Over there, later today, will be the second day of Wimbledon. For a moment, Adam diverts himself with the thought that, as ever, his mother will be glued to the TV coverage, and is sure to try to share her passion with the kids.

Behind the apartment block lies Yebna, a warren of rough, box-like dwellings, most of them thrown up to house the flood of Palestinian refugees who fled from Israel in 1948, when Gaza was still part of Egypt. Khader's drivers parked their trucks at a soccer field well beyond its perimeter, and Adam has accompanied his men's advance from there, the sandy floors of Yebna's alleys muffling their steps. Most of the Hamas soldiers carry only AK47s, though a few have heavier, more specialised equipment. None of them wear body armour. They seem well-drilled, and so far as Adam can make out, they are also highly motivated. Lit by the moon, their blue fatigues look grey. Most have put on some kind of camouflage paint, deepening their faces from brown to black. Not a building, not a street lamp, is lit.

236

More minutes pass, and Adam watches as the second team occupies the roof of a second building of similar height, just to the left of the block which supposedly contains Morgan. He silently repeats her name. Is she really there in front of him, less than two hundred feet away, behind those nondescript walls? What will she look like? What kind of shape, physical and mental, will she be in? Will he even recognise her, and what will he say? He has no answers.

Yet Adam feels as if everything he's done for the past three months has been impelling him towards this moment. He's barely tried to figure out why his need to be present is so overwhelming, and he knows that it's a little late to be recognising that he may be running an enormous risk: if he ends up losing his own life, many will call him irresponsible. But something inside him insists it is vital that he's here, not only to bear witness, but to help, though he cannot even dimly guess what such help might be.

On the roof, the moonshadows blur the men's silhouettes. Still working in silence, they are bolting together the sections of a ladder. Crossing from one building to another will take a steady nerve: it must be more than seventy feet from the flat roof's edge to the ground. At last their bridge is complete. It slopes downhill: the roof of the kidnapper's building must be somewhat lower down. The first man's journey is the most precarious, but once he's over, he holds the ladder for his companions, and one by one they crawl across. Adam counts them over. He hopes this isn't an omen: they are thirteen.

Can Khader's confidence that the kidnappers know nothing about the impending attack really be justified? His plan seems so elaborate, and Adam is amazed that the roof team seems to have reached its objective without disturbing anybody's sleep. Yet thus far, everything has been unrolling smoothly. The only movement he can see is from the Hamas men, and there is no sign that anyone else in Yebna is awake. Just a few more minutes, and as his new friends say, *insh'Allah* it will all be over.

Some of the men on the roof gather around the half-enclosed portal that marks the top of the stairwell, while the others take up positions along the parapet, scanning the gloom as they clutch their Kalashnikovs, like archers on a medieval castle's battlements. Adam checks his watch once again: four forty-five. Across the open ground, he sees the last of Khader's teams emerge from the alley behind the building and enter by the double front doors, altogether nine of them. The doors don't even squeak, and furtive as cats, the men vanish inside. Presumably now they're starting to climb the stairs. It shouldn't take them long to reach the apartment next to the kidnappers.

For a moment, the breeze increases in strength, sighing through the loose-fitting timbers of the shack and making them rattle. It makes Adam start. Apart from might have been a couple of shots just after they arrived, it's the loudest sound he's heard since leaving Khan Younis. He looks at his watch a final time and braces himself. Ninety seconds to go. The next thing he expects to hear is the sound of the stun grenades the men at the front of the two entry parties are carrying.

But it isn't.

There is an explosion: not inside the building, but, so it seems, on or just below the roof. Its blast wave catches Adam in the solar plexus like an undefended hook from a professional heavyweight, crushing his ribs against his lungs, while the boom scours his eardrums. It feels as if he's lost a layer of cells somewhere inside his head: the world is muffled, his entire sense of being knocked off balance. He looks at Rafiq. His eyes reflect his own shock and panic, while little by little Adam grasps that screams are now echoing across Yebna.

At first, the roof is hidden by smoke. Atomised debris, hurled up into the atmosphere, is starting to fall, accompanied by the barbecue stench of burnt human flesh. When the cloud starts to clear, it becomes apparent that the blast must have been carried upwards from somewhere inside the stairwell: the portal structure on the roof has been completely destroyed. Up there, no one is still standing. Adam assumes the men who poured down the stairs

238

must all be dead or horribly injured. So far as he can make out, two or three of the parapet sentries look as if they may still be alive. He sees one crawl away from the edge. Up there, nothing else moves.

It's been an eternal thirty seconds since the blast when Rafiq, suddenly jolted from his marble immobility, grabs his arm and issues contradictory instructions. 'Down! Mr Adam, get down! We are under attack! We must run!'

But nothing else happens. No one attacks, and no one fires a weapon. The tinnitus in Adam's ears is beginning to clear, and the screaming is becoming less muffled. He looks at Rafiq and pulls him to his feet. 'Come on!' he shouts. 'We must get in there! We need to know what's happening – and what they have done with my wife!'

Rafiq hesitates, his eyes still round with terror. Finally he beckons to the men on either side in the cordon. Adam draws his gun, and they advance towards the doors. He slides back the safety catch. It's not a Walther like the weapon he used at the range in Buckinghamshire, but a silver Smith and Wesson nine millimetre automatic.

Inside the lobby there is chaos. All or most of the apartments' occupants are already there or making their way down the stairs in their nightclothes: a panicking sea of children, babies, mothers, fathers and the elderly, shouting in Arabic, unsure whether they should be going outside or staying where they are, fearful of further danger. Where is Khader? Adam remembers that he wasn't with the rooftop group, but with the team who climbed from the lobby. Finally he sees him, struggling to deal with a trio of men who yell and jab their fingers, demanding answers which he cannot begin to give. Only four of the men who had been in his group are with him: the other five are missing, as well as all those who were on the roof.

Adam yells at him. 'Khader! Get everyone outside!' The building may be unsafe, it could collapse, and there may still be terrorists.'

Khader's uniform is dark with blood, but so far as Adam can see, it is not his own: he must have been protected by the men in front of him, and it was they who absorbed the full force of the blast. He staggers a little: he's dazed. But he accepts Adam's instructions, and somehow produces the first semblance of control, barking orders at Rafiq and the other Hamas men in the lobby, so getting everyone on to the wasteground by the tunnel outside. He tells two of the young militiamen to begin a search of the apartments to make sure everyone is out, though to go no higher than the third floor. Finally he steps outside, away from the noise and tumult. He takes out his cellphone, and, Adam guesses, calls to summon help. At last the evacuation is complete, and Adam joins him in front of the building.

'In a few minutes there will be a fire truck, and ambulances,' Khader says, his words coming in gasps. 'It was an IED. They left a tripwire at the bottom of the stairs going up to the roof, attached to a hand grenade. That was taped to a shell from a mortar. The wire went tight on someone's leg as they came down the stairs. It pulled the pin out. The grenade triggered the mortar shell. I was at the back. We were just climbing up. Four of the others are okay. I think all the others are dead.'

Khader's words sound more like sobs. 'I have not seen a bomb like this before in Gaza. It is like the bombs that al-Qaeda make in Iraq.' He pauses, momentarily overcome. 'And now they have killed so many Muslims.'

'What about Morgan? Where's Morgan? Khader, have you been into the apartment where she was being held?' Adam can't stop his own surge of panic. 'Was she caught in this? Is she dead too?'

'I have not entered he apartment. I was trying to get those who are not hurt down here safely. I am sorry. Now we will go to see. I have a flashlight.'

Followed by Rafiq and four of his men, they start to climb the stairs, their weapons at the ready. Even from the lobby, Adam hears men's groans floating down from above. Only Khader has a light, and behind him, the darkness is suffocating: they must navigate by touch. When they reach the second floor, the hard stone surface of the steps becomes wet. It's only the beginning of a sticky cataract of blood, a stream of gore from the shredded men higher up, who were caught by the brunt of the explosion.

Higher still, the fading moonlight and the first dawn glimmer deliver more illumination. The roof around the top of the stairwell has been blown out, leaving a crater with the top tier of stairs balanced precariously against its lip. On the third floor, right at the bottom of the next flight of stairs, two of the men from Khader's party lie motionless, apparently blown down bodily by the blast wave: they have no visible injuries. On the floor above, one flight of stairs below the roof, they reach the place where the bomb must have been situated. Here another seven or eight have been killed outright. Adam sees a scalp, with hair still attached; a hand; a blown-off lower leg. The bodies dam the blood collecting between them in pools, several inches deep, the springs where the cascade on the stairs begins. Saying nothing, Khader gestures to Rafiq that he should check the roof. From somewhere up there, Adam makes out a word being spoken by someone in terrible agony: '*ummu*,' 'mother.' There's something wooden up there too, and it smells as if it is burning.

Khader points beyond the bodies to the door of one of the fourth-floor apartments. The design of the landing is L-shaped, protecting it from the blast. 'This is the one,' he says. He starts to turn the handle.

At once a voice yells from behind the door in Arabic and English: '*Kef!*,' 'stop!'

Khader and Adam exchange glances. Khader lets fly a stream of invective in his own language, then gets a lengthy reply.

'He says there is another IED in the apartment,' Khader says. 'The tripwire is behind the door.' He yells up the stairwell to Rafiq, whose face appears at the edge of the roof crater. He tosses down a Swiss army penknife.

'We must cut the wire and make it safe. These scissors will be enough,' Khader says. 'The guy on the other side says it is made with dental floss. I think he's telling the truth. I have heard they use this when they are in a hurry.'

241

'For fuck's sake do it gently,' Adam says. Involuntarily he holds his breath while Khader opens the door. Thankfully it swings outwards. Khader bends down, pulls out the scissors from the penknife, and snips the white thread.

'You can come in.'

Adam follows him, holding his gun in front of him with both hands, waving it from side to side to cover the room, just as he's seen at the movies. The blinds at the windows are open, and outside the sky is turning from black to blue. In the middle of the room is a fortification made of sandbags, the nest for a heavy machine gun. The weapon remains unused. Besides himself and Khader, the room has just one other occupant, a sallow, bearded man in early middle age, who wears a stained, white *jallabiya*. He lies slumped against the wall, next to the IED. Blood oozes from exit wounds in both of his kneecaps. Judging by the quantity he's already lost, he must have been shot some time ago. He raises a hand in a pained and weary greeting.

'Welcome,' he says. 'My name is Abu Mustafa. You must be Adam Cooper. I have heard a lot about you. I am sorry. I'm so sorry for everything. Mrs Cooper is not here.'

'What have you bastards done with her? Where is she? What the hell has happened?'

'She is okay. She is alive, and she is not hurt, but they have taken her. Karim, Aqil and the others.' Abu Mustafa grimaces. 'They have all gone.'

'Taken her where?'

'To Egypt. Through the tunnel. I tried to stop them. I was going to shoot them with the machine gun but Karim was too quick. I think he had overheard me talking to your wife. He rushed into the room when I was not ready and held a gun to my head, while one of his men put bullets in my legs. Then I watched while they took Morgan, and they put the bombs by the stairs and the door to this apartment. They knew you were coming. Karim has a source in the Hamas *mukhabarat*. He knew you would try to attack from the roof. H~ ~as fr~ ~~

242

waiting on the Egyptian side in Rafah. I think they are Yemenis. They have a truck. I don't know where they will go.'

'The tunnel? How did they get her to the tunnel?' Adam is incredulous. 'It's out there, in the open ground, and the Hamas guys have been guarding it. I was there with them. Before that, they were watching it for hours. They can't have gone that way.'

Abu Mustafa shakes his head. Each time he speaks, it takes a greater effort. 'Not through the tunnel outside. That is for smuggling, for business. There is another one. Inside this building. Smaller. The opening is in the basement. Karim's clan. They live here. They made it. Please – I need water. There is a bottle.'

Khader brings it, unscrews the top and puts it to Abu Mustafa's lips. He takes a mouthful, sighs heavily, and it seems to revive him. He speaks up again, his voice stronger, as if he just remembered something. 'They have Abdel Nasser too.'

'Abdel Nasser?'

'Her Palestinian contact.'

So Morgan is with her lover. Even at this moment of crisis, Adam is assailed by emotions he had almost forgotten about: pain and jealousy. 'I know who he is,' he says thickly.

'They were keeping him in another apartment. I did not know he was here until just before they left. He is sick. Very bad smell. They shot his legs before, when they captured him. If Morgan will not talk to Karim, he will cut off his head. Before, when she made the video, he had a knife and threatened him. That is why she confessed.'

'When did they leave? How much head start do they have?'

'Not long. I am not sure, but I think less than one hour.'

'And you? Where do you fit in to all this?'

'I am nothing.' Abu Mustafa sounds utterly defeated. 'I want to go home. I have had enough. I want to go home. Amman.' His voice is fading again, and he looks as if he's starting to lose consciousness. He closes his eyes but his lips are still moving, and Adam strains to listen above the mounting tumult coming from outside: sirens, more shouts, the sounds of diesel vehicles

243

being driven at speed and then stopping. In a momentary lull he realises that Abu Mustafa is muttering the names of his wife and children, talking to them quietly in Arabic, as if they are here with him.

'Khader, we must get this man help. Whoever he is, he does not deserve to die.'

Khader nods. 'I will tell my men to make sure they give him first aid and take him to the hospital. But I have to tell you that right now, he is not at the top of my list of priorities.'

Back in the lobby, what must be the door to the stairs which lead to the basement is right in front of them, opposite the main opening on to the ground outside. There, Adam can see that two ambulances have already arrived from Rafah and Khan Younis, along with several trucks and SUVs – Hamas militia reinforcements. Men are pouring into the lobby and climbing the stairs, Executive Force members and Red Crescent paramedics. Khader steps outside and gets into the back of one of the trucks where he manages to change his clothes, swapping his bloodstained uniform for a plain black sports shirt and a pair of ill-fitting jeans. He also finds two big, heavy-duty flashlights. One of them he gives to Adam. In less than a minute, he returns.

'You are ready?' asks Khader.

'As much as I ever will be.'

Khader selects two of the men who have just arrived, and beckons to them and Adam to follow. He opens the door and they begin to descend, Adam holding the flashlight in his left hand, his gun in his right.

The stairs are steeper and narrower than those above, and as they go down, Adam is flooded by dread. How will they follow Morgan now? Khader has promised him they can go through the tunnel as far as Egyptian Rafah, but no further. He has contacts there, who may be able to give them information, but no transport, and in Egypt they would both be arrested: Khader because he is from Hamas, Adam because he has no Egyptian visa. In any case, his passport is back at Khader's headquarters in

Gaza City. Strange to think they left there only four hours ago. It feels like a geological epoch.

But his fears over what happens next are not the only source of Adam's anxiety. A deep trepidation is tugging at his bowels, an overwhelming sense of danger. He's heard of the animal instinct that makes the hairs on the backs of people's necks and forearms stand on end, and now it's happening to him. At last, after the stairs make a ninety degree turn, they reach the pitch-black basement room. The air is heavy, hot and hard to breathe. Adam struggles to stop himself hyperventilating.

In the middle of the concrete floor, there's a wooden frame, and set within it, a square, wooden trap door. It has a hand-sized slot cut in it to make it easy to lift, but when Khader bends to open it, it's jammed. He grips the handle and grunts with the effort while the others look on. Still the door won't open.

'I'm sorry,' he says in English. 'I'm sure this won't take long.' He lies down and shines the flashlight through the hole, then inserts his fingers again and tries to feel its underside. 'Aha. I think I've got it. There's some kind of bolt, keeping it sealed from the inside. I'll send one of the guys out to get an axe or something. We'll have to try to break it.'

As he starts to give the order in Arabic, Adam hears the noise of a door they have not noticed being quietly opened in the shadows behind them. He wheels round and shines his lamp. Ten feet from the trapdoor, there's a man, wild-eyed and bearded, dressed in a white waistcoat and pants: the final component of the three-stage trap which Karim has set in order to kill them.

The man starts to speak. Time has already slowed so much this night, but now it seems almost to stop entirely.

He utters his first two syllables in a high-pitched, melodious tenor. It sounds like an incantation: '*Allah.*'

In the time he takes to utter them, Adam takes in fully the appearance and design of his lethal device. Through his work as a lawyer, he's read a lot about suicide bombs, and this one conforms to the standard al-Qaeda design, propagated by its international academies of bomb-making, so that it hardly

245

varies from Iraq to the bazaars turned civilian slaughterhouses of the Northwest Frontier Province of Pakistan. Flat slabs of Russian PVV-5A military explosive encase the man's torso, easily visible beneath his waistcoat. Connecting each slab is a thick and deadly red snake: an ex-Soviet military fuse made of pentaerythritol tetranitrate, PETN. Adam guesses that encasing the slabs is a fabric sheet, into which has been woven thousands of steel pellets: shrapnel to increase the bomb's murderous power.

The bomber is wearing white because that is the colour worn by Muslim mourners, and that of their funeral shrouds, and he gives off a strong and distinctive odour. Before preparing himself to die, he has doused himself with *kafoor*, a perfume made from jasmine and camphor, used only for Islamic funerary rites. Beneath his left armpit, he holds the bomb's trigger with his right hand. It's another Soviet-era hangover, commonly found in Afghanistan and readily supplied elsewhere: a manual, spring-loaded detonator. If someone asks a bomber to raise his hands, he can pull the pin and trigger the explosion at the same time as he complies.

The man utters his third syllable, a single letter, or rather, a musical note: '*U.*'

This time, scenes from Adam's own life flash through his mind, and with each image, his will to continue it intensifies. He sees Charlie and Aimee, their bodies tanned and glistening as they emerge from a lake on a family summer vacation; then again wrapped in anoraks, safe in their helmets, on a skiing trip to Vermont. He sees a family row over Aimee's reluctance to do her school homework, and experiences anew his unexpected pride when her teacher called especially to tell him a poem she has written will be published in a national anthology. And he sees Morgan: that first day in Harvard Square; at their wedding; and in bed, damp and naked in the aftermath of the physical exultation that he suddenly knows with undoubting certainty they must and will regain.

The bomber's fourth syllable: '*Ak-*'

He gets no further.

Adam fires three times. The first shot hits the bomber squarely in the middle of the forehead, extinguishing all consciousness and severing in an instant the neural pathways that formerly connected his brain to his hand. The next gets him in the throat, and the third the top of his sternum.

He falls to the floor. Adam walks over and fires a final bullet into the side of his temple, then unclasps the man's lifeless fingers from the detonator.

'Khader,' he says, 'as well as a pickaxe, we're going to need a bomb-disposal expert.'

Chapter Twenty-one
Tuesday, June 26, 2007

Still trapped in the box in which they dragged her through the tunnel, Morgan feels herself being moved from a vertical to a horizontal position. The ascent of the shaft must be over, which means she is now in Egypt. The wood muffles the sound and the planks of the box admit almost no light, but so far as she can tell, they have ended up somewhere outside. There is very little space between her body and the lid, making any kind of movement difficult. But despite her claustrophobia and fear of total darkness, she knows she must not hyperventilate. The heat is all-enveloping, and her mouth is swaddled once again with the hated duct tape. Her living coffin has been infiltrated by fine sand, presumably from the tunnel, and the consequent irritation of her nasal passages means that suffocation is a real possibility.

All the way down the stairs from the apartment and into the tunnel, they kept her head pointing downwards. The pressure of the blood coursing through her skull was a new source of pain, and she felt herself on the brink of vertigo. But somewhere, through sheer necessity and willpower, she found the strength to fight it off. By the time they reached the top of what, to judge by the box's steeper angle, was some kind of ladder, she had overcome her panic. She feels a fierce thirst, but the only thing she finds almost overwhelming now is her own repellent stench.

She can hear the sounds of men greeting each other. Backs are being slapped as Karim greets the comrades who have apparently been waiting for him in Egypt. They seem to be indulging in rounds of mutual congratulation, using words she understands: '*mash'Allah*,' '*al-hamdulillah*.' Someone pats the top of her box. She hears the phrase '*CIA kufr*.' Does that mean there is a second box? She feels herself being lifted on to some kind of platform. After a moment or two, it starts to rumble and vibrate. She's been loaded on to the back of a flatbed truck. But before its engine grows any louder, she hears another sound she finds more troubling: the whimpering groan of a man in pain. He does not utter any words: presumably his mouth is also taped. But with a sharp pang she recognises the timbre of his voice: Abdel Nasser. He sounds as if he is lying very close. He must have been carried through the tunnel at the same time.

The truck starts to move, but they've hardly gone any distance before she hears another, much louder noise: the penetrating boom of an explosion. There's silence for several seconds, and then two other voices, very close by, emit a ragged cheer. Before they put her in the box, she watched Aqil boobytrap the apartment. Does the fact that his bombs have gone off mean she was about to be rescued? And are those who were trying to come to her aid now dead?

Where does Karim plan to take her? He has said nothing, but she can guess. For him, Egypt, with its American-aided dictatorship, will be only a little less hostile than Gaza. But the distance to any of its land borders is vast. They must be hoping to get her to the Sinai coast, to one of the channels that lead to the Red Sea, the Gulfs of Suez and Aqaba. If they can load her on to a boat at some lonely desert cove, they will be able to take her to one of several destinations from which her chances of re-emergence do not look so promising. Abu Mustafa said that Karim's new allies are Yemenis, so Yemen is the obvious choice. But Sudan is also possible, or even Somalia.

She feels hyper alert, her senses heightened by the fear and andrenalin. As the vehicle gathers speed, she reaches for the gift conferred by Abu Mustafa in the moments before he was shot: a pocket knife, which he left tucked inside the waistband of her filthy sweatpants. But now is not the time to use it. In any case, her movements are so constricted, she cannot begin to try to cut through her bonds. In time, she prays, that may change.

While one of Khader's men takes steps to ensure that the suicide bomber's device is fully disarmed, another attacks the trapdoor

249

over the shaft with a pickaxe. They have brought more lights, making the dingy basement bright. Adam can see where the bomber hid: a small room to one side of the main underground basement. It contains circuit-breakers and cleaning equipment, not so very different to the hallway closet under his parents' Oxford stairs, where Aimee keeps her new scooter. He feels shaky from the ebbing of the adrenalin flood which saved all their lives, and a little nauseous. But there is no time to pause.

'Are you okay?' asks Khader.

'Yes. I'm fine.'

'No one has ever done this before, *habibi*. Saved my life twice. Whoever it was that taught you to shoot, they did their job well.'

At last the top of the shaft is fully revealed: a dark, narrow rift hewn from the sandy bedrock, partially lined with planks and sheets of chipboard. Adam peers down and directs the beam of his flashlight. It looks at least sixty feet deep, and the only way to descend is by a home-made wooden ladder, its rough horizontal spars lashed and nailed to rickety uprights. Every fifteen feet or so there's a ledge, where one section of the ladder ends and another begins. The air is dusty. Evidently the sand has recently been disturbed, but it doesn't look as if the tunnel gets much traffic.

Adam starts to descend, grasping the rungs firmly. But he's only gone down two steps when Khader reaches down and grasps his wrist.

'Stop,' he says. 'We shouldn't do this.'

'But you promised we could go as far as Egyptian Rafah.'

'Not this way. Maybe they have booby-trapped this tunnel, too. Or they may have left someone waiting for us at the far end. We should go another way.'

Adam climbs back out and they leave the basement, returning to the lobby. Adam winces as he catches sight of the remains of someone caught by the blast's full force being carried on a stretcher down the last few stairs. According to Islamic tradition, his funeral must be held later this same day. But his face has gone: Adam hopes that Hamas militiamen wear dog tags, or he will not be easy to identify.

'We will go to the tunnel where you were waiting when this all began,' Khader says. 'There the operator knows he must cooperate with us and pay us taxes, or his business will close. I have a man on the other side. I will call him and tell him to meet us.'

They walk outside into the brightening daylight and approach the familiar shack. Inside, a short, unshaven man with red-rimmed eyes stands by the winch. Its winding drum is fixed directly above the round, black shaft, which is both wider and apparently deeper than the hole in the basement. Evidently alarmed by the events of the morning, he's sucking hard on a cigarette. He must have been in bed when the bomb went off, and has come out to check on the state of his source of income.

Khader speaks to him in Arabic. The man starts a diesel generator to one side of the shaft, and a row of lights inside it flicks on, illuminating what looks like professional wooden shoring. The man uses a hook to fix a wide, padded harness into a steel eyelet attached to the end of the cable, and hands it to Adam, indicating he should slide it under his buttocks. Adam stands at the lip, feels the cable take his weight, then swings into the middle of the gaping hole and descends, rather more rapidly than he expected. By the time he reaches the sandy floor, the mouth of the shaft is a mere coin of light, a hundred feet above his head. The tunnel, with sealed electric lamps every fifteen feet, lies ahead. The harness is hoisted skyward, then swiftly returns. This time, it contains Khader.

'This is one of the biggest and newest tunnels,' Khader says as he arrives. 'If the Israelis maintain their blockade, tunnels like this will be the only way to keep Gaza going.'

'This wouldn't be a great time for the Israelis to launch an airstrike, I guess.'

'No *habibi*. It wouldn't. Let's hope not this morning.'

They walk quickly, barely needing to stoop. The air is dusty, but there are fans to ensure it circulates. At this greater depth, the orange rock must be stronger: for most of the way, there's no shoring. Several hundred feet in, they hear a party of people coming the other way. The tunnel makes a bend, and they come into view. There are three men. One is pushing a shiny Yamaha motorcycle with its price label still attached, while the other two are struggling to manage a live, full-grown nanny goat. Khader greets them, and they move on.

Finally they reach the far end: another coin of light, another disappearing cable.

'We push this button,' Khader says, pointing. 'It gives them the signal we are here, and then they will winch us to the top.'

Time passes. It must be at least an hour since they left the Egyptian side of Rafah. Inside her dark, foetid, coffin, Morgan finds it impossible to judge. The sun must be rising higher in the sky, for the heat is becoming intolerable. Feeling new pools of sweat behind her neck and beneath the small of her back, she summons a mental map of the Sinai. The eastern side is surely too well developed for a clandestine handover, for the coast is punctuated by resorts, scuba centres and marine national parks. They must be heading southwest, towards the Gulf of Suez, an arid, sparsely-populated region inhabited mainly by Bedouin. But where along that shore? Most of the way down, there's a paved coastal road: a big risk for the kidnappers. Then comes a flash of insight, and Morgan guesses where she's headed.

From an another era of her existence, an unbidden memory materialises: an intelligence report that she studied a few weeks before she left for Israel. The work not of the CIA but its sister organisation based at the Pentagon, the Defense Intelligence Agency, it suggested that militants in Egypt had been forging links with extremist organisations further east. It pointed out that north of the town of El Tor, the main road leaves the coast and swings miles inland. In a cove near the empty headland of Abu Suwayrah, the DIA report went on, assets of the Agency's Egyptian liaison service had noticed a fishing *dhow* making landfall – although so far as they could ascertain, it never

252

did any fishing. Other sources had suggested that a *dhow* of this type was being used by AQAP, Al-Qaeda in the Arabian Peninsula. An accompanying, highly-classified memo to the National Security Council suggested this might be part of a weapons supply line, and recommended that steps be taken to develop these leads – perhaps by a US Marine intelligence unit which was about to be deployed in the general area. Maybe this AQAP cell are Karim's Yemenis.

As she bakes in her constricted, wooden oven, Morgan considers her mental map again. From Rafah to El Tor must be well over five hundred kilometres. Though most of the road is paved, it's certainly no highway: a winding, narrow blacktop across the Sinai mountains, and then, if the cove mentioned in the report really is the place where they're headed, a final off-road section to the coast, at least another fifteen miles. The journey is bound to take at least nine hours, but as yet, the day's heat has hardly begun. The conclusion is inescapable. If they don't stop soon to give her and Abdel Nasser some air and water and free them from their coffins, by the time they reach the *dhow*, they'll likely both be dead. She focuses on her breathing, trying to stem the rising tide of fear.

Khader's man is waiting in the shack at the top of the shaft in Egyptian Rafah: Hamas's local contact. He looks dishevelled, as if he hasn't had time to orientate himself since an abrupt, too-early awakening. As Khader moves to talk to him, Adam takes in his surroundings. They're in a neighbourhood of low, poorly constructed buildings, connected by sandy alleys: here the Egyptian side doesn't look very different from the Gazan one. From where they're standing, the Wall is invisible. Khader and his man confer in Arabic for several minutes. Finally Khader touches his arm and comes back to Adam. His face wears a look of defeat.

'I am sorry, *habibi*. We have reached the end of the line.'

'What did he say?'

'It wasn't the explosion which woke him. He lives just over there, less than two hundred metres away. At about four o'clock, he heard the sound of a truck engine. He got up to look: it was a white Mitsubishi pick-up. It had Egyptian tags, and it stopped just outside his house and waited. The driver stayed inside all the time, so my man kept watch: the situation was not normal. Then, just before the bomb, he saw a group of men loading two boxes on to the truck flatbed. He heard the driver talking to the men who brought the boxes, and he thinks he had a Yemeni accent. Then the bomb went off, and the truck drove away.' Khader clasps Adam's hand. 'We cannot stay here. The Egyptian *mukhabarat* almost certainly know we are here already. I am sure Morgan is on that truck, but we cannot try to follow it.'

'Surely we can do something! Khader, men have died to get us this far. There must be someone we can turn to, something we can do!'

'*Habibi*. If I truly thought there was anything, we would. But what? To the Egyptians, I am the enemy. If they find me here, they will put me in jail. If you try to talk to them, they will see you have no entry visa. They will arrest you first, and ask questions later. But at least we have some information. We know when she crossed, and the vehicle they are using. And we have a photo of the truck. Can't you tell your American friends? Can you call the embassy in Tel Aviv?'

'Not them.' Adam stops, thinking for a moment. 'But there is someone else. Before we go back through the tunnel, let me make a phone call.'

'As long as you are quick. But use my phone. To the people who monitor such things, a Palestinian number will be much less conspicuous than your American cellphone.' Khader hands his handset over.

Did Rob mean all that stuff he said in Oxford? Could he really deliver on it? There's only one way to find out. Adam's made sure he's memorised Rob's number. The ring-tone tells him he's still in England: he must have extended his trip. Rob picks up after the third ring, his voice thick with sleep. In Oxford, or London, or wherever else he is, it's only four in the morning.

'Ashfield.'

'Rob, it's me, Adam.'

'Shit. Adam. I'm sorry. I was in a deep sleep.'

'There's no need to apologise. But what you told me – that I was to holler if I needed help – well, I do. I'm in Rafah, Egypt, just across the border from Gaza. I followed Morgan through the tunnels, but I was too late. They've loaded her on to a truck. We don't know for sure where they're taking her, but the driver may be a Yemeni, and Yemen may be their ultimate destination. The vehicle is probably a white Mitsubishi pick-up.'

'Roger that,' Robert says. 'A white Mitsubishi pick-up. You know when they left?'

'It's hard to be sure, but it would have been before five, local time. Before a big explosion on the other side of the wall – that was the bomb the kidnappers left in the apartment where they'd been holding her. Someone must have picked that up with a seismograph. It made the fucking ground shake. And it killed a lot of people.'

'Okay. Roger that as well. I'm going to do what I can. I'm going to be passing this on to what I hope are the right people. This isn't the time for a catch-up, but... are you okay?'

'I'm fine. At least, I am in one piece.'

'And Morgan? Do you think she's still alive?'

'I think she is. She has to be.'

'Call me again in four hours. By the way, those kids are great. Just like their mom and dad. You must be so proud of them. I'm still in Oxford, by the way. At your mom and dad's house. Out.'

'Thanks Rob.' Adam feels himself slipping into Rob's military dialect. 'Over and out.' He manages a wry smile, a moment's response to his situation's perilous absurdity.

Until now, Morgan's ride has been smooth, but now she feels the flatbed jolting as the truck hits stones and passes over ruts. They must have turned off the road. Ten minutes more and the vehicle stops. The driver cuts the engine. She hears the cab doors open, and footsteps on the ground. Someone is climbing up on to the flatbed, making a metallic clang. The clasp of her

255

box makes a rattle and at last the lid is flung open. The hot morning air floods in, together with the brilliant sky. She's being pulled out by her bound wrists. As blood returns to her lower limbs, her calves start to cramp.

Karim is standing by the side of the truck. His voice is exultant. 'So, Mrs Cooper. It is nice day. Welcome!' He puts the emphasis on the word's second syllable. 'Welcome to Sinai!'

She can't reply. She's still wearing the duct tape gag. She's struggling to stay upright: the combination of heat and sudden elevation is making her feel faint

They're in what looks like an abandoned quarry, at the end of a dirt road. There's no vegetation, just brown and ochre-coloured stones and scree, and behind, craggy peaks of brown and red rock. A scorching wind blows relentlessly, whipping up swirls of dust. As the sensation returns to Morgan's legs, Aqil motions to her to descend from the truck. Another guard, whom she doesn't recognise, has removed Abdel Nasser from his box and is trying to get him to stand, but he's too weak. She catches sight of his face. He looks barely conscious. His hair and beard are ragged, his cheeks hollow. Yet his eyes meet hers, and, momentarily, his lips turn up in the trace of a smile. Another guard gets on to the flatbed and they lift him bodily, off the truck and then, with a guard's shoulder under each of his armpits, away to a black SUV. As they lead him away he turns his head and looks at her again. With a sudden pang, she wonders whether she'll see him again alive.

There's a second vehicle, a white Toyota Corolla sedan, ubiquitous throughout the Near East, behind the SUV. Karim leads her over, but before he gets in, he holds an animated conversation with the driver of the SUV. Morgan guesses they're discussing the details of their journey: the exact route, the time of their planned rendezvous, the distance the two cars should travel apart.

Karim's conversation is done. He opens the trunk of the car and brings out a black, Wahhabi-style *niqab*, a veil that leaves only a slit for her eyes, together with a long, Bedouin robe.

He places them over her head, without removing the duct tape round her mouth. Her hands are still bound. Aqil pushes her by the top of her head into the back of the car behind Karim, who's in the front passenger seat. It's as if he's a New York cop with his prisoner, playing to the cameras with his perp. He gets in beside her, and another man she doesn't know occupies the driving seat. She still has Abu Mustafa's knife.

Morgan is learning something new about Aqil: his stench is worse than her own. Sometimes he seems to be dozing, and then his body starts to loll, and his trunk-like thigh slips across the car's back seat, inching closer to her own. It can't be accidental.

Her head is beginning to throb again, and she realises it's been many hours since she had anything to eat or drink. Karim and Aqil both have water bottles. Her need to drink is suddenly overwhelming, and heedless of the consequences, she starts to make wordless noises through the duct tape and the *niqab* mask, grunts and squeals that indicate they have to listen to her properly. Karim seems to get the message. He speaks to the driver, and a mile or two further down the almost-empty desert blacktop, the car pulls over.

'Okay, I understand,' Karim says. 'I take off the tape, and I let you drink. But you try anything stupid, Aqil will shoot you.'

Morgan nods. Karim lifts the *niaqb* far enough to expose her nose and mouth, and with unexpected gentleness, he cuts off the tape that binds her lips with a pocket knife, then pulls the remnant from the back of her neck with a painful tug. He opens a water bottle, holds it to her mouth, and a little at a time, upends it. The last time, she takes a little too much, and splutters.

'Thank you,' Morgan says, when she has recovered. 'I needed that.'

Karim only shrugs. 'Is not special. I need you alive.'

'Where are you taking me?'

'To seaside.' His trademark giggle.

'To a boat?'

'You will see. You will learn. All very soon. Now you have choice. I put the tape back, or you say nothing. No more questions.'

Karim speaks to the driver again and they move off again. Judging by the sun it must be well after ten. There are many hours still to go. Aqil closes his eyes and she touches her knife, reassuring herself it's still there. She doesn't begin to know how she'll use it, but she makes herself a pledge: she will not go gently into their dark jihadist night. Come what may, she's not getting on that boat.

Adam is back on the sofa by the coffee table in Khader's Gaza office. It's eleven o'clock in the morning: just eight hours since they left. Everything feels surreal: Adam would pinch himself, if the helpless dread he feels in his stomach weren't so heavy. How can everything – at least by the standards of Gaza – seem so normal? In the hours since he last sat in this office, he has witnessed a bloody carnage, he has killed a man who would have killed him, and he hasn't slept. And despite everything, he has failed. Morgan is still a prisoner, now more remote than ever. He sips a bittersweet Arabic coffee and nibbles a pastry. He's suddenly assailed by exhaustion. The food and drink are the only things still keeping him awake.

'Thank you Khader, for everything,' Adam says. 'You did your best. And I am so sorry for the loss of your men.'

Khader looks as exhausted as Adam. 'Thank you. I appreciate your feelings. But it is my fault. I should have anticipated what Karim and his *takfiris* planned to do. And our intelligence was inadequate. We had no idea about the tunnel in the basement. We may have taken power in the Gaza Strip, but we do not have control.'

'What about Abu Mustafa, the guy they left behind? What's going to happen to him?'

'He is in the Al-Shifa hospital. I think he will live, so long as the Israelis have allowed some antibiotics through their blockade, so that we can prevent an infection. He has been a collaborator

258

with the Zionist entity. But he gave us accurate information about the truck, about the second IED, and the tunnel. He told us Karim had a source inside the Hamas *Mukhabarat*. We will interrogate him, find out everything we can about this source, and about Karim's group. And then we will let him go. We will send him back through Erez. I think he will live to see his home and family again.'

'I should be going to Erez myself. I'll call for a car to pick me up on the far side and take me back to Tel Aviv.'

'Stay for lunch. We both need to eat. Then I'll take you to Erez myself.'

'Thanks. I'll do that. But first I need to make a phone call.'

Adam dials his parents' home. His mother answers.

'Darling! How wonderful to hear your voice. Let me give you to Rob.' She knows this is not the time for chit-chat. His father-in-law comes on the line.

'It's me, Adam,' says Adam.

'I know it's you. Okay. So take a fucking deep breath. I can't tell you much, because I don't know much. But after we spoke, I managed to reach a well-connected two-star buddy I served with at Lejeune. He's in Washington now, attached to the joint staff. He got it: the urgency, the need to act. All I know for sure is that your intelligence is in the system. It's reached the right Pentagon intel nerd's in-box, and the will is now there to action it.'

Adam can only mutter his thanks.

'Save the mutual congratulations for when we get her back. Hopefully, the information that we – that you – have supplied is going to match something which is already there. Do not ask me what exactly the fuck they're going to do with it, because I honestly don't know. But I will make one promise: that as we speak, some very good guys are giving this all they can. Semper fidelis, Adam. Semper fi.'

The call has barely ended when Adam's cellphone rings. Whoever it is has blocked the number, but the voice that speaks when he answers it is female and American.

'Adam Cooper?'

'This is me.'

'Lieutenant Suzanne Shawcroft. I'm calling you from JICCENT, the CENTCOM Joint Intelligence Centre. You identified a possible target vehicle in your conversation with Colonel Ashfield. But there are a lot of white pick-up trucks in Sinai. First I want to be sure it was a Mitsubishi. Is that right?'

Adam turns to Khader. 'It's the US military. Is there anything more you can tell them about the truck?'

'The guy said it looked new, but it was dirty. Like it had been driven a lot off-road. Definitely a Mitusbishi.'

Adam passes the information on.

'Okay, stand by sir. We copy you. We think we have an image of it. We've been following it for several hours from a UAV – a drone, an unmanned aerial vehicle. It's on the highway heading for Cairo. We're liaising with our Egyptian colleagues.'

The adrenalin jolt to Adam's chest feels like a karate kick. He swallows hard. 'You think you've located her? You really think this is it?'

'I don't want to be definitive. Things can go wrong. But tentatively, yes Sir, we have her in our sights.'

'My God. Oh my God.'

'So keep your phone on. I'll let you know the minute we have news.'

'Okay. Okay. I copy you.'

'Just one thing. The truck we're following. To judge by its speed and position when we first picked it up, it left Rafah at about o-four fifteen, four fifteen this morning. That fits in with what you told Colonel Ashfield, right?'

'Er… yes, I guess so…'

And then it hits him.

'No! Wait! Shit, no! Shit, shit shit. It doesn't fit, it doesn't fit at all! The Mistubishi with Morgan on board can't have left Rafah until almost five – o-five hundred. Just before the explosion.'

'You're sure about this?'

Adam hastily confers with Khader, then comes back on the line. 'I'm one hundred per cent certain. Four-fifteen has to be way too early.'

Lieutenant Shawcroft's voice sounds a little panicked. 'Thank you, Mr Cooper, thank you for this input, I've got to go.'

'Does this mean…?'

'Sir, like I said, I'll be back the moment I have news. Right now I have to go, goodbye Sir.'

Adam doesn't really have to ask what it means. He knows. For the past few hours, an American UAV has been following the wrong truck. The hunt for Morgan is going to have to start all over again, and the chances of finding her are rapidly diminishing. After so much risk, so much bloodshed, he, Khader, Rob and apparently the collective US military, are all staring at failure.

Chapter Twenty-two
Tuesday, June 26, 2007

Karim must have told the driver of the other vehicle to stay well in front of them: for a long time now Morgan has not caught a glimpse of it. Presumably he thinks they will be less conspicuous if they do not travel in convoy, especially when the time comes to leave the paved road. It has been a long night and now a long day, and they have no food. The driver bought some chocolate and nuts when they stopped to buy gasoline, but Karim and Aqil ate it all immediately, and they have brought nothing else. She can only hope that hunger and fatigue will make their reactions sluggish. They seem to have run out of water, too, and the car's air conditioning is feeble. The journey feels interminable.

When she isn't dozing, Morgan ponders. How strange have been the paths that have led her to this final crisis! She thinks about her conversation with Abu Mustafa and his extraordinary disclosures, and the origins of this crazy 'operation' cooked up with the help of this Israeli, Amos. According to Abu Mustafa, it was Amos who recommended her as the target of the proposed kidnap. But that in turn means her name must have been proposed by Gary, because she knows exactly who this Amos must be – the man Gary once described to her as his 'closest brother in arms,' Brigadier-General Amos Pearlman, or as Gary liked to put it, 'the man from *Haman*,' Israel's military intelligence section.

Over the years, he and Gary have worked together several times. Back in the nineties, Pearlman ran his own unit, focusing his considerable skills and resources on Muslim extremists operating far from Israel's borders, in the era before 9/11 made such inquiries fashionable. She first heard his name when she was based in Sarajevo, usually mentioned disparagingly. Back then, the western European and American intelligence agencies

262

considered the Serbs to be politically radioactive, but Pearlman spent most of his time with them, drinking plum brandy with butchers like Arkan and Ratko Mladic, and with their senior intelligence staff. More recently, Gary has told her why. Pearlman realised the Serbs were monitoring the hundreds of visiting *mujaheddin*, many of them veterans of Afghanistan, who were coming to fight from abroad with their brothers in the former Yugoslavia. By becoming the Serbs' crony, Pearlman persuaded them to share their intelligence with him.

According to Gary, one of Pearlman's hallmarks was his ability to manipulate the news media– just as Abu Mustafa said the pair of them had planned to do after her own kidnap. 'You remember that time the Serbs massacred a bunch of women and children by firing on a Sarajevo market?' Gary asked her once, towards the end of an unusually boozy Vespers night at their Tysons Corner out-station. Of course she remembered: she was in the city at the time, and witnessed the terrible aftermath.

'It could have been very damaging, but suddenly stories began to emerge that the Bosniak Muslims had deliberately killed some of their own in order to increase the pressure on the international community,' Gary said. 'It was all just lies and bullcrap, but the media reported it. It kind of took the political sting out of what had happened. Guess who their source was: Comrade Amos. He was doing his Serbian buddies a favour.' Later, when a couple of British journalists came across a Serb concentration camp, Pearlman planted the idea with some of their rivals that the Brit reporters had faked their interviews and pictures, insisting as a senior intelligence operative that the camp was bogus. 'According to Amos, it was just a Bosniak propaganda exercise contrived to force NATO to start a war on behalf of the fucking Muslims,' Gary told her. 'Of course, the journalists hadn't faked anything. But thanks to Amos, the real story – that the Serbs were running their own version of Dachau – got buried. It became a media clusterfuck about journalistic ethics and the difficulty of discerning truth amid the fog of war.'

She hadn't been able to keep the disgust from her face, but Gary was having none of it: 'Morgan, don't be so naïve. That was how Amos earned his keep with the Serbs. In return, he got some very useful information: stuff he eventually shared with me, that went into our own databases. Those reports are still accessible on yours and my workstation. Ratko's intel guys were pretty reliable.'

Could it have been Pearlman who betrayed her mission in Montenegro by telling the Serbs about the KLA supply line? If Gary had shared the details with him, it was distinctly possible. Long ago, she asked Gary what had had happened, but he insisted he had no idea: 'If this was something that came from CIA, it was as the result of a decision made way above my pay grade.' She would never really know.

But if Abu Mustafa was telling her the truth, it seems that even Amos Pearlman wanted to abort the plan to have her kidnapped in Gaza, once he was told by Abu Mustafa that Karim knew who she was. And the way he recognised her – from a video shot by a camera hidden in Abdel Nasser's apartment! How much did he see? Did he pass on film to his handlers of her and Abdel Nasser making love? Morgan has so much else to worry about, but this is not a pleasant thought. It feels like a physical assault.

So Amos closed the border and put the whole thing on hold until someone – surely it can only have been Gary – insisted it should go ahead. She recalls telling Gary shortly before she left for the airport how vital it was that her return must not be delayed, because of Adam's Supreme Court case. 'That's fine, that's fine,' he said. 'If there's any problem getting into Gaza, or if you think the risks have become unacceptable, just come on home.' At the time, she pinched herself: she wasn't used to Gary being sympathetic to the problems she had in balancing the demands of her family and job. Yet he had known all along that she wouldn't be coming home for months, perhaps more likely never, and just to make doubly sure, he had somehow induced Pearlman to contrive the approach from Ben-Meir. She imagines his voice, his lilting drawl: 'Just do something to get her to make another trip to Erez, old friend, and this time, she has to get through. We've come too far to waste this operation. We've already spent millions of dollars, and the future of Palestine is riding on it. Don't worry, if things turn nasty for her, we'll send in the cavalry. Next time you're in town, I'll buy you a beer.'

How smart she thought she was being when she asked Ben-Meir to dinner, and persuaded him to use his contacts to get Erez opened in time for her to go in and still get home. No doubt he was just their instrument, a handy instrument who was being manipulated, just as she was. Maybe he owed Pearlman for something. And all they were both really doing was following Gary's tortuous script.

Her head still throbs, but now she recognises a significant fact with terrifying clarity: that her CIA boss, Gary Thurmond, is a classic, clinical psychopath: utterly self-centred, unafraid of the possible consequences of his actions, and programmed instinctively to lie and manipulate. No wonder his Agency career has been so spectacular. Now the last penny drops. He has been prepared to risk her life, and some of the Agency's secrets, as an act of revenge, a punishment for her temerity in daring to go to the Inspector-General about his proposed abduction of the Muslim cleric in Amsterdam. He did all this to get even with her. Inwardly, she reels.

She closes her eyes. Vivid images of Adam, Charlie and Aimee flood into her mind: vacations and other happy times past, and visions of the future; graduations and weddings, family occasions which she will attend only inside their memories. She feels a pang and fights to stifle the tears. But if she cannot have life, may she and her family one day find justice. She prays that Adam, after her death, will uncover this degrading conspiracy and expose what has really been happening. One day, perhaps, he will find a way to avenge her in the way he knows best – through the courts.

They've finally left the paved road behind, heading southwest towards the sea, a milky blue she occasionally glimpses in the distance. The shadows are lengthening. Sunset can't be far away. Ahead, there's a cloud of dust: she guesses it's the other vehicle, the SUV containing Abdel Nasser. They're heading down a broad, stony *wadi*, the baked, red-brown mountains behind them. The amazing thing is: Aqil is asleep, not just dozing but really asleep, his snores making the seat of the car vibrate. She closes her own eyes as, imperceptibly, she bends over a little and moves her hands, slowly freeing Abu Mustafa's knife from her waistband. Once or twice the jolting of the car has made the point prick her, so she knows it's quite sharp.

Karim too appears to be unconscious: he's tilted his seat back, so it presses against her knees. As for the driver, he's concentrating hard, focused on the track's stones and potholes. Some of the ruts are so big that it wouldn't be hard to roll the vehicle over or wreck it, and they can't be travelling faster than ten miles per hour. The heat is just a little less intense: the cooling effect of the sea. Gently she manages to twist the blade so that it strokes the surface of the plastic cuffs which bind her wrists. It's awkward work, and she drops the knife several times, catching it again in her lap. But she manages eventually to lever the blade in behind the plastic, and so makes faster progress. All the time, her actions are concealed by her robe. Ten, fifteen minutes pass. At last her hands are free. There are no restraints on her lower limbs: Karim trusts Aqil and his gun. She closes her eyes again, pretending to doze.

Aqil's woken up. He's speaking to Karim, a staccato conversation that sounds a little urgent. But surely, he can't be alarmed. Nothing's going wrong with their plan. They haven't been followed, and they haven't been stopped. If she really heard a drone all those hours ago, there's been no sign of anything since. From the kidnappers' perspective, everything is as it should be. She's the package. This is the delivery.

They're coming much closer to the sea. It's less than a mile away now, and she can see the lateen sails of a dark, narrow-hulled *dhow*, moored only a short distance from the shore. The SUV has stopped on the sandy beach in front of it. The cove is small, less than half a mile wide, framed by the brown rocky cliffs of the headlands on either side. The beach itself is almost featureless, except for few large boulders, which have evidently tumbled from the cliffs. The sun is dipping close to the horizon. Once the *dhow* leaves, whether she is on board or not, it will very soon be night.

They're closer still, and she catches sight of the welcoming party. There's a tall man with pale skin, well-built with a bushy red beard, dressed in a dazzling white robe and a dark turban. He stands on the beach, flanked by at least a dozen armed retainers. There are several men still on the dhow: the beach party has made landfall by means of a small rowing boat.

The bearded man has the aura of leadership, and she recognises him from Agency photographs: Abu Ibrahim al-Almani, also known as Siegfried Maier, the adopted son of a Mercedes auto worker and a kindergarten nurse from Dusseldorf. In earlier times, he might have channelled his many hatreds into a nihilist, left-wing cell like the Baader-Meinhof gang. Instead, as a student of political science in Hamburg, he converted to Islam, and having attended the mosque which served as the incubator for the 9/11 conspiracy, he joined al-Qaeda. He has fought in Iraq and Afghanistan, and is now believed to be running his own increasingly murderous operations from a base in Yemen, at the same time making assiduous use of the internet to gather further European recruits. Now the DIA intelligence report she read in America makes sense. A weapons and IED supply line from Yemen to Egypt and Gaza: just the kind of thing Abu Ibrahim might have organised, and just the kind of terrorist organisation that Karim would have tried to connect with once he had her confession video, and was trying to burnish his career as an international *jihadi*.

The car begins to slow. This journey is almost over, and Morgan knows one thing with overwhelming clarity: that if she surrenders herself to this man's custody, she will die, and probably slowly, after much suffering. Far better that if this is the way it has to be, she dies fighting now.

They stop, about twenty yards behind the SUV. The driver is opening the front passenger door and Karim is getting out, wreathed in smiles. It's his big moment, the moment he achieves recognition on the world jihadist stage, and he's walking slowly towards Abu Ibrahim, readying himself for his embrace. Aqil's still beside her but seems distracted, as if he's noticed something: in any case, he's not watching her. He's peering across to the headland on the far side of the *dhow*, as if he's noticed something. It can't be anything. He's imagining threats that cannot exist. Baseless or not, his unexpected anxiety provides her opportunity.

Morgan takes the stubby knife in her right hand, pulls up her robe with the other, and with the reflexive speed that once took her to the top of her Farm martial arts class, she plunges the blade into Aqil's right eye. When she feels it penetrate the surprisingly resilient membrane at the back of his eye socket and enter the reservoir of softer material behind, she moves the knife from side to side, slashing and gouging at Aqil's brains, then takes it out and thrusts it in again, first upwards, and afterwards once again slashing, rendering as liquid the fleshy pad beneath his chin, at the angle between his throat and the back of his jaw.

At first he tries to resist, putting up his arms as if to ward off the acidic pain eating at his consciousness, but in what feels like a very few seconds she feels him start to go limp. The end of the knife is inside his mouth, slicing pieces from his tongue, and the blood bubbles and gushes, a little red spring that drenches her hand. But he cannot scream, partly because she has rendered his frontal cortex as useless as mashed potato, and partly because he is starting to choke, drowning in his own blood.

Only a little while ago Morgan was considering the subject of revenge, and now she is exacting it. She says nothing, but inside she is exultant. This is for what he did to Zainab, and for the fear and privation she has endured these past three months, and it means that she can die happy. In the space of an instant she sees the light begin to fade from his remaining good eye. It's turning milky, opaque, like the eye of a roasted sea bass when the cooking time is done. There is a detached part of her mind that senses she should feel horror at what she is doing; that considers that if she were still a proper and responsive human being, she should be retching or be trying to vomit the meagre substance in her stomach. But there is no time for anything like that. She has chosen life, chosen action over passivity, and such choices have their consequences.

These swaggering, lazy, arrogant motherfuckers are so stupid: they have not fixed the child safety lock to prevent her from leaving the car. She grabs the handle and flings open the back seat door, diving from the vehicle while ripping the *niqab* from her head. She almost trips in the sand but recovers, running away from the water, and as she hurtles away from the vehicles it becomes apparent that the guards around the two terrorist emirs haven't seen what she's done to Aqil. For some inexplicable reason, they're not reacting to her running away. But they're bound to soon, though the further she runs, the longer she will have so long as they don't shoot straight. As she runs, she braces herself, waiting for the bullets and final oblivion.

The bullets don't come. Is she dreaming? She manages to rip off the encumbering robe mid-stride, and thus increases her pace. She's sprinting now, towards the rocks, her mind filled with a sudden flash of that day in the summer of 1988 when she won the two hundred metres at the Texas state high school outdoor championships with a winning time of less than twenty-five seconds. Amazing that after so long confined she can still run, still leap across the ground, so fast, so lithe. Her feet are bare and the stones on the beach are sharp, but she feels no trace of pain. She's so light, it's almost as if she's floating. In making what must be the very last, glorious movements of her life, she feels liberated, loose-limbed, unleashed. Just as when she raced, time means nothing: every stride brings new thoughts, new perceptions. Maybe she's already dead, and her personal paradise is simply to keep on running.

But through her athletic trance she hears a voice from the real world, the voice of an African-American male. It's yelling at her, as loud as it can, in English.

'Ms Cooper! Morgan Cooper! Get the fuck down, get the fuck down!'

Almost simultaneously she catches sight of what must have distracted Aqil: a glint of reflected light among the boulders, now less than two hundred yards ahead. Then the first of three astonishing and wonderful things starts to happen. The glint becomes what can only be the barrel of a sniper rifle. It starts to fire. She can't look round to see if anyone has been hit, because she's taking the voice's advice, and flinging herself headlong into the sand. But she can see straight in front of her, and there she sees the second wonderful thing: two US Marine Corps AH-1 Sea Cobra helicopters. They round the headland which has been hiding them, their noses into the wind. It must be the breeze which, until now, has stopped anyone from hearing them.

They're flying in close formation. She does look back now, as one of the helicopters swoops low over the beach, while the other attacks the *dhow*. The Cobra fires its gun, and the place where the rudder must have been at the back of the boat explodes in a pool of flame, followed almost immediately by the wheelhouse over the engine. The gunship rakes the hull. This *dhow* isn't going anywhere.

Extremely accurate fire is coming now from the sniper team hidden among the boulders. She hears a loud popping noise, and looking behind her again, she sees they've hit the engine block of the SUV. Another sniper round, and Abu Ibrahim, still standing stupidly in his billowing, pompous robe, goes down, the place where his chest used to be a cloud of red vapour. She hears the crackle of AK47s: finally, the kidnappers have started to react, and they're firing their Kalashnikovs. She doesn't know who or what they're aiming at, only that she doesn't want to be hit.

There's still one more wonderful thing to come. Streaking into the bay at more than forty knots, two rigid hull inflatable boats, each one bearing a Marine Corps special operations fire team. One of the Cobras is covering their approach, and as she lies in the sand, Morgan watches Karim visibly panicking. He's yelling at the Yemenis, whose fire seems wild and undirected, and at his own driver. The Corolla is still undamaged, and he pushes himself past the driver, barging into what was his seat: he's trying to get away. He starts the motor and the engine screams as he puts the stick shift into reverse and turns the car around. He sets off up the track which leads away from the beach. He's going much faster than the driver dared when they came here: twenty, thirty, soon even forty miles an hour, making the vehicle heave as it hits the ruts and stones, like a white-knuckle theme park ride or a rodeo bucking bronco.

There's something languid about the Cobra's response. It hovers for a moment, sways a little, and its gun fires just once. The car is utterly destroyed. Karim has been reduced to red, fatty particles.

Now the seaborne fire teams are beaching their boats and disembarking: one near the rocks, less than fifty yards from Morgan, the other in the middle of the cove, by the remains of the *dhow* and the vehicles. Some of the Yemenis look as if they're trying to surrender, putting up their hands and discarding their weapons, but a couple are still shooting. This one-sided firefight doesn't look as if it's going to last very long.

Then the awful realisation hits her. Abdel Nasser, weak and wounded, is still inside the SUV, and none of the men whose efforts make up these wonderful things has the least idea who he is. They are bound to assume that he is one of the kidnappers, and like Karim, will try to get away. There's still firing going on from both sides when she gets to her feet and starts to run back the way she came, waving her arms, trying ineffectually to gesture to the Marines that they shouldn't attack the second vehicle.

'That's Abdel Nasser! Don't shoot him! Please stop, stop, he's one of the good guys, let me explain-'

A bullet strikes the ground in front of her, and another just to her side. One of the Yemenis has decided she's a target after all, so she ducks and starts to weave, still shouting: 'Stop! For God's sake stop!'

271

But suddenly she's caught and can go no further: the huge, uniformed arm of one of the water-borne fire team members is round her waist, dragging her back to the ground.

'Lady, for fuck's sake, you trying to get yourself killed? Stay down, stay down!'

'You don't understand.' She's yelling, but she's trying to sound authoritative. 'The guy in that vehicle, he's not one of them, he's a-'

It's too late. The Cobra fires. When the dust clears, there's very little left, either of Abdel Nasser or the SUV. And the battle seems to be over. In place of the firing, there's near-silence: the Cobras have moved offshore. Morgan can hear the breeze, and it's starting to get dark. The Marine helps her to her feet, then offers her his arm. But she can no longer walk unaided. Her legs have crumpled and the Marine has to call over one of his comrades. They give her a lift under each of her armpits. As they half-carry her towards the boat, she can't stop the sobs escaping through her cracked and arid lips.

'You're safe. You understand? You're safe,' the first Marine says. 'It's over. We're taking you off by boat. It's going to be okay. Ms Cooper. Please, Ms Cooper, don't worry. There's no need to worry about a thing any more. Everything's going to be fine.'

Adam's in Tel Aviv. It's early evening. He's chosen to wait at a different hotel, the Park Plaza, right on the seafront, sitting on a sofa on its beach-side terrace, gazing with empty eyes towards the sunset. He's doing something he hasn't done for well over a decade: smoking his way through a pack of Marlboros, mixing them with bitter black coffee, glancing obsessively down at his cellphone on the glass table in front of him, willing it to ring. It's been hours without a word from Lieutenant Shawcross, and there's been nothing from anyone else. He could call Rob, but what can he say? They may have started by following the wrong truck, but at least he took his chance to put them right. Have they found the correct target now? Where is it heading? What will they do? He has no idea, and it doesn't really seem that Rob's intervention now will be helpful. But why won't they call and give him an update, or if it has to be done, tell him the terrible truth? He takes another cigarette and lights it, convinced to his marrow that no news can't be good news.

Then his phone does ring. There's an American voice that checks his identity, then says she's going to patch him through to a name he can't catch. A man speaks, says he has someone who wants to speak with him, and wherever he is, it sounds like an airport, or maybe a battlefield. He can hear a helicopter, loud and close, more male voices, and what sound like waves.

And then, finally, unmistakeably, her voice a little hoarse, Morgan. 'Adam? Is that you? It's me. I'm safe. They say I'm going to be safe. I'm okay.'

He can't speak at all for several seconds. 'Morgan? You're alive, you're still in one piece?'

'Just about.'

'Oh Morgan.' He can't say anything for several more seconds, because the tears are coursing down his cheeks and his sobs are almost choking him. 'Thank God. Thank God.'

Cerulean. She remembered the word from a translation of the *Odyssey*, and now, in the midst of her own voyage home, the colour was everywhere. A cerulean sky and cerulean sea, two barely distinguishable infinities. When she closed her eyes during one of the four or five showers she took every day, the shade she saw behind her eyelids wasn't the usual reddish-orange, but cerulean. She suspected that her tears and the water that came from the shower head were probably cerulean too. *Caeruleus*: the blue of heaven, *caelum*. Morgan knew perfectly well she hadn't died, and yet her existence aboard the forty-one thousand ton United States amphibious assault ship *Kearsage* felt no more real than a children's story of paradise. She was also aware how narrowly she had avoided going to hell. A couple of days into the voyage, after the ship emerged from the Red Sea, she went up on deck to watch the sunset and saw the dark silhouette of some mountains. She was gazing into Yemen.

Captain Melkessetian had given her his stateroom, a bland and far from enormous expanse of oatmeal carpet equipped with a desk, a steel-frame bunkbed, a plain round table and two windows on to the cerulean world outside. There was a shelf of books, mainly military histories and great men's biographies, but no computer. A Marine military policeman stood guard outside her door, and when she did venture beyond it, she encountered a pervasive smell: pine-scented cleaning fluid. The engines were almost inaudible, and the water invariably calm. But though the movement of the ship was almost imperceptible, she was permanently nauseous, a state she had long ago come to expect whenever she took to the sea.

In as much as she did feel able to eat, she took most of her meals alone in the stateroom. Ordinarily, liquor on US Navy vessels was prohibited, but the captain kindly sent her beverages from his own, personal store – an ice cold beer with her lunch; a glass of Shiraz or Cabernet with dinner. Alcohol, she found, she could keep down more easily than food. On her third evening, the captain had invited her to dinner with a few of his senior officers. After congratulating her on her bravery, they tried to engage her interest on some of the world events and sporting triumphs that had transpired during her missing months, but she had forgotten how to converse. Nothing they said seemed important or interesting, and she resented their apparent delight in dwelling on triviality.

They also gallantly informed her how well she was looking, but when she finally found the courage to appraise herself properly in her bathroom mirror, she was shocked, if not surprised. Her face was gaunt and bony, and the dark bags beneath her dull, tired eyes looked as if no amount of rest or expensive beauty products would ever remove them. Her hair, so glossy and sleek before her capture, was long and ragged, with new areas of white around her temples. But the biggest shock was her body. She must have lost thirty pounds, and the once-toned muscles of her upper and lower limbs had all but disappeared. Where her stomach had been firm, it was hollow. The skin around her breasts hung loose, and there seemed to be canyons between her ribs. No wonder she hadn't had a period since the early days of her imprisonment. She looked anorexic. She had spent so long in hot, dirty conditions wearing the same, filthy clothes that in places her skin was raw and chafed by a red, fungal rash, and it felt as if she would never again be clean.

After her high-speed boat ride from the beach, Morgan had spent her first night aboard the *Kearsage* in the sickbay. There she was fussed over solicitously by a pair of male nurses and a pretty, Indian-American doctor whose family – Sikh, not Muslim, as she quickly made sure Morgan knew – had settled in Michigan. 'You've lost a lot of weight and muscle, but so far as I can see, there's really not much else wrong with you – physically at least,' Dr Kaur told her next morning after running a battery of tests. 'You're vitamin deficient and short on calcium, and in due course you're going to need psychological counselling, but that will have to wait until we land.' She gave her a clip to hold up her hair, a gift for which Morgan felt disproportionately grateful. It relieved her neck of the pressure of contact with her mane of unkempt hair, and it meant that when she vomited – something she was doing at least twice a day – she had something to keep it back. The doctor had only one immediate piece of advice: 'you must try to get some rest.'

But though she was utterly exhausted, resting was the one thing Morgan could not do. Far more vivid than anything she was experiencing now were the unbidden scenes in her mind: the day of her abduction; her torture; Zainab's rape; killing Aqil; the final desperate moments on the beach when she tried and failed to save Abdel Nasser. Familiar with some of the academic literature on the 'complex post traumatic stress disorder' peculiar to kidnap victims and abused prisoners of war, she knew these visions might well persist for years. Her overwhelming sense of guilt would surely be equally resilient. She had survived, but her own loyal agent had been killed, and the fact his death was ultimately caused by what was sometimes termed 'friendly fire' made matters worse. She didn't know what, but she should have done more, and months earlier, before the kidnap, she should have been more vigilant: she should have seen the signs that their 'safe house' was anything but. She knew these thoughts had no rational basis, but she felt that the stain of these crimes could never be expunged. She must dedicate the rest of her life to finding ways of doing penance for them, and the high esteem in which the ship's crew seemed to hold her was baffling and incongruous.

Following their first brief exchange at the beach, her first proper ship-to-shore phone call with Adam had come less than half an hour after she arrived on the Kearsage, patched through by a Lieutenant Shawcroft at CENTCOM. She had known nothing of what he had been doing during her absence, and she was bewildered to hear that he was in Tel Aviv. As before, his joy on hearing that she was alive and in reasonable health was palpable. But when he told her that he had been to Gaza himself not once but twice, and had actually been there that morning, she could not control her emotions.

'You went to Gaza? What were you doing? You're an American lawyer with a Jewish grandmother, for heaven's sake! What did you figure the kids would have done if something had happened to you?'

In all the circumstances, as she later discovered, these were not well-chosen words.

'I felt I had to. Like I didn't have a choice. I had to do what I could.' Adam's voice had sounded thick. 'And in the end, I think it did do some good. Quite a lot of good, actually.'

Morgan knew the call was likely being monitored, and so she did not ask him how. The last thing her husband needed was to have some Arab *mukhabarat* goon eavesdropping on his account of the role he had played in her release. 'Well, let's not talk about that for now,' she said. 'Better to wait until we see each other.' Then she softened. 'And it will be so great to see you. Greater than you can imagine. Now tell me about Charlie and Aimee.'

Whatever was passing through Adam's mind, he managed to sound enthusiastic. 'I've got a surprise for you.' There was a click, and then the voices of her children filled Morgan's ears, patched through from Oxford. Of course, they had already been told she was safe. But as Aimee told her when she finally composed herself enough to be able to speak, until the moment they heard her voice, they had not dared to believe it. What had they been doing? Morgan asked. Granny had just bought her first trainer bra, Aimee told her excitedly; she had learned to play hockey at the Oxford ice rink and she hadn't missed her American friends at all. 'You'll find I've grown up a hell of a lot,' she added. 'I guess I've had to. I know I've sometimes been a brat but I won't be any more, mom. Now that you're coming back, I'm going to appreciate you properly.'

Charlie's news was less complicated. He knew none of the detail of her rescue, but the fact she was aboard a US Navy ship 'was just so, so cool, I wish I could be there with you.' He had won the class sprint race at his Oxford school sports day, and last weekend, he and a friend's family had gone for a picnic to a stream on the Hampshire Downs where they caught three trout. Long before the children rang off, Morgan's tears were flowing freely.

Later she regretted having taken that phone call before the conversation which immediately followed it – with James Mallon, the Naval Criminal Investigative Service special agent afloat. A seasoned counter-terrorism expert from New Jersey, Mallon explained that he had strict instructions: for the time being, she must say very little about her ordeal, either to him or to anyone else. It was vital to keep her account fresh and uncontaminated for the formal debriefing which would begin almost immediately, once she was out of the Middle East. Her information about the *Janbiya al-Islam* and its operatives was sure to be invaluable: no US intelligence officer had survived an abduction by an al-Qaeda affiliate before.

But there were a few things Mallon was authorised to tell her. The first was that she had been incredibly lucky. On the day of her rescue, the *Kearsage* had been due to leave for Dubai, having completed a lengthy tour of patrols and manoeuvres up and down the Red Sea, and in the waters off the coast of the Horn of Africa. Its crew and Marines were overdue some rest and recreation, and Dubai was one of the few relatively nearby places where the ship could dock for what the Navy termed a 'liberty' R&R – meaning sailors could get an alcoholic drink.

'We were about to set our course for the Gulf when this piece of intel came through unexpectedly,' Mallon told her. 'It happened to match some reports the ship's own intel cell had been developing, but couldn't quite nail: that an al-Qaeda group based in Yemen had been organising a logistics supply line through Sinai, using a *dhow* they were landing – where else? – at the beach where you were rescued. We'd even set up onshore surveillance there for a few days, but though our guys were well-hidden, they couldn't come up with anything concrete. They were just unlucky, I guess. Anyhow, once we realised that you might be showing up with a bunch of terrorists at the very location we'd been watching, the R&R was put on hold. The new information completed the jigsaw. It meant we knew where to head for, and we also knew just how dangerous the situation was. We changed course and, well, you know what happened. You were there. One day later, and there would have been nothing we could have done, however good the intel. We wouldn't have made it in time.'

'So by now I'd be in Yemen.'

'If that's where they planned to take you, yes m'am, you would.'

'Where did the new intel come from?'

'The details will have to wait. But I can tell you this: the critical piece was fed by your husband in Gaza – well, at the time he made the first call, I believe technically he was in Egypt. It came through to us very quickly, relayed by someone high up in the Pentagon via your dad. There was a bit of a hiatus when the intel guys started following the wrong pick-up truck. But it turned out the right one had already been noticed by a UAV, and once we knew the other vehicle had been eliminated, we were able to figure out where they must be taking you. Eventually we identified what we thought must be the terrorists' convoy. When we saw the *dhow*, that clinched it.'

Since that first call, she and Adam had spoken again at least twice every day. At an intellectual level, she was proud of him, just as she was proud of her dad. She had apologised for her first, hasty comments. Yet their exchanges felt stilted and distant. Muffled by her cerulean shroud, she was disconnected from her husband as she was from everything else.

The *Kearsage* was due to dock around noon next day. Then there would be nowhere to hide. Her retreat from the world was almost over.

Adam's luxurious hotel bed was making no difference, although he had had a long day. The government of the United Arab

Emirates did not permit direct flights from Israel, so forcing him to endure a pre-dawn check-in at Ben Gurion for a flight to Amman, eight tedious hours in the stuffy Jordanian terminal, and then a long line to clear immigration when he finally reached Dubai. But still he couldn't sleep. He felt as if he were facing an exam for a course he hadn't revised, or a court oral argument for which he was poorly prepared. Then, on the other hand, he could have left his bed, made coffee, and worked, but there was no last minute revision he could do to ready himself for coming face to face with Morgan. He wished he could have been able to bring the kids: they would have made things easier. But although his mother had offered to bring them over, the State Department and CIA officials now taking care of Morgan's rebirth had insisted this could not happen. Apparently the presence of a single additional member of the Cooper family on the shores of the Persian Gulf would constitute an unjustifiable security risk, and since they intended to fly her out in less than twenty-four hours, there was little point in their coming.

On the eve of his journey, he'd agreed to meet Mike and Eugene in Tel Aviv. Everything that happened from that moment on had to be strictly controlled, they said, because 'American lives may depend on it.' To be sure, Adam had done his bit, and done it fantastically: 'for an attorney, you sure showed some balls,' as Eugene put it, displaying his customary lack of skill in finding the *mot juste*. But now the professionals were back in charge. Morgan was going to have to spend a lot of time sequestered with shrinks and her fellow spooks, and there was nothing Adam could do about it.

'Are you trying to tell me we don't even get to spend a night together before you whisk her away?' he had asked in Eugene's unpleasantly familiar office.

'Sure you do. We just don't want you at the pier: that might be dangerous, and in any case, we'd like to keep the US military's role in this under wraps. So the reunion will happen at the Consulate-General. You'll get a little private time together before a media photo-op with a pre-prepared statement –

though naturally, no Q and A. Then the time will be yours. You can travel together to the Consul-General's residence, where you'll be her guests for dinner, and you'll spend the night in her residence.'

'It doesn't sound like we'll have much private time at all,' Adam said.

'Nope. Not for the time being, anyhow. And I'm sorry to say, no lie-in next morning, either. You'll need to be up by three-thirty for the flight back to England. You'll be on a military plane, flying into the Royal Air Force base at Mildenhall. That's where the children will be, with your parents and Morgan's dad. I'm sure they'll give you some privacy there for a while, but it won't be for long. We need to know everything that's inside Morgan's head, and we need to know it quickly. The Brits have lent us a safe house. Somewhere quiet and secluded. She will be able to call you, but for a week or two, no visits.'

'Jesus.' Adam was aghast. 'All these weeks, Charlie and Aimee have been without their mother, not knowing whether she's alive or dead, and now you're telling me she's still a prisoner! And if your precious debrief is so time-critical, why didn't you start it while she was on the fucking boat?'

'You can't just dive into these things. You need the right personnel, and they need some preparation. And all the medical advice says we needed to give her a breathing space, time to compute what's happened. I'm really sorry, Adam.'

Eugene tried to touch Adam's arm, a gesture of *faux* solidarity, but he pushed him away. 'Fuck you, Eugene. Fuck you and fuck your fucking Agency. You and your colleagues did absolutely nothing to free her, and you know it. You fed me high grade bullshit, week after week: you remember all that crap about the kidnappers being a Hamas front? You planted a chip in my passport, which might have got me killed. Even after all that, you sent Mike to Oxford to ask me not to go back to Gaza in order to give you more time: well, if I'd agreed to that, by now Morgan might well be dead. And someone – maybe not you personally, but someone I think we all know –

281

flung mud at her via some sleazy tabloid journalist, just to try to fuck me up. And now you say I have to stand back, and let you guys do what you want with her for more days and weeks? You're kidding me, right?'

This time it was Mike who spoke. 'Adam, I know the Agency hasn't exactly covered itself with glory. But however this mess started, it's ended well, extremely well, and now you've got to let us to do our jobs. I think we both know that if you were to ask your wife, she'd tell you that's what she wants. She's not just a professional now. She's a heroine.'

'A heroine. I'm so glad you think so. But you really think this ended well? With God knows how many people dead?'

'At least two high value targets have been taken care of,' Eugene said. 'That's pretty satisfactory, I would say.'

Adam glared at him. 'I do so hope you think it was worth the risk. Because I think you knew Morgan was going to be kidnapped. I don't know what elaborate game you were playing, but I think Gary, you and that guy Amos knew all along.'

'That's an outrageous suggestion!' Eugene said. 'Are you really suggesting we would arrange for a colleague to be abducted? We may not have got everything right here. We may have made mistakes. But we didn't do that, and you need to be careful what you say!'

Even then, Adam reflected later, cordiality might have been restored had it not been for Eugene's next remark. 'Look,' he said, 'I know that this further period of separation is going to seem especially hard because of some of the things that have gone down between the two of you. I realise you're desperate to see how things work out, and to figure out what went wrong – what I'm trying to say, and I know I'm not putting it very delicately, is that I do feel for you, and I really understand why it must seem that -'

Adam stood up, pushing his chair back from the conference table so violently that its opposite edge caught Eugene's stomach. 'I've already said this once. Fuck you, Eugene. Fuck you a thousand times.' He stared into Eugene's eyes. 'I am simply disgusted that you're trying to bring up the subject of our relationship. I don't know whether you're making some kind of threat, but this is something you stay out of from here on in. Do I make myself plain?'

Overall, it might have made Adam's life slightly easier if he and Eugene were still on speaking terms. But it wasn't his righteous anger which was keeping him awake. Nor was it the flashbacks which often crowded his mind: the charnel house inside the Rafah apartment building; the moment he shot the suicide bomber; Morgan's DVD. It was fear: a terror that having been focused on a single, practical outcome for so many weeks, its achievement had left him without a purpose or objective, while making it impossible any longer to dodge the 'indelicate' matters which Eugene had so clumsily raised.

His wife had been banging her agent because her relationship with her husband had grown chilly and distant, and now she had survived God knew what ordeal. There was also the small but perplexing matter of his own personal guilt, at having slept with the mother of his children's best friends. Adam might have learnt how to stop a bomber, but just how to deal with his marriage, he hadn't the faintest idea.

Chapter Twenty-four
Sunday, July 1, 2007

In the months since Morgan's kidnap, superstition – an irrational belief that if he envisioned their reunion too vividly, he would somehow prevent it from happening – meant Adam had tried deliberately not to think about the moment he might see his wife again. But in as much as he had pictured it at all, he had imagined it taking place beneath the palm trees outside some Gaza apartment building, after her kidnappers had surrendered or were killed, or – this version just for a day or two, when he heard she was safe on the *Kearsage* – on the Dubai quayside: a tight and glorious embrace under the dazzling sunshine as she stepped off the gangway from the ship. Instead, he was standing in the hallway outside the elevators on the twenty-first floor of the Dubai World Trade Centre, the undistinguished office tower that housed the American Consulate-General, flanked by armed agents of the Diplomatic Security Service.

Jennifer Perkins, an ash-blonde foreign service officer in her forties who served as the chief of mission, stood awkwardly beside him. 'It won't be long now,' she said. 'I'm sorry it has to be this way, but out here… well, though it always looks as if the Emiratis have everything buttoned up, we can't take any risks. I wanted you to be able to stand outside to greet the limo, but I have to take my Regional Security Officer's advice. Anyhow, they're on their way.'

She was flanked to her right by Wendell Fisher, the elderly, sleek ambassador, who had been driven up from his base in Abu Dhabi. He looked at Adam. 'You all set?'

'I guess so. As much as I'll ever be.'

The illuminated floor numbers of the left-hand elevator of the two dedicated to the consulate's use had started moving. Adam's pulse rate quickened. But when the doors opened, it was only to divulge more security men: a false alarm. It did seem a pity that Uncle Sam hadn't devoted such resources to protecting her before she was kidnapped: any more armed agents, and the hallway would be jammed. Now the right-hand elevator numbers were flashing. There was a collective hush. This time, it must be her.

Adam moved in order to stand opposite the middle of the elevator, trying to ensure that he would be the first thing Morgan would see. Not that he had much of a wardrobe to choose from, but he hadn't dressed up: he was wearing chain-store khakis and a plain dark blue polo shirt which he knew she liked. The elevator pinged, signalling its imminent arrival.

At last the doors parted. Adam's eyes met hers. She was flanked by more armed men in suits but he held out his arms, trying to ignore the surroundings. He didn't really take in her appearance: he just wanted to hold her. She submitted to his greeting, but even as he tried to squeeze her, he felt her stiffen.

'Hey,' he said, 'you're late.'

Suddenly she seemed overcome. He felt her exhale, and she shuddered: the ghost of a sob. Relaxing just a little, she dug her forehead into his shoulder. 'Hey,' she said. 'It's you. You okay?'

'I'm okay. You?'

'Better than you might expect.'

But they had no more time, because Morgan was being mobbed. The ambassador was walking towards her, taking pains to ensure that she followed protocol by shaking his hand first, so forcing her to slide away from Adam and turn to him. Jennifer Perkins was next, uttering inanities about what an enormous pleasure it was to welcome her to the consulate. Adam found himself jostled, trailing four paces behind, separated from his wife by the platoon of security agents.

Morgan knew she had no real choices. America had rescued her, albeit with some unofficial help, and that meant that for the time being, her country owned her. The Agency had decreed what was going to happen to her now, and over the coming days, for reasons she understood. That didn't stop her hating it. She'd been promised some time alone with Adam before anything else. Instead, he'd barely been able to give her a hug before the ambassador, who in his previous life in business had given generously to Republican Party funds, was claiming her for himself. As for the irritatingly solicitous Consul-General, with her fussy little bob and fake Chanel suit, her main concern seemed to be to make sure she stuck close enough to Morgan to be in all the photographs. No doubt she believed her career would benefit if she were to be publicly associated with her release.

From the hallway, they took her straight to a briefing room, where a phalanx of reporters and camera operators had been waiting for some time. Ambassador Fisher motioned to her and the Consul-General: he would take the podium's centre spot, with Morgan and Perkins on either side. They walked up and the cameras clicked and whirred. They had sent an outfit for her to the ship: a yellow satin blouse that was never going to match her colouring, and some baggy, powder blue jeans. Still, better to appear dressed like that than in US Navy sweatpants. Meanwhile Special Agent Mallon had given her one very strong piece of advice: on no account should she open her mouth, other than to state how happy she was to be free, and to thank the Dubai mission for its hospitality.

The ambassador started to read his statement. 'I am delighted to report to you that Morgan Cooper, a career foreign service officer with the State Department Bureau of Democracy, Human Rights and Labour, has now been released from captivity. She was kidnapped by terrorists more than three months ago in the Gaza Strip, and is here with us today. She is, as you can see, in good health.

'The investigation into her kidnap has been carried out to date by several United States government agencies, and it is continuing. I want to thank those agencies for the enormous efforts they have made to secure her release. However, I cannot now disclose anything further as to how this took place, because to reveal operational details might jeopardise the safety of others.

'For the record, I will make just a few points. In accordance with longstanding policy, the United States has not paid a ransom for Mrs Cooper, and it has not conducted negotiations with any terrorist group.

'The United States utterly condemns those who perpetrated this outrage, and we will show no mercy in bringing them to justice. We will remain vigilant to protect the lives of all our citizens, especially those, like Mrs Cooper, who serve the public good. She has shown tremendous courage, and we thank God for her safe release.

'I'm afraid we will not be taking any questions, and I ask you all to exercise forbearance as she and her family start to recover in the months ahead. Thank you.'

As Morgan had expected, there was a barrage of shouted questions, the ambassador's announcement there would be no Q and A notwithstanding. She paused long enough to smile at CNN's camera and to tell a proffered microphone she was 'glad to be here, and feeling fine,' before dutifully following Fisher and Perkins from the room. Adam was somewhere behind her again. They were walking down a corridor, towards the opposite side of the consulate, as far as they could get from the reporters.

Morgan turned to Jennifer Perkins. 'Are we done now? Do I finally get to talk to my husband?'

'In just a moment. There's someone who needs to speak with you. Mr Cooper, you come with me while they talk; I'll get us some coffee.' They reached a half-open, heavy metal door. 'Here we are. Morgan, please, if you could just go in here. We'll see you again very shortly.'

Gary Thurmond was the very last person Morgan had expected to see. She knew that as her boss, he would not be allowed to play any part in debriefing her, and she had assumed that arranging to meet her before it started would be beyond even his manipulative powers. Yet there he was, tanned and dapper in a blue linen blazer, beaming from ear to ear.

'Morgan.' He stood and held out his arms. 'Close that door, then no one will catch us while I give you a squeeze. Welcome, trooper. Welcome to the Company hall of fame.'

Her mouth was open, her astonishment palpable. 'You. Of all people. How the hell did you get yourself in?'

'Wendell Fisher and I are old friends. More than friends, as a matter of fact. Back in the day, when he was in the oil business, he used to do a little work for me.' Gary looked down, and blew across his nails. 'And in any case, all I want to do is convey the admiration of all your friends and colleagues. You're the toast of headquarters, the name on every young officer's lips. Great job, Morgan. You pulled it off. You nailed the hardest assignment imaginable – and that after years away from the field.'

Had she not already deduced that Gary was a psychopath, Morgan would simply not have known what to say. As it was, a single thought filled her mind: that there was no limit of human decency he would not breach.

'So what are you trying to tell me here? That first you almost had me killed, but now I'm some kind of heroine?'

'Sure you're a heroine. And I don't know what on earth you think you mean by saying I almost had you killed: I've actually been spending all my waking hours for the past several months trying to save your goddamn ass. But, boy, did you turn this thing to your advantage.' He gestured expansively. 'Sit down. Let's talk. And by the way, we can't be overheard. In case you hadn't figured it out, this room is a SCIF.*'

She did sit, glaring at him across the pine table. 'I know what you did Gary. And I know why.'

'Okay. So surprise me. Before we get on to whatever crazy notion you've acquired about what I'm supposed to have done to you, do, please, explain my motive. Why would I want to hurt you? By the way, just let me say: you're looking great, Morgan.

---

*   SCIF: Sensitive Compartmented Information Facility, a soundproof room
     regularly swept for bugs, as found in many US government buildings.

For a woman who's just spent three months as a prisoner of al-Qaeda, you're looking really terrific.'

'I went to the Inspector-General,' she said, ignoring his barbed compliment. 'About your rendition operation in Holland. My role was supposed to stay confidential, but as I always guessed it might, somehow it leaked. And so your plan got nixed. You could simply have had me transferred, and written me a lousy appraisal. But that wasn't enough for you. You had to make me really suffer: not just to punish me, but to encourage the others, to make it plain what happens to someone who crosses Gary Thurmond.'

While she spoke, Gary was shaking his head, quietly laughing. When she finished, he let out a sigh. 'Morgan. This is nuts. Nuts. I don't know what it is that's made you think this way, but I guess you've have been spending too much time on your own, brooding and making two and two make five hundred. Listen to me. Yes, it's true I found out you'd been to the IG. But baby, you did me a favour. Frankly, I'm relieved we never did pick up that guy in Amsterdam. It would have been nothing but a headache. And as you so wisely realised some time before I did, extraordinary rendition really isn't the way we should operate. It had its place, but it's kind of passé.'

Morgan folded her arms. 'Bullshit, Gary. You cared about that operation. You put a lot into it.'

Gary shrugged. 'Maybe I did. But like I said, you did me a favour. Who needs the press and the oversight committees on their back, let alone the human rights brigade warriors like your own dear husband? Anyhow, rendition's not the way of the future. The way your own assignment ended – well, that's what is.'

'My assignment? What on earth are you talking about?'

'I'm talking about the fact that when our friends from the Marine Corps managed to rescue you, they also took out two extremely unpleasant high-value targets. Where Karim Musleh and that motherfucker white trash German are now, just happens to be beyond the scope of the Great Writ of *habeas corpus*. It really doesn't matter who wins the next presidential election. John McCain, Rudy Guiliani, Hillary fucking Clinton, even, God forbid, that radical liberal black guy from Chicago. It won't make any difference. The policy is changing. We're in a war, a war that's set to last a long time. And in a war, you don't want to capture your most dangerous enemies. You want to kill them – in a smart way, of course, with the Agency in the lead, using UAVs and special forces, and with minimum collateral damage. Well, that's what happened on that beach in Sinai. So thank you for your efforts, and get ready to receive a medal.'

Morgan was silent for many seconds. 'I see,' she said finally. 'But surely even you can't get away with claiming you had all this planned. My "assignment," as you put it, was a giant, sadistic fuck-up. And you weren't just risking my life, you were risking the Agency's secrets. Who knows what I might have given up if the guy interrogating me most of the time hadn't happened to be a friendly Jordanian agent? You could have been endangering agents' lives. And what if Karim had taken me to Yemen?'

Gary smiled. 'Well he didn't, did he? As for the excellent Abu Mustafa, he was the guy interrogating you, wasn't he, and I'm sure you'll be pleased to hear he's doing fine in a Hamas hospital. Let's hope he doesn't have any unfortunate accidents on his way home.'

'You making a threat?'

'Of course not. Just wishing him good health. And expressing my relief we can trust him to keep his mouth shut.'

'Gary, I was tortured, almost killed several times.'

'I know you were. And you've come through it magnificently. That's another reason why we're all so proud of you.'

'And what about your famous Fatah coup? Your plan to crush Hamas?'

'I guess the historical forces we were trying to fight were just too strong – as your own reports from the field indicated. Shit happens. We should have listened to you more carefully. Yet another thing to be proud of. Anyhow, fuck Hamas. We don't much like them, but they're no direct threat to US interests.

Al-Qaeda in the Arabian Peninsula, on the other hand – well, they damn well are. And one of their biggest cadres just got whacked, along with that wannabe, Karim. So the objectives of your mission had to shift a little. Sometimes you have to show flexibility.'

Morgan was having none of it. 'I already told you, Gary. I know what you did. You knew Karim had recognised me, and you had the chance to abort the operation. But you made sure I went to back Gaza, knowing I was going to be kidnapped. You must have known the likelihood was I wasn't going to come back.'

Gary's voice remained low and evenly-modulated. But there was no disguising its tone of menace. 'Ms Cooper, my advice to you is to be more judicious in your choice of words. I know you have been under extraordinary stress. But you are making wild allegations for which you have not a single shred of evidence, and if you repeat them, they will not be believed.'

'Are you sure about that, Gary? Aren't you running an enormous risk?'

Gary folded his hands and laid them on the table, smiling. 'Here's the thing. I don't just know you were fucking your agent, Abdel Nasser. I have a DVD of you doing it. A CIA porno, starring you. So this is how it's going to work. So far, only three living people know about that video – myself, Eugene and Mike. Doh! I almost forgot: your husband has seen it as well. When it first arrived at the Agency station in Tel Aviv, Eugene was sloppy enough to play it while Adam was in his office, before checking its contents. Well, I'm happy for things to stay this way: our secret. We will say nothing. You can go home, get your medal, and decide whether you want to resume your career. If you want to switch to another section, I'll write you a fabulous reference.

'On the other hand, you can go to the IG or whomever else you like, and you can repeat these false allegations. In which case, I will not deny that there is a possibility of that DVD circulating right across Langley, where, if I recall correctly, having sex with an agent while working under cover is generally considered a grave enough transgression to get an officer fired. And who knows where else it may end up? It seems a British tabloid newspaper has already had a hint of it – ask your husband. Well. I've said enough. No need to let me know your decision. But it's your call, Morgan. Your call.'

Morgan was in the bathroom again. Ever since her private meeting at the Consulate, her face had been pale, and she had said almost nothing. During the absurd, formal dinner at Jennifer Perkins's residence, she had left the table three times – almost certainly, Adam thought, to be sick. Now he had confirmation: he could hear her retching, though it sounded as if there was nothing left in her stomach. She flushed the toilet, and seemed to be making an attempt to hide the smell by brushing her teeth. At last she emerged and crossed the tiled floor of their guest room, wearing a set of loaned pyjamas. Adam had closed the wooden Venetian blinds, blocking out the view of the palm-fringed pool and the twinkling towers of the city. Aside from the low, king size bed, the only other furniture was a modern Scandinavian wardrobe and a small, stained pine desk. Morgan was dabbing with a towel at her face. Her eyes, Adam noticed, were still moist.

'I'm sorry,' she said. 'I'm not used to all this rich food. Still, better to get rid of it now than have to deal with it on the plane.'

He stood and made as if to embrace her. 'Recovery is going to take time. Given what you've been through, it's hardly surprising you're finding it hard. But we've got time. As much time as you need. Come here.'

She pushed him away. 'No, Adam, I don't want you to hold me. Leave me alone. We've got to be up in just a few hours, in any case. Let's just try to get some sleep.'

'I'm trying to help. I love you, Morgan. Please, let me in here. If we start to share this stuff, it can only get easier.'

'Forget it, okay?' A sudden blaze of anger. 'You warned me something like this would happen, and I wouldn't listen. So then it did. You were right, as always. Vindication must be sweet.' She sat down on the bed and he followed her, perching cross-legged against the headboard.

'Morgan, I hardly think the fights we had before you went to Gaza matter very much now. They're behind us. What matters is getting you well, getting you over this. And then we'll see about trying to seek redress – from the people really responsible for getting you kidnapped.'

'Save the attorney-speak, okay? It's not going to happen. As for getting over it, I'll talk to my Agency shrink. Adam. It's time to stop pretending. What's just been proven in the most horrible way is that we no longer have a marriage. I appreciate what you did to save me. Without you, I'd probably be dead. But that doesn't mean we should have a life together. Let's face the truth for the once. We have nothing in common any more. Let's not prolong the agony, or make it any worse. Admit it. We're done.'

It had been obvious to Adam from the moment he saw her outside the elevator that rebuilding their relationship was going to be a daunting task. Yet it seemed apparent that Morgan's distress and anger had a fresh, specific source: some new factor which had not been present earlier.

'Did something happen in that meeting? When you went into that room after the press conference?'

'Yes. Something happened. I saw my boss, Gary Thurmond. I believe you are acquainted with him, too. As ever, he was very persuasive.'

Adam swallowed. He could guess what was coming. 'So what did he say?'

'Like I said a few moments ago, it's time to stop pretending. I know that you know that I had an affair, and as you must also realise, Gary does too. In rather more detail than is good for anyone. As it happens, I wasn't really in love with the man I slept with, but I found him sweet and brave, and he swept me off my feet. And the thing we have to face is that ultimately, the reason I had an affair was that our marriage was already dead. Until today, when Gary Thurmond told me, I had no idea how you found out, and for that, I am truly, deeply sorry. But in the end, we both have to take responsibility that it happened.'

'I know why you had an affair,' said Adam. 'And yes, I was a self-obsessed arsehole, who always put myself first. I know I have to change. But give me the chance to work with you, Morgan. I didn't do all I could to save your life just to lose you afterwards. We can get over this.'

'Easy to say, Adam. Easy to say. A lot more difficult to execute. How many times have I heard you promise that things will be different – only to find they never are? At least for once it's you who has a reason to end it.'

There was something he had to ask, although he dreaded the answer. 'Is the reason why you're saying that you're not even willing to try that you still have feelings for Abdel Nasser? Do you think you have a future with him?'

She froze. 'You mean you don't know?'

'Know what? Are you pregnant or something?'

'Jesus, Adam! What is it with you? Of course I'm not fucking pregnant! But Abdel Nasser is dead. He was killed by the Marines who rescued me, because they thought he was one of the terrorists. And all of it was my fault. Never mind the fact he was my lover. He was also my agent, and I failed to protect him. His safety was my responsibility, and I totally let him down. And that's another reason I want to separate. Even if I hadn't been through what I have been, making our marriage function again would probably have been impossible. As it is, I don't have the energy, and frankly, I don't deserve it. I ought to be on my own.'

'Oh Morgan.'

She was weeping now, her body convulsed by her sobs. Maybe a hug would have made her feel better, but he made no move: he knew she would push him away again. They were both alone in their grief.

'It wasn't your fault,' he said finally. 'It was Gary, and all those other bastards who were working with him. So let's get them! Let's make sure they pay for what they've done.'

Her tears were subsiding, and at last she turned to face him again. 'You still don't get it, do you? I can't do anything. That's what my meeting with Gary was about. He made it crystal clear: that if I say anything to anyone about what I think he's done, that DVD will be everywhere – not just all over the Agency, but in the press. Never mind my career. Think what that would do to the children. Somehow he always manages it: however many lives have been lost or shattered, Gary comes out on top.'

Adam held his face in his hands. For once, he had no rebuttal. Meanwhile, he still had to make his own confession. 'This doesn't mean we have to end our marriage. There's so much good still there: we just have to rediscover it. You talk about the kids, but you know as well as I do how much they would hate it if we were to give up now. But since we're levelling with each other, you need to know I haven't been entirely blameless myself.'

'For heaven's sake! Are you finally going to fess up that you fucked one of those hot young paralegals when you were on one of your trips in the South? Really, don't bother. Save your breath. I guessed you did that a long time ago. It isn't important.'

'Actually you're wrong about that, and you always were. But what I need to tell you is more recent. In fact it happened right after I saw your DVD. I was feeling pretty cut-up. I'd been in Gaza only a day or two earlier and got caught in a firefight. Almost got myself killed. So I guess I was in a vulnerable condition.'

'So. What happened – not that I'm in any position to judge you.'

He took a deep breath. 'I slept with Ronnie Wasserman. She was in Tel Aviv. It only happened once, and the sex really wasn't that great, but there it is.'

He had not expected Morgan's response: she began to laugh. 'Ronnie? Ronnie bake-sale Wasserman? Oh Adam, do you really think that I don't know she's been after you for years? I said I'm no position to judge you, but you're telling me you fucked Ronnie Wasserman while I was a hostage? I have to say, I expected better of you than that.'

'I know you can't stand her. But she's really not that bad. Earlier, when I was still back home and you had just disappeared, she was a rock for us all.'

'She was a rock, was she? Ronnie Wasserman, who's never managed to do an honest day's work in her life, except in order to get a man? Listen. I know she's a fabulous cook and all, and I'm sure she told you you're the greatest lawyer since Justice Learned Hand, but trust me, baby, after our divorce, you really can do better than that. I know you were feeling hurt, but you must have been really desperate. Jesus. While I was being tortured by a homicidal lunatic, you were having revenge sex with a soccer widow.'

'Well, I had to tell you.'

'I'm not mad about it. Only disappointed. But it also confirms everything I've been saying. If you can get off with Ronnie Wasserman, you really shouldn't be with someone like me. But now, if you don't mind, I need some sleep. I'm facing a flight and then a long debrief, and I'd like to be fresh. So enough now. Like the Arabs say: *hallas*.'

Morgan lay down, turned off her bedside light, and closed her eyes.

'Goodnight. I love you, Morgan,' Adam said. 'And I really, really don't want a divorce. Just so you know.'

Morgan said nothing.

He didn't to try to touch her. He lay down on the bed's opposite side, a wide gulf of mattress between them. He heard her breathing become more rhythmic, but he knew she wasn't asleep. He always slept on his front, but he lay on his back, motionless, ready for another waking night. The worst of the many thoughts spinning in his head was that Morgan might be right.

Chapter Twenty-five
Friday, July 21, 2007

'We seem to be trapped,' Adam says. 'I reckon there's more than a hundred of them. Your first and last day picking up the kids from Phil and Jim, and it looks like we're going to be late.'

After days of grey invisibility, the afternoon sun is making the damp earth steam. Free at last from the MI6 safe house in Suffolk – or rather, safe Jacobean mansion – Morgan has joined her husband for a stroll before they collect their children at the end of the school term. Since being driven to Adam's parents' home at the beginning of the week, she's kept a low profile: while she's still in England, the Agency doesn't want her to be recognised. But to go to the school just once doesn't seem like so much of a risk, and anyhow, she's wearing sunglasses. At least she'll get to see where they've been studying, and it's her final chance: they're all booked on a United Airlines flight to Dulles on Monday. Sherry and Rob will meet them at the airport, and then stay a few days while they settle back in. At last they'll be together: the former victim and the team who facilitated her rescue, her husband and her dad.

Unfortunately, before beginning their present adventure, she and Adam didn't quite foresee the consequences of recent meteorological events. Three days ago, more rain hit southern England's already-saturated soil in just a few hours than would normally fall in a month. At this time of year, Port Meadow, the broad plain through which the Isis flows a couple of miles above the centre of Oxford, ought to be a glorious expanse of grass and flowers, with the river a shining ribbon at its heart. Instead, Thames Water has had to open the sluice gates upstream lest the city be inundated, and the meadow has become a vast, grey sheet of murky water. The cows that graze there have been pinned into a narrow strip of grass around the edge, where any nourishment to be had has rapidly been eaten.

297

Just above the water level there's a narrow, concrete causeway, which leads from the dry portion of the meadow to Burgess Field, a nature reserve, whose slightly higher altitude has also kept it dry. Grazing there is forbidden. But when they saw Morgan and Adam walking down the causeway, the hungry beasts began to follow them. The reserve's main, cow-sized gate is locked: Adam and Morgan slipped in via the narrow kissing gate to its side. Where the first cows led, all have followed. Having completed their stroll around the reserve, the two human beings have returned to the gateway to find the only path out blocked by thousands of tons of bovine flesh. The stench is strong. As they stand dumbly on the causeway, the flood waters on either side, many of the animals have been emptying their bowels.

Adam stands on the five-bar gate and waves his arms. 'Bleurghh!' he yells. 'Go home! Bleurghh, aaghh, yalla!'

Nothing happens. He tries cow language: 'Moo! Ummhh! Moo!'

One or two cows moo back. He picks up a hefty stick, and stretching out across the gate, he taps the rump of the nearest animal. 'Yee ha! C'mon now! Bleurghh!'

Very slowly, the cow begins to advance, tottering a little on its hooves. Its nose brushes the haunches of the beast in front, and almost imperceptibly, a ripple of forward movement begins, like a line of cars getting out of a highway traffic jam. It's going to take a good many minutes before the path is clear.

Adam turns to Morgan. She's laughing and smiling unaffectedly, not only with her mouth, but her eyes. It's a sight he hasn't seen for many months.

'You tell them, cowboy,' she says. 'Easy to guess that you weren't raised on a ranch. Still, it's good to know that once again, I'm no longer a prisoner.'

Morgan's debrief, she has to admit, went much better than she had feared. Charrington House, the facility provided by MI6, turned out to be a haven, with lavish grounds in which to walk when it wasn't raining, a heated swimming pool and a well-equipped gym, where every two days she was given a dreamy therapeutic massage. Her bedroom, with three big leaded windows, a gigantic bed and one of the new flat-screen TVs, would not have disgraced a five-star spa resort. The food – exquisitely prepared by a young, security-vetted chef from Northern Ireland – was not only delicious, but chosen carefully to ease her battered digestive system's re-entry to the world of civilised cuisine. She has stopped vomiting, and after sixteen days there, she has put on seven pounds. Thanks to the regular exercise, her muscle tone is coming back: she is starting once more to acknowledge her body as her own. One afternoon, she was taken to a hairdressing salon in Woodbridge, where a local stylist made a decent job of her hair. The patches of white are there to stay, but Morgan has resigned herself to joining the millions of women with highlights. In times gone by, Charrington House was used to house Soviet defectors, and it amuses Morgan to think that she has occupied the same lodgings as some of the Cold War's most notable spies.

To her delight, Adam and the children were allowed to visit her three times, driven across to Suffolk in an MI6 car which picked them up from Oxford. But most helpful of all have been her sessions with Eva David, an Israeli psychologist experienced in handling abused POWs, who seems to possess an intuitive understanding of what has been distressing her most. She has none of the awkwardness Morgan might have expected in a Brit, and tackles matters head-on: 'You are blaming yourself for your agent's death. This I have encountered with people in your profession many times. But punishing yourself will not bring him back, and nor will punishing other people close to you. Eventually, you will embrace this at a fundamental, emotional level. For the time being, rationalise it, and when you feel yourself sliding into self-destructive melancholy, fight back – just as you did against your captors when you were a hostage.'

It does not take the pain and guilt away, but it makes them easier to deal with. Dr David has also taught her some simple, cognitive-behavioural techniques. Thus armed, Morgan battles her demons. Naturally, she hasn't told Dr David that Abdel Nasser was her lover: in the CIA, she suspects, patient confidentiality is a somewhat malleable concept. On the other hand, it does seem that for the moment, that particular secret is still safe.

The intelligence component of her days at 'Charrers,' as some of the MI6 personnel there called it, was also tolerable. She had never come across the officers who debriefed her before, and unless she finds herself in a similar situation, they assure her, she probably never will again. Joel, an intense young New Yorker, and Peggy, a matronly soul from Nebraska, had researched her case with impressive diligence before they started, and took pains to ensure that their meetings did not add to her stress. They never lasted more than two hours, and took place in a comfortable, airy drawing room, with plenty of excellent coffee and a choice of sodas always on hand.

In the face of Gary's threat, Morgan has decided to capitulate. There was simply no other choice. How she hates this, but sometimes, she reasons, bullies are simply too strong, and so she has said nothing to Joel and Peggy about her first trip to Erez, her meetings with Ben-Meir, and her last conversation with Abu Mustafa. But then, these are not the issues which interest them. They want to know everything she can tell them about her kidnappers' identities, backgrounds, means of organising themselves, rhetoric, communications, liaison with the Yemenis, and – most critically – all she can remember of what she gave up under interrogation. All of it, they must assume, was passed on by Abu Mustafa to Karim, and thus in turn to the global jihadist network.

When she told them about the day she was waterboarded, they sounded suitably impressed. 'Not many people can deal with that,' Peggy said. 'There are cases from the literature, but they're few and far between. And of course they would have cut off your agent's head in front of you if you hadn't finally given in. As I don't have to tell you, that's how they roll. At least you gave the poor guy a chance.'

300

As for Zainab, when Morgan described her rape and abrupt departure from the Rafah apartment block, she could sense her debriefers salivating: was she someone the Agency should pitch as a recruit? 'Leave her alone,' Morgan said. 'Hasn't she been through enough? But if you really want to do some good, get her a US visa and a college scholarship. If anyone deserves the chance to make a new life, she does.' Joel promised he would look into it. Somehow, Morgan doubts whether anything will come of it.

Towards the end of her stay, they asked her about how she saw her future with the Agency. If she chose to stay, they said, she could have her pick of assignments. 'I still can't begin to think about it,' Morgan said. 'It's just too soon.' The Agency, she reflected later, is not the only department of her life to which that statement applies.

Since his wife's arrival in Oxford, Adam has sensed the changes in her. There are still periods when she seems irritable or morose, but they have not returned to the subjects they discussed on that agonising night in Dubai.

Her recovery, he knows, has only just begun. During his last visit to Charrington House, while Morgan ambled in the garden with the children, Dr David took him aside and warned him that she would never be without the mental scars, and that how she would feel six or twelve months later was still impossible to tell. He ought to seek advice in dealing with the psychological legacy of his own experiences, too, she said. It was not every Washington lawyer who had been forced to kill in order to save his own life, though that, as she gently pointed out, was something he and Morgan had in common.

Over the past few days, they have gradually told each other everything. Learning how close Adam came to being killed seemed to make Morgan appalled. At the same time, she could not help but admit she was impressed that a man who had previously found his triumphs in citing obscure legal opinions stepped up in the way that he did. She has come to accept that in the end, what he did was right. 'I know I ran big risks,' he told her one night, as they sat on the garden deck together, finishing a bottle of Sauternes. 'And as you're well aware, I'm an atheist. But I somehow had this belief that I was going to be alright; that something was protecting me. In the end, that's why I didn't hesitate.'

When he said this, Morgan shuddered.

'You getting cold?' Adam asked.

'No. I'm fine.. It's just… well, I had the exact opposite feeling. I never quite articulated it to myself, but right through that last trip, in the days before I was kidnapped, I had this sense of dread; if I'd had the courage to listen to my instincts, I'd have been on the next plane home. But for all the shitty reasons you know too much about, I couldn't. I had to see it through, whatever the consequences.'

That night, for the first time since her release, Adam tried to make love to her.

But though she let him hold her, she said she wasn't ready. 'Not yet. I don't know when. I'm sorry, I just can't fully relax.'

Today, just before they left for their stroll, Adam checked his email to find a message from Ronnie. He shared its contents with Morgan as soon as he read it.

'Dearest Adam,' it began, 'first I can only apologise for what I said on the phone when last we spoke. You were going through a terrible time, and the last thing I should have done was add to the pressure.

'Anyhow, I wanted to let you know how thrilled I am at the news of Morgan's release, and I know it must mean the world to the kids. I'm sure you must have played a part in it, and that she must be very proud. Please pass on my warmest regards: I hope we can all be friends again when we're back in Bethesda.

'Meanwhile, I'm still in Israel, and my big news is that I've started dating someone. His name's Ya'acov, and he's a widower who works in a high-tech start-up. We met one night four weeks ago, when Rachelle asked some friends for dinner. I guess she was trying to set me up. Anyhow, it worked. Who knows?

Maybe I'll be an adoptive sabra, too. See you at the wedding (lol)! Bye for now, and have a good flight home. Love to Charlie and Aimee, xxoo Ronit.'

'A widower, huh?' was Morgan's first response. 'Well, I'll keep my mouth shut on the subject of Ronnie, or do I mean Ronit. Except to say: do the math. If she met Ya'acov nearly four weeks ago, she didn't take long to get over you, did she? It did break my heart to think of her grieving over losing you. And I'm so looking forward to us all being friends in Bethesda: my God, the woman has no shame. Well, let's hope the sex is better with Ya'acov than it seems to have been with you.'

At last the cow jam has thinned enough to allow them to make progress down the causeway, and they gingerly pick their way along it between the steaming piles of ordure.

'We've still got a few minutes,' Adam says. 'The school is just across the railway bridge, and then you're right there.'

When they arrive at the line of modern, red-brick buildings, there's already a swelling crowd of parents and children outside the open gates, squinting in the unfamiliar sunlight, clutching bags of sports kit, lunch boxes and artwork. They make their way into the playground outside the classrooms. Farewells are being said all round them, and vacation plans discussed.

Aimee emerges from her classroom first, holding hands with Alice. Charlie runs up a few moments later, in the company of Tom.

'You guys had better be saying goodbye to each other,' Adam says. 'Alice, Tom, in case you don't know, we're going back to America on Monday. Thank you for looking after Aimee and Charlie and helping them find their feet. You've made things much easier for them, and I want you to know how much I appreciate it. And by the way, here's someone I'd like you to meet. This is Morgan, their mum.'

'Wow!' says Tom. 'You must be so brave, like a heroine or something.' He holds out his hand. Morgan takes it, smiling broadly.

'I'm pleased to meet you Tom. And thank you for teaching Charlie how to fish. He's hardly stopped talking about it from the moment I came back.'

Alice proffers her hand, too. 'How do you do, Mrs Cooper. I'm so pleased you're back safe – all of Aimee's friends are. But we're going to miss her very much.'

'Mommy?' says Charlie, 'I know we've got to say goodbye for now, but can't we all come back for a visit? I mean, like maybe for Christmas or Easter or something? Granny and grandpa won't mind if we come stay. Not just us and dad this time, but you as well. We can have another anglers' picnic!'

Adam and Morgan exchange glances.

'I'm just not sure,' she says. 'We'll see how things go. The flights are very expensive, and dad's had to take a lot of time off from his job. But we'll see. I'm not saying definitely yes, but if we can make it work, sweetie, we will. If we can make it work.'

'So can we go to Bunters now?'

'Bunters?' Morgan looks at Adam again, this time quizzically.

'It's the little supermarket and candy store on the other side of the canal. It's become a bit of a tradition: we stop there to buy them something on the way home every Friday.'

'In that case of course we can. Come on.' Morgan takes Charlie's hand, and they join the throng of families making their way across the old, narrow bridge, Adam and Aimee just behind.

'Mom, you'll never guess,' Charlie says. 'They've got white chocolate Magnums.'

Author's Note

This is a work of fiction, but the background to its story is real. There really was a covert US operation to supply and train Fatah's forces in Gaza planned with the intention that they would crush Hamas in the spring of 2007, and its discovery was the trigger for the successful Hamas coup. Much of the detail is set out in my article *The Gaza Bombshell*, published in the April 2008 issue of *Vanity Fair*. Among the things that Hamas discovered once it seized power was that its Palestinian enemies had made secret video recordings of the sex lives of their opponents, usually as a means of blackmailing them. In the chaotic, bloody months before the Hamas takeover, there was a spate of kidnappings by jihadist groups, most notably of the BBC reporter Alan Johnston. Hamas secured his freedom soon after the coup. His account of his ordeal, *Kidnapped*, is published by Profile. The USS *Kearsage*, an amphibious assault ship, was on patrol in the Red Sea during 2007. There really was a US Marine Corps operation which saved Sunni tribal fighters from Al-Qaeda at the town of Al-Qaim in May 2005, and it was launched thanks to an American seed merchant who called his Marine contacts from his porch. However, his name was not Rob Ashfield but Ken Wischkaemper. SS Philip and James is a primary school in Oxford, where the deputy head teacher, Kelly Brain, not only has a marvellous name, but is also an inspirational teacher. All other characters in this book are fictitious, and any resemblance they may have to real persons, living or dead, is coincidence.

There are many people I must thank without whose help this novel could not have been written. Rebecca Nicolson and Chris Anderson first gave me the confidence that I might be able to write fiction, and to Chris, who read each draft chapter as I completed it, I owe a particular debt. Paul Janiczek and David Davis gave me critical help with the details of the military equipment and operational methods described in the closing chapters. Several members of the American, Israeli and British intelligence communities, who would prefer not to be named, also gave me invaluable assistance: they know who they are. Others with experience of the Middle East, Washington and other relevant aspects of life gave generously of their time as readers and made many helpful criticisms. In no particular order, they include Harvey Boulter, Alison Phillips, John Lupold, Michael Murphy, Ina Parker and Amanda Craig.

Since the time of the Gaza coup, my many journalistic visits to Israel and the Palestinian territories have been facilitated and illuminated by the help and warm friendship of my translator and fixer, Nuha Musleh, and her family, Khader, Zainab and Abdel Nasser. If I have gained any insight into Palestinian politics, life and culture, it is down them, and I thank them for their hospitality from the bottom of my heart. All visitors to Ramallah should make a point of visiting their extraordinary oriental art, antiques, carpet and jewellery boutique, Gallery Zainab. In Gaza, Hassan Jaber, a warm man and a superb journalist who somehow keeps smiling in very difficult circumstances, has played a similar role.

Jill Grinberg, my agent in New York, has represented me for many years, and her role in the gestation of this book was immense. She gave generously of her time from the beginning, supplying vital editorial advice, the support that kept me going, and later, when the thing was almost finished, enormously perceptive suggestions for fine-tuning the text. At Quartet, Naim Attallah and Gavin James Bower responded to the manuscript with the care and enthusiasm which every writer covets.

Finally, but also first, I thank my wife, Carolyn. Although her own life, thanks in part to the sons to whom the book is dedicated, can be quite busy, she not only commented on every draft of every chapter, she proof read them. More important, she sustained both this project and its author with her love.